D0519252

# Duane's
# Depressed

# By Larry McMurtry

Comanche Moon
Dead Man's Walk
The Late Child
Streets of Laredo
The Evening Star
Buffalo Girls
Some Can Whistle
Anything for Billy
Film Flam: Essays on Hollywood
Texasville
Lonesome Dove
The Desert Rose
Cadillac Jack
Somebody's Darling
Terms of Endearment
All My Friends Are Going to Be Strangers
Moving On
The Last Picture Show
In a Narrow Grave: Essays on Texas
Leaving Cheyenne
Horseman, Pass By

# By Larry McMurtry and Diana Ossana

Pretty Boy Floyd
Zeke and Ned

# Duane's Depressed

LARRY McMURTRY

ORION

Copyright © 1999 Larry McMurtry

The right of Larry McMurtry to be identified
as the author of this work have been
asserted by him in accordance with the
Copyright, Designs and Patents Act 1988

All rights reserved.
No part of this publication may be
reproduced, stored in a retrieval system, or transmitted in any
form or by any means, electronic, mechanical, photocopying,
recording or otherwise without the prior permission of the
copyright owner

This edition first published in
Great Britain in 1999 by
Orion
An imprint of Orion Books Ltd
Orion House, 5 Upper St Martin's Lane,
London WC2H 9EA

A CIP catalogue record for this book
is available from the British Library

The characters and events in this book are fictitious
Any similarity to real persons,
living or dead, is coincidental

Typeset by Deltatype Ltd, Birkenhead, Merseyside
Printed and bound in Great Britain by
Clays Ltd, St Ives plc

*For Karen Kennerly*

# BOOK ONE

# The Walker and His Family

# 1

Two years into his sixties, Duane Moore – a man who had driven pickups for as long as he had been licensed to drive – parked his pickup in his own carport one day and began to walk wherever he went.

The carport was a spacious affair, built to house six cars in the days when cars still had some size; now that cars had been miniaturized – as had horses – the carport could accommodate ten vehicles and might have accommodated as many as a dozen if the vehicles had been parked with some care; but care, defined as a capacity for attention to such things as order and propriety, was not something that most members of Duane's large family had proven to be capable of or interested in – not so far, at least. In the Moore carport cars tended to stack up behind one another, so that the person who had parked in front could rarely get his or her car out without a bitter quarrel, sometimes involving fisticuffs, with the person or persons whose car or cars were parked behind theirs.

In fact – and it was a fact that had vexed Duane for years – the spacious carport mainly housed a collection of junk: welding tools, old golf clubs, fishing equipment, baby carriages whose tires had been flat for several years, couches and chairs that had stalled, somehow, on their way to the upholsterer, and towering pyramids of objects acquired by Karla or one of the girls at garage sales, department stores, swap meets, or discount malls – objects that had evidently fallen in their purchasers' esteem before they could even get into the house – though the house too contained comparable pyramids of objects that had made it through the doors but not much farther.

Contemplation of his own misused carport was one of the reasons Duane parked his pickup one day and began to walk, but it was not the only reason, or necessarily the most important. He had spent almost fifty years of his life in the cab of a pickup, racing through the vast oil patch that extended over much of West Texas, hurrying from one oil-soaked lease to another; but now he was sixty-two and the oil game had lost its thrill, the chase its flavor. He didn't want to be in the cab of a pickup anymore, because being in the cab of a pickup suddenly made him wonder what had happened to his life. It occurred to him one day – not in a flash, but through a process of seepage, a kind of gas leak into his consciousness – that most of his memories, from first courtship to the lip of old age, involved the cabs of pickups. His long marriage to Karla, their four children, their nine grandchildren, his booms and his busts, his friendships and his few love affairs had somehow all happened in the few brief periods when he hadn't been in the cab of a pickup, somewhere in the Texas oil patch.

So, one day in February, with a blue norther cutting through the pastures of dead mesquite like a saw, Duane parked his pickup in the southernmost parking spot in the carport and hid the keys in a chipped coffee cup on the top shelf in the kitchen cabinet. Nobody used that coffee cup anymore – it had sat untouched on the top shelf for years. All Duane hoped was that the keys could be hidden in it for a year or two – that way none of the grandkids could steal his pickup until they grew adept enough to hot-wire it, which ought to be a while.

Then, pleased with his decision and even rather enjoying the crisp cut of the norther, Duane took the first walk of his new life, a short one of some three-quarters of a mile along a dirt road to his office. His departure was observed only by Willy, the grandson Julie had presented them with only a few days prior to her seventeenth birthday; now Willy was nine. The prospect of great-grandchildren was never far from Duane's thoughts – or Karla's either. Willy sat in front of the living room TV, playing a video game called Extreme Rampage – he was merely resting his fingers for a moment when he saw his grandfather walk off down the dusty road. The sight struck Willy as being slightly odd, but he loved Extreme Rampage too much to allow anything to distract him from it for long. He forgot all about his grandfather until his grandmother came into the living room a few minutes later, looking puzzled.

'Willy, have you seen Pa-Pa?' she asked. 'I thought sure I heard his pickup drive up, and his gloves are in the kitchen, but I can't find him anywhere.'

'Pa-Pa walked off.' Willy said, his fingers dancing expertly on the buttons of the video game.

'What?' Karla asked, supposing she had heard wrong.

'Pa-Pa walked off down that road – that road right out there,' Willy insisted. He didn't point – matters on the screen were critical – indeed, domination of the world was at stake. He couldn't spare a hand.

'Willy, I've told you not to lie to me,' Karla said. 'Just because your little sister lies to me constantly don't mean you have to start.'

'It wasn't a lie!' Willy protested indignantly. Unfortunately the brief shift in his attention proved fatal: the Ninja Master kicked him off the cliff.

'Oh no!' Willy said. 'I was winning and now I'm dead.'

His grandmother was unmoved.

'I'm gonna talk to your mother about you, young man,' she said. 'I think you spend too much time playing those dumb video games. They're screwing up your cognition or something. Pa-Pa's never walked anywhere in his life, much less on a day when there's a norther.'

Willy saw no point in arguing with his grandmother. Grown-ups who were that old could never be convinced of anything anyway – indeed, all grown-ups had a tendency to deny the plainest facts. One of the few things he and his sister, Bubbles, agreed on was that grown-ups were weird.

Just as his grandmother was about to leave the room the phone rang and she picked it up.

'Maybe it's Pa-Pa – he might be on the cell phone,' she said, but instead it was Julie, mother of Willy and Bubbles. Julie was just returning from visiting her boyfriend, Darren, who was in jail in Lawton, Oklahoma, awaiting trial on a charge of armed robbery and aggravated assault, a charge Julie was convinced was unjust. Julie was making the call from the edge of her parents' driveway; she was not about to rush into the house without making a few inquiries, not after what she had just seen.

'Did you and Daddy just have a big fight?' Julie asked. 'If you did I'm going back to Wichita Falls and spend the night in a motel.'

Karla was too surprised to answer right away. She had just put in a peaceful morning watching the international table tennis championships on cable – it was amazing how fast a little Ping-Pong ball could travel if someone from China whopped it.

'It's bad enough seeing Darren in custody just because he hit some old fart with a wrench,' Julie said. 'I shouldn't have to come home and be a witness to parental violence.'

'Julie, Darren was *robbing* the old man he hit with the wrench,' Karla reminded her. 'Darren's a criminal. That's why he's in custody.'

'I don't want to talk about that – I want to talk about you and Daddy,' Julie insisted. She was close enough to the house to be able to see into the kitchen, but was not close enough to be able to tell whether there was blood on the walls.

'Honey, your father and I haven't been violent in years, and then it was just me throwing things,' Karla told her. 'Bubbles is watching Barney and Willy is right here playing video games.'

'Then why is Daddy walking down the road?' Julie asked.

Karla threw Willy a quick, slightly guilty glance, but Willy was in space, trying to keep aliens from destroying planet Earth.

'*Duane's* walking down the road?' she said. 'Are you sure it's him – a lot of men look alike from the back.'

'I guess I know my own daddy; he's been my daddy my whole life,' Julie said.

'I told you Pa-Pa was walking down the road,' Willy said, without taking his eyes from the TV screen. 'You should apologize for calling me a liar.'

'I *do* apologize for calling you a liar,' Karla said. 'I just hope I don't have to call your mother something worse. There's all kinds of dope available in those Oklahoma jails. I don't think your mother's lying but she could be hallucinating.'

'Momma, all I took was a little speed so I wouldn't fall asleep driving and leave my children without a mother,' Julie said. 'I'm not hallucinating! *My daddy is walking down the road! Get it?*'

'Then oil prices must have really tanked, or else somebody's died,' Karla said, suddenly convinced. 'There'd be no other reason why Duane would get out of his pickup and go walking down a road.'

'Momma, I wish you'd just ask him,' Julie said. 'He hasn't gone very far.'

'Oh, I mean to ask him,' Karla said. 'What does he think he's doing, scaring us this way?'

# 2

Before leaving to go chase down her husband, Karla put in a call to Mildred-Jean Ennis at the beauty parlor – Mildred-Jean was the person to check with about sudden fatalities in the community, the reason being that her beauty parlor was right across the street from where they parked the local ambulance. Karla was so upset by the thought of Duane walking around in a norther that she felt a panic attack coming on – calling Mildred-Jean might be a way to keep herself on an even keel until she found out what lay behind her husband's strange behavior. When it came to local disturbances Mildred-Jean was at least as reliable as the Weather Channel was about the weather. It didn't take ambulance-level emergencies to prompt her interest, either. She was a solid source of information about adulteries, and even mild flirtations seldom escaped her notice.

'My antennae are always out; that's what antennae are for,' Mildred-Jean liked to say; besides that she was a psychic, who sometimes gave card readings when she wasn't styling hair.

Mildred-Jean hailed from Enid, Oklahoma, a garden spot by comparison with Thalia, in her opinion, but, unfortunately, she had ended up in Texas when her passionate romance with a crop duster named Woody suddenly lost altitude and deposited her on a dusty corner by Highway 79.

'Well, I just thought somebody might have died this morning,' Karla said. 'Most people seem to die in the morning rather than the afternoon – I don't know why that is.'

'Nope, nobody died – not that there ain't two or three ignorant sons-of-bitches around here who deserve to have their asses killed.' She was thinking particularly of Woody, who lived a few blocks away with a redhead he had formed an unseemly relationship with.

'Well, I just wondered. Bye,' Karla said, and hung up. She didn't want to give Mildred-Jean an opportunity to start in about Woody –

hearing about other men's treachery was not likely to help quell her panic attack, not while her husband, a male himself, was wandering the streets.

'Maybe aliens came down in a spaceship and took possession of Pa-Pa's mind,' Willy offered, helpfully. He was resting his fingers again.

'It could be aliens but I bet it's oil,' Karla said. She raced into her bedroom and shot the TV by her bed all the way up the cable to the Financial Channel, convinced that the Saudis had opened the floodgates at last, producing a tidal wave of oil that would drop the price of West Texas crude to around two dollars a barrel, ruining everybody in Texas, or at least everybody in Thalia. Anxiety about the Saudi tidal wave had been a constant in the oil patch for years; nobody knew when it would come but everyone agreed that once it *did* come, ruin would be complete: no more platinum AmEx cards, no more frequent-flier miles, no more fun trips to Las Vegas or Bossier City.

Apparently, though, the tidal wave still hadn't come. The commentators on the Financial Channel evinced no sign of panic.

If it's not death and it's not oil I guess he wants a divorce, Karla thought. No sooner had the notion entered her head than the last few barricades separating reason from panic were swept aside. He wanted a divorce: she knew it, should have known it immediately. There wasn't anything wrong with Duane: he just wanted a divorce and was too chicken to come in the house and spit it out.

Julie was in the kitchen making herself and Bubbles bacon sandwiches when Karla wandered in, looking for her car keys. Now that she knew what the truth was she was in no special hurry to go chase her husband down.

'Bacon sandwiches, I love 'em,' Bubbles said. 'I wish they'd kill every pig in the world so there'd always be plenty of bacon sandwiches.'

Bubbles, eight, had frizzy blonde hair and a blue-eyed gaze that melted the hardest hearts.

'I don't think the world needs to lose a whole species of animal just so you can stuff yourself with grease, Miss Bubbles,' Karla said.

Bubbles regarded her grandmother coolly. They did not always see eye to eye.

'You shut up that talk or I'll never hug your wrinkled old neck again,' Bubbles said, although without rancor. She was dipping a table knife into a big jar of Miracle Whip and licking the Miracle Whip off the knife blade.

'Thanks a lot. Who bought you that stupid purple dinosaur you sleep with?' Karla said, as she stood in the door. She glanced at Julie, hoping her daughter would offer Bubbles a word or two of correction, but Julie was gazing absently out the window, wondering what she was going to do for fun until Darren Connor got out of jail.

'If she's this rude at eight, what's she going to be like at fifteen?' Karla asked. 'You need to be thinking about things like that, Julie, instead of just wasting your life on violent criminals.'

'Bacon and Miracle Whip and Barney are the three best things in the whole world,' Bubbles said airily, waving the knife around as if it were a wand.

Julie was wishing her mother would leave, so she could pop an upper – handling her kids in the morning was really tiring work.

Once in her little white BMW, Karla found that her panic attack was subsiding a little. Duane's sudden desire for a divorce was annoying, but it probably wasn't the end of the world. She whirled out of her driveway in a cloud of dust, as usual, but then sat with the driver's-side window down, smelling the dust and feeling the cut of the norther, wondering *why* he suddenly wanted a divorce. He hadn't been especially restless lately – Karla was even reasonably sure he didn't have a girlfriend. One of her many spies would have immediately alerted her to any romantic development. He must already be in his office; there was no sign of him on the road. She had known Duane for much of her life and had been married to him just over forty years. They had never in their lives been strangers to each other, she and Duane; but, once she thought about it a few more minutes, sitting in her car with the motor idling, she realized that the part about them not being strangers wasn't quite true. Living with Duane *had* become sort of like living with a stranger: a pleasant stranger, to be sure, and an attractive stranger, but not a person she could truthfully say she knew very much about. They still lived in the same house, ate at the same table, talked about the same kids, worried about the same crises, even slept in the same bed, but what did they know of each other now, really? Not much, it seemed to Karla, a thought that aroused only a faint sadness in her. Somehow forty years of constant intimacy had betrayed them finally, in some sly way. The very fact of being together so long had imperceptibly swirled them farther and farther apart. If such a realization had come to her sooner, *she* might have been the one to act, the one to ask for a divorce.

Coming out of a panic attack was not much different from awakening from a nightmare. Once you woke up and realized you were really lost or dead, then the things of the earth slowly settled back into place. By the time Karla had made the short drive to Duane's office she had begun to feel a little like a fool. Duane might not even want a divorce. He might just have been low on gas and walked back to the office to get something he had forgotten. He might have sneaked off on foot so as not to stir up the grandkids, who were pretty demanding where their Pa-Pa was concerned. Reassured, Karla gave her hair a lick or two with a comb before going into the office.

Ruth Popper, the old secretary whom Duane refused to push into retirement, sat in a chair in one corner of the office, peering through a big magnifying glass at a book of crossword puzzles. Ruth had a dictionary balanced on one knee and a pencil between her teeth. The big magnifying glass was attached to the chair Ruth sat in. The whole office staff and even a few of the roughnecks had chipped in to buy Ruth the big magnifying glass, but it soon became apparent that they had wasted their philanthropy.

'Hell, she couldn't see a crossword puzzle if she was looking at it through the Mount Palomar telescope,' Bobby Lee said, putting the matter caustically. A year or two back, testicular cancer had forced Bobby Lee to surrender one ball, a circumstance that had rendered him notably testy. Bobby Lee, the drilling company, and to a degree everyone in Thalia were almost as anxious about the other testicle as they were about the coming tidal wave of Saudi oil. If the cancer should come back and force him to surrender the other ball, the general view was that Bobby Lee would get two or three young women pregnant just prior to the operation and then buy an assault rifle and shoot down everybody he had ever quarreled with, which was, in essence, the whole population of Thalia.

'If he sees he's gonna lose that other ball I expect him to fuck up a storm and then get seven or eight guns and take us all out,' Rusty Aitken told Duane. Rusty was the local drug dealer, though officially he just ran a body shop on the west edge of town. Karla didn't like Rusty Aitken, largely because her own children had done their best to make him a rich man, and had largely succeeded.

Bobby Lee was right about Ruth and the magnifying glass, though.

All she could see when she held the crossword puzzle book under the glass was an occasional wavy line.

'It's all right,' Duane invariably said, when some busybody pointed out that he was employing a blind woman who sat in a corner all day pretending to do crossword puzzles. 'Moving the magnifying glass back and forth gives her a little something to do.' A young secretary named Earlene did all the actual secretarying. Earlene and Ruth did not have a harmonious relationship, mainly because Ruth would sneak over during Earlene's lunch break and hide whatever lease orders Earlene had been working on when she left for lunch.

'I'm just testing her,' Ruth said, when Duane chided her about this habit. 'A good secretary ought to be able to find anything in this office in three minutes, hidden or not.'

'Even if you hid it in your car?' Duane asked – though almost blind, Ruth still drove herself to work, making use of a tortuous network of back alleys and avoiding all contact with what she called the 'big roads.' The worst she had done so far was knock down a row of garbage cans.

'Well, if it's in my car I guess it's stuff I need to work on myself, in the peace of my home,' Ruth informed him. She did not enjoy having her methods questioned – she never had.

'Where's Duane?' Karla asked, peeking into the office.

Earlene was typing and Ruth was swiveling her magnifying glass back and forth. She had just caught a glimpse of the word 'Mississippi,' an excellent word, and she wanted to count the letters and see if she could fit it into her puzzle anyplace. Karla's sudden entry caused her dictionary to fall off her knee.

'Ain't here; he just stuck his head in the door and said he was going to the cabin,' Earlene said, without lifting her eyes from the lease contract she was typing.

The cabin was just a frame shack Duane had built a few years ago, when all their kids and grandkids were temporarily living at home. Nellie, Dickie, and Julie were all in the process of quarrelsome divorces, and Jack – Julie's twin – was serving a twelve-month probation for possession of a controlled substance, in this case four thousand methamphetamine tablets. All the grandchildren liked living in their grandparents' big house, though Nellie's two oldest, Barbette and Little Mike, preferred living in a commune in Oregon, where they had been for the last three years. The children themselves hated living at home and were constantly at one another's throats.

Karla, who was auditing a few courses at Midwestern University at the time, audited one in art history and came home one day eager to explain a few new concepts to Duane.

'Now Baroque came along in real old-timey times,' she explained one morning, after an evening when they had both underestimated the force of some tequila they were drinking, with the stereo in their bedroom turned up high enough to drown out the sounds of Nellie screaming at T.C., her boyfriend of the moment.

'I don't know what you're talking about,' Duane said. He didn't mind Karla auditing courses – in fact, he encouraged it – but he did mind having to audit her auditings, particularly when he had a hangover.

'Baroque, Duane – Baroque,' Karla said. It always pleased her to learn a complicated new word that no one else in Thalia knew the meaning of.

'I heard you. What does it mean?' he asked.

'Well, it kinda means "too much," you know?' Karla said, thinking that was probably the simplest way to explain it to someone like Duane, who had never given ten seconds' thought to art of any kind, unless it was just pictures of cowboys loping around in the snow or something.

'Okay, too much,' Duane said. He was slightly addicted to antihistamine nose sprays at the time – he quickly squirted some nose spray into his nose before Karla could stop him.

' "Too much" is like our family,' he said. 'Would it be fair to say our family is Baroque?'

'Duane, of course not, our family is perfectly normal,' Karla said. 'They might have a few too many hormones or something but otherwise they're perfectly normal.'

'Nope, if "Baroque" really means "too much," then our family is Baroque and I'm leaving,' he informed her.

Ten days later he and Bobby Lee hammered the cabin together, on the edge of a rocky hill on some property Duane owned a few miles out of town. It was built in a place with no shade and lots of rattlesnakes, so many that none of the grandkids were permitted anywhere near it, at least not in the warm months. Karla had only set foot in it twice, and the only satisfaction she got on either visit was to confiscate two or three containers of nosespray.

Rough and lonely as it was – or perhaps *because* it was rough and lonely – Duane loved the cabin and spent many weekends in it. The only regular visitor was Bobby Lee, and he only became a regular visitor after the trouble developed with his testicle, when he became so depressed and in need of company that Duane didn't have the heart to turn him out.

The existence of the cabin had always made Karla a little uneasy, though – it still did.

'I'd just like to know what you find to do out there all by yourself,' she asked, several times.

'I don't do anything,' Duane explained.

'Duane, that's worrisome to me,' Karla said. 'It's not normal for a healthy man to sit off on a hill and not do anything.'

'You could at least get a telephone,' she said later.

'I don't want a telephone,' Duane said. 'I've got a radio, though.' He thought he might throw his wife that small crumb of normality, a quality she had come to put a great deal of stock in, now that she was plunging on through middle age.

'Big deal,' Karla said. 'What if I need you quick? What do I do?'

'Call the radio station and have them page me,' he suggested.

'Duane, don't be perverse,' Karla said, the perverse being a concept she had learned about in a psychology class she had audited.

'Now you made me drop my dictionary and lose my place,' Ruth Popper complained, while Karla was snooping around the office seeing what she could find.

'I'm sorry, Ruth – what word were you looking up?' Karla said, picking up the dictionary.

'I was looking up "Nepal," ' Ruth said. She always had a few good words like 'Nepal' ready when busybodies asked her how she was coming along with her puzzles.

Karla opened the dictionary to the Ns but before she could find the word 'Nepal' her sense of something not being quite right returned. It wasn't a full-scale panic attack, just a sense that a gear had slipped, somewhere in her life.

'If Duane went to the cabin what did he drive?' she asked.

Earlene stopped typing – she looked blank.

'Why, his pickup, I guess,' she said.

'No, his pickup is parked in the carport,' Karla said. 'Could he have taken one of the trucks?'

Earlene shook her head.

'The trucks are where the rigs are,' she said.

'He didn't take a truck; he's walking it,' Ruth said.

'Ruth, he couldn't be walking it,' Karla said. 'The cabin is six miles out of town and there's a norther blowing.'

'Don't care – he's walking it,' Ruth said, wishing everybody would leave her alone so she could start counting the letters in 'Mississippi.'

'Maybe he borrowed your car,' Karla suggested to Earlene.

Earlene shook her head. Her car keys were right there by the ashtray on her desk. Nonetheless she got up and ran over to peek out the door, just to make absolutely sure her blue Toyota was still there. If there was one thing Earlene couldn't tolerate it was the thought of being afoot.

'He's walking it,' Ruth said again. 'If you don't believe me go down the road and you'll see.'

'Oh lord, I guess he *does* want a divorce,' Karla said, thinking out loud. Her first instinct had been right; the situation was now crystal clear.

Her remark proved to be an immediate showstopper. Ruth Popper forgot about Nepal and Mississippi. Earlene ceased typing. Her fingers were still poised above the keys, but she wasn't moving a muscle. Earlene had long had a crush on Duane – perhaps, at last, there was a chance. Wild hope sprang up in her heart.

'Oh well, I'm surprised it lasted this long,' Ruth said. 'You two never did have a thing in common.'

'Nothing in common – what about those nine grandkids?' Karla asked. For a moment she felt like strangling Ruth Popper. Maybe after the murder she could plead temporary insanity and be put on probation like her son Jack.

Heartened as Earlene was by the news that Duane was finally divorcing Karla, she didn't believe for a minute that he was actually walking around in the street.

'We forgot about the toolshed,' she said. 'He's probably out there playing with wrenches or something. I'll go look.'

'I'll go with you,' Karla said. She was well aware that Earlene had a crush on Duane.

But the toolshed proved to be cold, oily, and empty. There were plenty of wrenches on the workbench, but Duane wasn't playing with any of them. Earlene had convinced herself that Duane – for the moment her boss, but soon, possibly, her beau – must be in the toolshed. Now that it was clear that he wasn't, she didn't know what to think. Only three cars had been parked at the office that day: her Toyota, Ruth Popper's Volkswagen Bug, and Karla's BMW. All three were still there. The unpleasant possibility that Ruth was right and that Duane actually *was* walking to his cabin had to be faced.

'I guess the divorce must have really got that man torn up,' she said.

'I don't know, Earlene,' Karla said. 'People get divorced every day, I guess.'

'I know it – *I* even got divorced,' Earlene said. 'And I'm Church of Christ, too.'

'If you ask me, a simple divorce is no excuse for doing something crazy, like walking six miles in a norther,' Karla said.

The thought that Duane, her favorite boss of all time, might be crazy was not a thought Earlene really wanted to entertain. Karla didn't want to entertain it either, but the fact was, Duane was gone and the cars weren't. What else were they to think?

The two women, who had rushed out to the toolshed eager and hopeful, convinced that they would find Duane in it, trudged back to the office depressed and uncertain, while the cold wind blew dust against their legs.

# 3

Duane, meanwhile, was walking briskly along the dirt road toward his cabin, the collar of his Levi's jacket turned up against the norther. He had skirted the downtown area, such as it was, slipping through some of the same alleys that Ruth Popper used on her way to and from work. He was well aware that the fact that he was walking would attract attention, so he chose an obscure route out of town – a route along which there would be little attention to attract.

Even so, by the time he reached the city limits, a dozen passing motorists had stopped to ask if his pickup was broken down. All twelve offered him a ride.

'No thanks,' Duane said, twelve times. 'I'm just out for a walk.'

'Out for a what?' Johnny Ringo asked – Johnny was a wheat farmer who owned a fine patch of cropland in the Onion Creek bottoms.

'A walk, Johnny,' Duane repeated.

Johnny Ringo was a tough old bird who took little interest in the doings of his fellowman. Of the twelve people who stopped to offer Duane a ride, he was the least disturbed by the notion of pedestrianism.

'Well, a walk's something I never tried,' he said. And then he drove off.

Duane knew that it would take a while to accustom the citizens of the county to the notion that he was tired of driving pickups and just wanted to walk around for a few years. By his reckoning there were fewer committed pedestrians in the county than there were followers of Islam. Pedestrians, by his count, numbered one – himself – whereas two lonely and diminutive Muslims had somehow washed up in the nearby town of Megargel, where they worked in a feed store. Anyone who cared to visit Megargel could see them struggling with huge sacks of grain, their turbans covered with the dust of oats and wheat.

Duane walked on into the dun countryside, obligingly stopping every half mile or so to explain to a passing cowboy, or pickup full of roughnecks, that no, his pickup hadn't broken down, he was just walking out to his cabin, enjoying the February breeze. Although annoyed to have to explain himself to every single car that passed, he was not surprised and took care to preserve his amiability. The county had slowly come to accept C-SPAN and computers – in a few months they could probably be brought to accept a walker, too. Then his walks would get easier, more pure. A day would finally come when none of the roughnecks or the hunters would stop at the sight of him walking – not unless he waved them down. He could walk in peace, think, be alone.

Even now, on what was essentially the first solitary walk of his life, there were pleasant stretches when the road ahead was empty, free of pickups and trucks coming and going from the oil fields or the ranches. There was just the cold blue winter sky, and the whip of the wind, so strong when it gusted that the weeds by the fences rattled against the barbed wire. He could walk along, keeping a lookout for deer, or coveys of quail, or wild turkeys or wild pigs, all of which he and his son Dickie occasionally liked to hunt.

He had passed through much of his life paying only the most casual attention to the natural world, noting only whether it was cold or wet or hot, an obstruction to his business or otherwise. He had not delved much into nature's particularities, knew the names of only a few trees, a few birds, some insects, and the common animals. The thought of his own ignorance made him feel a little guilty. He knew scarcely a thing about botany, could identify only a few of the plants he was passing as he walked. He thought he might purchase a book about weeds and flowers, and maybe a book about birds; he could at least educate himself to the point where he recognized the plants he was passing, as he walked here and there.

Rounding a bend in the road, at about the halfway point between his cabin and the town, he happened to notice a coyote, standing only twenty yards away in the pasture. The coyote, unalarmed, was watching him intently, its head cocked to one side.

'No, my pickup ain't broke down,' Duane said. 'I'm just out for a walk, if you don't mind.'

He walked a little farther and then glanced back. The coyote was still standing there, looking at him.

# 4

Once she left the office Karla headed for the post office, meaning to see if any interesting catalogues had come in the mail.

Halfway there, she realized she didn't care. If there was anything she wasn't in the mood for just then it was one more J. Crew catalogue. Why bother to buy anything, if her husband wanted a divorce?

Nonetheless, from force of habit, she drifted on toward the post office. But when she got a block from it she noticed that seven or eight miscellaneous citizens were standing out in the wind, talking, as they might if there had been a bad accident on the highway. As soon as one of them noticed the BMW coming, eight faces looked her way, a sure indication, in her opinion, that they had spotted Duane walking and knew about the divorce. For a moment it pissed her off: half the town already knew her husband wanted to divorce her and the son-of-a-bitch hadn't even bothered to mention it to her!

A second later she decided it might be a good day to skip the post office; J. Crew could definitely wait. She didn't feel up to trying to explain to half the people in town why her husband was walking down the road. Explaining why he was leaving her would be easier: any two people who had been together forty years might one day just elect to say, 'Enough!'

Karla blazed on past the post office, to the considerable disappointment of several people who had been hoping to ask her a few questions – discreet questions, of course. When and if it came to a showdown of some kind between herself and Duane, she was not really sure that the good citizens of Thalia would come down on her side. Duane was outrageously popular, always had been. He was president of the school board at the time, and vice president of the Chamber of Commerce. Karla, by her own admission, had had a few years when she could fairly have been described as wild and unruly.

Quite a few of the people who had known her then, many of them just as wild, had paid for their wildness and were dead and gone; but some of them were still alive and they had long memories.

Of course, most of the women in Thalia had *always* hoped Duane would divorce her, so they could marry him themselves, or at least sleep with him without violating the Seventh Commandment – or whichever Commandment it was that forbade adultery. The fact that most of these women were now long in the tooth didn't mean that they had entirely abandoned these hopes. Even chubby little Earlene, back at the office, had hardly been able to conceal her excitement at the thought that Duane might soon be an eligible divorcé.

Annoyed as she was by Duane's sudden bad behavior, Karla's view of *that* matter was that the women who allowed themselves to think along those lines were in for a big disappointment. Duane wasn't by nature much of a womanizer – so far as she knew he hadn't had a fling in years, and the few that had occurred in earlier days had mainly been forced upon him.

'You don't dodge quick enough, Duane – that's the whole story of you and women,' Karla had told him, years before, when dodging or not dodging had been a constant part of both their lives.

She started to drive out the road toward the cabin and have it out with him then and there; all her life she had been a confronter, and this was certainly an issue that needed confronting, but for some reason her instincts had gotten in a scrambled state. It was just possible that something physical had gone wrong with Duane; it might be that what was occurring had nothing to do with any sudden desire for a divorce. He could have had a small stroke, causing Alzheimer's to come on him so suddenly that he had forgotten how to drive; he might even have forgotten where they lived. Maybe the divorce theory, which had seemed reasonable at first, wasn't reasonable at all. Maybe Duane had just had a stroke and lost his mind, in which case she was going to need help when she brought him home. Dickie, their older son, was back in rehab, trying to overcome his cocaine problem, and Jack, the younger boy, was off in the next county, trapping wild pigs, a profession that suited him perfectly. Jack baited horse trailers with acorns and sold whatever pigs he trapped for five dollars a pound to someone who shipped them to Germany or somewhere.

That left Bobby Lee as the likeliest male who might have some influence with Duane in his deranged state. Karla zipped back to the office and soon had Bobby Lee on the CB.

'Bobby Lee, what are you doing?' she asked.

'Oh, not much. I just shot my little toe off,' Bobby Lee said, deadpan as ever.

'Drop everything then and come to the office,' Karla said. 'I need some help with Duane.'

'What'd he do, beat you up?' Bobby Lee inquired.

'I'd rather not talk about it on the CB. Could you please just come on to the office?' Karla asked.

She assumed the part about shooting his toe off was one of Bobby Lee's little weird jokes, but when his pickup bounced up to the office ten minutes later he was holding the driver's door open with one hand and dangling a bloody foot out the door.

'Oh my God, what has that stupid little idjit done now?' Earlene said, whereupon she fainted, falling face forward onto her electric typewriter, which immediately emitted a wild keening sound.

'It's all right, it was just my little toe,' Bobby Lee said, when Karla came running out. 'I guess Duane didn't beat you too bad, you don't have no black eyes, or else if you do you're using real good makeup.'

'I never said he beat me,' Karla said. 'Now Earlene's fainted right on her typewriter – I bet she's ruined that whole contract.'

'Well, big deal, I ruined my whole foot,' Bobby Lee said. 'And a foot's more important than a contract. There's a hose hooked to that faucet there by the corner of the office – if you'll just turn it on and hand it to me I'll sluice off some of this blood and we'll be on our way.'

'On our way where?' Karla asked. 'I never said we were going anywhere.'

One of the reasons Bobby Lee was so hard to communicate with was that he never removed his sunglasses, no matter how light or how dark it was. Once long ago a woman he was madly in love with called him a cross-eyed runt. Despite the fact that, in the years since the insult had been delivered, hundreds of people had assured him that he *wasn't* cross-eyed – a fact he could see for himself, in the privacy of his own bathroom, every morning when he shaved – Bobby Lee had refused to take any chances. He kept his dark glasses on at all times, in case cross-eyedness struck unexpectedly.

'Oh, come on, Karla,' he said. 'Everybody knows Duane has left you. The CB's been cracklin' all mornin', about him walking off. Ten or twelve people have offered him rides, but he won't get in no car. You two must have had the fight of a lifetime, for him to take it into his head to walk six miles.'

'Nope, no fight. I haven't even seen him since breakfast,' Karla said. 'He just parked his pickup and walked off.'

'Well, that's not what they're saying on the CB,' Bobby Lee assured her. 'Are you going to bring me that hose, or not? I don't want to get blood on my pickup.'

Karla brought him the hose, but declined to watch him wash his mangled toe.

'What were you aiming at that you hit your little toe?' she asked.

'A bug,' Bobby Lee said. 'I was so fucking bored I tried to shoot a bug and hit my toe.'

'I guess I better go wet a washrag and see if I can bring Earlene back to life,' Karla said.

'If it don't work I guess I could always give her mouth-to-mouth,' Bobby Lee said. He found Earlene appealing – who cared if she was a little chubby?

'I guess you would, you lech,' Karla said. 'I expect I can revive her without any help from a man so stupid he would try to shoot a bug.'

But reviving Earlene proved more difficult than she had expected. Even when Earlene regained a measure of consciousness she was far from out of the woods.

'I'm all right, I'm all right, I just need a little air. Everybody stand back,' Earlene said. Her voice was wobbly but not as wobbly as her legs. When she attempted to walk across the room and get what she referred to euphemistically as her 'nerve medicine' – it was actually Paxil, a fact Karla had determined long ago by sneaking a look in Earlene's purse one day when she was in the bathroom – she began to list heavily to the left. Before anyone could grab her and set her back on course she flopped into the watercooler, knocking it over. The water bottle, which had just been refilled that morning, went rolling across the floor, gurgling as it went, and gushing nice fresh springwater freely onto the rug.

Ruth Popper, who had been deep in a nap and unaware of any commotion, woke up from her nap with the conviction that her feet were wet, which they were, the rolling bottle of water having come to rest against her chair.

'I'm soaked – what's going on here? Has everybody in this office gone crazy?' she asked.

'No, but I guess you could say we've had a few setbacks,' Karla admitted. Earlene's head had hit the corner of the watercooler when she fell, opening a gash that took nine stitches to close. Karla left Bobby Lee in charge of the office while she ran the hysterical Earlene down to the clinic.

'It's gonna take plastic surgery, I know it is,' Earlene sobbed. 'No man will ever look at me again if I have a big ugly scar.'

'Earlene, you just bumped your head on the watercooler. Calm down,' Karla said. 'A little cut like that will heal up perfectly fine.'

'Will you pray for me – I figure prayer's my best hope,' Earlene begged.

'You've got pretty good health insurance – I expect that's all you'll need,' Karla said. She did not want to commit herself to praying for a little cut on Earlene Gholson's head. Her own husband might be wandering around the country with Alzheimer's, for all she knew; what little credit she might have with the higher powers had best be saved for members of her own immediate family, she believed.

Once Earlene finally got her stitches, screaming all the while as if she were being tortured by Comanches, Karla took her back to the office, to discover that Bobby Lee and Ruth were at each other's throats. Bobby Lee, sulking because his own injury had been neglected in favor of Earlene's, had refused to accept any responsibility for Ruth's wet feet and at some point in the discussion had told her to go to hell.

'If I do go to hell there you'll be, roasting on a spit,' Ruth told him.

'That's probably true, and it could happen in the next few days if I get gangrene from this injured toe,' Bobby Lee countered.

'You can't get gangrene from your toe because your toe's not there,' Karla pointed out, but her logic, however impeccable, was lost on Bobby Lee when he was in one of his sulky moods.

Karla, knowing she would never hear the end of it if she didn't offer Bobby Lee at least as much attention as she had offered Earlene, took him to the clinic too. The young doctor, who had just moved to Thalia and didn't really know the local ways, was annoyed with Bobby Lee because he had made no attempt to find the shot-off toe and bring it with him.

'If you'd just brought it with you I'm sure I could have sewed it back on,' the doctor said testily. 'Frankly, I would have liked the practice.'

'Then shoot your own toe off and practice on it, you dumb fuck,'

Bobby Lee said, after which the doctor's ministrations grew noticeably perfunctory.

'Bobby, why would you insult a doctor when he was trying to help you?' Karla asked, as they were driving away from the clinic, Bobby Lee sporting a nice clean bandage.

'It's a doctor's duty to heal the sick, no matter how rude they are,' Bobby Lee replied.

'Yes, but people don't always do their duty,' Karla reminded him – the sentiment prompted her to remember Duane, her sick-in-the-head husband, who must have long since walked to wherever he was going.

'Will you just ride out with me to the cabin, so I can see if Duane's there?' Karla asked. Bobby Lee, now that he was cured, had a familiar, selfish look on his face, the look that meant he was seriously considering parking himself in a beer joint and drinking beer for a day or two.

'It's kind of late,' he said. 'I'm sure Duane will show back up when he gets good and ready to.'

'Does that mean yes, or no?' Karla asked. 'I sure hope for your sake it means yes.'

'Why for my sake?' Bobby Lee asked. 'It's for my sake that I'm trying to be a little careful. Getting in the middle between a husband and a wife can be dangerous, you know.'

'Yes, but not as dangerous as refusing me on one of the rare occasions when I work up to asking you a favor,' Karla said.

'That sounds like a threat,' Bobby Lee said.

'Bobby, it *is* a threat,' Karla assured him. 'If you're too selfish to help me in my hour of need I'm going to wait until you're drunk or looking off and then I'm going to kick you as hard as I can right in your one good ball.'

'Oops, let's go right now,' Bobby Lee said, and without any more discussion, they went.

# 5

They had just rounded the first curve going out of Thalia when they saw a man walking toward them, backlit by the orange winter sunset.

'That's Duane, I know his walk,' Karla said.

'You're right,' Bobby Lee admitted. 'I didn't really believe it until now. Duane's about the last person you'd expect to see walking along the road.'

Karla had always been a confident woman, secure in her convictions and sure of her powers, but for some reason the mere sight of her husband walking down a country road right at sunset threw everything she had ever felt and believed into question. It stripped her of all confidence, and made her feel alone and confused.

'I think you ought to be the one to ask him if he'll get in the car, Bobby Lee,' she said.

'Me, uh-uh, no way,' Bobby Lee said. 'I done lost a toe today – I don't need to lose a job too.'

'Why would he fire you just for asking a question?' she asked.

Bobby Lee was silent for a while. He too was nervous about whatever was about to happen.

'A man that would get out of a perfectly good pickup and just go walking off is not in his right mind,' Bobby Lee said. 'He might fire me over nothing.'

Duane had already spotted his wife's BMW in the road ahead. Its appearance did not surprise him; what surprised him was that Karla had waited until almost sundown to show up. Karla usually jumped on a problem immediately; she had rarely been known to hesitate. The fact that she had waited nearly half a day to come looking for him probably meant one of two things: either she hadn't actually missed him until a few minutes ago, or she had missed him but hadn't been able to get away sooner because of one or more calamitous events. With all the grandkids living at the big house,

calamitous events were not rare; two or three a day was about the norm. Duane's guess was that his wife had had such a hectic day that she was just now getting around to him. Several cowboys and a couple of hunters had offered him rides on his walk back from the cabin, all of which he had amiably declined. He knew that the cowboys and the hunters would have spread the word that Duane Moore, president of the school board and vice president of the Chamber of Commerce, had lost his mind and was walking around on foot. That was the sort of news that spread quick.

The BMW had stopped in the road, a few hundred yards ahead, which just meant that Karla didn't know what to make of the sight of him walking. If a grandkid had swallowed a fishhook or something equally awkward to extract she would have known exactly what to do, but this new development was more complicated, and there was no precedent for it – not unless you counted a few tennis lessons he had invested in long ago, during the heady days of the boom – it was a time when many members of the West Texas oil community briefly convinced themselves they had risen into the leisure class, when in fact they hadn't.

Duane walked on toward the waiting car. Though he had only been walking a few hours, he had already developed a good deal of confidence in his pace. Given a few days in which to time himself from location to location, he felt sure he would arrive wherever he was supposed to be pretty much exactly when he was supposed to be there – at least he could if he didn't overreach and make an appointment in Olney or somewhere. Olney was eighteen miles down the road; it might be a month or so before he was ready for the eighteen-milers.

By the time Duane came even with the car, Karla was in such a state of nerves that she could not sustain the icy demeanor with which she usually greeted her husband when she was mad at him. Instead she rolled the window down and blurted out the fear that was uppermost in her mind.

'Duane, if you wanted a divorce why didn't you just say so?' she asked, when he stopped. 'Why did you have to scare us all this way?'

'What are you talking about, honey?' he asked. 'I don't want a divorce.'

Karla was flooded with relief. Her husband seemed to be perfectly sane, and he didn't want a divorce. But that fact, once she took a moment to consider it, made his behavior all the more puzzling.

Duane leaned down and looked in the car. Bobby Lee, inscrutable behind his sunglasses, sat in the passenger seat, staring straight ahead.

'What are you doing here?' Duane asked. 'I thought you had a job.'

'I do, but I shot my toe off,' Bobby Lee remarked, adding no details.

'Uh-oh,' Duane said. 'Target practice at bugs again?'

Bobby Lee just nodded.

'Duane, could you please get in, I've had a hectic day,' Karla said. 'Earlene fainted at the sight of Bobby's toe and when she came to she fell and split her head open on the watercooler, and then Ruth got her feet wet and so on.'

She paused. 'Just get in and let's go home,' she said.

'But I *am* nearly home,' Duane said. He glanced at his watch. 'I'll be there in fifteen minutes.'

'Duane, I wish you wouldn't be stubborn over this,' Karla said. 'Just get in the car. You've already embarrassed me enough, walking around all day.'

'I don't want to get in,' Duane said pleasantly. 'I'm enjoying my walk.'

'Well, good for you, nobody else is enjoying themselves much today,' Karla said. 'Get in just this once and we'll talk about it later.'

'I don't think there's much to talk about,' Duane said. 'Walking is a normal activity – anybody with two good legs can do it. It's also good for your health – lowers the risk of heart attacks and strokes.'

'It doesn't lower the risk for me,' Karla pointed out. 'I could get a stroke right now just from being mad at you.'

'Why would you be mad at me for taking steps to improve my health?' Duane asked. 'Isn't this better than having me keel over in the cab of a pickup somewhere?'

Karla considered those remarks for a while.

'It's just like you to try and make something unreasonable sound reasonable,' she said.

'I'm not the only person in the world who walks,' Duane reminded her. 'I'm not even the only person in Thalia. There's probably four or five women down at the track right now, taking their walks.

'What I'm doing is a lot healthier than shooting at bugs,' he added, with a glance at Bobby Lee.

Karla was growing more and more irritated, as she often did when Duane got in one of his reasonable moods. At such times he always seemed able to make what he wanted to do seem completely rational, something everybody else would be doing if they had just thought of it themselves. It was true, for example, that several town women, and even one or two men, could be seen walking in the early mornings, before the day's work started. But the women who walked were mostly just housewives or secretaries or else retired. Probably the only reason most of them were walking was because they were too tight to buy StairMasters or other machines that would allow them to exercise in their homes. Karla owned several exercise machines herself and would have been happy to buy a few for Duane if he had given her any indication that he felt the need for exercise.

'Duane, there's plenty of ways you could exercise at home without upsetting everybody and making them think you've lost your mind,' Karla said, but when she looked up to see what response he would make she discovered that she was just floating words out an open window; Duane had continued on down the road – she could see his retreating back in her rearview mirror.

'What do you think of that, the son-of-a-bitch didn't even hear me out,' Karla said, turning to Bobby Lee.

'Can't we just go home – my toe hurts,' he said.

'I don't want to go home,' Karla said. 'I want Duane to get in the car. If we don't nip this development in the bud there's no telling where we'll end up.'

'It's not a crime to walk,' Bobby Lee pointed out.

'If he went all the way to the cabin and now nearly all the way back, that's twelve miles he's walked today!' Karla said, to emphasize her point.

Bobby Lee had to admit that she had come up with an impressive calculation – twelve miles was farther than anyone in Thalia had walked in living memory, at least as far as he was aware. He himself had once had to walk nearly two miles when he got his pickup stuck while duck hunting one morning. Twelve miles, by his rough calculation, was six times as far as two miles.

'Just thinking about all them miles makes my feet hurt,' he admitted.

'But it's still not a crime,' he added. 'And it don't necessarily mean he's crazy.'

'I don't like it that you're weakening,' Karla said.

'It's because my toe hurts,' Bobby Lee assured her.

Karla slowly turned the BMW around in the narrow country road.

'You didn't even ask him to get in,' she said to Bobby Lee. 'He never does anything I ask him to do but he might get in if you asked him.'

'Doubtful,' Bobby Lee said.

'Won't you even try?' she asked.

Bobby Lee was silent, a response Karla took to mean no. Disgusted, she shoved the pedal to the metal. By the time she passed her husband she was going eighty-six. If her husband was determined to refuse her perfectly polite offer of a ride, then she wanted to see that he ate a little dust.

'Slow down, there's a bridge; we'll be airborne if you hit it going this fast,' Bobby Lee said, regretting, once again, that he had allowed himself to be drawn into a controversy between a husband and a wife.

Duane tucked his chin into his jacket when his wife went roaring by. The dusty cloud she raised was still hanging over the road when he crossed the pavement. What was left of the sunset showed yellow through the drifting dust.

# 6

When Duane stepped into his house the kitchen was a maelstrom, as it usually was when dinnertime approached. Little Bascom, Nellie's two-year-old, had managed to claw his way up on the kitchen counter and was cramming one fist into a big jar of peanut butter and then proceeded to lick it off, an activity which evidently enjoyed the approval of Rag, the elderly cook, who was frying round steak and making what she liked to refer to as her 'signature cream gravy,' all only a foot or two south of Little Bascom.

'Why are you letting him do this?' Duane asked, immediately setting Little Bascom back on the floor where he belonged. Then he spun off some paper towels and managed to get the little boy's fist more or less free of peanut butter.

'Because he was whining, that's why,' Rag said, without looking up from her task. 'I can't cook my gourmet food with whiny kids underfoot.'

'Then you've taken the wrong job,' Duane informed her. 'We've got a large surplus of whiny kids around here.'

'Little Bascom was starving, that's my analysis,' Rag assured him. 'Nellie drifts around listening to her Walkman all day and lets her kids fend for themselves.'

'I didn't say she was a perfect mother,' Duane countered. 'Just make him a peanut butter sandwich next time, okay? Who knows what else he's had his fist in.'

'I know, the poo-poo,' Bubbles said.

'Shut up, you snitch!' Willy said. The two of them were already at table, waiting politely for the food to be served.

'Hi, kids,' Duane said. Not only were his grandkids beautiful; they had healthy appetites as well.

'I'm mad at you, Pa-Pa,' Bubbles said. 'I didn't want you to go crazy.'

'Shut up, he doesn't look crazy to me,' Willy said.

'It's not polite to say "shut up" to a person,' Bubbles informed her brother.

Rag emitted a sound that was somewhere between a laugh and a bellow.

'Polite. I ain't seen much of that since I took this job,' she said. Rag's main problem as a gourmet cook was that she was almost too short to see over the stove.

'You could try setting an example,' Duane told her. 'Be a role model, you know? Someone the kids could look up to.'

'They only look up to me while I'm cooking,' Rag said. 'They know that if it weren't for me they'd starve. But once that food's on the table it's dog-eat-dog.'

'What makes you think I'm crazy, honey?' Duane asked, sitting down by Bubbles.

'Because you walked,' Bubbles said. Personally she didn't see anything wrong with Pa-Pa taking a walk, but her grandmother was in her room sobbing so there must be a bad element to it that no one had explained to her.

'Grandma's cryin',' she said.

'That's too bad, unless they're crocodile tears,' Duane said, easing off his new walking shoes. They were first-rate walking shoes, but, even so, his feet had not quite been ready to do twelve miles. They hurt.

'It's hormones,' Rag volunteered. 'You taking it into your head to go walking around all day has set off a hormone storm. There's no telling where this will end.'

'Hormone storms are just part of life,' Duane said, massaging his left foot.

'Female life, you mean,' Rag said. 'Males only got one hormone to worry about and once it's dribbled out that's the end of that story.'

'What story, Raggedy?' Willy asked. Rag was always making remarks like that and then never explaining them.

'Never mind, it's a song you'll be singing soon enough,' Rag told him.

'I thought you said it was a story,' Willy reminded her. 'Now you say it's a song.'

'Grandma's crying,' Bubbles said again, in case her grandfather had somehow missed this vital piece of information.

'Well, maybe she just needs to cry,' Duane said. 'Let's eat supper.'

28

He was determined not to let Karla overdramatize his decision to become a walker. He knew she would immediately try to enlist the kids and the grandkids in her effort to get him back in the cab of a pickup, but he meant to meet whatever campaign she launched with reasonableness and calm. He would explain that walking was a particularly good exercise for a man his age – it was something that would help keep him in good health. He didn't intend to let Karla stampede the household into believing that the simple act of walking was tantamount to insanity – though he had no doubt she would do just that and had probably already started.

'Don't you even care that Grandma's cryin'?' Bubbles asked. She was extremely curious about her grandpa and her grandma. If her grandpa really didn't even care that her grandma was crying, then that was a significant clue.

'Oh sure, I care a bunch,' Duane said, easing off the other shoe and massaging the other sore foot.

'Then why don't you go kiss her and make her well?' Bubbles asked.

'I doubt she wants me to kiss her, honey,' Duane said.

'That's right, she don't,' Karla said, marching into the room with Baby Paul in her arms – he was Nellie's youngest, seven months old, almost. Baby Paul grinned at the sight of his grandfather, exposing his new tooth. He loved his grandfather and held out his arms, indicating that he would welcome a transfer, but Karla walked him around Duane and popped him into his high chair so briskly that his happy look turned to one of dismay.

'Sit there and deal with it,' Karla told him, when he looked as if he might cry.

'Mean,' Little Bascom said, to the table at large.

'No comments out of you, unless you want me to spank your little butt,' Karla said.

'My tasty gourmet food is almost ready,' Rag informed them cheerfully. She always tried to be extra cheerful when she felt domestic tension building; and she certainly felt it building just at that point.

'I just don't want to rush my signature gravy,' she continued, when no one responded to her first cheerful remark.

'Take your time,' Duane said. 'We've got lots of it.'

'Speak for yourself, Duane,' Karla told him. 'If I have to spend my declining years dealing with a crazy husband, then I doubt I have much time to spare.'

Before he could answer, Julie wandered in, wearing the sleepy look she wore when she was smoking dope rather than the wired look she sported when she was taking speed. The fact that her own brother, Dickie, was in rehab for the third time, leaving his own three children to the tender mercies of his spaced-out wife, Annette, was not enough to discourage Julie from sampling a wide range of drugs.

'I wish you all weren't so mean to Annette,' she said. 'It's a lot jollier around here when Annette and those kids come to supper.'

Annette, at the moment, was living in a trailer house at the far west end of the property – the trailer house had been bought for Rag to stay in, but Rag – who had once made the mistake of telling her sister that she felt like Raggedy Ann and had been called Rag ever since – soon decided that she would survive in her job longer if she lived a little farther from work. That way she wouldn't be available if Jack showed up drunk or stoned at three in the morning, under the delusion that it was breakfast time.

'We're not mean to Annette,' Duane said. 'I like Annette a lot.'

'I like her too but it's hard to give your full approval to a daughter-in-law who makes her living robbing convenience stores,' Karla said.

Annette did in fact have two convictions for armed robbery, but she was so appealing that the judge's heart had melted both times, causing her to pile up twice as much probation time as Jack; but the good part was she had only served three or four nights in jail.

'Why do you always have to bring that up?' Julie asked. 'She just took the petty cash, both times. Can't I just ask her if she and the kids would like to come in and eat? I hate to think of the four of them sitting out in that trailer house eating junk food.'

'Bring 'em in, they can have gourmet cooking,' Rag said.

'Annette's part of the family,' Duane said. 'Of course you can go invite her to dinner.'

'But if she doesn't want to come you hurry on back,' Karla said. 'I don't want you sitting out there half the night, smoking dope and watching porn.'

'Mom, we don't watch porn,' Julie protested. 'It's just that on cable sometimes people are naked.'

'Naked,' Little Bascom said. His vocabulary was growing by leaps and bounds.

'Do you want a drink, Duane?' Karla asked. Annoyed as she was, it was hard to stay totally mad when Duane was sitting around with his grandkids, looking sweet.

'A splash of bourbon might taste good,' Duane said. 'Little Bascom was poking his fist in the peanut butter when I got home.'

'That's your fault, for not taking the ride I offered,' Karla said.

Duane let the remark float by. He was determined not to be goaded into some hasty retort that would just raise Karla's temperature. He decided to wait for Annette and her kids to show up before making a statement announcing his intention to become a walker. He would explain calmly that at his age he needed lots of exercise and fresh air. Walking, by definition, was a beneficial activity that would keep him outdoors and reduce his desire to smoke cigarettes or pursue any of the unhealthy desires that could overcome a man who spent too much time in the cab of a pickup. He wasn't naive enough to suppose that his reasonableness would sway Karla, who was rarely swayable once she took a position. But he thought he could probably get most of the grandkids on his side, creating a lobbying force that would keep it from being such a him-against-them kind of thing.

While he sipped his bourbon, rehearsing in his mind a few of the points he meant to cover in his statement, Julie came back, trailed closely by Annette and the three kids she and Dickie had produced in ten years of an off-again, on-again union: Loni, Barbi, and Sami, it being Annette's desire that all her kids' names end with i. Loni was nine, Barbi six, and Sami four. Annette was a willowy brunette, the tallest woman in Thalia; she went through life wearing a dreamy smile that reflected her good nature, and also the fact that she smoked a lot of dope. Even the convenience store managers that Annette had robbed reported that she had continued to smile pleasantly and remain perfectly courteous while holding them at gunpoint.

Of the children, Loni and Sami were as good-natured as their mother, but Barbi, a dark midge of a child, was the opposite in all respects of the doll she had been named after. All the other grandkids thought Barbi was a witch, and the older three had only just been prevented from burning her at the stake. The UPS man, who was at the house virtually every day, delivering things Karla had ordered from various catalogues, noticed that something weird was going on and raced over and stopped it just before Bubbles and Willy could get the kindling to light. Barbi, silent and malevolent, had been tied to a fence post.

'Hi, Annette,' Duane said, when the group walked in. 'Why, there's my Sami.'

'And there's my Loni and my Barbi,' Karla said. Grandparental favoritism, where Dickie's children were concerned, had divided along the lines of gender.

'I think it's stupid that that old rehab center won't even let Dickie make a phone call,' Annette said. 'I just miss him to pieces. What could one little phone call hurt?'

'Plenty, because he'd make it to the drug dealer, not to his loving wife,' Karla reminded her. 'That's what he did last time he was in, remember?'

'Shut up talking about dope – here comes my gourmet cooking,' Rag informed them. Soon the large kitchen table was covered with all the things Rag liked to cook: platters of round steak for the masses, bowls of her signature cream gravy, hominy, black-eyed peas, sauerkraut – a personal passion of Rag's not shared with much intensity by the people she fed – okra, a mound of baked potatoes, grilled onions, and hot rolls.

'Sit down and eat with us, Rag,' Duane said. 'I hate to eat when somebody's working.'

He said it every night; asking Rag to eat with them was a prelude to every meal, as grace had once been, but Rag had no interest in eating her gourmet cooking. Instead, she repaired to the little pantry, where she smoked and watched *I Love Lucy* reruns on a small TV, occasionally popping back in to pile more food on the table or check on the cobbler she held in readiness for dessert.

'In my day the help didn't eat with the family,' she said, when Duane asked her to sit down and eat.

'What if we adopt you, would you eat with us then?' he once asked, out of curiosity.

'No, because if I start eating my gourmet cooking I'll get fat and lose my figure,' Rag replied. The truth was that she preferred to stop by the Dairy Queen and pick up a cheeseburger and a few tacos to munch while watching the midnight reruns, her favorite being *The Mary Tyler Moore Show*, all one hundred and sixty-eight episodes of which she had seen at least once; she could recite whole episodes almost verbatim, and would, if asked. She could do passable imitations of Mary, Phyllis, Lou Grant, Rhoda, Ted, Georgette, and Murray. All the grandkids listened attentively but the one most won by Rag's performances was Little Bascom, who would roll on the floor laughing hysterically, although he had never seen *The Mary Tyler Moore Show* and had no idea what Rag was doing.

Although both Julie and Annette were professing vegetarianism at the time, they each forgot their vows and ate several pieces of round steak, washing it down with beer.

'If either of you are pregnant you oughtn't to be drinking that beer,' Karla informed them sternly. 'We have enough addicts in this family without producing any little alcoholic fetuses.'

'Mom, don't talk about things like that, it's creepy,' Julie said. 'I don't even want my kids to know what a fetus is – they're too young.'

'We already know. Don't you ever watch the Discovery Channel?' Willy asked.

'A fetus grows in the uterus,' Barbi said, in her dark way. 'And it's sperm that makes them and sperm lives in the balls of the male.'

'That's right – I think I've already got some in *my* balls,' Willy said.

'Balls,' Little Bascom said. 'Balls, balls.'

'Now see what you started,' Annette said to Karla. They had never been close.

'Yes, but I started it for a good reason – so you won't drink when you're pregnant and produce some little baby that won't never have good math skills,' Karla said. 'Anyway, as soon as kids get big enough to watch television now they know all about the facts of life.'

'And penises and vaginas too,' Willy said.

'Daddy, stop him,' Julie said. 'I don't want him talking about dicks at the dinner table.'

'Okay, Julie's right, everybody shut up about the facts of life,' Duane said. 'Anyway I need to talk to all of you about a decision I made today.'

'Uh-oh, I knew this was coming,' Karla said. 'I think we ought to get the children to bed before we get into this.'

'Not on your life,' Duane said. 'I particularly want the children to hear what I have to say.'

'Oh sure, so you can brainwash them into believing that anything you do is just fine and dandy,' Karla said.

'There's free speech in this country – I have the right to say what I want to say to my own children and grandchildren, don't I?' Duane demanded to know.

Karla refused to answer, but there was a chorus from the crowd and the chorus was in favor of hearing what Duane had to say. Rag, intrigued, turned down *I Love Lucy* and stuck her head out the pantry door so she could listen.

'You can talk,' Karla said, reluctantly. 'But then I get the last word, okay?'

'Okay – but on condition you don't interrupt me until I've finished,' Duane said. 'I want you to shut up until I've said what I have to say. Then we can all talk it over.'

'If you go off the deep end and start brainwashing my grandkids I guess I have the right to interrupt,' Karla said. 'What kind of democracy is this, anyway?'

'Shut up, Grandma, I want to hear what Grandpa has to say,' Willy said.

'As for that, you ain't too big to spank, young man,' Karla said.

She looked severely at Willy, but then, noticing that everyone at the table was frowning at her, and realizing that Duane, with his gift for sweet reasonableness, was costing her whatever advantage she might have in the court of public opinion, Karla quickly shut up.

# 7

'I guess some people in town and maybe one or two people in this house were a little upset with me today because I decided to take a walk,' Duane began.

'Right, Grandma freaked out,' Willy said.

'Right, 'cause you went crazy,' Bubbles said.

'You should have taken me. I like to walk and nobody ever lets me,' Barbi said.

'I don't walk, I run,' Sami said.

Loni, the shy one, who rarely spoke, as usual kept her own counsel.

'I didn't go crazy, Bubbles,' Duane said. 'You don't have to be crazy just to want to take a walk.'

'Yes, you do,' Bubbles insisted. 'You want to walk away and leave us all to starve, that's what my momma said.'

'It was a joke, Bubbles,' Julie said, horrified that her own daughter would betray a casual comment she had happened to make.

'You kids shut up, and you too, Julie,' Karla said. 'Let Pa-Pa finish.'

'Thanks,' Duane said. 'It's simple, really. Walking is very good exercise, and a man my age needs exercise. Walking keeps people from having strokes and heart attacks, whereas riding around in pickups smoking cigarettes is a good way to get lung cancer and keel over and die.'

'Don't *die*, Pa-Pa!' Bubbles said, horrified at the prospect.

'Well, I won't, honey, if everyone will just leave me alone to do my walking,' Duane assured her. 'All of you are little right now, but I want to live a long time so I can see you grow up and meet who you marry and see what kind of kids you have. Don't you think it would be nice if I could do that?'

All the children nodded, even Little Bascom and Baby Paul, neither of whom had any notion as to what was going on. Little Bascom and Baby Paul continued to nod, long after the others had stopped.

'Of course, nobody would really starve – not as long as I'm here to do my gourmet cooking,' Rag said.

She had taken the remark as a slight on her loyalty.

'I didn't say anything about starving,' Duane assured her. 'I just want everybody to think about this calmly. Just because walking isn't a popular thing around Thalia doesn't mean it's crazy. Actually it's a smart, healthy thing to do. It just means I have a good attitude and want to stay healthy and live a long life.'

He stopped and surveyed his audience.

'There's nothing wrong with that, is there?' he asked.

'No, but you don't have to stay alive to see what kind of kids I have because I hate girls and I'm not going to have any,' Willy informed him.

'I hated them too, when I was your age, but I changed my mind and you might change yours,' Duane said. 'I'd just kind of like to stay alive to see what happens.'

'Okay,' Willy said. 'I don't mind, Pa-Pa.'

'If I just keep walking people will gradually get used to it and then they'll notice that I'm losing weight and looking a little healthier – some of them might start walking too,' Duane said.

'That would be good,' Barbi said. 'There are too many people with fat ugly butts in this town. They all need to get liposuction on their big fat asses.'

'My lord, where did you hear about liposuction?' Duane asked.

'From Grandma,' Barbi said.

'Duane, I was just discussing it in the abstract,' Karla said.

'All your friends are too fat, Grandma,' Barbi said, pressing on. 'Bobbie is fat and Candy is fat and Jolene is the fattest of all.'

'That's not a kind way to put it, Barbi,' Karla said. 'But some of them *are* a little heavy, I'll admit.'

'I know,' Bubbles said. 'Pa-Pa can take all the fat people with him when he walks and pretty soon they won't be fat anymore.'

'Fat chance of that,' Rag said, to Duane's relief. He had no intention of leading a pack of fat walkers, but to say so directly would damage his case, just when he thought he pretty well had it made.

'So, does everybody understand now?' Duane said. 'Walking doesn't mean I'm crazy – it just means I want to be healthy and stay alive a long time.'

'What if it takes you too long and you get lost in the weeds?' Barbi asked. She was good at spotting possible flaws in whatever arguments came her way, particularly the arguments that came her way from her parents, when they wanted her to do something she didn't want to do. Often she was able to convince them that for her to do what they wanted would mean almost certain death – of course, that worked best when both her parents were too stoned to think clearly.

'I'm taller than the weeds; I won't get lost,' Duane said.

'Yes, but what if a bad witch made the weeds grow taller than the water tower, then you might get lost,' Barbi said.

'Well if that happened Grandma could just hire a helicopter to come and rescue me,' Duane said.

'Shut up, you're the only witch around here, you little slut,' Willy said. Barbi was always talking about disasters bad witches could make and some of them sounded so real he had bad dreams about them.

'Don't be calling your own cousin a slut, little boy,' Annette said.

'Now see what you've done, Duane – you've got all these kids talking ugly,' Karla said.

'Honey, they're kids,' he reminded her. 'They can talk ugly without any help from me.'

'What about Six Flags? Have any of you kids thought of that?' Karla asked.

'What about Six Flags, are we going?' Willy asked.

'Yeah, are we going?' Bubbles asked, and the others chimed in, all except Barbi, who refused to join the clamor. Baby Paul banged his spoon and threw his carrots off his high chair.

'The reason I mention it is because Pa-Pa is the only person I trust to drive on those Arlington freeways and Arlington's where Six Flags is,' Karla said. 'If he won't drive we can't plan trips to Six Flags because it's too far for all of us to walk.'

'Hey, that's not fair, I'm the grandparent,' Duane said. 'It's the parents' job to take kids to amusement parks.'

Nonetheless he and Karla were usually the ones who took the grandkids to Six Flags. When Julie and Jack and Nellie and Dickie went they left the kids at home.

'We wouldn't have any fun ourselves if we took the kids,' Nellie said, succinctly summarizing the prevailing attitude.

Duane noticed that all the young eyes had swiveled in his direction. The thought that his walking might deprive them of trips to Six Flags put the whole matter in a different light.

'Well, it's really no problem,' he said. 'The next time you kids all want to go to Six Flags I'll just hire a limo. And Grandma can ride along with you to chaperone.'

'Oh boy, a limo ... a limo!' Bubbles said, so ecstatically that Duane congratulated himself on the clever way he had trumped Karla's ace.

It was a clean victory, too. All of the kids had seen limos galore on TV but none of them had ever ridden in one. The consensus was that riding in a limo would be even more fun than Six Flags itself – after all, they had been to Six Flags quite a few times already.

Karla, who knew when she had been trumped, didn't say a word. If Duane turned out to be serious about walking, then it was going to be a long campaign. Better to fight and run away, and live to fight another day.

'Cobbler time!' Rag announced. 'There's not many things better on earth than blackberry cobbler.'

'Riding in a limo is better,' Willy assured her.

'I hope the driver is a member of the Mafia,' Barbi said. 'I hope he wears a dark suit and is a member of the Mafia.'

'Why would you want to be driven to Six Flags by a member of the Mafia, honey?' Annette inquired. Sometimes the things that came out of her daughter's mouth shocked her a little. She never had that problem with Loni, who was so quiet she often wouldn't even say what color socks she wanted to put on in the morning.

'I love the Mafia. I want to join it when I get big,' Barbi said. 'It's my favorite thing in the whole world.'

Then, while everyone was absorbed with their cobbler, Baby Paul somehow managed to push with his feet and tip his high chair over backward; when it hit the floor he popped out of it like a living cork and went sliding far across the kitchen floor. The fall didn't hurt him at all but when everybody rushed over to see if he was injured he got rattled and began to shriek at the top of his lungs.

'I told Nellie that high chair was no good; she just doesn't listen,' Karla said.

'Shrieks and screams, typical day,' Rag said, contemplating the mess of dishes she had to clean up.

# 8

Duane had put a sliding glass door along the wall of the master bedroom, so he could step outside at night and gauge the weather, sniff the breeze, look at the stars, or just sit in a lawn chair for a while, relaxing. On a dark night, when there were no stars to look at and no moon to light the patio or the yard, accidents could happen. Once when Duane left the glass door open a little, a granddaddy rattlesnake, almost eight feet long, sidled into the house and made itself comfortable on the bed. Karla noticed it just as she was about to throw back the covers: she let out a shriek that could have been heard in Wichita Falls. The sight of a huge rattlesnake – the largest anyone had seen around Thalia in more than twenty-five years – on her very own bed so unnerved Karla that she slept on the couch in the living room for the next two months. The snake had been killed, stuffed, and given to the county museum, where it was on permanent display, but even so Karla was a long time freeing herself of the conviction that the big snake or one of its kinfolk was under her bed or in her walk-in closet. The incident scared her so badly that she had every object taken out of every closet in the house, to be sure no snakes were lurking among them. The house contained seventeen large closets; the objects they disgorged while Karla was hunting for snakes made a pile the like of which had not been seen by anyone in Thalia, ever.

'They didn't even have this much stuff in Babylon, Grandma,' Barbi said. She had only been four at the time, but, even then, she had a good vocabulary.

'Where'd you hear about Babylon, honey? You don't even go to Sunday school,' Karla asked. The answer, of course, was the Discovery Channel.

'I don't know about Babylon but this is too much stuff,' Duane observed. 'No wonder I've already been bankrupt twice.'

'Duane, it just kind of filtered in – you know, like sand does when there's a sandstorm,' Karla said.

After contemplating the great pile for a few days, Karla decided there might be something to be said for the simple life after all. Rather than try to fit the thousands of objects back in the seventeen closets, she and the girls indulged in an orgy of weeding, carried a whole pickup load of designer clothes to an orphanage in Waco, and got rid of much of the rest in a gigantic garage sale which drew patrons from as far away as Odessa.

'That old snake had a good effect after all,' Duane observed. 'Now I can go in my own closet and look for some clean underwear without suffocating.'

'Duane, don't even mention that snake, I might get a migraine,' Karla said.

That night, though, it was far too cold for there to be any rattlesnakes about. The sky was inky, the stars like white diamonds. Though the norther had mostly blown itself out, it still sighed and whistled a bit; the wind chimes Annette had hung up behind the trailer house tinkled in the distance.

Duane, in his bathrobe, blew in his hands a few times and considered the various places he could walk on the morrow. He knew every road in the county, from his years in the pickup, but there were plenty of them he had yet to traverse on foot. The decision to walk for a while, made on the spur of the moment, had already changed his perspective and improved his attitude. Instead of going to bed with the dull sense that he would just have to get up in the morning and do the same things he had done more or less every day for sixty years, he had a new experience to look forward to.

'Duane, get in here; it's too cold for you to be standing out there,' Karla said, sticking her head out the glass door for a moment.

Duane obeyed, yawning. He felt invigorated, rather than sleepy, but he yawned anyway, hoping Karla would just let him go to bed with no more discussion of the walking. He didn't expect it to work, but he gave it a try, anyway.

Sure enough, it didn't work.

'Duane, if you're that depressed maybe you should just get counseling,' Karla said.

He didn't respond.

'Lots of normal people go into counseling now – it's not a stigma, like it used to be,' she said.

'If it's not a stigma, why don't you get it, instead of liposuction?' Duane suggested, slipping into bed.

'Duane, I'm not the one that's depressed,' Karla said.

'Maybe you *are* depressed and you just won't admit it,' he said. 'A few trips to the counselor might teach you a few things about yourself.'

'Candy says what you're doing now is a strategy, Duane,' Karla said. 'We weren't talking about me, we were talking about you. Candy says that's a strategy depressed people always use. They try to pretend that it's the person who's trying to help them that's depressed.'

'Even if it's a strategy it could be true. Good night,' Duane said.

'Don't just roll over and go to sleep,' Karla said. 'We need to talk this through. Why can't you just be normal and get up and get in your pickup and drive off, like you've done our whole marriage?'

'Because when I'm in my pickup I *am* depressed,' Duane admitted. 'Just the thought of having to be in my pickup makes me depressed. Don't you understand? I've spent my whole life in a goddamn pickup and what do I have to show for it? Just the thought of having to get in a pickup makes me feel crazy.'

The vehemence in his voice surprised him a little. He hadn't realized, until he started talking, how much he hated pickups.

The same vehemence surprised Karla a lot.

'Duane, don't talk so loud,' she said meekly. 'It scares me when you talk loud.'

But, now that he was started, Duane found it hard to stop.

'What I'd really like to do is burn my pickup!' he said. 'I'd like to burn my pickup and burn all my trucks, too. I never want to ride in any of them again.'

Then he stopped, realizing that he must, indeed, sound a little crazy. Pickups were the commonest vehicles in that part of the country. Almost everyone he knew owned one or two. If someone at the filling station heard him talk about wanting to burn his pickup they would probably consider that he had lost his mind.

As for his wife, she just looked shocked.

'Okay, okay, I'm sorry I mentioned it. Go to sleep,' Karla said.

# 9

Duane woke at three. Karla had the bed light on and was reading catalogues. She didn't seem particularly upset.

'Remember when Neiman's offered those his-or-her camels in their Christmas catalogue a few years back?' she asked.

'I think I remember hearing something about that,' he said. 'Why?'

'Oh, I don't know,' Karla said. 'I was just wondering if those camels were still available. I think I'll call Neiman's and ask them, as soon as it's time for the store to open.'

'That won't be for seven hours,' he pointed out.

'I know, but I was just thinking that if we had a pair of camels to ride around on maybe you wouldn't be so depressed,' she said.

Details of the Neiman Marcus offering of matched riding camels were beginning to come back to him – or rather one detail in particular: the price.

'Honey, those camels cost a hundred and seventy-five thousand dollars, and that was years ago,' he said. 'If I had to pay a hundred and seventy-five thousand dollars for two animals I don't even know how to ride I'd be a lot more depressed.

'Besides, camels spit on you,' he added, by way of a clincher.

'Oh well, it was just a thought. I bet you'd look cute on a camel,' Karla said. 'Besides, if you're depressed enough that you're thinking about burning your pickup, then something needs to happen quick.'

'It won't be riding camels,' Duane said. 'I know you're just grasping at straws, but maybe you ought to try grasping somewhere besides the Neiman Marcus catalogue. Their straws are too expensive.'

'Okay, forget the camels,' Karla said. 'Do you think it's because of our sex life that you're depressed?'

'What sex life?' Duane asked, and then immediately wished he had phrased his response differently.

'That's what I meant,' Karla said. 'We don't have one. Maybe you're just so pent up that you're trying to walk it off.'

'If I was pent up I think I'd know a way to get unpent,' Duane said. 'We've probably had more of a sex life than any ten people you can name in this town.'

'Yes, but beautiful memories aren't enough,' Karla said.

'I wish I hadn't waked up,' Duane said. 'If there's one thing that's not going to make me less depressed it's talking about sex.'

'I know, but right now I can't think of anything else to talk about,' Karla said.

'We've had slumps before,' he reminded her. 'A slump now and then has to be expected when you get to be our age.'

'That's not what it says in my health magazines, Duane,' Karla mentioned.

He politely refrained from asking what it said in her health magazines. He didn't want to know about tanned, healthy, perfectly adjusted old couples who had sex constantly, even at advanced ages. Besides, he had a feeling Karla was going to tell him anyway, and she did.

'It says in my health magazines that people who have healthy bodies and good attitudes can go right on having sex until they're eighty-five or ninety or so,' she said.

'Yeah, but those health magazines don't have anything to do with real life,' Duane pointed out. 'They're just magazines. In real life people have slumps all the time.'

'I guess they do, but that doesn't mean I like just having sex on my birthday,' Karla said.

'Oh hush,' he said. 'We've had sex since your birthday.'

Then, once he thought about it, he couldn't really be sure they *had* had sex since her birthday, and her birthday was nine months back. Sex was one of those things that seemed to inhabit a no-man's-land beyond explanation or excuse. It had been there for a long time and now it seemed to be gone. He had no desire to make love to Karla or any other woman – not at the present time.

'Couldn't you just try a teeny little bit of counseling, just for me?' Karla asked. 'My birthday is coming around again. It could be like an early birthday present or something.'

'I'm going to take a walk now,' Duane said. 'I'll think about the counseling while I'm walking.'

'Duane, it's three-fifteen in the morning; you can't take a walk now,' Karla said, alarmed that he would even consider such a thing.

'Sure I can,' Duane said. 'All it takes is two good legs. The time of day doesn't have a thing to do with it.'

In fact he couldn't wait to get out of the house, into the cold air – couldn't wait to be alone in the night with his thoughts, walking by himself, beyond the reach of expectation or demand.

'If you ask me you're clinically depressed or you wouldn't even think of such a thing,' Karla said. 'It's the middle of the night. People don't just go walking around in the middle of the night – not in this part of the country.'

'It's not against the law, though,' Duane pointed out. 'There's nothing out there that's going to hurt me.'

'I guess a truck could hurt you if it was coming around the corner real fast and didn't expect to see a crazy man walking in the road,' Karla said. She was growing indignant at the mere thought of Duane walking around the streets at three-fifteen in the morning.

'No truck is going to come around the corner and hit me and I don't want to talk about this anymore,' he said, sliding out of the bed and grabbing his new walking shoes.

'Where do you think you're going to walk to at this hour?' Karla asked. 'It won't even be light enough to see good for three hours.'

'I don't mean to be walking anywhere but in the road,' Duane said. 'I think I can see well enough to stay in the road.'

'If it was summer you might step on a snake,' Karla said – realizing, though, that February was not the summer.

Duane didn't bother to answer. He quickly shaved and showered, got dressed, and carefully tied his walking shoes. By the time he was ready to leave Karla was sitting at the kitchen counter with a cup of coffee and a stack of health magazines. She felt disoriented, on the whole. It was three-fifteen in the morning and her husband was about to go walking away.

'Suppose one of the grandkids needed a blood transfusion real quick,' she said. 'What good would you be if you were walking around somewhere out on the road?'

'Not much good,' he admitted. 'I doubt that's going to happen, but if it does, call nine-one-one. That's what it's for.'

'Duane, I'm really upset; you're just not in your right mind anymore,' Karla said. 'You're clinically depressed, only you're too stubborn to admit it.'

'We can talk about it later,' he said, not looking at his wife. He had an overpowering desire to be out of the house, beyond questions, speculations, marriage, business, all of it.

He pulled on his gloves and left, leaving Karla sitting unhappily with her pile of magazines.

# 10

Once outside his house, Duane immediately felt a huge swelling of relief. He had a feeling he had never had before in his life: that the whole world was there before him and that he was free to walk through it. He might walk through Egypt, if he felt like it, or India, or China. If he had to use airplanes or boats in order to cross the great waters that lay in his way it would only be until he was back on land. From then on he would trust to his two feet again, walking everywhere, in no hurry, free. All that he had been too busy to see or do in his life so far he could now investigate, without haste, at his own pace, on foot. It was a wonderful feeling – he stood by his garage for a few moments, savoring it. There sat the pickup that had been his prison; but it was his prison no longer.

Happily, he set off through the town. Though he felt as if the whole world were spread before him, his actual location was a small town on the West Texas plain, the town where he had lived his whole life. He had never before, even in boyhood, really wandered around it much at night. Walking through it would be, in a sense, to discover it afresh. The wind had died completely – it was no longer very cold. Duane soon warmed up sufficiently that he felt he could do without his gloves, which he stuffed in his hip pocket.

Although most of the houses in town were dark, a few had lights in their kitchens, or bedrooms, or dens. From some the only light was the glow of a television set, faintly lighting a window. Evidently he and Karla were not the only people awake with things on their minds at three in the morning.

A dog barked at him, here and there – to the south a coyote yipped. From the north-south highway that ran through town there was the drone of a truck – from the sound of the motor Duane thought he recognized it as one of his own.

When he turned north he passed the small house where Lester

Marlow, once the local banker, now lived in gloomy penance. Five years back Lester had lost track of the fact that, while he might be president of the bank, he didn't own the money in it. He began to embezzle; then, in an effort to conceal what he had done from the watchful auditors, he had decided to blow up the bank. He constructed a bomb in his garage, put it in the trunk of his car, and was on the way to the bank with it when the bomb went off, blowing up, not the bank, but a brand-new Cadillac and, to some extent, Lester. The blast in effect scalped him; it also blew him through the windshield and cut off one of his ears. The blast, which occurred only a block from the bank, created such confusion in downtown Thalia that no one noticed Lester had lost an ear. Lester had always been considered funny looking; he had been in the hospital nearly three hours before a nurse noticed that he only had one ear. A hasty search of the bomb site failed to turn it up. The loss of the ear didn't seem to bother Lester much but he *was* bothered by the loss of his hair. Much of his time since he had been released from prison was taken up with various experimental hair transplants, none of which made him look any less funny looking.

Fortunately his loyal and attractive wife, Jenny, stuck by him, even though they were now forced to live in much reduced circumstances. The only evidence of their former affluence was a wall-sized television set. When Duane walked past their little house he noticed a glow in the window far brighter than any that emanated from the other houses where only a TV was on. Lester, intent upon regaining his financial position, was probably watching the Financial Channel on his wall-sized TV.

Over the years Duane had come to have a real fondness for Lester Marlow, even though during the terrible oil bust of the eighties Lester had foreclosed on his deep rig and several other pieces of his property. Even though the embezzlement soon came to light, once the bomb had gone off, nobody in Thalia particularly wanted to see Lester go to prison – he had been absurdly generous with loans, during his years as a banker – but his eccentricities were so pronounced that several thought he belonged in the nuthouse, perhaps permanently. Karla was of that school.

'Duane, he was always good at chemistry,' Karla said. 'For all we know he might get broody and set off another bomb.'

Duane paused a moment in front of the small house with the giant, glowing TV, with half a mind to knock on the door and sit a minute with Lester. But it was still only three-forty-five, a little early for visiting no matter how eccentric your host happened to be. Lester could just have forgotten to turn off the big TV before he went to bed.

Duane strolled on through the quiet streets. When he crossed the highway he saw that the truck he had heard droning through town was indeed his own. It was parked in front of the twenty-four-hour Kwik-Sack. The driver, Jimmy Savory, was probably heating himself up a burrito or two in the microwave. Duane hastily slipped across the street and hid in shadows by the Baptist church. If Lonesome Jimmy Savory came out of the Kwik-Sack munching a burrito and saw his boss afoot on the street at such an hour he might have a heart attack, from shock – or else he would run back inside and ask Sonny Crawford, who owned the Kwik-Sack and usually took the night shift himself, what in hell was the matter with Duane.

Long ago, in high school, Duane and Sonny had been best friends. But they hadn't stayed best friends; now, for no clear or particular reason, they preferred to avoid each other altogether. Sonny hadn't made any bombs, but he had spent three stretches in the mental hospital himself, and now preferred to see as few people as possible. He owned a small house but kept the shades drawn winter and summer. He worked the night shift at his Kwik-Sack seven nights a week, winter and summer; so far as anyone knew, that was all he did. Duane's kids all thought of Sonny as an uncle, and Karla, once every month or two, would discover that she was out of Bloody Mary mix, and would run by and visit with him a little. When Duane asked her how Sonny seemed, Karla had little to say.

'Like he's seemed for the last forty years,' Karla said. 'Depressed.'

Sonny, once a very good-looking man, had been puffy for years, from the various drugs he had been given in the mental hospital. Julie and Nellie had both tried to get him to go to the dentist; his teeth were in dreadful shape. But Sonny resisted all efforts to get him to take better care of himself.

While Duane watched from the shadows, Lonesome Jim Savory, a lanky string bean wearing an old dozer cap and tennis shoes whose loose laces flapped when he walked, came out of the Kwik-Sack, lit a cigarette, got in the truck, and was gone.

Far up the street the town's one stoplight winked in the inky darkness like a low red star.

Before Duane turned to leave, Sonny came out of the store carrying the long thin measuring stick that he used to check gas levels in the big tanks beneath the two pumps. He moved slowly, and, even from a distance, looked puffy, old, discouraged.

Duane turned away, slipping across the dark parking lot. He had intended to get a half pound of bacon to take to his cabin, but the rapidly rising level of Karla's gloom had made him anxious to get out of the house as quickly as possible, and he didn't want to go in the Kwik-Sack and buy bacon from Sonny Crawford. He decided just to make do with coffee, which he had plenty of. When he stopped once more to look back, Sonny was squinting at the long measuring stick, trying to read the gas level. Probably one of the reasons he had to squint was because he only had one eye. Duane himself had put the other eye out in a brief, intense fight over a girl, Jacy Farrow. The fight had occurred when they were eighteen. For much of his life Sonny had worn an eye patch; but in the last few years he had ceased to bother.

Now the cause of that long-ago fight, Jacy Farrow, a minor actress who was the town's nearest approach to a celebrity, was five years dead, lost somewhere in the snows of the North Slope. She had gone north of the Arctic Circle to film a beer commercial, fallen in love with a young bush pilot, and flew off with him one morning hoping to spot a polar bear. Though it was a clear morning when they left, neither Jacy nor the pilot was ever seen again. Two years later a pipeline crew found the plane in a snowdrift. The cockpit was empty, except for a small bag containing Jacy's cosmetics. No trace of the lovers was ever found.

The loss haunted Karla for years – she and Jacy had once been good friends.

'Either she froze or a bear ate her,' Karla said. 'I know it was one or the other.'

Duane made no comment, but Karla continued to brood about Jacy's life and death.

'First her child gets killed and then she goes off and gets eaten by a bear,' she remarked from time to time. 'It wasn't such a fun life, was it?'

Once on the dirt road that led out to his cabin, Duane walked a little faster. He wanted to be out of town, beyond the reach of the ghosts that lived in his memory. He didn't want to think about Jacy, or about Sonny Crawford as he had once been. He wanted to hang on to the new, uplifting feeling of possibility that he had felt when he first stepped out of his house: the feeling that he had a new life to live, a life of walking, of unburdened solitude, or a different way of looking at the world.

He had just turned the corner past the last house when he and a deer startled each other. The deer, confused, jumped out of the ditch and ran right past him, so close that he could have touched it. He heard it crashing through the dry weeds as it fled. If he hurried he could be at his cabin by first light. The coyotes would be yipping, the quail would be whistling, and nobody would be able to call him on the telephone.

# 11

Karla waited patiently for the hour of seven to roll around, that being the earliest hour that she could feel it would be polite to rally her troops – that is, her girlfriends. However sympathetic her girlfriends might be, they weren't likely to appreciate being awakened from their beauty sleep before 7 A.M. – at least not for any crisis short of a fatality.

Duane wasn't dead, he was just depressed, so Karla waited, idling away her time by looking through her files of old health magazines. She was hoping to glean some clues about male depression, but almost all the articles in her health magazines were about women, not men. She did find one short piece from years back that claimed men went through menopause too, although, of course, since they didn't have periods, it was different for them than for women. How different, the article didn't say. Nonetheless the concept of male menopause provided at least a clue as to what might have gone wrong with Duane.

At 7 A.M. on the dot she called her flamboyant redheaded friend Candy Morris, a new arrival to the Thalia scene. Candy hailed from Las Vegas. Not long before, she had married a high-rolling Texas oilman named Joe Don Morris, on the assumption that he lived someplace glamorous and exciting. Thalia had been a big disappointment to Candy, but she hadn't fled the marriage just yet. Joe Don, very rich, was building her a vast mansion that, he assured her, would combine many of the best aspects of Las Vegas and New York City. Candy had her doubts about that but, so far, was sticking around to see how the house turned out. It was modeled on the Temple of Luxor, which, Candy understood, was not in America. She made the time pass by drinking a lot of vodka, or perhaps tequila, if she was in more of a tequila mood.

'Candy, have you ever heard of male menopause?' Karla asked, cutting right to the chase when her new friend answered the phone.

'No, but I've known a lot of men to pause just when you want 'em to ... , if you know what I mean,' Candy said. 'Joe Don's bad about pausing just at the wrong time.'

Though Joe Don was a full twelve years younger than Candy she had dropped more than one hint that his energies, in some respects, were not all she had hoped they would be.

'Well, how is Joe Don?' Karla asked. She thought she ought to be polite and inquire before moving along to her own troubles.

'Scared. I just had a fit over nothing,' Candy admitted. 'I think the little chickenshit is hiding in the sauna.

'That sauna just got finished yesterday,' she said. 'Just in time for my little wimpy husband to hide in it.'

'I guess I'll have to ask a doctor about this male menopause,' Karla said. 'I think Duane might have it.'

'I heard he did something weird but I can't remember what it was,' Candy said. 'My brain don't seem to work till I have my makeup on and I don't have it on yet. You sound real stressed. Have you been crying, or what?'

'Duane walked out at three-fifteen this morning – he left on foot,' Karla said, unable to hold back the dread truth any longer.

'That's right, he was seen walking down the road, that's what it was,' Candy said. 'One of our roughnecks offered him a ride and he wouldn't take it. What's got into that man?'

Personally Candy felt that she could easily learn to overlook a harmless little flaw like a tendency to take walks if she could have a man as sweet and as good looking as Duane Moore. He looked better to her than her Temple of Luxor new house; it had even occurred to her that if he was really out walking around by himself she might want to get out and get a little fresh air herself. She might even join him on one of his little saunters if he didn't mind.

She didn't say that to Karla, of course. Karla was in shock, which was only normal under the circumstances. In a hicky place like Thalia people just didn't take walks at three-fifteen in the morning, though of course it was common practice in Las Vegas, particularly if you were walking around inside a casino.

'I think Duane's just real depressed right now,' Karla said. 'He just seems to have lost his sense of motivation or something.'

'If there's one thing I can't stand it's a man who's down in the dumps and won't do anything about it,' Candy said. 'Oops, here's my architect. What's he doing here this early? I better go put on my face so my brain will work.'

Actually, it wasn't her architect, it was just a young carpenter with a real good bod that Candy had been hoping to get a little better acquainted with, and one good motto she had brought with her from Las Vegas was that there was no time like the present.

Karla found herself holding a phone that had nobody to talk to on the other end. She felt like she had been hung out to dry, to some extent, and reminded herself that people from Las Vegas just probably weren't brought up to have very good manners. The fact that Candy had married Joe Don Morris, a twitchy little nerd who couldn't even dance, indicated that her judgment was a little bit off, in some respects.

Karla dialed the phone again, and this time got Babe Collins, an old friend and a person who had spent much of her life in Thalia, as Karla had. Babe was twice widowed; she had a tendency to marry men who drove too fast while they were drinking too much – but the fact that Babe had kept on trucking so determinedly that she had just managed to snare a third husband, Randy Harcanville, meant that she knew at least a little bit about the temperaments of men from the north-central-western part of Texas. Randy Harcanville wasn't much to look at, but was a fine dancer nevertheless.

Babe, too, had heard about Duane's deviant behavior, but felt that it didn't do to rush to judgment where Duane and Karla were concerned. The death of their marriage had been predicted many times, by various and sundry; many of the predictors were now dead and buried but Duane and Karla were still married. Maybe they had just had a particularly bad fight. Duane might have just wanted to walk around for a while, licking his wounds, like an old dog might do.

'Duane's sensitive, honey,' she offered, when Karla called. 'Maybe you hurt his feelings and didn't realize you had hurt his feelings.'

'I've hurt his feelings a million times and he's never done nothing like this,' Karla pointed out. 'Usually when we have a fight he gets in his pickup and goes to a bar and drinks beer.'

'There aren't many good bars around here,' Babe said. 'Maybe he just got tired of doing the same old thing.'

'But, Babe, we didn't have a fight,' Karla said. 'Things were going along real smooth, and now look.'

Though Babe was polite, it was soon clear to Karla that her friend didn't take this walking crisis very seriously, which might actually be a sensible reaction. Of course, people would gossip about it at the post office, but that didn't mean it was really all that important. People as hard up for excitement as the people in Thalia were would gossip about anything. The wild extravagance of Joe Don's new Temple of Luxor house had been the main subject of local gossip for months. Maybe Duane was just doing everybody a favor by giving them something fresh to turn their attention to.

Nonetheless, when she hung up the phone – feeling slightly ridiculous – and let Babe go back to her new life with Randy Harcanville, Karla experienced a momentary spasm of pure hopelessness that she knew herself was way out of proportion to anything Duane had actually done. Probably part of the hopelessness was the knowledge that she wasn't going to pick up much sympathy by complaining about Duane to her friends. Everyone in Thalia, men and women alike, knew she had the best husband in town. People who saw him walking down the street wouldn't necessarily assume that Duane had gone crazy; quite a few of them might assume that she had been so mean to him that he couldn't take it anymore and just walked out the door and left.

The main part of her spasm of hopelessness, though, had nothing to do with public opinion, which was bound to be fickle at best. The core of her disturbance was the suspicion that some fundamental change had just occurred in her husband – a change that left her out. It was not totally unheard of in Thalia for couples to exercise together. Couples, fat or skinny, could sometimes be seen jogging around the track, or, if the weather was pretty, walking along the street. She herself owned walking shoes. She wouldn't have minded taking a stroll with Duane, if he had asked her – but he hadn't.

About that time she heard a yell from Baby Paul, and Little Bascom straggled in, dragging a blanket and a stuffed squirrel. Though Baby Paul kept yelling there was no sign that anyone was responding to him, so Karla hurried in and plucked him out of his crib. Rag was in the kitchen making Little Bascom Cream of Wheat when Karla returned with the baby.

'You look like you've been crying already today,' Rag said amiably. It was clear to her that things were not quite right in the Moore household – they rarely had been in the ten years that she had worked there. Of course, with kids as wild as Dickie, Nellie, Julie, and Jack, quiet times and peace and harmony were not really to be expected. Still, it was a little unusual for Karla to look so upset at breakfast time.

'He walked off at three-fifteen this morning – what if we never see him again?' Karla asked, plopping Baby Paul into his high chair, taking care to position it far enough from the table that he couldn't tip it over as he had the evening before.

'Oh my lord, so the man went for a walk in the early A.M.,' Rag said. 'It's not a hanging offense, is it?'

Nonetheless, something of Karla's disquiet communicated itself to her. When a man left the house on foot at three-fifteen in the morning, it was a sign of something. But what?

In her distraction she forgot what she was about for a minute or two and scorched the Cream of Wheat.

'Oh my lord, now look ... I don't do that once a year,' Rag said.

# 12

Duane had not hurried his walk. In Thalia there had been a few scattered streetlights, but along the dirt road it was very dark. An oil rig strung with lights, seven or eight miles away, provided the only challenge to the starlight, and that a faint one. Besides the startled deer there was a surprising amount of game along the road. The country was thick with small feral pigs – twice he saw families of them snuffling in the underbrush. Crossing a river bottom he thought he heard some wild turkeys flush, but he couldn't see them. A family of coons waddled ahead of him for a while, and, just before he reached the cabin, with only the faintest light beginning to show in the east, he heard the beat of wings and looked up to see some Canada geese, rising from a small lake nearby.

When he walked across the narrow gravel road that ran along the edge of the hill to his little cabin he thought he saw something move in front of the cabin door. His first thought was that a coon was trying to break in, to forage in what few foodstuffs he kept in the cabin, leaving the kind of mess that coons leave.

A second later, though, he realized that the animal sniffing around his cabin wasn't a coon, it was a low-slung little dog. It was Shorty, a Queensland blue heeler, the sixth in a ragged and uncertain line of descent from the first Shorty – the first blue heeler that Duane had owned. Shorty, who had been Duane's constant companion for nearly ten years, not only had offspring all over Thalia; he had offspring all over the oil patch as well.

Shorty the Sixth, as he was sometimes called, had been a very winning puppy, and they had kept him at home until he began to exhibit the same tendencies that Duane's blue heelers always exhibited, that is, a tendency to herd children in the same way they would have herded cattle or sheep: they nipped their heels. Shorty the Sixth had shown himself particularly eager to nip Little Bascom's heels – in his view Little Bascom was essentially an erratic, two-legged sheep. After Shorty the Sixth's nips had broken the skin of Little Bascom's heels the third time, Karla insisted on dispatching him to the camp of some wetbacks who lived north of town, sustaining themselves by fixing fence for a number of ranchers in the area. The wetbacks had no children for Shorty to attempt to herd; besides, they were lonely men, and grateful for the company of a little blue dog.

The only problem with the arrangement was the same problem that had prevailed with the other five blue heelers, and that was that no man, whether wetback or Anglo, could compare in their eyes with Duane. Even though the descent from the original Shorty was ragged and irregular, an intense loyalty to Duane, and Duane alone, somehow got passed down the generations. Shorty the Sixth was perfectly nice to the three wetbacks, but at least once a week, he would decide it was time to go back to Duane – and he went. It was only four miles from the wetbacks' camp to Duane's spartan cabin. Shorty the Sixth knew the way, and there he was, waiting patiently, when Duane came walking up.

'Oh hell, you again,' Duane said mildly.

Shorty, as always, shuffled around submissively; it was too dark to tell much about his expression but he probably looked slightly guilty. An air of slight guilt was typical of all the Shortys.

Despite the danger to Little Bascom's heels, Duane was glad to see Shorty. He liked having a dog – intense loyalty of the sort Shorty displayed was hard to resist. Besides, now that he had become a walker, having a loyal pet to walk with might make what he wanted to do a little more acceptable to the general populace. He decided not to bother taking Shorty back to the wetbacks.

'Come on in,' he said. 'I guess Juan and Jesus and Rafael will just have to look for a new dog.'

When dawn spread its cool clear flush over the meadows and fields and thorny pastures to the north and east, Duane pulled an old lawn chair out of the cabin and sat down to watch, cradling a cup of coffee in his hands. It was chilly enough that he threw an old poncho over his lap.

Shorty, deeply content, lay at Duane's feet, his chin on his front paws. He kept his eyes open, though, just in case an intruder of some sort – a coyote, a bobcat, a skunk, or a wild pig – strayed into Duane's territory.

Duane too was deeply content. He had cracked pecans for breakfast

– the pecans were left over from last year, but they were still tasty. Nuts and coffee and the peace of the country were all he needed, anyway. It certainly beat the morning clangor of his home, with Karla or Rag or Julie yelling at this kid or that, and the TV blaring as the same old celebrities spoke their brief pieces on the various morning shows. The phone would usually ring, announcing a crisis at this rig or that, or a banker would call, just to give him a friendly reminder that one of his notes was coming due. All that occurred so noisily at his home was, he knew, just the sound of ongoing life, as his wife and his hired help, his children and his grandchildren each struggled to get a little bit of what they wanted out of the day or the hour.

They were all doing more or less exactly what they should be doing – wanting, living, getting, squeezing as much as possible out of their little moments, just as Rag squeezed as much as possible out of the two dozen oranges she turned into juice every morning. Deep in his heart Duane wished them well, wished them luck, wished them happiness, wished them love and money, wished them honesty and grace, wished them strength, wished them hope.

He didn't think, though, that he would be contributing much more to their efforts or their achievements. He had stepped out of the flow of ongoingness. He had other things to do, though it would not have been easy for him to say what the other things were. Indeed, finding out what he *really* wanted to do was his first task – all he knew at the moment was that his desires lay somewhere in the spacious realm of unsatisfied curiosity. All his life he had worked too hard to allow himself the time to be curious, to learn things that were interesting rather than merely useful. He had always meant to learn a little botany, a little agronomy, but had just never really taken the time. He had only a vague, layman's knowledge of weather patterns, of how the jet stream worked, or the Gulf Stream. He knew a lot about machinery but very little about animal habitats or the rhythms of bird migration. He knew a little about rivers, but nothing about oceans. He could cook simple foods but had never made biscuits from scratch or baked a pie or cake. He had read very few books, and had not even attended very closely to the newspapers – he had always just got the broad outlines of what was going on in the world from radio or television. He had a certain curiosity about the Siberian oil fields, and also about the oil fields of the OPEC nations – after all, the latter had controlled his financial destiny for much of his life – but he had never been to Russia or the Middle East. A piece about the pyramids, read in an airline magazine, intrigued him enough that he had cut it out and saved it, but he had only seen the pyramids on the Discovery Channel. It struck him as a little sad that in sixty-two years he had only acquired firsthand knowledge of one place – the very place he could see from his lawn chair, where the new sun was just beginning to shine on the distant buildings of Thalia. He only knew one place, and an unremarkable place too, of the thousands of places there were to see and know.

Of course, he had grown up poor – the struggle to make a living had taken his youth. But he hadn't been poor in a long time – in debt, yes, but not poor. He could have afforded, anytime in the last thirty-five years, to go see the pyramids, or the Siberian oil fields, or the lands of sand. His own secretary, Ruth Popper, who certainly wasn't wealthy, had taken wing when she was about seventy – Ruth and a younger sister had gone to Egypt, Scotland, China; he, who wrote her paycheck each week, had never seen any of those places. It was only lately that he had begun to feel negligent in some vague way. He had just gone along, like everyone else, doing what he was supposed to do – but no more than he was supposed to do. Without realizing it, he had been wasting time – years and years of time, time that would never be his again. He had failed to take advantage of the diversity of opportunity that had been, all along, available to him.

'So now what?' he asked, out loud. Shorty looked up at him expectantly.

But it had merely been a question put to himself. He was sixty-two. People were living a lot longer than they had once lived. One old man and three old women of his acquaintance were still walking spryly around the streets of Thalia, all of them in their early nineties. If he could hang on to enough vigor to be walking around on his own when he was in his nineties, then he still had thirty years – and thirty years gave him time enough to do at least some of the things he had never done. He was in good health and needn't feel, yet, that he had totally cheated himself where his unsatisfied curiosity was concerned. In thirty years a person could do a lot, learn a lot, see a lot. There was no need to panic – not even much need to rush. He meant to take a slow, relaxed approach to his new life. Mainly, to begin with, he wanted to walk around for a while.

Though he had only left his home to walk to the cabin a few hours earlier, it already seemed that he had been gone a long time, and it seemed, also, that he had traveled a good deal farther than six miles. In a way he felt he had crossed a border, entered a new country in which the laws and customs were different from the laws and customs he had lived under all his life. Nothing about his new life was defined very clearly – not yet – but that didn't bother him, really. His new life, after all, was still less than twenty-four hours old. It had been almost noon of the day before when he had parked his pickup in the cluttered carport and set out on foot to find peace.

It seemed to Duane, sitting in his lawn chair, warm under his poncho, watching the sun rise higher in the clear winter sky, that he had been lucky to find the contentment he felt at that moment so soon and so easily. It was only a six-mile walk from his old life to his new. He had a stove and a small refrigerator in the cabin. He could provision himself for a while with no more provisions than would fit in a backpack. The first thing he had done when he arrived that morning was disconnect the small radio. He did that immediately, before he even brewed coffee, because he knew it would be just like Karla to call the radio station and concoct some kind of emergency, a sick child or something, so that the radio station would page him.

But he didn't want to be paged: didn't want to be answerable. He had been answerable long enough. Now what he wanted was to sit and think, walk and think, lie in bed and think; and not to be in any hurry as he was thinking. He had done what was expected of him all his life, but he didn't feel that he had to do the expected any longer. He wanted to establish his own priorities and then act on them. Should he go to Egypt first? Or learn to make biscuits first? He had always had the notion that it would be interesting to follow some great river from its source to the sea. Maybe that was what he should do first, take a long trip on a long river.

One thing he knew already was that he wanted to pare down, rid himself of things he didn't need, such as his pickup. What he was doing at the moment, sitting in a lawn chair, watching the sunrise, was simple and basic. The first thing he wanted to do was eliminate what was unnecessary and excessive. The cabin he sat by was already as simple as it needed to be. There was a stove, a small fireplace, a refrigerator, a single bed, a card table, two chairs, a nail to hang a coat on, two fishing rods, an almanac, a twenty-two, an axe for cutting firewood, and some overshoes. The radio was the only thing in the cabin that he really didn't need, and he had already unplugged the radio.

Duane knew already that simplicity was a big part of what he was seeking now, in his life. For as far back as he could remember he had spent his days wading through clutter, fighting for air in a way. His home, his office, his pickup each contained an overabundance of clutter. Just stepping into his office and seeing the piles of bills, envelopes, mail, circulars, catalogues, contracts overwhelmed him. At the cabin he had exactly what he needed: a dog, a chair, coffee, a warm poncho, and no more. He even had a small bathroom, a luxury put in at Karla's insistence – the cabin at first had had no bathroom.

'No bathroom?' she said. 'Ye gods! What if I'm paying you one of my rare visits and need to go?'

Duane shrugged. 'There's six sections of land here,' he said. 'You could probably go find a place to go somewhere on it.'

'Yes, and get snakebit, ye gods!' she said.

Rather than argue about it for years he had put in the commode and the shower. But he would not allow Karla to hang curtains.

'Duane, what if somebody was to drive by and see you?' she asked.

'The only way they can drive by and see me is if they drive off this hill,' he pointed out. 'And if they drive off this hill it won't matter if they did see me, because they'll be dead.'

Karla raged about the cabin for about a year and then gave up. The only improvements Duane had added since then was to drive two more nails in the wall, to hang coats and slickers from.

Now, so far as he was concerned, the cabin was perfect. There were windows on all four sides, to let in the light and allow him to see what the weather was doing. The windows also made it easy for him to keep an eye on the flats below. Road hunters had to be watched – they didn't always honor the season and would sometimes pick off an unwary deer if they thought they were unobserved. From now on he meant to keep a stern watch on them.

The sun rose higher, the morning wore on; Duane finished one cup of coffee and then a second – except for the few moments it took him to pour the second cup of coffee, he didn't leave his chair. Well to the northwest a dark layer of cloud was forming; it might be that colder weather was hurrying down the plains. It occurred to him that he probably ought to chop a little firewood that afternoon; there was a mesquite thicket a couple of hundred yards to the south that would provide him all he needed. It was too bad he had forgotten the bacon, though. With a half pound of bacon and a can or two of beans he would be set up fine, if it should happen to get sleety or wet.

After a lengthy nap Shorty got restless and decided to investigate the rocks just off the edge of the hill, where a family of ground squirrels burrowed. Shorty considered the ground squirrels intruders, and the ground squirrels considered Shorty a bothersome pest. One of the squirrels would sit on top of a boulder and scold Shorty roundly, chattering in indignation.

'Live and let live, Shorty,' Duane said. 'Those squirrels got here first.'

Gradually, as the morning wore on and the dark clouds to the northwest edged closer, a thought with equally stormy implications began to edge into Duane's mind. When he walked off that morning at three-fifteen he had assumed he would take a long walk, perhaps spend most of the day at his cabin, and then walk back in and eat dinner with his family. That would be his new pattern: alone, exploring the country during the day, and a meal with his family at night. He made himself a can of tomato soup for lunch, and, while he was eating it, realized that he didn't want to go back and have dinner with his family. He didn't want to go back and spend the night in his home in Thalia. He didn't want to go to his office and see what checks or bills might have come in the morning's mail. The change he felt in himself was more profound than he had first supposed it to be. His larder was undersupplied – it consisted of three more cans of soup, a can of English peas, and some coffee. He was going to have to walk in and buy food and some toiletries at some point. He kept a toothbrush at the cabin but no razor. The stormy thought that came to him was simple enough: he didn't want to live at the big house with his family anymore. He wanted to live in his cabin, alone except for Shorty. The process of change that began when he had locked his pickup and put the keys in the old chipped coffee cup was more serious than he had supposed. He hadn't been just walking for amusement: he had been walking away from his life.

When the conviction struck him that he wasn't going back, he felt again the feeling of relief that had come to him that morning when he first stepped out of his house. He had walked away from his life – and it seemed to him that he had waited until the last possible minute to do it, too. He didn't know why he felt that way, but he *did* feel that way. Any later, even a few weeks, and he might not have been able to do it. He might have stayed trapped in the same strong fishnet of routine and habit that had bored him for at least the last twenty years, if not longer. As he felt himself flooded with relief for the second time that day it seemed to Duane that his legs had simply taken independent action. While he had been sitting calmly at the dinner table, explaining to his grandchildren that walking was just healthy exercise, his legs and feet had been preparing for revolutionary action, and now they had taken it. Karla, in her shock that he would leave the house on foot at three-fifteen in the morning, had been right, her instincts sound. It wasn't just a momentary restlessness that had carried him out the door and out of town. Without exactly knowing it he had reached a point in his life where he had to live differently if he was to live at all, and his feet and legs, somehow recognizing that fact before he had been able to face it consciously, had hurried him away and saved him.

Although geographically he had only gone six miles – in fact he could look out of the south window of the cabin and see not only the town of Thalia but the very roof of the house where he had slept last night – he knew that in emotional terms he might already be in Egypt or India. It had never before struck him so forcibly that distance was not really a matter of miles. His family, most of them probably just about to begin their normal day of television and fights and trips to Wichita Falls, had no idea yet that he had ceased to live among them. Only Karla knew it, and even Karla just suspected it. She couldn't know it for sure, because he himself had just come to realize it within the last few minutes. Walking away was exactly what he had intended to do, but the intention had been so well submerged inside him, deep in his feelings, that he hadn't realized it was there until, in the quiet of the cabin, it had suddenly surfaced, and surfaced powerfully, like a whale rising.

Then the sun vanished – the clouds from the northwest had just arrived. The little cabin was not well insulated. In a few minutes Duane felt the temperature begin to drop. He put on his coat and picked up the axe.

'Come on, Shorty, let's go cut some firewood,' he said. 'You and me had better get to work.'

Shorty, excited to be going somewhere with Duane, his favorite person, briskly led the way to the thicket of mesquite, on the slope of the hill to the south.

# 13

'We ain't as well equipped as I thought, Shorty,' Duane said, an hour later. Despite the plummeting temperature he had worked up a good sweat cutting the abundant mesquite limbs into fireplace-size chunks. He had a respectable pile of nice burnable mesquite, but the cabin was two hundred yards away and he had no way to transport the firewood to the cabin except in his arms.

'We need a good wheelbarrow, or maybe a wagon,' he said to the dog, who was watching a hawk circle low over the hill, hoping to surprise a quail or a small rabbit or even a good-sized rat – there were plenty of rats living under the vast archipelagos of prickly pear which dotted the plain to the south. Shorty knew he couldn't get the hawk but kept an eye on it anyway.

'Maybe I could fix up a travois – make you a sled dog,' Duane said, but, for the moment, Duane filled his arms with as much mesquite as he could carry and walked to the cabin. He came back and got three more loads before he had a pile of firewood that satisfied him. With a wheelbarrow or a small wagon he could have moved as much in one trip. It was mildly aggravating to realize how many basic tools it took just to enable one man to live a simple life.

Then he went back six more times to the woodpile he had created at the edge of the thicket. He decided his reflection about tools had been incorrect. It had been based on the premise that there was some kind of hurry, and that convenience, not simplicity, was the basic, prime good in life. He was so used to that way of thinking, had proceeded on that premise for so long, that he had to twist himself around mentally in order to see that it didn't have to be that way. A huge abundance of firewood was only a short walk away. In an hour or less, each day, he could carry more than he could possibly burn. In a week of steady work, even without a wagon or a wheelbarrow, he could have firewood stacked almost to the roof of his cabin. There was no reason to hurry about it, or to spend money on tools, when the one tool he really needed – his axe – he already had. The one thing he needed to get, next time he was home, was a file, so he could sharpen the axe.

'An axe don't stay sharp forever,' he said to the dog, who decided he was being told to get those ground squirrels. Shorty went flashing off. He was so happy that Duane hadn't put him in the pickup and taken him back to Juan, Jesus, and Rafael that he couldn't refrain from frisking as he went about his duties – or what he supposed to be his duties.

The hawk that had been hunting near the mesquite thicket had been joined by its mate. Just as Duane was stacking his last armload of firewood the two hawks sailed by him and dipped off the edge of the hill. He looked down on their backs as they rode the wind and scanned the valley below.

The only paper in the cabin was a little notepad that dated from the year the cabin had been built. In the first months he had occasionally had two or three of his fishing buddies in – once or twice they played cards, using the notepad to keep score, if they were playing a card game that involved a score. Such visits had only occurred a few times. Duane soon discovered that what he came to the cabin for was solitude.

But it was good that he had the notepad, and two or three ballpoint pens. Now that he intended to walk to town when he needed something, and would only have a small backpack to carry his supplies in, it behooved him to make careful lists before he went shopping. His first list only consisted of four items: matches, bacon, chili, and a file. He stood for a long time, looking out at the scudding clouds, trying to think of something else he might need on his trip in. Finally he added one more item to the list: twenty-two shells. He debated in his mind whether to bring a short shotgun back with him. Quail, duck, and wild turkey were all still in season – and the wild pigs were always in season. With a shotgun he could provide himself with a variety of succulent fowl, at least until bird season closed.

But in the end he decided against the shotgun. He wasn't a back-to-nature crank, after all. He didn't have to kill everything he ate – canned goods would suit him fine, for the most part. If he developed a sudden hunger for game he would just have to sneak up close enough to something to kill it with the twenty-two.

The clouds lay so low above his hill now that he could no longer see the buildings of Thalia, or, indeed, much of anything. It would be dark in a few hours. Between his relaxing and his wood chopping he had used up much of the day. If he intended to walk to town to pick up the file and a few groceries he had better get started. He couldn't tell what the clouds intended. If it started to sleet or snow everyone at home would freak out all the more when he told them he was going to walk back to the cabin and spend the night.

Then, watching the two hawks scout the valley, he sat down in his lawn chair again and covered himself – to the chin this time – with the thick poncho. It was a little too cold to be sitting out on a hill in a lawn chair; the heat that he had generated with all his wood chopping had begun to leave him: better to go inside and build a fire with some of the wood he had chopped. Shorty, by dint of frantic effort, had managed to scramble up on the boulder where the old ground squirrel had sat when it scolded him – but the old ground squirrel, at the moment, was snug in its burrow. Shorty stood triumphantly on top of the boulder, yipping at nothing. Then a jackrabbit appeared, well west on the hill, and Shorty was off in hot pursuit.

After a time Duane went inside and built a good fire in the little fireplace. There wasn't going to be a sunset to watch that evening – just a slow fade from dim to dark. The moment for hiking into Thalia had passed. There was nothing he needed that he couldn't do without until the next day. He still had the soup, the can of English peas, some crackers, and plenty of coffee. The axe was thoroughly dulled, but then he didn't need to chop any more firewood for a while. He had an abundance, stacked right by his door. If part of what he was attempting to do was free himself from habit, then making a habit of walking to town every single day was no way to start.

After a time Shorty came back, rabbitless, and Duane let him in and brought the lawn chair in too. He realized well enough that there were still a few impediments to his enjoyment of the simple life – a few barriers that still had to be removed, the main one being his family. When he left that morning to walk to his cabin it hadn't dawned on him that what he really wanted to do was live in the cabin permanently. He just told Karla he was going for a walk. He didn't tell her he was leaving her because he hadn't realized it himself until he had sat in the lawn chair for a few hours and thought about things. She may have had her apprehensions but she didn't really know what was going on with him, since he didn't know himself, really. The one thing he knew for certain was that he didn't want to live even a single day as he had been living, driving around in his pickup and going through the motions of a life that had long since ceased to interest him. Other than Karla, no one at his house had a clue about his feelings. His little speech about walking for his health had seemed to satisfy whatever concerns the others might have. They wouldn't particularly miss him if he didn't show up for supper, probably wouldn't particularly miss him for a week or two. They would just assume he was on a fishing trip or a business trip or something. Willy and Bubbles would eventually begin to wonder what had become of Pa-Pa – but that wouldn't occur for a while.

When he tried to think of what he might say to Karla, to make her realize that he was unlikely to be coming back, his brain felt as dull as the axe he had just used to cut the mesquite. The fact was, he felt a little tired – more tired than hungry. He couldn't really be expected to rethink his whole life – not in one day.

He didn't imagine Karla would show up looking for him, either. She had had a wary look in her eyes, when he left the house that morning. Though by nature a confronter, Karla had been married to him a long time; she mostly knew when to test him and when to let be. Of course, she was also impatient – she never let be for long, but she was not so impatient that she couldn't let a day or two slide by before she decided to bring some crisis to a head. It was not particularly unusual for him to spend a night in his cabin. His failure to appear at suppertime wouldn't cause too much comment – less, probably, than if he showed up, got a file, and walked away in the night. Karla, once she had had time to think about it, would probably lay back, leave him alone, let him have a day or two to come to his senses.

Just as he had convinced himself that that was likely to be the case, and had opened a can of soup for his supper, he saw a pair of headlights coming across his hill.

'Just when we don't want company we're getting company,' he said, to Shorty. But he opened the can of soup anyway, and was trying to decide whether cream of chicken soup would go well with English peas, when Bobby Lee stepped into the cabin, his sunglasses in place, as dark as clouds.

'Goodness me, what's for supper?' he asked. 'If it's cream of chicken soup can I have a bowl?'

'Help yourself,' Duane said.

# 14

'If you're just going to sit there and act nervous I wish you'd leave,' Duane said. It didn't take long for the two of them to consume a bowl of soup and a few crackers; while they were eating Bobby Lee did an unusual amount of twitching, sniffing, shuffling his feet. After such a peaceful day it took very little in the way of human anxiety to set Duane's teeth on edge.

'I didn't move all this way out here to eat soup with nervous people,' he added.

'Why *did* you move out here, boss?' Bobby Lee asked. 'You own the best house in this whole part of the country and here you are out on a hill, living in a shack with a dog.'

'I moved out here to get away from people who are so nervous they can't even sit still long enough to eat a bowl of soup,' Duane said.

'Want me to take Shorty back to the wetbacks?' Bobby Lee asked. 'I bet they're missing him by now, and even if they ain't it would be an excuse to leave.'

'Shorty is not going back to the wetbacks,' Duane informed him. 'He lives with me now. I'm going to be his foster parent.'

'You could have adopted me instead of him,' Bobby Lee said. 'I've been needing a foster parent ever since I lost my left nut.'

'Unless I'm mistaken it was your right nut you lost,' Duane reminded him.

'It might as well have been both nuts, for all the pussy I'm getting,' Bobby Lee said.

'I hope you didn't drive all the way out here to talk about your sex life,' Duane said. But he offered him a cup of coffee, moved by the sad look Bobby Lee had worn ever since the loss of his testicle.

'I take that back,' Bobby Lee said. 'As long as I've still got one nut I might get some pussy eventually.'

'Don't wait too long,' Duane said. 'You might get to the point where you don't want any.'

'Women don't look twice at a man with one ball,' Bobby Lee said. Even before his operation he had been prone to sudden plunges into bottomless self-pity.

'It's not the women, it's you,' Duane said. 'You're a goddamn baby. You go around feeling so sorry for yourself that you don't try.'

'If you tried as hard as you used to, at least the law of averages would be on your side,' Duane added.

'Ain't you got any hamburger meat?' Bobby asked. 'I have to work tonight. That cream of chicken soup may not stick to my ribs very long.'

'I plan to acquire some groceries tomorrow,' Duane said. 'I didn't get time to go shopping today.'

'Karla said you was so lonesome you'd probably appreciate any company you could get, but that was wrong,' Bobby said. 'You ain't even lonesome, are you?'

'Nope,' Duane said.

'Why not? You got to admit this is a lonesome old hill.'

'I think it's a nice hill,' Duane said. 'If it was higher it would be too high, and if it was lower it wouldn't be a hill, it would just be a ridge. It makes a fine place to retire.'

'Oh, are you retired now?' Bobby Lee asked. 'If you are, you should have told them at the office. They're under the impression that you're still running a business.'

'I'll tell them tomorrow,' Duane assured him. 'I had to chop my wood today.'

Bobby Lee was quiet for a while, thinking. He extracted a cigarette from a pack, looked at it, and then stuck it behind his ear.

'I get the feeling your retirement home is a smoke-free environment,' he said.

'No, you can smoke,' Duane said. 'One of the benefits of retirement is that you get to stop making rules for other people. Other people can go to hell anyway they want to.'

'Hell is not having but one ball and wondering if you're going to get cancer in the good one,' Bobby Lee said.

'I thought we weren't going to talk about this anymore,' Duane said.

'I was sent out here by Karla – she instructed me to snoop. I guess you know that,' Bobby Lee said.

'You don't work for Karla,' Duane reminded him. 'You're not her employee. You don't have to do her dirty work, you know?'

'I don't guess I really know what's happening,' Bobby Lee said. 'I thought I was your employee, but now you say you're retired. Who's going to run the oil company if that's the case?'

'Dickie and you,' Duane said. 'He'll be out of rehab next week. A little more responsibility might be good for him. It might encourage him to let the drugs alone.'

'Maybe,' Bobby Lee said.

After that they sat in silence for a long time.

'What do you want me to tell Karla?' Bobby asked.

'Tell her I'm fine,' Duane said.

There was another silence.

'You're fine – that's it?' Bobby inquired.

'You're sitting there looking at me. Don't I look healthy to you?' Duane asked.

'Yes, but you could be seething underneath,' Bobby Lee said.

'I'm not seething underneath. I was just enjoying a quiet evening in my cabin when you showed up.

'I'm fine,' he added.

'It may be true but she's not gonna want to hear that,' Bobby Lee said. 'She thinks you're racked with guilt for deserting your family.'

'My family's six miles away,' Duane reminded him. 'If something bad happens somebody can run out and get me.'

'Bad ... what do you mean, bad?'

'Oh, like a murder, or maybe a car wreck,' Duane said.

Bobby Lee stood up, took the cigarette from behind his ear, tapped it on his wrist, and put it back behind his ear.

'I don't know, I just feel kind of fraught up about all this,' he said.

'Why?'

'I guess because nobody expected you just to suddenly leave home,' Bobby Lee said. 'It ain't really like you.'

'Well, I didn't plan it,' Duane said. 'It just occurred. And it is like me. It's like the new me.'

'Oh, the retired you?' Bobby asked.

'The me that's at peace,' Duane said.

'At peace?' Bobby Lee asked.

Duane nodded. Shorty had gone to sleep.

'Then I guess that means you were at war, only none of us knew it,' Bobby Lee said.

'Something like that. One way to explain it is that I got tired of pickups, and all that goes with them.'

'All that goes with them – you mean like family life and stuff?'

Again, Duane nodded.

'You ought to appreciate that yourself,' he said. 'You've never liked family life, particularly. You spend most of your life in a pickup, drinking beer and smoking.'

'And listening to the radio,' Bobby Lee reminded him.

'I just meant you're not Mr Average Dad,' Duane said.

'I know it. I never learned not to marry them cruel women,' Bobby Lee said. 'I've had to lead a life of driving around, just to escape them.'

'All women are high maintenance,' Duane said. 'When you get right down to it that's the bottom line.'

Bobby Lee considered the remark in silence for a moment.

'Fuckin' A,' he said, just before he went out the door.

# 15

Karla was in the den watching Comedy Central when Nellie came in, dragging two suitcases and several large bags full of tropical doodads. She had just been in Cancun with a new boyfriend, Tommy, but the romance had not quite survived the long unromantic flight back to DFW. Tommy had not felt like defending her right to drag the large bags onto the airplane, the result being that Nellie had been forced to check them – then, wouldn't you know, her bags had been the very last to come off the plane, which meant that she was at the very end of the Customs line. The Customs agents had become unreasonably suspicious, perhaps because she and Tommy were the last ones in line. By the time they finally got through Customs Nellie was so fed up with Tommy that she brusquely informed him that she never wanted to see him again, an action which necessitated taking a taxi home all the way from Dallas, a distance of one hundred and twenty miles.

Nellie was surprised to see her mother up at such an hour, but glad too – she had spent her last cent in Cancun and couldn't pay the taxi driver.

'Mom, do you have two hundred dollars? I had to take a taxi home,' Nellie said. 'It was a black man that drove me – he was real nice.'

'I guess I'd die of surprise if one of my kids showed up not needing money,' Karla said. She riffled through three or four purses and a jacket or two and finally found enough twenties to pay the bill.

'You want to come in and have coffee?' she asked the black man, waiting patiently in her driveway. 'It's two hours back to Dallas. Or I could just pour you some in a paper cup if you're in a hurry.'

The driver gratefully accepted the coffee and drove off.

'You look like you got a nice tan, honey – how'd it go with Tommy?' she asked, giving her daughter a quick once-over.

'That boring little shitheel, I can't remember why I even went with him,' Nellie said. 'How come you're up so late, Mom?'

Something didn't feel quite right in the house. Nellie thought it might be jet lag on her part, but actually she felt pretty peppy. She just had a feeling that something was a little off.

'I'm grown, can't I stay up late if I want to?' Karla asked. 'Anyway, you have to stay up late if you want to see the best comedy acts – they don't put 'em on while normal people are awake.'

'That's true, but it don't explain why you look like you've been crying,' Nellie said.

Like her mother, she preferred to cut right to the chase.

'Well, now that you mention it, your father left me,' Karla said – why hide the truth from your own child?

'Oh no, another midlife crisis,' Nellie said. 'When he comes back let's try to get him on Paxil. It sure helped me right after I came out of rehab.'

Karla opened her cabinet and studied the various whiskeys available to her, deciding on tequila, in honor of her daughter's safe return from a land where it was so popular.

'Your daddy's too old for a midlife crisis – at least, he is unless he's planning to live to be one hundred and twenty-four,' she said. 'He's sixty-two. People have midlife crises when they're in their forties.'

She poured herself a nice slug of tequila and held the bottle up for Nellie to see.

'Want a little of the hair of the dog that's been biting you for the last few days?' she asked. Nellie was the only child she had who would drink with her. Dickie and the twins preferred drugs.

'Maybe just a dribble,' Nellie said. 'Just enough to remind me of Mexico. It's a drag coming back to a place where there ain't no beach.'

She thought about the feeling she had, the feeling that something wasn't right in the house.

'Is there another woman involved ... is that why Daddy left?' she asked.

Karla shook her head but Nellie remained skeptical.

'Just because you don't know who it is yet doesn't mean there isn't one,' she said.

'Well, I don't think so,' Karla said. 'He left yesterday morning, on foot.'

'On foot. Why?' Nellie asked. 'You didn't throw his car keys in the septic tank again, did you?'

She remembered the septic tank incident vividly because her mother, once she calmed down, had tried to bribe Fug, her boyfriend of the moment, to dive into the septic tank and hunt for the keys. But Fug was too chicken, and those particular keys were never found.

'I didn't throw his keys in the septic tank – we didn't even have a fight,' Karla said. 'I thought we were getting along fine.'

Before Karla could elaborate Nellie suddenly remembered that she was a mother. She sprang up and ran down the hall to take a quick look at Little Bascom and Baby Paul, both sleeping like the angels they were. Then she peeked in the master bedroom, just to be sure her father wasn't there – and he wasn't.

'He's gone all right,' she said, when she got back to the kitchen. 'Start from the beginning and tell me all about it.'

Karla was glad to have her daughter home. Nellie was usually sympathetic when it came to troubles with men – she had had plenty of them herself.

'I don't know what the beginning was,' Karla admitted. 'Day before yesterday he showed up about noon, parked his pickup, and just walked off. He didn't say a word to anybody.'

'Where'd he walk to?' Nellie asked. 'If he left he had to go somewhere.'

'Out to the cabin,' Karla said. 'Walked back in, had a nice meal with the grandkids, told them he was mainly walking for his health, and left again at three-fifteen the next morning. He told the kids he wanted to stay in good health so he could live to see them grown up and married ...'

She had to pause briefly in her narrative, choked up at the thought of her own grandkids being grown up and married. Even dark little Barbi might grow up and marry, someday; then she would have no kids living at home, unless, of course, there were divorces at the grandkids' level.

'He didn't seem mad or anything, when he left,' she went on. 'The only crazy thing he said was that he'd like to burn his pickup.'

'Mom, it could be senility,' Nellie said. 'I've heard that senile people hide things and burn letters and stuff.'

'Letters, sure, I'd burn letters if my boyfriends had ever written me any,' Karla said. 'But I never heard of anyone wanting to burn their pickup – how's he supposed to run an oil business without a pickup?'

Nellie had to admit that was a puzzler. Pickups were the first facts of life, where they lived. She was beginning to feel a little anxious. What if her father really had gone for good? Pretty soon all the grandkids would be whining because they missed their Pa-Pa. The very thought made her wish she was back on the clean white beach of Cancun, wearing the string bikini that had brought her so many admiring looks and made Tommy afraid to leave her side for more than about twenty seconds at a time.

'So, is he at the cabin?' she asked.

'Yep – Bobby Lee had supper with him,' Karla said. 'All they had was soup and crackers.'

'Mom, that's okay, there's nothing crazy about having a light meal once in a while,' Nellie said.

'No, but Bobby Lee said he was just real distant,' Karla said.

'Oh well, who wants to talk to that little shrimp anyway?' Nellie asked. 'All he wants to talk about is how good he can do it even though he's only got one ball.'

'How would he know? He hasn't had a girlfriend since he had the operation,' Karla said. 'I'd feel sorry for him if he wasn't so whiny. He shot his little toe off yesterday – that's one more thing that happened while you were gone.'

'Maybe they could page Daddy on the radio and let him know I'm home,' Nellie said. 'If he knew I was here he might come back. I've always been his favorite – you said that yourself.'

'Won't work. Bobby says he's unplugged the radio; he's real cut off,' Karla told her. 'Anyway he knows when you were due back – we marked it right there on the calendar.'

The calendar hung on the wall right beside the microwave. Nellie went over to look, and sure enough, her return date had been recorded in her own neat hand, in contrast to the rest of the calendar, which was just a mass of scribbles, most of them scribbled by Rag. The scribbles mainly seemed to involve dental appointments for the grandchildren, but they were constantly missing their appointments because nobody but Rag could read Rag's handwriting, and she sometimes couldn't read it herself.

'What does Rag think about Daddy leaving?' Nellie inquired.

'Oh, it suits her fine – it's one less mouth to cook for,' Karla said. 'I'm the only one here in despair. Julie and Annette stay stoned all day – you know how they are. I can't expect much support from them.'

'I know, they're dopeheads,' Nellie said. She suddenly felt very, very sleepy – the fatigue accumulated in a week's round-the-clock partying in Mexico had begun to wash over her, like a great warm wave.

'But *I'm* home now,' she added. 'It'll be all right, Mom. Daddy will get tired of the cabin and walk back in a couple of days.

'You need to not overdramatize,' she said. Then she gave her mother a good long hug and a kiss and went to bed.

# 16

When Nellie went to bed Karla rolled up in a blanket and channel-surfed until she struck the Weather Channel – it was by far her favorite channel for late-night viewing. After a certain hour she grew tired of weird comedians and brassy talk show hosts: she just wanted some nice soothing weather. The pleasant thing about the Weather Channel was you really didn't have to watch it or even listen to it – you could just sort of absorb it, like the weather itself. Karla often let it play all night, while she lay on the couch, flipped through magazines, or dozed; the Weather Channel allowed her to inhabit a comfortable country between sleep and wakefulness. She got to hear the sound of human voices without having to engage with a human personality. Also – although she knew this wasn't a Christian trait – the worse the weather was in some remote part of the world, the cozier it felt to lie in her blankets and drowse. If the weather was *really* bad elsewhere, with whole towns sliding into the surf in California, or floods causing people to have to sit on the roofs of their houses in Missouri, or to rescue their half-drowned pets in Arkansas, then the better it felt to be dozing on a nice dry couch in Thalia.

Of course, on this occasion it would have been a lot cozier to drowse on the couch if her husband, Duane, had been asleep in the bedroom, where he usually was when she turned on the Weather Channel. Of course, he was only six miles away: he wasn't experiencing terrible weather in Missouri or California, but he wasn't where he belonged, either. Where he belonged was in their bed.

Despite two healthy slugs of tequila, Karla didn't feel relaxed enough to drowse, didn't feel interested in flipping through catalogues, and, for once, didn't feel soothed by the sight of a storm front moving in on Detroit. Despite the tequila, the weather, and her daughter's safe return, Karla could not seem to settle down in her mind – and she couldn't understand why. Duane had always needed to be by himself from time to time; there was really nothing new about that. The thought occurred to her that it might be no more than that. Their house, admittedly, was a noisy place – it would be perfectly normal for a man to want to be someplace where it was quiet for a day or two. Earlier in their marriage Duane had spent a good deal of his time in a boat fishing, for the same reason. Sitting in a cabin on a hill and sitting in a boat fishing were not such radically different things; Karla could not get a clear fix on why the former bothered her while the latter didn't.

All she knew was that the two things felt totally different. Lots of men fished, some of them probably for no better reason than that it gave them an opportunity to escape their domestic lives, or whatever. That was perfectly normal – she herself had taken many a soothing shopping trip to Dallas for essentially the same reasons. Getting away from it all was a motive she certainly understood – it was Duane's decision to *walk* away from it all that threw the whole picture out of kilter and caused her to feel that she was dealing with a whole new phenomenon. Very few men of her acquaintance had ever walked six miles for any reason whatever, and very few would choose to sit by themselves in a bare little cabin that didn't offer much in the way of creature comforts – not when they could have been staying in what was, by common consent, the most comfortable house in Thalia.

In her gut, Karla knew something had changed. This wasn't a mood she was dealing with: this was something more fundamental. Why it had struck just when it had, she had no idea. But there it was, like a pregnancy: something new had started growing and she had no choice but to deal with it.

A little before dawn she threw on a robe, took her car keys off a peg by the door, and whipped her BMW out of the driveway. In a minute she was on the dark road that led to Duane's cabin. In five minutes she was parked on a hill with a view of the cabin, her lights off, her motor idling. In case Duane's craziness took the form of walking around before it was light, she didn't want him to see her. If he thought she was snooping he would be twice as difficult. There were a lot of things Duane liked about her – forty years of marriage had convinced her of that – but one thing he definitely didn't like was her determined snooping. Karla wanted to know everything that was going on, always had, always would. If Duane wanted to keep something from her he had to be pretty sly to do it – and he knew this. Over the four decades they had been together each had honed their skills – snooping and antisnooping – to a fine degree. Karla's ambition was to snoop so skillfully that she left no track – several times she supposed she had done just that, only to have Duane, through the exercise of some sixth sense, find her out. It was a game they both continued to play. Several times Karla had promised him she would never snoop again, only to break her promise immediately. Duane expected her to snoop, which didn't mean he *wanted* her to. Their cat-and-mouse games had always been serious and still were.

'Duane, I *have* to snoop,' Karla told him many times. 'It's a matter of survival. If I didn't snoop and find out things you try to hide from me I wouldn't know anything about you at all, and what kind of marriage would that be, where the wife don't know nothing about the husband?'

'Better than what we've got, from my point of view,' Duane said. 'Why can't you just give privacy a chance?'

'I just can't,' Karla admitted.

This morning, particularly, she didn't want Duane to find out that she had been snooping around the road that led to his cabin. She cut her lights before she even rounded the last bend in the road, so as not to flash even the most distant light on the hill where her husband was sleeping. Fortunately the BMW was a quiet-running car – a kind of stealth car compared to the rattly pickups that made up most of the traffic along that route. The road was a faint white track ahead of her; she purred along it slowly and stopped at a point where she was fairly sure she could see the light in Duane's cabin when it came on; there she paused. Duane had good hearing. If she turned the motor off he might hear it when she turned it back on to leave, so she left it running. She got out of the car and listened – even from twenty yards away she could barely hear the motor running, and the cabin was several hundred yards away, up across the hill. There was no likelihood that Duane was going to detect her snooping this time, not unless he did it by ESP.

Karla got back in the car, rolled one of the windows down, and sat and waited. She felt a little silly and even a little guilty. Why couldn't she just let her husband have a little time to himself? Living with her and most of the kids and all the grandkids could have just been a little bit more than he bargained for. Snooping on him in the middle of the night smacked of paranoia, or whatever. It was pretty unlikely that he had a girlfriend tucked away in the little cabin, which had no TV and only a single bed with an old sleeping bag for a comforter. Of course some women would put up with less than that in order to have an affair with Duane, but Karla felt pretty sure that he was past the girlfriend stage – perhaps a little too far past it. A man who had reached the point in his life where he would rather walk than have sex was a man who needed counseling, Karla felt, even if the propaganda in her health magazines about eighty-five-year-olds screwing constantly wasn't strictly a true thing.

Then, just as Karla resigned herself to a long wait, a miracle happened. The light came on in Duane's cabin – it was just a tiny yellow spot in the darkness but the sight of it brought an immediate relief – deep relief. Duane was right there in the cabin, where Bobby Lee said he was; all the walking wasn't simply a complicated dodge to throw her off the track of a love affair or something. Duane was in his cabin – he was probably about to make himself some coffee. Bobby Lee had assured her that there seemed to be plenty of coffee.

Once she saw the light and knew her husband was all right, Karla immediately turned the BMW around in the narrow road. She had to back and turn, back and turn, two or three times before she got headed back toward town. She crept back along the same dark road, careful not to turn her lights on until she had rounded the first bend.

As she turned into Thalia she saw the lights of the Dairy Queen wink on: it was 6 A.M. She hesitated a moment, torn between the mood for company and the desire to catch a few more winks of sleep before Little Bascom and Baby Paul woke up and began to demand attention.

The desire for company won – she could always lock herself in the big bedroom and let the kids pound on the door and scream until they gave up and crawled away. After all, Rag could tend to them, not to mention their mothers.

By the time she drove the half mile to the Dairy Queen there were already six pickups parked in front of it. A cluster of oilmen, wanting to postpone their day's work as long as possible, sat at the long table in the rear of the room. Karla rarely hit the Dairy Queen that early – when she swept in, in her bathrobe, several of the oilmen looked at her askance.

'What's the matter, J.T., never seen a woman in a bathrobe?' she asked one who was pouring himself a cup of coffee.

J.T., disturbed enough at the mere sight of Karla, was more disturbed at being asked a direct question.

'Scared I'll bite, or what?' Karla inquired.

80

'I'm divorced, remember?' J.T. reminded her. 'I *have* seen a woman in a bathrobe, but not in a while.'

'I ain't either seen one and it's not a pleasant sight,' Dan Connor informed her. Dan fancied himself the leader of whatever pack he was with – he had always had a smart lip.

'You could have combed your hair,' he added.

'Well, I would have if I had known you were going to be here, Dan,' Karla said. 'Mind if I sit down?'

The request took the six men aback. Though most of them had known Karla for much of their lives the thought of having her right there in their midst was more than they were prepared to deal with at such an early hour.

'Ha, ha, just kidding,' Karla said. 'I didn't mean to paralyze you.'

'You talk too fast, that's the only thing,' J.T. said. He liked Karla, but had not been prepared for her early arrival. Now he faced the problem of how to strike a balance between being friendly and being too friendly.

'We might want to talk about men stuff; you might be embarrassed,' Dan Connor informed her.

'I haven't been embarrassed in ten years,' Karla said. 'Maybe it would be a thrill.'

She took her coffee and walked over to a booth by the window, as far as she could get from the men. She hadn't really wanted to sit down with them – she had just invited herself in order to see them flinch.

Outside there was a screech of air brakes. Two eighteen-wheelers had just pulled off the highway. Soon three cowboys, wearing chaps and spurs, came crowding in behind the two truckers, both of whom were broad in the beam. The cowboys had several horses in one of the long horse trailers that had become popular in the last few years. It was cold out – Karla could see the horses' breath condensing in great puffs of steam over the long horse trailer. It was a gray day. When Nellie woke up she would be despondent, not only because she was in a place where there was no beach but because she was in a place where there was no hint of sun.

Before she finished her coffee all the oilmen got up and trailed out. A couple of them smiled at her and nodded as they left.

'Bye, boys,' she said, watching as, one by one, they got in their muddy pickups and drove away.

# 17

When Duane first stepped out of the cabin to stretch and assess the weather he saw a spot of red back down the road. Then he saw it again, twice more. It looked like a brake light: somebody was turning a car around on the road west of his hill. His first thought was that it might be a deer poacher. But if someone had shot a deer he would have heard the shot, and Shorty would have barked.

His second, more accurate thought was that it was his wife, unable to resist the temptation to snoop yet again. Probably she had been sitting in the road for an hour, determined to find out if he was really in the cabin. In a way it was annoying, and, in another way, kind of touching. Even though Bobby Lee had probably given her a full report, it wasn't good enough for Karla. She had to see something with her own eyes before she would believe it.

Later in the morning, once he had walked into town to pick up the file and a few groceries, he couldn't resist mentioning it to Karla, who was working in the little greenhouse they had built behind the garage, the main point of which was to grow winter tomatoes.

'I saw you on the road this morning – couldn't resist checking on me, could you?' he said.

It was a wild shot – after all, it could have been a deer poacher with a silencer whose taillights he had seen.

Karla was amused and even a little relieved that Duane brought it up. If he still objected to her snooping, then that was something, at least.

'How'd you know it was me?' she asked. 'I was in my stealth car.'

'Because your stealth car has brake lights,' he said. 'I saw you when you turned around in the road.'

'If that road had been wider, so I wouldn't have had to back up to get turned, you would never have known I was there, would you?' she asked.

'Nope,' Duane said. 'How's everything?'

'Why would you need to know? You left,' Karla said. 'Dan Connor insulted me in the Dairy Queen. Next time you run into him I hope you'll knock him on his fat ass.'

'I doubt he meant to insult you,' Duane said. 'He's just awkward with women.'

'Okay, don't knock him on his fat butt if you don't believe me,' she said. Paradoxically, after spending most of the night wishing Duane would show up, she found that she was a little annoyed now that he had. Working with her tomato plants put her in a good mood. The fact that her husband had left her had ceased to seem like such a big deal. But now, there he stood, looking annoyingly healthy and fit. It was just like a man – now that she was getting used to the fact that he was gone, there he was again, not gone, expecting her to get used to the fact that he was back.

'What brings you to town, Mr Hermit?' she asked.

'I needed to get my file – the axe is dull,' Duane said. 'I wouldn't mind a few tomatoes, either, if you've got some that are ripe.'

Karla handed him a tomato that was no larger than a pecan.

'These tomatoes ain't even as big as nuts,' she said. 'I don't know what's wrong. It was a sunny winter too.'

Duane wished he had just dug the file out of his toolbox and left. He had actually been glad to see Karla – for almost his entire life he had been glad to see Karla. He liked her energy, always had. But now, after only a minute's conversation, it seemed as if the tentacles of habit were snaking out toward him like a vine. Here they were talking about the fact that their winter tomatoes were stunted. It was a subject that came up year after year.

Karla seemed to feel the same way. She had stopped poking amid the vines and just sat, hugging her knees and looking at him.

'What's the deal? Just tell me,' she said. 'Are we over, or what?'

Duane had been about to leave, but he stayed where he was for a minute. His wife had just asked him a serious question – he felt he ought to make her some kind of answer.

'That's way too big a question – I just came to pick up my file,' he said. 'I want to stay in the cabin for a while. I'd just as soon pass on the big questions until I've done some walking, if you don't mind.'

'I wish I knew what it was about, this walking,' Karla said. 'That's the most worrisome part.'

'It's just so interesting,' Duane said. 'When you ride in a pickup you don't really see anything but the pickup – and I've done that nearly all my life.'

'I know you're trying to make it clearer, but you're not making it clearer,' Karla said. 'You must be real depressed. What if you tried acupuncture? That's a remedy that's thousands of years old.'

'Try it for what?' Duane asked.

'Or you could just try plain old counseling,' she said. 'Right now you're in denial.'

'Oh, bullshit, I'm not either,' he said mildly. 'I'll see you in a day or two. I'm going back to the cabin.'

'At least go in and kiss Nellie – she got back last night and she'll be real upset if you go off without kissing her.'

Duane felt the tentacles of the vine snaking toward him again.

'What time did she get home?' he asked.

'It was late – she broke up with Tommy and had to take a taxi all this way,' Karla admitted.

She walked into the garage with him and waited until he got his file, a pair of pliers, and a small set of wrenches out of his toolbox.

Shorty, the blue heeler, was waiting patiently by the back steps. His intent was to go right in the house and herd Little Bascom – all he needed was for someone to open the door. When he saw Karla he hunkered down. Karla was the harshest critic of his efforts to keep Little Bascom in the playroom, where all the toys were. She had administered several harsh scoldings and had been the one to pitch him in the car and haul him off to the camp of Juan, Jesus, and Rafael.

'What's that dog doing here?' she asked. 'Don't tell me you've taken up with that dog again.'

'He's just sitting there, honey,' Duane said. 'He came to the cabin and I let him stay. What I like about Shorty is that he don't make any demands.'

'Oh great, so now I'm too demanding,' Karla said.

'Not particularly, but any human being is more demanding than Shorty,' Duane said. 'It's snaky on that hill. When it gets warm he can find the snakes before I step on them.'

At that Karla looked sad. She shook her head a few times, as if in bewilderment.

'The snakes won't be out for a couple of months, Duane,' she said.

'Well, or six weeks, if it warms up quick,' he said, realizing his mistake.

'Six weeks, two months, I don't care,' Karla said. 'It just sounds to me like you mean to make that cabin your permanent home. Is that correct?'

'I can't say,' Duane replied. 'I don't have any timetables. Timetables is another thing I'm tired of, like pickups and the oil business and a few other things.'

'Would family life be one of the few other things?' Karla asked. 'This is beginning to sound serious.'

'It doesn't feel that serious,' he said. 'It just feels like something I need to do.'

Karla shook her head again.

'You may not even know how serious it is,' she said. 'You may be right in the midst of a complete nervous breakdown – only you're so quiet about everything that it just doesn't show.

'You've always been able to fool most people, Duane,' she went on. 'Everybody thinks you're the most normal man in town, but you aren't.'

'I've never claimed to be especially normal, have I?' he asked. He had found his old backpack in a cabinet in the garage – he put the few tools in it. The backpack was a relic of an earlier era, when he had done a good bit of camping. It still had a couple of pieces of jerky in it, purchased nearly ten years earlier.

Karla seemed to have lost interest in the question of his normalcy. Her shoes were muddy from working in the greenhouse after she had just watered the tomatoes. She was trying to knock the mud off them with her trowel.

'You can't get many groceries in that backpack,' she observed. 'You ought to try to eat healthy food even if you are going crazy.'

'I'm not going crazy – I'll see you in a few days,' Duane said. 'Come on, Shorty.'

'Acupuncture really does work,' Karla said, when he was at the edge of the driveway. 'You could at least think about it.'

'Okay,' Duane said. 'I'll think about it.'

He was two blocks away before he realized he had forgotten to go in and kiss Nellie. He looked back at his house for a moment, wishing he hadn't forgotten. But the house seemed a long way back down the road, and, also, it was the place where the vines of habit grew the most thickly. In his house one familiar thing led to another familiar thing – if he went to kiss Nellie he would be unlikely to slip past Little Bascom, or Baby Paul, or Rag, or even Bubbles, Willy, and Barbi, all of whom tended to hang out in the kitchen in the mornings, annoying Rag and doing everything they could to avoid getting ready to go to school on time. His children had once held the all-time local record for tardies, but his grandchildren had already broken it by a wide margin. If he walked in just as Rag was trying to assemble all their lunches it would only make a bad situation worse. All the children would want to tell him about the most recent injustices that had been visited on them, and if Rag's car wouldn't start – it frequently stalled just as the tardy bell was about to ring – he would be the one who would have to fix it. It was too much to risk just to kiss his daughter, who was welcome to come out to his cabin and be kissed anytime.

'I doubt she's up, anyway – she got in real late,' he said, as if he were required to excuse this omission and had no one to excuse it to except his dog.

A few minutes later he saw a dust cloud on the road where he had just been: it was Rag, racing the bell in her old Chevy, which was packed with his grandkids. They didn't make it, though. Before they even reached the school yard Duane heard the tardy bell ring.

# 18

As Duane was passing Lester Marlow's house he saw the former banker himself, sitting on his own front porch in a green bathrobe, aiming a twenty-two at something in his own yard. Before Duane could get close enough to make out what he was shooting at, Lester fired off three quick rounds. There was some torn-up earth and quite a few clods in Lester's yard – when Duane got a little closer it became apparent that Lester was shooting at the clods, an unusual thing to do even for someone who had spent several lengthy stretches in the mental hospital, and also the kind of thing that might attract the attention of the authorities. After all, it was morning – kids had just been walking to school.

When Lester saw Duane he put down his rifle and walked out to the gate to greet him. Just as he did his wife, Jenny, came whipping out of the driveway in her small black Yugo, the only Yugo in Thalia. Jenny had flown to Newark, New Jersey, to pick up her car. What with Lester's legal bills, doctor bills, and expensive medication, Jenny had to see that they watched their pennies, and a car that claimed to get one hundred and thirty miles to the gallon was nothing to sneeze at. Jenny worked as a court reporter now – when she sped out of the driveway she was holding a coffee mug that seemed almost as big as the car. It left her no hand to wave with, so she nodded at Duane instead.

'Jenny loves her Yugo,' Lester said. He was proud of his wife's thriftiness, in going to such lengths to get a car they could afford. He himself, despite extensive counseling, had never managed to attain thrifty habits. When Lester got money he still spent it immediately. Now and then, to his wife's distress, he even spent it before he got it, due to some tricks he was able to play at the ATM machines.

'Why are you shooting at clods, Lester?' Duane asked, when he walked up.

'I wasn't shooting at the clods, I was shooting into the ground,' Lester said. 'There's a mole down under those clods, somewhere. I figure if I keep plunking bullets into the ground I'll get him sooner or later. Want to sell me your pickup cheap?'

'What would you want with my pickup?' Duane asked. 'I've never thought you were the pickup type.'

'No, but I'm thinking of taking a booth at that big swap meet in Fort Worth,' Lester said. 'I need a pickup to haul the junk I plan to sell. You can't get much junk in a Yugo.'

Duane stepped into the yard and examined the clods, which looked as if they had been rooted up by an armadillo, a creature that was known to have a bad effect on lawns.

'You're hunting the wrong animal – all this rooting was done by an armadillo,' he informed Lester.

'Could be,' Lester said. 'That business about the mole is just what I tell the new deputy sheriff, when the neighbors complain about my plinking. I've got the man convinced there's a mole in my yard. Basically I just like to shoot at clods. It's a harmless pursuit.'

'Well, it is, unless you hit a neighbor,' Duane said.

'Come on, I've only nicked one neighbor in all these years,' Lester said.

'I know, but the one you nicked was Karla, which is the wrong one to nick,' Duane said. Years before, when she was interested in photography, Karla had been trying to take a picture of a roadrunner when a bullet fired by Lester ricocheted off a fire hydrant and blew the flashbulb out of her camera. Though Lester had been half a mile away at the time and didn't know she was trying to photograph roadrunners, Karla had given him so much hell over the incident that Lester tried to claim he had been shooting at a mad dog, a claim no one believed, even though a mad dog showed up in town a day or two later and bit an old man who was mowing his lawn.

'Karla holds grudges, don't she?' Lester said. 'Is that why you walked off?'

'No, I just started walking because I like it,' Duane said.

'That's the same reason I shoot at clods,' Lester said. 'It gives me a feeling of peace to shoot at things.'

'You could join a gun club,' Duane suggested.

'If you're going to be walking all over the place, keep an eye out for things I could sell at the swap meet,' Lester said.

'I haven't noticed much swap-meet-quality material along the roads,' Duane told him. 'What sort of things do you mean?'

'Haven't you ever been to a swap meet?' Lester asked. 'People bored enough to go to swap meets will buy anything. They'll even buy interesting rocks if they can't find anything else to spend their money on. Surely you can find an interesting rock, once in a while.'

Duane was beginning to wish he hadn't walked by Lester's house. Now and again he would begin to feel slightly guilty where Lester was concerned; then he would convince himself that he was being a bad neighbor or a bad friend, for visiting Lester so seldom. For all he knew Lester was more depressed than ever – without a visit now and then to lift his spirits he might have to go back into the hospital. He might even kill himself, which would be a terrible blow to Jenny, who loved him, despite all.

'Bullshit,' Karla always said, when Duane confessed that he was feeling bad about not seeing much of Lester. 'Some crazy people are perfectly happy being crazy. And they like it that all the sane people they know feel guilty about them.'

That remark had been made years ago, long before Karla had ever dreamed that her own husband would ever do anything that might cause people to think he was unbalanced – abandoning his brand-new pickup in favor of foot transportation, for example. She had merely been trying to discourage Duane from hanging around Lester's too much. It was widely known that Jenny Marlow had a big crush on Duane. She had had it since the first grade, or maybe even longer.

Whenever Duane weakened and went by Lester's house to check up on him, he invariably regretted his decision, usually within minutes. Before Duane had even been there ten minutes Lester would somehow manage to off-load his depression onto him. Duane would arrive feeling noble for being such a good, loyal friend, but would always depart feeling miserable, as if he were about to come down with the flu or something.

It always happened, and it happened this time as well. He had been walking along in a pretty good humor and had merely stopped by Lester's to see what he was shooting at, and now Lester was trying to get him to sell him his pickup, so he could haul junk to a swap meet in Fort Worth.

'Just think about it while you're walking along,' Lester suggested.

'Be on the lookout for chairs people have thrown out beside the road. People are always throwing out ratty old chairs.

'One man's junk is another man's treasure,' he added. 'That's the first principle of swap meets. If you see any pocketknives people have dropped, pick them up. Pocketknives sell real quick at a swap meet.'

Duane couldn't remember ever having found a pocketknife that somebody had dropped – but then his eyes had only been operating at ground level for the last couple of days. There might be dropped pocketknives everywhere, for all he knew.

'If your grandkids have any video games they're tired of, ask them if they'd mind if I borrowed them,' Lester said. 'I've only got about two – Jenny won't buy me any more, even though my psychiatrist says I really need to recover my inner child.'

'Why won't she buy you any more?' Duane asked.

'Too expensive,' Lester said. 'Some of those video games cost almost as much as her car.

'Nobody told her to go off to New Jersey and buy a Yugo,' Lester added, as if it were a point that had just occurred to him. 'She could do what you're doing – walk. It's not that far to the courthouse.'

Duane had no comment. The only way to get out of a conversation with Lester was to leave in the middle of it, so he began to amble off. Lester followed him, but only as far as the corner of his yard.

'I don't think Jenny agrees with my shrink about the inner child stuff,' Lester said. 'Jenny's always telling me to grow up. But how can I grow up if I'm supposed to encourage my inner child? Who do I mind, my wife or my shrink?'

Duane didn't answer. He wished he had chosen to walk down another road. The road to Lester's house was the road to the too familiar, and the too familiar was exactly what he was tired of. The day no longer seemed as fresh and lovely as it had that morning when he walked into town. A problem that occurred to him was that almost everyplace he could reach on foot, starting from where he had started from, was too familiar.

For a moment, the thought made him feel stupid – his spirits dropped. What did he think he was accomplishing, by walking rather than riding? What it really meant was that he was just being forced to take a slower look at the very things he didn't want to see. Here he was on foot, halfway between his home and town, and he didn't feel free and purposeful anymore; he felt confused and uncertain. His walk was not a rich pleasure anymore: it was just something he had to go on with until he got to someplace where it made sense to stop – and that place was his cabin.

He stopped at the Kwik-Sack only long enough to buy a loaf of bread, bacon, peanut butter, four more cans of tomato soup, Fritos, and a small sack of dog food. Sonny Crawford had gone home for the day, which was good. Just seeing Lester Marlow had lowered Duane's spirits enough for one day.

Once he got back on the dirt road and was well out of town he began to feel a little better, though not as good as he had felt only a couple of hours ago, when he was walking in. Something had changed. For two days he had felt really happy, and now he didn't.

As he was crossing a short wooden bridge over a shallow stream he stopped for a moment and looked down at the shallow brown water. Somebody had thrown an old car battery off the bridge. The battery was just on the edge of the stream. A mud turtle sat on it. If Lester saw it he would probably try to drag it up and take it to the swap meet.

Standing on the bridge, watching the brown stream play around the abandoned battery – just an ugly piece of debris – Duane remembered something he had paid no attention to at the time, which was that Karla had said he was depressed. She felt it so strongly that she had driven out and waited in his road at night just to check on him. Karla was not always entirely right, but she was seldom entirely wrong, either, where her family was concerned. Maybe he was depressed?

One thing Duane knew for sure was that he hated the fact that the battery was in the water. In that part of the country people habitually threw their junk off bridges, to get rid of it in the quickest way. Cross almost any small bridge in the county and you would see the equivalent of the battery with the turtle on it. People took the easy way, when it came to disposing of possessions. They stopped on the bridge and threw whatever it was they no longer wanted out of their pickups. It had been going on all his life. It was unsightly – always had been unsightly – but the unsightliness had never particularly bothered Duane before.

Now it bothered him so much that he would have liked to see huge fines levied against anyone caught throwing junk off a bridge.

'I'd like to kill him,' he said, to Shorty – referring to the man who had thrown the battery off the bridge.

Then he realized he had just said something crazy, and to a dog, at that. Littering was a nuisance – it wasn't a capital crime. If he didn't like the sight of the battery in the creek, he should just go and remove the battery, instead of threatening to kill the man who threw it off the bridge.

Duane walked off the bridge and crawled through the barbed-wire fence near where the battery lay. When he did the mud turtle plopped into the water. The stream was too shallow to cover the turtle completely. It swam out a few feet and stopped.

Finding a place to stuff the battery, so as to prevent it from being an eyesore, was not easy, but Duane walked along the creek bank until he found a good-sized hole, a kind of cave-in. By good luck the battery fit the hole like a hand fits a glove. Duane threw four or five good-sized rocks on top of the battery, covering it completely. He became a little obsessive about covering the battery; he didn't want any part of it to show. If he piled dirt on the battery the next rain would just wash it away, so he searched until he had enough rocks to build a good-sized cairn over the hole where the battery was concealed. Then he walked around the pile of rocks several times, making sure that no trace of the ugly battery was visible from the road.

While he was doing that Shorty flushed an old mother skunk, with four skunk babies trailing her in a line. Shorty barked furiously at the family of skunks, but he had been skunked a number of times in his life and had learned his lesson where little black-and-white animals were concerned. He barked, but he didn't engage.

Hiding the battery made Duane feel a little better. He felt he had made a small but important contribution to the beautification of the landscape. But as he was crawling through the fence to get back to the road he saw something worse: on the other side of the bridge, in the same creek, somebody had thrown out a car seat. He hadn't noticed it when he crossed the bridge because a post-oak limb obscured it, but from creek level there it was, plain to see. Almost all the stuffing had been pulled out of it, leaving an ugly tangle of spring. No doubt the pack rats and other small animals had made good use of the stuffing: what had once been padding for a car seat now probably lined many small dens in the pastures the creek ran through.

What was left, though, was every bit as ugly as the battery, and much larger and harder to hide. There was not likely to be a hole anywhere around large enough to hold a car seat. For a moment Duane felt the same murderous hatred of the person who had chosen to dispose of a car seat by throwing it off a bridge. It was terrible, trashy behavior; and yet he was uneasily aware that one of his own employees might have done it: Juan and Jesus and Rafael, for example. The wetback fencing crew had owned a number of verminous, rattly old station wagons, which they would frequently trade in for others just as bad. Of course, you couldn't really blame men as poor as the three Mexicans for disposing of an unwanted car seat in the easiest way. The men worked hard, and they were honest, but they had no energy to spare for the beautification of the land they would never own. His own son Dickie had once tried to dispose of a whole pickup by shoving it off a small bluff into a lake. Dickie's intention had been to claim that the pickup had been stolen, so he could collect the insurance money and spend it on drugs. But the lake at the point where the pickup went in was only four feet deep – all Dickie got for his troubles was a wet pickup full of water moccasins and turtles. Six months later, when Dickie was in jail, Duane and Bobby Lee had winched the pickup out of the lake and sold it for junk.

It was pretty muddy where the car seat was, but Duane managed to hook it with a long stick and pull it up on the bank. Several tiny frogs hopped out when he did. It was a wretched, peeling thing that he couldn't immediately decide what to do with – finally he tucked it as neatly as possible behind a big clump of chaparral. It was pretty weedy where the chaparral grew – a person would have had to be walking right by the chaparral to be able to see the car seat. Probably only cattle and an occasional coyote would ever be that close to that spot.

Still, Duane wasn't fully satisfied. He became as obsessive about the car seat as he had been about the battery. He didn't want the slightest trace to show. There weren't enough rocks around to cover the car seat with rocks, so he began to drag up brush and small logs to pile around it. It occurred to him that if Sam Tucker, a taciturn old rancher whose land he was on, had happened to come by and see him going to such lengths to conceal a cast-off car seat, the man would think he was crazy. Sam Tucker had a low opinion of the mental stability of his fellowmen, anyway. He had been sheriff of the county for twenty years, during which time he had had ample opportunity to see human nature at its worst.

Though several pickups whizzed by while Duane was at work covering the car seat, no one noticed him.

Pretty soon he had the car seat so well hidden that only a rat or a snake could have located it. If the car seat had been on his own land he would have burned it and then stuffed the springs in a hole, but he couldn't take such a liberty when he was on Sam Tucker's land. As it was, Sam would probably be a little puzzled by the piled-up brush by the chaparral thicket. Duane meant to explain it to him if a suitable occasion ever presented itself.

Once he was finished, Duane felt a little better. He had done what he could for the landscape, even though, in a junk-ridden county, it was the merest drop in the bucket. At least he had rendered a small stretch of one creek more pleasing to the eye. It was, in its way, a good morning's work. Feeling less depressed, he picked up his backpack, whistled at Shorty, and continued his walk. Fortunately there were no more creeks and no more bridges between where he was and the cabin.

# 19

When Duane got back to the cabin he unloaded his few groceries and his few tools. He was home, but he wasn't entirely calm. When he sat down with his file and began to sharpen the axe, he stopped after only a few strokes because he felt shaky, as if he had had an adrenaline rush and had to try to relax and come down from it. He supposed it was from the anger he felt when he saw the trash in the creek – the battery and the car seat. Probably both objects had been in that creek for months; he must have driven over that bridge at least fifty times and never noticed them; he had even walked over it a couple of times without noticing them. It was unlike him to let himself become so disturbed over something so trivial, just two pieces of common trash in a creek; yet fury had taken possession of him for a few moments, fury so intense that his hands were shaky from it. The trash wasn't even on his land – it wasn't even polluting his stretch of creek. He had nearly had a fit over common litter, which seemed to lend strength to Karla's complaint that he had grown more and more irritable in the last few months.

'Could be too much caffeine. Maybe I better cut down on the coffee; what do you think?' he said to Shorty, who was dozing by the woodpile. The dog didn't wake up.

Duane spent the afternoon sitting in his lawn chair, covered by his poncho. He liked being outside, and also liked being warm as he looked off his hill and watched the hawks circling over the scrubby plain below it.

A day or two earlier he had been trying to decide where to start, when it came to investigating some of the things he was curious about: botany, biscuit making, the pyramids. There was, after all, a bewildering abundance of things he might do. There were skills he had not mastered; he was, for example, only an indifferent wood-chopper, as he had discovered the day before when he was cutting firewood. He could begin by spending a week or two perfecting his skills with an axe. He wouldn't have to go very far from the cabin to do that, and sticking close to the cabin appealed to him. Biscuit making would have to wait until his next trip to town, which might be a few days – he had forgotten to buy flour that morning.

After an hour in his lawn chair Duane began to recover the comfortable feeling he had when he first walked out and settled into the cabin. The cabin felt like the right place – as opposed to the town, which definitely felt like the wrong place. Somehow, from being in town that morning, he had received a kind of bruise to his spirit, but that bruise was healing – his spirit was beginning to feel healthy again. It was hard to say what had caused the bruise, since all he had done was walk in to pick up some tools and a few groceries. He had chatted with his wife for a few minutes, which hadn't really been unpleasant. Karla had been concerned and a little sad, but not rancorous. Then he had listened to Lester Marlow babble for a while – it was depressing, but visits to Lester were always depressing. Lester was just a selfish, slightly crazy man who was too big to spank. The law hadn't even spanked him very hard, although he had stolen over one hundred thousand dollars and broken every rule in banking.

Nothing that had occurred in town should have depressed him to the extent that it had, and neither should the trash in the creek. He realized that for the first time in his life he had too much time to think; of course, he had *wanted* more time to think, but that was probably because he hadn't realized how tricky thinking could be. Probably thinking was a little bit like mountain climbing – you had to give yourself time to adjust to the altitude. He wasn't used to thinking – particularly not to thinking about himself. He had probably tried to think too much, too soon, without giving himself time to adjust to the altitude it required. He would have to slow down with the thinking, not do too much of it at one time, and maybe learn to avoid dangerous areas of thought, areas that could bruise the spirit. Probably thinking should be approached in an orderly way, done with a little care.

The wind came up, a sharp wind. He had to tuck the poncho tighter around him. Tumbleweeds were beginning to roll across the road below him. He did not want to be like a tumbleweed, sent skittering in his mind by every sharp breeze that life blew up.

Soon the temperature began to drop. It was February – spring was still a month away. Even with the poncho to cover him the lawn chair ceased to be a comfortable place to be, so he whistled at Shorty and followed him into the cabin.

He had meant to pick up some form of literature while he was in town – maybe a road atlas or a fishing magazine or something about boats – just something to distract his mind a little. If he had a road atlas he could study it and plan a trip or two. There was a rack of magazines in the Kwik-Sack but he had been so overwhelmed by the need to get out of town that he hadn't bought any.

He had also meant to pick up a tablet and a couple of ballpoint pens. He thought he might make a list, write down some things he wanted to learn to do, some places he might want to go, and some problems he needed to grapple with.

But, thanks to his sudden depression, he had made a poor showing at the Kwik-Sack. He had meant to pick up enough stuff to render him self-sufficient for a week or two; the thought of a long stretch in the cabin, with no visits to town, appealed to him. How could he make any progress on a new life if he had to keep going back to Thalia, the old place with the old problems? He liked the simplicity and the order of his cabin, where he had a chair, table, bed, stove, fireplace, shower, and nails to hang his clothes on, each in its ordered place.

The cabin was the opposite of town – there, everything was disorderly: his kids taking drugs and neglecting *their* kids, his oil business crew growing more deranged every year. Of course, Karla did keep a neat greenhouse – he had to give her that, even if the winter tomatoes were only the size of pecans. But the town churned with disorder, and what he wanted for himself was order. He wanted each tool in its place at the end of the day.

Once inside, Duane surveyed his domain and decided that the oversight he regretted most from his shopping trip was the forgotten tablet. He only had three sheets of notepaper left, and the only ballpoint pen that still wrote showed signs of playing out. Until he secured a new tablet and a better pen he had to be efficient with his list making.

'Help me think, Shorty,' he said. 'We've only got three sheets of paper left.'

He tore the three sheets of paper off the tablet and sat down to make his list, using one of the old fishing magazines as backing. He decided that the way to proceed was to use one sheet of paper for things they needed, one sheet for possibilities he wanted to consider in terms of places to go or skills to attempt to master, and the third sheet for problems he might need to deal with, if he could isolate any.

On the first sheet, after some thought, he wrote:

1. Flour
2. Magazines
3. Road Atlas
4. Spade

– this last because he now realized how useful it would be to have had a spade that morning, when he was trying to bury the battery.

On the second sheet, at the top, he wrote:

'Things to Do.' Then he put down:

1. Make biscuits
2. Pyramids in Egypt
3. Meteor crater
4. Read about World Wars

Number three, the meteor crater, near Holbrook, Arizona, was something he had always meant to go see, just as the world wars were things he had always meant to learn something about. His grandfather had been in the first war, his father in the second, but both of them had died before they could share many memories with him. Millions of people had died in those wars, one of which had occurred in his lifetime – he wanted to read something that might explain why they had come about.

His last ballpoint pen was fast running out of ink. The item about the world wars was faint on the page, but then he only had one sheet of notepaper left, the one on which he had been intending to list his problems.

After staring out the window for a few minutes he made the number one on the small piece of paper. After it, in very faint letters, he wrote the word 'depression.'

# 20

For the next three days Duane stayed away from Thalia. Each day he took a long, slow walk around his property. One day he walked all the way around the edge of the hill where the cabin sat. He took his time, poked around, surprised a badger and two armadillos, took note of several holes that looked as if they might be entrances to a snake den, found a nice flint arrowhead, saw three wild pigs. Since he intended to live on the hill for as far ahead as he could foresee, he wanted to begin to develop a certain intimacy with it.

The second day he took an even longer walk, along the banks of the small river that snaked through the north end of the property. On that walk he twice surprised wild turkeys, and flushed a pair of prairie chickens, which pleased him a lot. Maybe the prairie chicken was going to make a comeback into the south plains.

Though seeing the turkeys and the prairie chickens pleased him, the condition of the creek bed didn't. There were all kinds of trash in it, nothing as heavy as the battery or the car seat but many cans and bottles and miscellaneous junk. Obviously people had formed the habit of cleaning out their pickups on the bridge that crossed the little river, and their debris floated down onto his property before washing up on the banks or lodging in the shallows.

There were beer cans, beer bottles, cans that had once held motor oil or transmission fluid, empty antifreeze jugs, a toilet seat, several cardboard boxes, an old boot, a muddy dozer cap, and – the very thing Lester had told him to look for – a chair with the bottom busted out. It had been a rainy winter. High water spread the debris all along the creek, from where it entered his property, on the west side, to where it left it, on the east.

Duane didn't immediately try to clean it up: there was too much, and it was on both sides of the creek, which was too high to wade. Besides, he had no way to collect such a variety of trash. He didn't become angry, as he had the day before, but he did feel melancholy as he made his way along the creek bank. People were just messy – it was that thought that made him melancholy. They went about their lives creating waste materials and then just threw them off the handiest bridge. At one point he pulled a plastic bag out of the mud, to discover that it held several syringes. People were messy and they took drugs – at the moment the messiness bothered him more than the drugs.

When he got back to the cabin, about sundown, he added trash bags to the list of things he needed to get the next time he found himself in a store. Then he added the word 'large.' With some good big trash bags he could clean up the riverbank in a day or two. It wouldn't cure the problem of human messiness, but it would make the riverbed look a little nicer for a day or two.

On the third day, late in the afternoon, he saw a small, bright red car turn onto the hill. It was Nellie's little Saab. From the moment she acquired a driver's license, Nellie had favored red cars. 'More sporty,' she said.

Duane had been half expecting his daughter to show up. He had always been closer to her than to his other three children: there was no explaining it, it was just there. He could hear her radio before she even got halfway across the hill. Nellie was not interested in the quiet life, never had been.

'Shoot, I like to drink that José Cuervo and kick up my heels,' she said. 'What's the point of living if you don't drink tequila and kick up your heels?'

Once she turned onto the road that led to the cabin she slowed down and inched along. Although it was a perfectly good road, with only one or two tricky places on it, both Nellie and Karla liked to pretend that it was a treacherous, boulder-strewn track into the wilderness.

'If I was to go any faster a rock might shoot up right through the floor of my car,' Nellie said, when he teased her about her caution. 'I got to take good care of this vehicle – if it breaks down I won't have no way to get to a bar.'

Duane had been sitting in his lawn chair, watching a flock of geese, high to the northeast. A small plane, probably some oilman looking for a leak in a pipeline, was going in the same direction, but the plane was only a hundred feet off the ground and the wild geese were way up there. Their flight was so pure, so graceful, that it made the little airplane look tacky. It was as if a lawn mower were trying to fly.

Nellie had the radio on so loud that the car seemed to be pulsing. She waved at her father, but didn't get out immediately – Nellie wanted to hear the rest of the song. Shorty, who liked Nellie, ran up and tried to jump in the car, but Nellie yelled at him to get lost. 'I don't want dog hairs in my car!' she yelled, over the sound of the song.

When the song finally ended – Duane had his fingers in his ears by that time – Nellie got out and ran over to him, gave him a kiss and a nice long hug.

'Daddy, what's the deal?' she asked, looking him over to see if he looked all right.

'I got home from my trip with that miserable scumbag and you wasn't there,' she added.

But, to her eyes, her dad looked fine.

'Nope,' he said. 'You're always zombified when you get back from Mexico. I figured you'd just want to sleep.'

'I did, but I sleep better when you're around the house somewhere,' Nellie said. 'It's just total chaos around that house when you're gone.'

'I know, that's one reason I moved out,' Duane said. 'Got tired of chaos.'

Once inside the cabin Nellie did a quick scan to see if she could detect any sign of a female presence. The cabin was neat as a pin. There was really no sign of *any* presence, not even her father's. In fact, it was a cozy little place. There was a nice fire in the little fireplace. The dishes were washed, the bed made. The axe was leaning against the fireplace; a shirt or two hung on a nail. It all looked real basic to her. The only sign of anything unusual was that the radio was unplugged. She herself hated silence. Her own radios – she had several – were on twenty-four hours a day. Sometimes she turned them up, sometimes she turned them down, but she never turned them off. In her view, being without music was like being dead. But then her father was a lot older – he might be tired of music. Still, that unplugged radio was a little worrisome.

'It's a nice little cabin but I can't see that there's much to do out here,' she said. 'Don't you get bored?'

'Haven't so far,' Duane said.

Nellie was always active. He knew it must puzzle her that he would just like to sit around.

'I've worked my whole life,' he reminded her. 'I was a roustabout when I was thirteen. I guess I'm just ready to do some sitting and thinking.'

'Well, that makes sense, I guess,' Nellie said – although it really didn't. Her father seemed fine, just to look at, but she was beginning to learn that you couldn't always tell what was going on with a man just from looking. Maybe he wasn't as content as he appeared to be. Maybe he was real depressed, like her mother claimed, or at least a little wrought up inside. Her father had always been the most normal and the most dependable person she knew. Her mother was a pretty good mom, but she was definitely flighty, changeable, prone to pretty intense moods. Her father had always just been pretty much the same, didn't have too many moods, just sort of hung in there year after year in a real stable way. The thought that he might be going crazy or something was pretty disturbing. The Moore family spent most of its time teetering on the brink of hell as it was. If her father went crazy, then the likelihood was that the whole family would break to bits, or something.

'Don't you miss us all none?' she asked. Her father frowned slightly, probably because she hadn't used very good grammar.

'I'd probably miss you more if you used good English,' Duane said, but then he smiled. Part of Nellie's appeal was her artlessness; she had a good brain but had not taken the trouble to train it, and she seldom subjected it to even the slightest discipline. None of his children had spent any more time than was necessary with their textbooks. Fortunately – with the exception of Dickie – they were as healthy as horses and had an abundance of energy.

'I know I ain't supposed to say "none" and stuff,' Nellie admitted. 'Sometimes my talk just comes out country – too much time in honky-tonks, I guess.'

'You ought to go back to college and finish your degree, honey,' Duane said. 'Right now you're getting by on being young and pretty, but that don't last forever.'

'It does if you go to the right spas,' Nellie said. 'We're all trying to get Mom to go to a good spa. She could go to the Canyon Ranch or the Golden Door or somewhere and eat right and get massage. She might pep up, if she'd just go to a good spa.'

'Is she low?' Duane asked. He felt silly asking the question. After all, he had been living with Karla only a week ago. He ought to know how she was himself.

Nellie decided just to be blunt with her father. She was in the habit of saying exactly what was on her mind, even if the grammar of it wasn't too correct.

'She don't think you're ever coming back,' she said. 'She thinks you want to just live in this cabin from now on, or else move to a foreign country or something.'

'I might visit a foreign country,' Duane said. 'I might go to Egypt and see the pyramids. But I don't think I'll move to a foreign country.'

'So, do you think you'll ever move back in with us?' Nellie asked. 'Everybody thinks you'll come on back except Mom. She don't think you'll ever be back.'

'Ever and never – that's looking a long way ahead,' Duane said. 'I'm not looking that far ahead, just at this time. I want to be alone for a while. I want to think about some things I can't seem to think about when I'm crowded all up with you.'

'I can understand that,' Nellie said. 'I can't think two thoughts in a row myself without the phone ringing or some kid squalling somewhere in the house.'

'I've just been out here about a week,' Duane pointed out. 'I need some time to myself, and I like walking around. It's good exercise.'

'You could join a health club,' Nellie said. 'All these gyms are giving big discounts now.'

'I don't think I'm the gym type,' Duane said.

Nellie decided not to press the matter of the gym, or the matter of when her father might come back and rejoin the family, either.

'But if I really needed you I could run out here and get you, couldn't I?' Nellie said, thinking out loud.

'Sure,' Duane said. 'I'm only six miles away. Six miles is not very far.'

'It's not far but it's dusty,' Nellie said. Although casual about her own appearance, she liked for her little red Saab to be dust free. The car wash in Thalia had no better customer than Nellie Moore. Even if the sand wasn't blowing she liked to pop her car into the car wash every day or two. In fact, looking at her car, she thought it seemed a little grimy – it occurred to her that she should probably hit the car wash on the way back home.

Duane walked out with her.

'You didn't really answer the question about whether you were ever coming home, did you?' Nellie asked.

'Nope – it's too big a question,' Duane said.

'Well, couldn't you take a guess?' Nellie asked.

'Nope,' he said. 'It's not really as important a question as you think it is. You're too old to be living at home, but you're living at home. You asking me when I'm coming back home is like me asking you when you're moving out.

'You're a grown woman,' he added. 'It's probably not a particularly good idea for you to be living with your parents.'

'I know,' Nellie said. 'I get in your hair, and so does Dickie and that bunch, and so does Julie and her two. Momma's always threatening to kick us out, but she never goes through with it.'

'Some mothers like their own kids better than they like anybody else,' Duane observed. 'Besides, your mother likes lots of company. I'm different. I can do without company for a while, now and then.'

'I guess that's why you don't mind living out here on this hill,' Nellie said. Her father's remarks depressed her a little. He was right. What was she doing living at home, at her age? She always got jobs easily – she just usually didn't keep them very long, and she had none at the moment. But there was the problem of the babies. Who would watch them if she moved away and got a job? Little Bascom was about ready for play school, but Baby Paul had just been born. It wasn't easy being a mom if you lacked a dad, and neither Billy Deeds nor Randy McGregor, the fathers, respectively, of Little Bascom and Baby Paul, had been heard from in quite a few months. Neither was lavish with child support, either. Nellie had waited a good long time to start having babies again after her first two husbands, the fathers of Barbette and Little Mike, had also been stingy with child support. One reason she waited was because she wanted to be mature and make good choices the next time around – and yet she *hadn't* made good choices. She had just ended up having her babies by two more cowboys who happened to be good dancers. It didn't hurt that they had good butts, too. In fact she had had her first date with Randy McGregor the night he won the Best Wrangler Butt contest at a nearby honky-tonk. But life was a cruel thing. The fact was, a woman could get tired of even the best butt, and the getting tired, in Randy's case, had only taken her about three weeks, in the middle of which she had somehow gotten pregnant with Baby Paul.

Seeing her father, who seemed as sane as ever and was leading a well-ordered life in his little cabin, reminded Nellie a little too sharply of how little she had done to establish any kind of satisfactory life for herself.

Besides that, there was definitely dust and grime on her car. Nobody had taken it to the car wash while she was in Mexico. The garage had a door, but no one ever thought to shut it, so a lot of dust had undoubtedly blown in. She had meant, every day since her return, to run it over to the car wash but something had happened to distract her – mainly just Tommy calling to beg her to please take him back. Some of Tommy's pleadings went on for as long as four hours, him begging every minute of it. Even though he was no fun to go to bed with, Tommy *was* somebody to talk to; by the time she finally got him off the phone she would be too worn out from his entreaties to take her car to the car wash. What she mainly did, when she wasn't on the phone with Tommy, was sit in the kitchen and listen to Rag tell stories about disasters that had befallen her in her long and varied life: tornadoes, oil booms, spousal abuse. Rag had experienced it all.

'Daddy, I guess I'll go,' Nellie said, the thought of the car wash uppermost in her mind. 'Is there anything you want me to tell Momma?'

'Oh sure – just tell her not to worry, I'm fine,' Duane said. 'You can see that for yourself.'

'I guess you are,' Nellie agreed, reluctantly. 'It's just hard to get used to the idea of you living way out here by yourself.'

'Well, it's quiet,' Duane said. He thought he had explained enough.

'Okay, bye,' Nellie said. She gave him a real big hug, a tight hug. For a moment she felt like asking if he'd just get in the car and come home with her. She knew he didn't want to, but she felt like asking anyway. Things just seemed so much more normal when her father was at home.

Nellie knew that things changed – they changed, they changed – but she didn't like it. Driving back to town along the country road she suddenly started to cry so hard that for a second she got confused and thought she must be in a cloudburst. She couldn't see a thing, but when she turned the windshield wipers on they only scraped the dust on her windshield. The cloudburst wasn't outside, it was inside, and it was all because her father didn't want to live at home – not anymore.

# 21

After Nellie left, Duane made himself some soup and had crackers with it. The crackers had probably been in his cupboard for at least a year, but they were still tasty.

After some thought he added 'Fried Pies' to the list of groceries he needed to pick up next time he went shopping.

Shortly after eating, he went to bed. It occurred to him that he was leading a go-to-bed-with-the-chickens life, only he had no chickens. A banty hen or two might be good company, but he'd have to bring them in at night if they were to survive the coyotes, owls, and bobcats; hens weren't neat housemates, either, so he decided to table that idea.

Duane fell asleep immediately, but two hours later came wide awake. Out his window he could see the lights of an oil rig, to the northwest. Now and then a pickup would rattle along the road, roughnecks either going out to the rig or coming in from it. Many times, throughout his life, he had ridden out to a rig at night, to deal with one problem or another. The scurryings that went on in the oil business were incessant, nocturnal as well as diurnal. The roughnecks and tool pushers were night animals, as much so as the coons and possums. Karla too was a night animal – she rarely turned off the TV before two in the morning.

'Why sleep, if you don't need to?' she asked. 'Why just lay there, letting your life pass?' she would say, if he tried to get her to go to bed a little earlier.

'But your body needs sleep,' he said.

'Speak for yourself, mine don't,' Karla said. 'There could be something important happen, and if I was asleep I'd miss it.'

Now, it seemed, he was the one who didn't need sleep, although he was walking several miles a day and by rights should have been tired.

'No tension in the environment, I guess,' he said to Shorty, who was sleeping beside the fireplace.

Duane realized, as he sat in bed looking at the lights of the distant oil rig, that he didn't miss his family at all. Even Nellie's visit had produced mixed emotions in him. Of course, he loved Nellie – that would never change. Despite her day-to-day approach to life she was an appealing girl, who, in the main, had normal instincts. It was unlikely that she would ever go bad. He wasn't sure he could say as much for Dickie and Jack, his boys, both of whom were a little too enamored of the notion of being bad – not that either of them had ever done a really bad thing – not so far, at least.

He realized, sitting in his bed, that he was rapidly speeding away from his family – he didn't know why. Halley's comet had just gone past the earth and was now speeding away from it, and it seemed to Duane that he was doing the same thing: speeding away, speeding away. So far Karla had been the only one in his family to intuit how he really felt, which was that he had left a place to which he would never be likely to return. Karla couldn't help wanting to understand why. A why, even if it was a why she didn't agree with or even really grasp, would give her a place to put her feet in relation to this unexpected and puzzling event. Karla liked for there to be reasons for human actions.

'I'll take a wrong reason over no reason,' she had told her children often, when they misbehaved, when they did something inexplicable. So the kids invented reasons, to keep their mother happy – a mistake, since once Karla got them telling lies she would soon track through the lies to somewhere near the truth.

Sooner or later, he knew, Karla would try the same tactic with him. She would try to get him to confess to an affair he hadn't had in order to get him talking: once she got him talking she would find her way to a reason that explained the matter to her satisfaction.

Duane knew such a conversation was coming, but he didn't think it would work this time. He didn't know why he had left. He hadn't been getting along badly with Karla, or the children or his employees or anyone in his life. What had happened to him had nothing to do with a deterioration in his major relationships. Even to say something simplistic, such as that it was time for a change, would not be stating the matter accurately. It wasn't that it was *time* for a change, particularly; it was that he had just *changed*. He had driven his pickup into his carport, gotten out, locked the pickup, put the keys in the old chipped cup, and, at about that moment, *changed*. He didn't become a different man, but when he stepped out of his house he found himself in a different life. He hadn't given any forethought to taking a walk, or to living a different life, either. For the first few minutes of his new life he felt a distinct surprise at finding himself walking, but it was a *pleasant* surprise one with no dark shadows in it. He had been riding – now he was walking. It seemed to be a very simple, very satisfying change; but he knew it could hardly have seemed simple or satisfying to the people he left. His forty years with Karla had contained many surprises, but probably none as major as this one. He had just walked off: with no animosity toward anyone, with no intent to harm, wishing everybody well – just walked off. He knew it must seem puzzling to everyone, but he couldn't help that. The change had just come, as naturally as a change in the weather – one day cloudy, one day fair. He could imagine that his future life would take many unexpected twists and turns, but what he couldn't imagine was going back home. Over the years he had adjusted to a great many things – in some cases difficult things – for the sake of other people; now it was the other people, his nearest and dearest, who would have to do the adjusting, because he couldn't. His old skin, or his old self, no longer fit. It would mean a sadness for his family, for a while at least – there was no getting around that fact.

What was evident, as day came – with a glowing line in the east – was that he still needed groceries. He got up, cleaned up, put the list of things he needed into his shirt pocket, and prepared to walk to town. When he first stepped outside, the lights of Thalia were like a sprinkle of fallen stars. He dreaded going there – he would just have to buy his supplies from the same old people, who would wonder why he wasn't in his pickup. He paused for a moment, as he was about to turn off the hill, not reluctant to walk but reluctant to walk in the direction of Thalia. It was stronger than reluctance – it was dread: he didn't want to go to Thalia, and his resistance to going there was solid enough that he considered just trying to live for a while off what he could shoot with his twenty-two. There were ducks on most of the little creeks and ponds, and besides ducks, there were rabbits and quail and wild pigs. No species would be endangered if he lived off game for a while.

For a moment this option excited him, but then he began to feel silly. Did he think he was a mountain man or a survivalist or something? The little twenty-two was just for plinking – it didn't have a scope. It was ridiculous to suppose he could live off game; and anyway, he didn't like duck, and wild pigs were tough meat.

Then, just as he was about to trudge off to a place he didn't want to go, he remembered the Corners, a small crossroads store on a farm-to-market road seven or eight miles to the northwest. It never closed – indeed, had been in business twenty-four hours a day long before the notion of round-the-clock convenience stores had taken hold. The Corners existed mainly to serve the needs of oil field workers who didn't have time to drive to Thalia or Wichita Falls to eat; it was a dim little two-lightbulb store run by a cranky old man named Jody Carmichael, who ran it alone, twenty-four hours a day, seven days a week, three hundred and sixty-five days a year. Jody Carmichael rarely bathed, and even more rarely slept.

'Nope, my nerves got mangled on the Burma Road,' he informed those who considered it odd that one man could run a twenty-four-hour convenience store year in and year out with no help. Jody spent his life on an old couch behind the counter, catnapping when there were no roughnecks in the store microwaving burritos or wolfing down the variety of junk foods that Jody carried. Lately, Jody – who had been valedictorian of his class before getting drafted for World War II – had become a compulsive sports gambler, doing his gambling on a tiny computer he had set up behind his counter, next to an equally tiny TV set. Jody Carmichael was perhaps a little demented, but he wasn't dumb. Duane always enjoyed chatting with him when he was out that way, grappling with a problem on one of his rigs. He remembered that Jody had once been married to a beautiful heiress from somewhere in the panhandle – he had seen them at rodeos a few times in earlier years, and remembered, or thought he remembered, that they had a daughter. The rumor in law enforcement circles was that Jody was the mastermind behind a string of methamphetamine labs that snaked through the oil patch. It was a rumor that Duane didn't credit. Jody Carmichael was obviously smart enough to be a drug baron, and the Corners was remote enough to make a good headquarters, but Jody's interests just seemed to lie elsewhere: keeping up with forty or fifty horse races a day via his computer, or betting on South American soccer matches. Jody never bragged about his winnings, if any, but his dull blue eyes suddenly lit up and began to dance around in his head at the mention of horse races or South American soccer.

Duane took his list of needs out of his pocket and studied it a minute – it was just light enough to make it out. To his relief he discovered that he didn't need to go to Thalia at all. Jody Carmichael would have everything on the list, with the possible exception of large trash bags – the few residents of the Corners area were not overly concerned about proper trash collection.

The Corners was two miles farther than Thalia, but it was in a direction Duane had never walked and distance was not a problem, in any case. He felt sure he could walk all day, just as long as he didn't have to see people he didn't want to see while he was walking. The very notion that he was going dead away from Thalia, rather than toward it, was enough to put a spring in his step. He had a packet of the old crackers in his backpack, and ate the crackers as he walked along. Several pickups passed him, some coming and some going, but no one stopped to offer him a ride. In only a week's time he had managed to convince people in that part of the country that he didn't want a ride. They might think that he was crazy, but they no longer stopped and pestered him to get in the pickup.

Duane had never gone directly from his cabin to the store and soon realized that he would have to zigzag a little, if he hoped to get there by staying off the paved roads. He had to swing east through a large pasture and then back west past some fields where the winter wheat was just greening. He figured he had walked almost nine miles when he finally came in sight of the Corners. Along the way he had seen a field full of white cattle egrets, standing in a greening wheat field, with no cattle to attach themselves to. The delicate white birds made a pretty picture against the deep green of the sprouting wheat. A little later he saw two gray herons standing in a kind of bog – one of the herons was almost as tall as he was. When he passed, both the huge birds flapped away, rising as slowly as small airplanes, barely lifting above the line of the mesquite. Still later, the same small airplane that he had noticed the day before sputtered overhead and flew east, above the line of trees that bordered the little creek.

When he was within a mile of the Corners he began to see an increase of litter in the barditches. Beer cans, bottles, empty cans of motor oil, Styrofoam cups, packing, spent shotgun shells, abandoned packing crates large enough to have contained a washing machine or a refrigerator lay beside the road. He saw a car radiator, and an old pink plastic hair dryer that someone had thrown out. Duane began to get angry again, at the sight of the litter. In contrast to the white birds in the green field, the tawdry spectacle in the ditches seemed the

110

more deplorable. Fifty large trash bags would hardly have sufficed to bag the trash just from that one stretch of road, and it wasn't even a paved road. Duane had driven past such sights every day of his life and given them no thought, but walking past them was an entirely different experience. It suggested that the people who drove along that road had no pride, either in themselves or in the place they lived. They consumed trash and then excreted it, indifferent to what they were doing. The sight grated on Duane so much that he thought he might start doing his grocery shopping at night, so he wouldn't have to see what he was walking past – the Corners was a twenty-four-hour establishment, after all.

The whole back wall of the little store was hidden by a towering pyramid of empty beer cans and beer bottles, the creation of at least two generations of all-night rig crews who decided to drink their fill right behind the store. It was a well-known pyramid of empty beer cans – Jody Carmichael had finally built a little fence around it for the express purpose of discouraging can collectors.

'What's mine is mine, and it's always going to be mine,' he told people who asked if they could poke in the pyramid of cans.

'What's mine is mine, and it's always going to be mine,' he told anyone who had the gall to point out that he had already been paid for the cans once – that is, when the customers bought the beer. 'They were discarded on my property, which means they still belong to me, and what's more, they ain't for sale. I don't intend to sell the same beer can twice, if I can help it – and I can help it.'

Not far to the west of the store Jody had installed a giant satellite dish, the largest and most sophisticated satellite dish in that part of the world. With the help of the dish Jody could bring in most sporting events in the Western Hemisphere, though the little TV he brought them in on only had an eight-inch screen. Somehow the discrepancy between the enormous dish and the tiny screen bothered Bobby Lee, who was often with Duane when they got hungry enough to drive to the Corners to microwave a burrito.

'If you're going to have that big a dish, looks like you'd at least have a regular-sized TV – I'd ruin my eyes squinting at that little old screen,' Bobby Lee told Jody once.

'Ain't you got anything smaller than a twenty?' Jody asked, noting that Bobby Lee's purchase only totaled a dollar and a half.

'You didn't answer my question, and my change is all the way out in the pickup,' Bobby Lee said. 'I keep it in a paper cup.'

Jody made the change with some reluctance, but did not respond at all to Bobby Lee's question, which ticked the latter off.

'You need to learn to mind your own business,' Duane told him, as they were driving away.

'I just asked a question; is that a crime?' Bobby Lee complained. 'You and Jody Carmichael are two of a kind, if you ask me.'

'Two of what kind?' Duane asked.

'The closemouthed kind,' Bobby Lee said.

Bright sunlight was glinting off the hundreds of cans and bottles as Duane approached the Corners; the great white satellite dish was still pointed toward the southern sky. Shorty flushed a pack rat but the rat got under the building before Shorty could get him. Shorty didn't give up, though. He was still scratching madly, trying to get under the house and get the rat, when Duane stepped inside the store.

# 22

Jody Carmichael was restocking the barbecued potato chips and hot pork rinds when Duane walked in. A Portuguese soccer magazine lay on the counter – at least, Duane assumed it was in Portuguese, since it was in a foreign language that looked different from Spanish. Among the locals Jody had the reputation for being a highly educated man. Duane had the vague sense that after World War II Jody had gone off to Michigan or somewhere and gotten his schooling on the G.I. Bill.

'Ah, it's our pedestrian. Good morning to you, sir,' Jody said. When he was in a good mood he was apt to indulge in flowery talk – flowery, at least, by roughneck standards.

'You got pack rats under your house, Jody,' Duane informed him. 'I just saw a big fat one run right under it.'

'And pack rats carry the hanta virus, is that your point?' Jody asked. One of his bets must have come in – his eyes were dancing.

'Well, and bubonic plague and a few other things,' Duane said. 'I just thought I'd tell you.'

Jody finished filling the trays with pork rinds and barbecued potato chips and came back behind his counter. He cast a quick glance at his computer before turning to Duane.

'Brazil, now there's a country – the whole society is soccer mad,' he said. 'Screwing and soccer, those are the national pastimes in Brazil. What's on your mind today?'

'Oh, I need a few things,' Duane said. 'I was hoping you stock those large trash bags – somebody's made a mess in my creek.'

'I stock everything, but that don't mean I can find everything I stock,' Jody said. 'The lawn-and-leaf bags are over in the corner there – the corner where the light don't quite penetrate.'

Sure enough the bags were there – Duane took all six packages. Jody Carmichael had settled comfortably back on his couch. He raised an eyebrow when he saw his entire stock of lawn-and-leaf bags piled on the counter.

'You must have a noble mess in your creek, to need three hundred large white trash bags,' he said. 'That means I'll have to reorder, pronto. What do you think about the Unabomber?'

'I'm not expecting any packages from him,' Duane said. 'I haven't given him that much thought.'

'I figure he's some old nut like me, stuck off somewhere in Kansas or Wyoming,' Jody said. 'When he ain't restocking groceries he makes bombs and sends them off to big shots who are ruining people's minds with these computers.'

'Why would he be in Kansas?' Duane asked.

'Oh, there's plenty of wild men in Kansas,' Jody said. 'I figure he's off somewhere between Wichita and Salina, where the country is real flat. An excessively flat landscape can do bad things to the human personality, and lord knows it's flat up there north of Wichita.

'It's flat enough right around here,' Jody continued. 'That could be why you've started acting like Thoreau or somebody. Walking off from your family and cleaning up creek beds and such. That could be the actions of a mind unsettled by too much exposure to flat countryside.'

Duane remembered that Karla had brought home a Thoreau book or two, some years back, when she was auditing literature courses at the university in Wichita Falls. All he personally knew about Thoreau was that he had lived at a place called Walden Pond – developers were trying to develop it and a bunch of rock stars and country singers were trying to stop the development. That much had been in the papers.

'Of course it ain't really *that* flat around here,' Jody said. 'The land's got a gentle roll to it, so you probably won't get as crazy as this Unabomber fellow. You've got all the roughnecks worried, though.'

'Worried about what?' Duane asked.

'The rumor I heard is that you've got a sniper's rifle with a nightscope on it,' Jody replied. 'The roughnecks figure that a man with a sniper's rifle and a nightscope might get the urge to use it some night when they're on their way to the rig.'

'Those roughnecks must have a little touch of this flat disease you're talking about,' Duane said. 'I don't have a sniper's rifle.'

Then he remembered that in fact Dickie did own such a rifle – he had won it shooting craps in the back of a pickup somewhere. Duane had never seen the gun himself, but Bobby Lee had mentioned that it had a nightscope. The rumor that he was likely to snipe on roughnecks was to him just an example of how paranoid people could get when they took too much speed – a not-unheard-of practice among roughnecks.

Jody watched with interest as Duane fitted the trash bags into his backpack.

'You don't sell spades, do you?' Duane asked. He was happy to have found the trash bags and a few other groceries he needed, and wanted to get back on the road.

'You bet. I sell spades and sling blades too, and I think I've got a posthole digger or two and several pickaxes and crowbars, if you're needing hardware,' Jody said. 'They're all out in my hardware shed. I don't make a practice of keeping heavy items where somebody who wasn't right in the head could pick one up and whack me with it. There have been people in this store who weren't entirely in their right minds. I expect one of them would have laid me out by now if there had been a spade or crowbar handy.'

'Good point,' Duane said. 'Mind if I look in the shed?'

Jody handed him a key affixed to a short piece of wire – then he went back to watching his soccer game. Duane heard a faint roaring, like the sound of the sea in a seashell, the cheers of a wild crowd in faraway Brazil.

The padlock on the old rusty metal shed behind the store was reluctant to open at first, but Duane persisted and finally got it unlocked. He switched on a light – bright, in this case, not dim – and was startled to see that he was in a well-organized miniature hardware store, one that was as neat and carefully arranged as the other store was cluttered. All the items Jody had mentioned were there, plus adzes and awls, two anvils, giant wrenches and tiny wrenches, hammers, sledgehammers, saws, a wheelbarrow, screws and nails, and all manner of wires and tubing, all of it neatly arranged on hooks or on shelves. The equipment was so clean it looked as if it had been polished. One shelf held a selection of carpentry tools so old that they might have been in a museum. He puzzled over some of the older tools for several minutes, trying to figure out what they could be used for. The shed was so clean and well organized that being in it was almost shocking. Duane chose a spade, a hammer, and a saw, but mainly he just stood and looked. Where had Jody Carmichael found the time to organize his toolshed so well? The attractive array of hardware suggested not just another man but another life. Yet the shed was only ten yards from the store – it was as if the man had split himself somehow: he brought order to his hardware and let disorder spread among his groceries.

After the shock wore off, Duane began to feel better than he had felt all day, just from looking at all the good equipment he could have if he needed it. If he decided to make major improvements in his new living quarters he could easily get all the equipment he needed just a short walk from his cabin. He decided it was lucky that he was on foot – if he had been in his pickup he might have bought half the items in the shed, just to have them in case of future need.

'That was a surprise,' he told Jody, when he handed him back the key. 'You've got a regular hardware store back there.'

'Not only that; things out there are easy to find,' Jody said. 'My daughter done that. The shed was in as big a mess as the store until she moved back here. She claims she's going to do the same for the store, one of these days. Honor can't tolerate messes – no sir, no messes.'

'I thought I remembered that you had a daughter,' Duane said.

'A fine daughter, too,' Jody said, with evident pride. 'She's the one thing her mother and I did right. We're both proud as hell of Honor.'

'What does she do when she's not cleaning out sheds?' Duane asked.

Jody gave him a sort of sly look and pointed to a little tray of business cards sitting by the cash register. In the dim light Duane had not seen them. He took one and sought a better light in which to read it:

Honor Carmichael, M.D.
Counseling, Psychiatry, Psychoanalysis
900 Taft Street
Wichita Falls, Texas 76302

Duane was momentarily flabbergasted at the thought that Jody Carmichael's daughter had become – of all things – a psychiatrist, though he didn't know why he was so startled. So far as he could remember he had only seen Jody's daughter a few times, when she was a little girl in pigtails. Psychiatry was just not a profession many people in that part of the country went into – particularly not if they were women.

116

'Good lord,' he said. 'I guess you would be proud of her, if she can do all that and arrange hardware too.'

'Yes, I'm real proud,' Jody said simply.

'Where'd your daughter go to school?' Duane asked.

'Baltimore,' Jody said. 'She moved back here a few years ago, mainly so she could get better acquainted with her old dad. You ought to make an appointment, Duane. A session or two with Honor might clear your head.'

'Me?' Duane said. 'I don't know that my head is cloudy enough that I need psychiatry – though I guess some people think so.'

'You might not be too crazy now – but you could always get crazier,' Jody said. 'I did – went crazy and started betting on these soccer games. Honor could probably help you figure out why you started acting like Thoreau.'

'Or I could just go to a library and get a book by the man and read it,' Duane said. 'Maybe I could puzzle it out for myself, if the writing's not too complicated.'

'Doubtful, very doubtful,' Jody Carmichael said. 'If people could really figure themselves out, Honor wouldn't have such a booming business.'

Duane tucked the card into his shirt pocket, slipped on his backpack, and picked up his spade.

'I don't know about psychiatry, but I'll probably be back to look over the hardware again,' he said. 'You've got some real nice hardware.'

Jody had picked up the Portuguese soccer magazine and was leafing through it. He seemed to have lost interest in Duane, who, for some reason, felt a little reluctant to leave.

'Is that magazine in Portuguese?' he asked. Jody seemed surprised by the question.

'Sure is, why?' he asked.

'I just wondered,' Duane said. Then he waved and went out the door.

# 23

Duane had a fine walk home – somehow the little bit of conversation and the knowledge that there was a plentiful supply of tools available only a few hours' walk away had put him in a good mood. The minute he came in sight of his cabin he began to think of improvements he might make, using all the tools he could buy from Jody's nicely arranged hardware store.

There was not a shade tree anywhere near the cabin – it sat on a bare knob. Sitting out in front of it in a lawn chair would work fine in the cool months, but the cool months would soon be over, after which sitting out on the hill in a lawn chair would be a warm experience. The notion that came to him was that he might put awnings around three sides of the cabin. Then he could sit wherever he pleased and be reasonably assured of shade.

Duane was so pleased with the notion of awnings that, once he got home, he immediately wanted to take some measurements; then he discovered that he lacked a tape measure. The discovery didn't upset him too much – at least he had remembered to buy a tablet and some ballpoint pens. What he needed to do was make careful plans, draw up a more comprehensive list, walk back to Jody's the next day, and add to his arsenal of essential tools. He had been tempted to buy a wheelbarrow on his visit that morning, but had held off mainly because he thought that if he had a wheelbarrow he'd go on a buying spree and fill it up with things he didn't really need. Then, too, the notion of walking along a public road pushing a wheelbarrow struck him as being a pretty eccentric thing – perhaps a little too eccentric. The roughnecks who expected him to snipe at them with a sniper's rifle would really think he had gone around the bend if they saw him pushing a wheelbarrow filled with hardware along one of the roads where they were expecting to be assassinated.

Once he *had* a wheelbarrow, though, he could transplant a few little saplings from down in the river valley and eventually grow his own shade trees. That would take a few years, admittedly, but it wouldn't hurt to go on and get started with a few schemes to give the outside of the cabin a more pleasing aspect. As it was, the grandkids wouldn't be able to visit him at all in the summer months without risking both snakebite and heat stroke. He hadn't given the grandkids a thought since leaving home, but he knew that could change. The time might come when he would want to have his grandkids, or his kids, or even Karla out to visit.

Duane was so pepped up by the idea of improvements on the cabin that it was all he could do to keep from hiking off back to Jody's, to buy himself a tape measure, the wheelbarrow, and perhaps a T square and a leveling tool. He restrained himself, though. One trip a day to the Corners was really enough. He napped a little and woke up so refreshed that he decided to walk to the Corners and come back with the wheelbarrow after dark. If a pickup full of roughnecks came barreling along he could probably conceal the wheelbarrow in the barditch until they passed.

This time, with the luxury of a thick tablet and a good ballpoint pen, Duane began to make a lengthy and careful list of items it would be good to have around. Of course, Jody Carmichael couldn't be expected to stock awnings – but he might be able to order some for him. Duane listed a dozen items and his mind suddenly went blank. He began to feel saggy, although only a few minutes before he had felt refreshed. After all, a walk to Jody's store and back was at least a sixteen-mile round trip. Twice in one day would be more than thirty miles, a long walk by any standards. Besides being tired, he began to feel a little foolish. Did he really need a wheelbarrow badly enough to walk thirty miles just to buy one? If Karla knew he was even contemplating such a thing she would no doubt laugh her head off, a thought which made him miss her. Karla was never more appealing than when she was laughing her head off about some hilarious act of human folly – which, he had no doubt, was how she would consider his thirty-mile walk.

Just thinking about Karla's reaction caused Duane to conclude that he was too tired to make another trip to the Corners that day. He sat with his tablet a good while, considering other staples that might go on his list. While he was thinking he remembered Jody Carmichael's daughter, the psychiatrist. He took her little card out of his pocket and propped it against the salt and pepper shakers. He remembered how Jody had beamed when he spoke of his daughter, and how moved he had sounded when he said he was proud of her. The little girl Duane had seen only once or twice at rodeos long ago had gone off to school and made something of herself. Now she was a licensed doctor, qualified to help people with their emotional problems, an endeavor that undoubtedly took brains and judgment.

He thought of his own children, whose erratic lives stood in harsh contrast to Honor Carmichael's success. Not one of them had finished college, or even come very close to finishing. Nellie and Julie would occasionally enroll for a semester, when the mood struck them, but would casually drop out again if they ran up against a course that was too hard for them, which could mean any course that actually required study. They were all smart – but they were also all ignorant, a reflection that saddened Duane, since he considered that it was partly his fault. Neither he nor Karla had really pressed the matter of education with them; when they did prod one of the girls to get back in school and finish a degree, their efforts were halfhearted. He himself had never been near a college, and Karla had only attended sporadically – though in the last few years Karla had audited a wide variety of courses and sometimes gave some thought to actually entering a degree program.

'You could too,' she pointed out. 'It's never too late to go to college. I bet you'd make all As if you'd just try. If you had something to engage your mind with, maybe you wouldn't be so bored.'

'Who says I'm bored?' he asked. 'I've never been bored in my life.'

'Bullshit,' Karla said. 'You're too bored even to have love affairs, which is pretty bored, in my book.'

Sitting alone in his cabin, he realized that his wife had been right. He *was* bored – perhaps had been bored since sometime in his late forties, which was the point at which the oil business had ceased to engage him. He considered himself to be a skilled professional oilman, but by his forties he had acquired as great a proficiency as he was ever likely to have. If he rose much higher it would be because of some particularly lucky strike. He wasn't going to get any better, and he couldn't pretend that what he was doing particularly interested him, once he had passed a certain point. He might get more of a kick out of learning to make good biscuits than he did out of drilling oil wells.

Honor Carmichael's plain little business card bespoke real accomplishment. Crazy old Jody and his estranged wife had at least managed to see that their child got a first-rate education, whereas he and Karla had let the same opportunity dribble away. He decided to sit his boys down, the next time he saw them, and attempt to convince them that they were not too old to acquire good educations – maybe Karla could have a session or two with the girls, on the same subject.

Just before turning off his light, Duane reread his list. He wanted to be off for the Corners at first light and didn't want to forget anything. While he was checking it he munched most of a fried pie – it claimed to be apricot but tasted more like peach – and gave the crust to Shorty. A small gray mouse sat in plain view near the fireplace, nibbling a crumb, but Shorty was so intent on getting at least a taste of the fried pie that he hadn't noticed.

'There's a mouse, do your job,' Duane said, but Shorty merely gulped and waited for more crust.

At the bottom of the list Duane decided to add one more item: a book by Thoreau, the one about living at Walden Pond. He wasn't sure about the spelling of the name – he thought it probably ought to have an $x$ at the end – but the list was for his own eyes anyway. He left it as it was and went to bed.

# 24

The next morning while Karla was in the shower she began to have the uneasy sense that somebody was prowling around the house somewhere. There had never been a prowler around her house, but, as she often pointed out, there could always be a first time. She had often asked Duane for a pistol but he resolutely refused to allow it.

'There are too many grandkids in the house and they can all climb,' he told her. 'Even if you hid it on the highest shelf Willy or Sami or somebody might climb up and get it and start firing.'

When she came out of the shower, well swaddled in her cherry-colored bathrobe, she tiptoed silently from room to room, so as not to startle the prowler, if there was one.

Then the prowler turned out to be Duane – he had changed his mind about hurrying back to the Corners and was poking around in the books that were shelved over the TV. Outside, it was only just beginning to be light. None of the grandkids were awake, and the younger grandkids were early risers. Rag wasn't even in the kitchen yet, and Rag was usually in the kitchen before sunup.

'I thought we had a Thoreau book here somewhere,' Duane said. 'Didn't you read it in one of your classes?'

It seemed so natural to wake up and find her husband in the den that Karla went over and started helping him look for the Thoreau book. The fact that he had walked six miles before it was even really light was a little matter she decided to ignore, at least for the moment.

'I had that book but I never read it,' she said. 'I had it about the time Bobby Lee had his operation – thinking about someone we know only having one ball kind of threw me off, as a reader.'

'Why would that have thrown you off?' Duane asked, a little annoyed. He had awakened at three-thirty, firmly convinced that the Thoreau book was somewhere in the bookshelves above the TV – the conviction was so strong that he had walked to Thalia to get the book, rather than to the Corners to get the wheelbarrow and the other things on his list. He had a clear mental picture of exactly where the book was – only, now he was standing right in front of the shelf where he remembered seeing it and it wasn't there. All kinds of books were there – books by John Grisham and Dean Koontz and Danielle Steel, but there was no book in the bookshelves by Thoreau.

'Well, it was kind of hard to read, and that plus Bobby Lee losing his testicle just kind of threw me off,' Karla admitted.

'It must be a famous book or they wouldn't be teaching it in a college class,' Duane said.

'There's lots of books they teach in college that I can't read ten words of,' Karla said. 'That's one reason I don't audit as much as I used to: got tired of being embarrassed by my own ignorance. Why do you want this particular book all of a sudden?'

She could tell Duane was on the verge of being irate, because he had walked all the way into town and now couldn't find what he was looking for.

Duane didn't answer – he just kept looking through the shelves. He had himself convinced that the book was there, though it wasn't.

'It's probably in one of the girls' bedrooms,' Karla said. 'Little Bascom could have carried it off. He likes to chew on books.'

'Why do you let him?' Duane asked. 'Books aren't for babies to chew.'

Despite his determination to be calm, his irritation was rising. He had meant to slip into the house before anyone was up and get the book. He didn't want to see anyone, or disturb the household in any way. All he wanted was the book. Jody Carmichael was not dumb. If Jody thought he was behaving like Thoreau, then Duane wanted to know what he meant by such a remark. The book had been right there, for years, but now, because a little boy was allowed to wander around chewing on books, it was gone, just when he needed it. If he was going crazy, as a number of people seemed to think, then it was because his family's sloppy, undisciplined ways were driving him crazy.

'Duane, it wasn't just me that let him chew books,' Karla said. '*You* let him chew books. Nellie let him chew books.'

Duane was uncomfortably aware that she had a point. He was as guilty as the rest of them. The whole household took the line of least resistance, where the children were concerned: never spanking them for chewing books, never demanding that the older children do their homework, never punishing with any severity any of the hundreds of disciplinary lapses that occurred every week. It was a lax household. The children didn't take their parents seriously, or their grandparents either. Everyone just did as they pleased, and no one had a college degree.

'I know it – and it needs to change,' Duane said. 'Next time somebody sees him chewing a book they ought to spank his little butt.'

'I agree, but I don't expect it will be you,' Karla said. 'You can't spank a child from six miles away.'

Duane didn't answer. He continued his fruitless search of the shelves.

'Duane, just calm down,' Karla said. 'There's plenty of those old Thoreau books in this world. There's a lot of them in the college bookstore. If we can't find this one we can just drive to Wichita and buy one.'

'I can't drive to Wichita because I've stopped driving,' Duane reminded her. 'Jody Carmichael says I'm acting like Thoreau and I'd like to read the book and find out what he means.'

'Okay, but it's pretty poky reading, like I said,' Karla told him. 'I'll go look in the girls' bedrooms. It might just be under a bed.'

Just then Little Bascom, the book chewer, waddled in. His face lit up when he saw his grandfather but it clouded again when Duane pointed a finger at him.

'Don't you ever let me catch you chewing a book,' Duane said. He didn't yell, but he spoke in a stern voice. Little Bascom burst into tears and ran to his grandmother.

'He's not even awake good,' Karla pointed out. 'It don't do a bit of good for you to suddenly start lecturing him. You need to wait until you catch him chewing a book and then spank his little butt.'

Again, Duane knew Karla was right. But being with his family – or even a tiny portion of it – made him feel suffocated, and, at the same time, guilty. He wanted to get the book and leave, but Little Bascom was so upset that Duane took him from Karla and carried him outside so he could pet the dog, which immediately restored his good humor. The little boy was hugging the dog's neck when Rag drove up in her belching old Chevy.

'That car's eating up the ozone; you ought to have your exhaust system checked out,' Duane told her.

'I don't even know what ozone is, but I know you look skinny, from not eating my gourmet cooking anymore,' Rag countered. 'I don't need no criticism from an anorexic this time of day.'

'Doggie,' Little Bascom said.

'It's a doggie all right, and it's probably covered with fleas and ticks,' Rag said. She started into the house and then turned to Duane.

'Are you eating with us, or not?' she asked.

'I'm eating, but not here,' he said. 'I just came in to look for a book.'

Karla came out on the back steps, no book in her hand.

'Rag, have you seen that Thoreau book I bought when I was taking that class?' she asked. 'It's just like a book to disappear the minute somebody wants it.'

'I have no idea what you're talking about,' Rag said. She went in the house, followed closely by Little Bascom, who knew her to be a reliable source of juice in the early part of the day.

'Want anything from the greenhouse?' Karla asked. It was clear that Duane was restless and wanted to be on his way.

'Maybe a few of those midget tomatoes,' he said. 'They're better than no tomatoes.'

'I wonder why your own family has started making you nervous, all of a sudden,' Karla said. 'Do you think it's just a phase?'

'It could be – but then life itself is just a phase,' Duane said.

'Duane, don't be saying pessimistic things to me when I'm upset anyway,' Karla said. 'I like to try and be hopeful, if you don't mind.'

'I'm sorry,' Duane said. 'I'm not fit company right now. That's why I moved out to the cabin. Is Dickie back from rehab?'

'He's in the trailer, sound asleep,' Karla said. 'He always sleeps for a week when he comes out of rehab. I think they must give them downers.'

'When he wakes up tell him to come see me,' Duane said. 'I'm putting him in charge of the oil company. There can't be no more of this drug addiction.'

Karla found a sack and put some of the small tomatoes in it. Duane tucked them carefully into his backpack.

'I hope you don't squash your tomatoes, walking home,' she said.

'Did you hear what I said about Dickie?' he asked. 'He's perfectly competent to run the company, if he'll do it. It's time Dickie clicked in, don't you think?'

'Oh sure, past time,' Karla said. 'It's past time he clicked in. But just because it's time don't mean he can. I guess we'll just have to see.'

'Tell him to come see me,' Duane repeated.

'I will, but don't be too hard on him,' Karla said. 'He's always a little scared when he first comes out of rehab.'

'I won't be hard on him,' Duane said. 'I've never been hard on Dickie. That may have been the problem.'

'It may have been, but it's too late to switch now,' Karla said. 'Go away. You're making me depressed.'

'I'm sorry,' Duane said. 'Remember that girl of Jody Carmichael's?'

Karla felt like crying but managed to suppress all but a sniffle or two.

'I knew he had a little girl but she was never around much,' she said. 'They sent her off to school. She came to Nellie's birthday party when Nellie was about five, but I don't think I've seen her since.'

'She's a psychiatrist now,' Duane said.

'She *is?*' Karla said. 'How'd you find that out?'

'I walked over to the Corners to buy a spade,' Duane said. 'Jody gave me her card. She studied in Baltimore. Jody's real proud of her.'

'I guess he would be,' Karla said. 'If one of our children made a psychiatrist I'd faint.'

Then she shook her head, in a gesture of despair.

'What'd I say now?' he asked, disturbed.

'It's just the thought of you walking that far to buy a spade,' Karla said. 'We've got a shed full of spades. It must be eight or nine miles over to the Corners. That's a sixteen-mile walk. That's crazy, Duane! What's wrong with you?'

'I don't know,' Duane admitted. He felt foolish for having revealed that he had walked so far just for a spade, when, as Karla said, he had a shed crammed with spades at home. He felt bad about having upset her, and he didn't even have the Thoreau book to show for it.

Karla ran back in the house – she was clearly getting ready for a cry. Toward the back of the property Loni, Barbi, and Sami filed out of the trailer house in their school clothes and headed in for breakfast. When they saw their grandfather they all looked startled. When he waved at them Loni and Sami waved back. Barbi, the one who had to be different, didn't wave, but Duane thought she looked glad to see him anyway. Annette, his tall daughter-in-law, came out of the trailer house for a moment and sat on the steps, smoking. Annette didn't wave, either. She was a mother, enjoying a moment of quiet after getting her children ready for school. Some people considered Annette standoffish, but Duane liked her. Her children were dressed neatly and they all did well in school, and he thought Annette did her best with Dickie, who was a handful. Duane started to walk over and chat with her for a moment – perhaps ask her how Dickie seemed – but he changed his mind. It might be better to leave her in peace. And, besides, he wanted to leave, to seek a little peace himself, of the sort that he could only seem to find when he was by himself, walking alone down an empty road.

# 25

The peace of the road was not to be his quickly. As he was approaching Ruth Popper's house – the one house in town he could saunter by at an easy pace, because he knew Ruth was too blind to see him – he saw Ruth come out her door. Her arms, as usual, were full of dictionaries and crossword puzzle books. Duane slowed a little, to give Ruth time to back out and turn toward his office – even though she couldn't see him she might intuit him if he got too close.

Ruth put her books in the backseat, got in, fastened her seat belt, and hit the ignition. The car – almost half as old as Ruth herself – started immediately.

Then Ruth sat for two or three minutes, listening to the engine purr. Duane had about decided to attempt to sneak on by, since Ruth appeared to be daydreaming. He felt tense, and was in a hurry to get into the country, where he could relax.

But before he could attempt to walk past her, Ruth woke up, wrestled the car into reverse – she had long complained that the Volkswagen's reverse was in a bad place – and suddenly shot backward across the road and into the opposite barditch. It was a fairly steep barditch too – the Volkswagen's front end was pointed almost straight up.

'She must have tried for the clutch and hit the foot feed,' Duane said, to Shorty. It was the only way he could account for the car's backward spurt. He had never seen Ruth drive that fast before. He knew that the peace of the road had just receded, because Ruth Popper was stuck. Even though she hadn't spotted him, he couldn't very well walk by and leave an old woman stuck in a ditch. He walked over and tapped on the window – Ruth squinted at him and then rolled it down, with some reluctance.

'Did you lock your house?' he inquired.

'Oh, the deserter,' Ruth said. 'Why'd you push me into this ditch?'

'Hey, I didn't push you,' Duane said. 'I think you just hit the foot feed a little too hard when you started to back up.'

'Why would I do that?' Ruth asked. 'I back out of this driveway every morning of my life and I've never done this before. I think you made it happen so I'll be late for work and you can dock my pay.'

'I haven't got time to argue with you,' Duane said. 'I'm going in your house and call Earlene. If she's there maybe she can find Bobby Lee. He's got a good winch on his pickup – he can have you out of there in no time.'

'Bobby Lee hates my guts,' Ruth said. 'Why would he do me any favors?'

'He does not hate your guts, Ruth. He just gets a little impatient with you, from time to time,' Duane said.

'He's only got one ball and he hates my guts, that's the way I see it,' Ruth insisted.

'Okay, he hates your guts,' Duane said. 'But he still works for me and if I tell him to come pull you out of the ditch I expect he'll do it.'

'You're behind the times,' Ruth said. 'Nobody works for you, because you aren't there to work for. Why would anybody work for a deserter and a turncoat?'

'Because even a deserter and a turncoat can still issue paychecks,' Duane reminded her.

Ruth had locked her front door, but her back door was unlocked. Duane made the call, keeping it as brief as possible.

'Earlene, Ruth backed into the ditch in front of her house,' he said. 'She's stuck. See if you can locate Bobby Lee and tell him to get over here and winch her out.'

'We'd be better off leaving her there, if you ask me,' Earlene said. 'She's just in the way around here.'

'Earlene, nobody asked you,' Duane said, wishing Earlene were a little nicer.

'Just do what you're told,' he added, reinforcing his point.

'Oh sure, bawl me out, why don't you?' Earlene said. 'There's a million people want to talk to you and I don't even know where to tell them to call.'

Then she burst into tears.

'There's no place they can call,' Duane said. 'Starting next week they can talk to Dickie – he'll be running things.'

'Oh lord help us, that'll be the end of us all,' Earlene gasped. Then she began to sob hysterically, so Duane hung up.

'I hate being late for work,' Ruth said, when he returned to the car. 'Over the years I've maintained a laudable attendance record, only no one lauds me.'

'If I were you I'd go back in the house and wait for Bobby Lee to show up,' Duane advised.

'He won't show up because he hates my guts,' Ruth said. 'I told you that but you never listen to me.'

'What else have I done for the last thirty years, except listen to you?' he said.

'I don't know – cheated on your wife, I guess,' Ruth said, a little startled by his comeback.

'That reminds me,' he said. 'I accidentally made Karla cry this morning. When you get to work call the flower shop and have a big bunch of flowers sent over. Make it a real nice bouquet.'

'Maybe seventy-five dollars' worth,' he added.

'Must have been some fight, for you to spend that kind of money,' Ruth said.

'No, it wasn't a fight, it was just a misunderstanding,' Duane said. 'But please don't forget to send the flowers.'

Ruth considered her position. She was looking straight up, into the heavens, which were clear at the moment.

'I doubt anyone will come,' she said. 'I imagine I'll just sit here all day. If it comes a flash flood it'll drown me.'

Duane looked up. There was not a cloud in the sky.

'You're not trapped,' he pointed out. 'You could go back in your house and wait for the tow truck.'

'No thanks, I think I'd rather be a martyr,' Ruth said.

Then she looked at him with cloudy eyes.

'Duane, you're really depressed,' she said. 'I can sense it. I wish you'd see a psychiatrist. *I* saw one, and I wasn't really the psychiatrist type.'

'Well, did it help?' Duane asked. 'Did you find out anything important?'

Ruth considered the question. The way the Volkswagen was tilted skyward made it seem that she could just drive straight up, perhaps into heaven. She wasn't a very orthodox Christian, didn't believe in pearly gates or streets of gold, but she supposed there might be a place somewhere where virtuous spirits gathered – the spirits of people who had done their best all their lives, as she had. She was thinking that it would be nice just to drive off in her Volkswagen to the place of virtuous spirits – and that would be what dying was.

Then she remembered that Duane had asked her something.

'What was the question again? I was thinking about heaven,' she said.

'I asked if you learned anything important when you went to the psychiatrist,' he repeated.

'Well, I learned that my husband had never loved me – I guess that was important, since I was married to him a long time,' she said.

'Jody Carmichael's daughter is a psychiatrist,' Duane said. 'I've been thinking I might see her.'

'That's good,' Ruth said. 'A woman would probably be better for you than a man.'

Duane wanted to go. He didn't want to get in a long conversation about psychiatry – or anything else – with Ruth Popper. Besides, if Earlene had actually made contact with Bobby Lee he was apt to show up at any time, wanting attention. Duane really wanted to get out of town before he had to dish out any more attention. But Ruth's comment startled him.

'Why would a woman be better for me than a man?' he asked.

Ruth shrugged. 'That's just my opinion, Duane,' she said. 'I suppose it's because you've never been much like other men.

'You're not exactly one of the guys,' she added. The sun through her windshield was hot – she was fanning herself with a crossword puzzle book. Ruth enjoyed fanning herself. It was a way of keeping active.

Duane felt as if he had one foot stuck in glue – the glue of human relations. He really wanted to be walking down the road, back to his solitary cabin, but somehow he had got stuck in a gluey conversation with Ruth. Every time he thought he saw an opportunity to leave, Ruth said something that held him again, like glue.

'Ruth, I'm president of the school board,' he reminded her. 'I'm vice president of the Chamber of Commerce.'

Ruth didn't respond.

'Those are normal things, aren't they?' he asked.

'Oh, as far as they go, but it still doesn't make you one of the guys,' Ruth said. 'I think it's good that you're going to see a woman psychiatrist.'

Duane walked away. Ruth was like Lester, like Karla, like Bobby Lee, like everyone he knew. The only way to get out of a conversation with any of them was to leave. He walked home at a good clip, feeling anything but at peace. As soon as he got home he sat down at his table, opened his tablet, and wrote two short letters of resignation, one to the school board and the other to the Chamber of Commerce.

Then, feeling a little better, he tore the two letters out of the tablet, folded them neatly, and closed the tablet. He had neither envelopes nor stamps – he would have to get some the next time he went to Jody Carmichael's, which might be as soon as later that day.

Though he couldn't immediately mail them, just writing the letters had the effect of easing his mind. He had done something he wanted to do, taken what he considered to be a strong, positive step – he was getting his feet out of the glue. He began to relax, ceased to feel quite so tight in his chest. He took his lawn chair outside, covered himself with his poncho, and just sat, relaxing, breathing better, watching the wide sky.

# 26

Later in the day Duane walked a mile and a half south of the hill to a large stock tank – he sat by the tank most of the afternoon, watching the ripples on the water as the wind blew across it. The stock tank was nothing much, as man-made ponds went in that country, but it had a line of nice willow trees across the north side. In his bass fishing days he had often sat in the shade of the willow trees, casting idly for bass and throwing back most of what he caught.

It was windy and brisk but sunny; he was still tense, and had walked over to the water to be soothed by the quiet lapping sound it made when the low waves struck the shore. Alone, with no one to argue with or banter with, he had no difficulty in admitting to himself that he felt confused. In a short space of time he had ceased to be able to interact comfortably or amiably with anyone. He couldn't stand to be around his family, around his employees, or around his old friends. Twice during the morning, first with Karla and then with Ruth, he had actually grown short of breath, just from having to talk to them. He had often been angry or irritated with both women, over the years, but he could not recall that just talking to them had affected his breathing before.

Something had changed – it was just difficult to say what. He didn't want to be with his family, or even be in the town where he had spent his whole life. He could only relax when he was alone. And yet nothing obvious or dramatic had occurred to bring about the change. He wanted to be where he was, sitting on a hill or by a stock tank, alone. Not only did he not want to be with any of the people he knew, he didn't feel that he could even survive if he had to be. He had been a stable citizen, parent, husband, friend for a long time, and then it had ended. He had no more stability to offer. He knew that it would be a while before his family and the townspeople accepted the change, but eventually they would have to, if only because he couldn't do differently, couldn't be, again, what he had been.

While he sat at the edge of the pond, his back against one of the willow trees, a flock of mallards banked out of the east and settled on the pond, right in front of him. If he had brought his twenty-two he could have had duck for dinner – the ducks were only fifteen feet away. Later, just as he was rising to walk back to the cabin, seven wild pigs snuffled out of the underbrush on the other side of the pond – one piglet waded into the shallows and flopped down on his belly, as if exhausted. Duane sat back down and watched as the pigs nosed through the scrub oak, foraging for acorns. A little before sunset a heron landed in a muddy inlet west of the main pond. It was smaller than the herons he had seen beside the road to the Corners. The ducks were quacking, bobbing down into the water, shaking their feathers, making a racket, but the heron was silent. Some doves came into the water. Then, as he was walking home, along the rocky south side of the hill, he noticed a covey of blue quail, scuttling from bush to bush.

Duane had never paid much attention to the animal life around him. Sometimes he hunted, but not avidly. Now and then his eye might be arrested by a line of geese in the sky, or the dash of a bobcat, or the flutter of wild turkeys along a creek bank, but his response to animal life had been occasional and brief. Now he found the company of animals soothing. They were all small animals, too – they weren't doing anything dramatic. The blue quail seemed as modest as nuns as they hurried through the scanty cover. He decided that the study of animal life would be his new pleasure. While the family he had left behind watched television he would be keeping an eye out for the beasts of the field.

On the walk to the pond that afternoon Shorty had run off, in overpersistent pursuit of a jackrabbit – Duane considered it just as well. If Shorty had been with him at the pond he would just have barked at the wild pigs, or the ducks, or the heron.

As he approached the cabin Duane saw Shorty running around with a stick in his mouth. The dog disappeared onto the north side of the cabin and then reappeared as the same stick came flying through the air. Just then the stick thrower – Dickie – stepped into view and waved at his father. Duane waved back, but he immediately felt his chest begin to tighten. He had wanted to talk to Dickie, needed to talk to Dickie, but at the same time, didn't feel ready to talk to Dickie.

What he felt was a little tinge of sadness at the memory of his son's long battle with drugs.

Dickie was tall and good looking, friendly and competent – everybody in Thalia liked him. He had had as much promise as anyone coming out of that high school, and yet, with Dickie, normal high school hell-raising had segued into bouts of addiction that had eaten up his youth. Dickie was thirty-five and, except for a decent wife and three nice children, had nothing to show for a third of his life. Duane and Karla both felt guilty about it. Both felt that, as parents, they had somehow nodded just when they should have been alert. They felt they should have done something more effective than paying out money to doctors and clinics as nearly twenty years of their son's life slipped by in a haze of drugs.

There the boy stood, as handsome and as likable as ever – only he wasn't a boy now, he was a middle-aged man, a fact Duane had a hard time remembering or believing.

'Hi, Dad,' Dickie said, when Duane approached. He held out his hand and Duane shook it. He gave his son a close look but, in the dimming light, couldn't tell much. One puzzling facet of Dickie's long self-abuse was that it didn't really show. He looked good, always had – probably it was a metabolic gift inherited from his mother. Karla had had some hard-drinking years, but it had never affected her looks – it still didn't. Lookswise both Karla and Dickie always managed to look unblemished, no matter how wild the weekend.

'Hi,' Duane said. 'I was by this morning but decided to let you sleep.'

'Boy, I needed it,' Dickie said. 'Rehab's draining. I guess it's all that talking.'

'I just hope it drained all the bad stuff out of you, this time,' Duane said.

Though Duane had twice flown to Arizona to check his son into the famous and expensive rehabilitation facility there, and had then gone back for the obligatory family day, in which Dickie and his siblings had spent several hours blaming one another for their problems – blaming him and Karla too, although not quite so venomously – he had not gained much insight into the actual day-to-day procedures of the place, or into the process of rehabilitation either. Once or twice during the high-stress days of the boom he himself had drunk too much whiskey. Karla had even urged him to go into rehab, but he had taken up bass fishing instead and found that it worked just as well – maybe better. The more he fished, the less he drank. Being alone on the water then had had the same soothing effect as being alone by the pond had now. He had needed to be calm, rather than to be drunk, and floating alone in a bass boat had seemed to calm him down.

'I'm glad you came out – let's go inside,' Duane said. 'There's not much to eat, but I can offer you a good hot bowl of soup.'

'Can't. Annette's cooking dinner,' Dickie said. 'She thinks I'm too skinny – she wants to put some meat on my bones.'

'You've come back with a good tan,' Duane said, once he looked at his son in good light.

'That Arizona sun,' Dickie said, looking around the cabin. 'So, Momma says you're kind of a hermit now. How long has that been happening?'

Duane was heating himself a can of clam chowder.

'About ten days,' he said.

Dickie was silent, waiting for his father to explain himself, but Duane didn't. He just went on heating the chowder, stirring the chowder.

'So, what's going on?' Dickie asked, a little nervously. 'Was it a big fight with Mom, or what?'

'No, your mother and I have been getting along fine,' Duane said. He stirred some more, not sure that he could find the language in which to explain himself accurately to his nervous son.

He poured the soup, turned off the stove, sat down at the table, and looked at Dickie.

'I want a different life,' he said. 'I already have a different life. I know it's going to take a while for people to adjust to that fact – your mother particularly – but you'll all just have to do your best to adjust. I want to live alone now. I don't want to be a family man anymore, and I don't want to be an oilman, either.'

Duane paused. Dickie was listening – waiting to hear what his father had to say.

'The oil business is what I need to talk to you about,' Duane said. 'Starting tomorrow it's yours to run.'

'What do you mean?' Dickie asked, startled.

'I said exactly what I meant,' Duane said. 'You're home, you're healthy, and the oil business is now yours to run. You're the boss man – starting immediately.'

'Gosh,' Dickie said. 'I just got out of rehab and I'm supposed to run our oil business?'

'That's right,' Duane said. 'It's not Exxon or Texaco, you know. It's just a little family oil business. You grew up with it. You've worked every job connected with it – except mine. Now you need to take over and do what I've been doing, because I've done it all my life and I don't want to do it anymore. From now on you make the deals, you hire the crews, you tell who to go where, you check on the rigs, you see that the leases get pumped properly. You see that the trucks are kept in good repair, you go over the contracts, you see that the bookkeeper and the accountant get the information they need. You see that the crews don't go to work drunk and don't go to work stoned.'

Dickie chuckled. 'Dad, I've been in rehab three times. The crews are going to laugh in my face if I tell them not to take drugs.'

'Maybe at first, but that's just something you have to deal with,' Duane said. 'You're clean and you need to stay clean. If you do, the crews will behave – or at least most of them will. You're not going to find a crew that's so perfect everybody behaves.'

'Gosh,' Dickie said, again. 'I'm not saying I can't do it, but it's a big responsibility and it's sort of sudden.'

'It is, but I can't help it,' Duane said. 'Sometimes things just happen sudden.'

'But what if I screw up?' Dickie asked. 'I mean, I don't think I will, but what if I do?'

Duane shrugged. 'It's yours to run, like I say,' he said. 'If you fuck up, you just do. I can't be involved with it anymore. Maybe you'll fuck up and lose every cent we have. I don't think you will, and I hope you don't, but if you do, that's just tough shit. I'll give you advice now and then, but otherwise I'm not lifting a finger.'

'Gosh,' Dickie said again. Then he took a deep breath.

'Maybe I can do it,' he said. 'Maybe I can do it fine.'

'Maybe you can even do it better than I can,' Duane said. 'I hope so. It's been twenty years or more since I really had much interest in it. Everything you do for a long time gets old – I guess that's one reason I feel like being a hermit for a while.'

'You think it's just for a while, Dad?' Dickie asked. 'I mean, it's fine about the oil business, I think I can do it. But what about you?'

'What about me?' Duane asked.

'Momma doesn't know what to think,' Dickie says. 'She says you just kind of walked off.'

'That's a fair description,' Duane said. 'In fact, it's a perfect description. I just kind of walked off.'

'But you've never done anything like that,' Dickie said. 'It's got everyone confused.'

'Well, but I did do something like this,' Duane said. 'I used to fish, remember? I used to fish a lot.'

'I know, but at least you drove out to the lake,' Dickie said. 'At least you had a vehicle. You didn't just hoof it.'

'Is there something wrong with walking?' Duane asked. 'It's a pleasant thing to do. I've just reached a point where I enjoy a slow pace.'

'Nellie says you're thinking of going to Egypt or somewhere,' Dickie said. 'What's that all about?'

'Curiosity,' Duane said. 'I want to see the pyramids. That's not so strange, either. Thousands of people go to see the pyramids every year.'

'Are you depressed?' Dickie asked. He had his mother's impatience. He liked to cut to the chase.

Duane smiled. 'I don't know,' he said. 'Your mother thinks so, but I'm not sure.'

Dickie looked confused.

'Seems like you'd know, one way or the other,' he said. 'I sure know when I'm depressed. That's when I go looking for the stuff.'

'Which you can't do anymore,' Duane said firmly. 'You've done enough stuff. Now you've got an oil business to run, and the family fortune's in your hands.'

'It upsets everybody to think of you sitting out here depressed,' Dickie said.

Duane smiled again. 'You'll all just have to deal with it,' he said. 'Go on about your lives and let me worry about whether I'm depressed enough or not. If I am it's my problem.'

Dickie sighed – he looked uncertain.

'In rehab they teach you that all problems are family problems,' he said. 'So if you're depressed it's our problem too.'

Duane shook his head. 'This ain't rehab,' he said. 'This is just life. My problems don't pertain to anybody but me. I'm not unhealthy. I'm not suicidal. I'm not drinking or doping. There's nothing wrong with walking as a pursuit. I'm not harming myself or anybody else. I don't want anybody coming out here preaching to me. I'm going to live the way I want to live, for a while, and I don't see why I shouldn't. I'm not in dire straits and neither are any of you.'

'You've kind of got a peace-be-with-you attitude, don't you?' Dickie said. 'I had a counselor like that. I guess there's nothing wrong with it.'

'No, not that I can see,' Duane said. 'I'll give you one piece of advice about the oil business, the one you're going to be running starting tomorrow, and that's return your phone calls. Don't put it off and don't skip any, even if you think the person you're supposed to call is an asshole or a flake. Make sure Earlene keeps a good list, and the minute you get to the office return those phone calls. All of them.'

He ate the last swallow of the clam chowder and put the spoon neatly in the bowl.

'That's the secret of success,' he said. 'Just return all your phone calls, and the sooner the better.'

Dickie, across the table, noticed Honor Carmichael's business card propped against the salt and pepper shakers. He picked it up and looked at it – a psychiatrist's card was a surprising thing to find on his father's little table.

'Gosh!' he said, for the fourth time that evening. 'Are you actually seeing a shrink?'

'Not at the moment,' Duane said. 'Jody Carmichael gave me that card – that's his daughter. She made a head doctor and he's real proud of her. He wants everybody to know his daughter made something of herself.'

A little later, Dickie left. When he drove off Duane went back inside, picked up Honor Carmichael's business card, and slipped it into his billfold. He didn't want anyone else to casually pick it up, as his son had, and be shocked.

# 27

The next day Duane gave some thought to hitchhiking to Wichita Falls, largely in order to buy the book by Thoreau. A secondary purpose, which he also weighed, would be to use a pay phone to make an appointment with Honor Carmichael – counselor, psychiatrist, and psychoanalyst. He considered making the appointment for the same reason that he considered traveling to Egypt: curiosity. He was curious about the pyramids and also curious about Honor Carmichael. On the complex question of his depression, he remained undecided: whether he was in a depression, whether he wasn't, whether it really mattered, either way. He was not as convinced as Karla and everyone else that he was seriously depressed – but he *had* experienced two or three fits of irrational rage and had felt sad and weird when the rage subsided.

He considered himself to be a mature adult, with at least some capacity for making realistic judgments. Life was not all pie in the sky; some days were bound to be better than other days, and still other days were likely to be downright hard to get through. Some depression seemed normal to him – life was the sort of affair that, sooner or later, for one reason or another, would pull anybody's spirits down. He didn't know any adults who weren't sometimes depressed. Bobby Lee was depressed because he had only one testicle. Lester Marlow was depressed because his wife wouldn't buy him any new video games. Earlene was depressed because she had a scar from splitting her head open on the water fountain. Julie was depressed because her boyfriend would likely be in jail for three years. Karla was depressed because her husband had left her for no good reason – or none, at least, that she had been given. And in Africa and the Balkans people were depressed because they were being massacred in horrible ways, or being driven from their homes, or both: *their* depression was visible on CNN practically every night.

Seen in such a context, Duane didn't believe that his depression was anything the world needed to worry about, or even notice. As long as he kept to himself he felt sure he could handle it fine. Also, it seemed little enough to ask. Nobody in his family was either starving or sick. There were several young women and a couple of highly experienced older women available to take care of the grandkids. Dickie's situation vis-à-vis drugs would remain touchy for a while, but at least there was reason to hope.

Duane considered that he had pretty well fulfilled his duties as a father, a provider, and a citizen. He had done a reasonable percentage of the things he was supposed to do – now he just wanted to be left alone, and he didn't feel that the question of whether he was depressed or happy was anybody's business but his own. He had a warm house and warm clothes; anything he needed he could buy. Fortunately he had won about twenty-five hundred dollars in a poker game the night before he set out to be a walker – he had the cash in his pocket and could buy what he needed from day to day. Though he had splurged a bit on tools over at Jody Carmichael's he still was a long way from having exhausted the twenty-five hundred dollars.

Still and all, Duane was aware that such reasonable thoughts didn't necessarily represent the whole story. Several times lately he had felt a piercing sadness, a sadness that always took him by surprise. The sadness might pierce him while he was walking along, or while he sat in his lawn chair, or even while he was in bed. He didn't understand where these sadnesses came from, or why they were so deep and so sharp.

Also, his dreams had become intense and often painful. Three times lately he had had a calf-roping dream which puzzled him a good deal. In all the dreams he was a calf roper who had an easy throw and the prospect of winning time – only he always missed the calf. In all three dreams his horse put him in perfect position, and yet he missed. The loop he threw at the calf seemed to dissolve, somehow, just as it was about to settle around the calf's neck. Then he would be sitting on his horse watching the calf trot on across the arena, unroped, a sight that made Duane feel sad, intensely sad. Why had he missed the calf?

Another puzzling aspect of the dream, an aspect as curious as the dissolving rope, was the fact that there were no people in the stands to see his humiliation. Only he saw it – and his horse. The bleachers around the arena were empty. The spectators, if there were any, had all flocked to the snow cone stand at the same time.

Duane found the roping dream both puzzling and troubling. The first time he dreamed it he shrugged it off. Anybody could dream anything once. He himself had never owned a roping horse and had never competed in a rodeo; but he had seen a lot of rodeos and knew that it was not particularly uncommon for even a skilled roper to miss a calf now and then. It was something that happened to the best of them, though of course it happened less often to the best of them.

Then Duane dreamed the dream twice more – and each time, at the moment when the calf went trotting off, he felt an intense disappointment. He remembered all three dreams quite vividly when he woke up, too. The dreams were so painful, in their way, that waking brought him the kind of intense relief that comes when you wake from a nightmare and realize that whatever bad thing had happened had only happened in a dream. Yet in all three of the roping dreams his sense of humiliation was so intense that he kept recalling it throughout the day.

Of course, three bad dreams didn't necessarily mean that he was in a big depression. He had heard – or perhaps had read somewhere – that dreams might actually be a mechanism for getting rid of depression. The source of that theory, once he thought about it, was Mildred-Jean Ennis, who cut men's hair as well as women's. Sometimes when Duane felt shaggy he would go in and let Mildred-Jean cut his hair.

'Yep, that's the way dreams work,' she assured him. 'The worse the dream, the better you feel the next day. Dreams are God's way of helping you get rid of feelings you don't need to be carrying around.'

'If that's true, then I wish he would send me a dream that would help me get rid of the feeling that I'm going broke,' Duane said. 'I've been carrying that feeling around for a good many years. If I could have a dream that would help me get rid of it I'd be inclined to put a twenty-dollar bill in the collection plate.'

The main disadvantage to getting haircuts at Mildred-Jean's was her perfume, which she splashed liberally over her large person. Sometimes the perfume was so strong that Duane got a sore throat just from smelling it, but, otherwise, he liked Mildred-Jean.

'It don't work to ask God to get too specific when he's helping you to get rid of bad feelings,' she told him. 'Some of those bad feelings are put there to help you be a better person, Duane. If God helped you get rid of them too soon you might just go right on in the same old sinful ways.'

'I don't think I'd be any more sinful than I am if I could relax about going broke,' Duane said.

Then he went to the café and had a cheeseburger. He wasn't particularly hungry but the smell of grease cooking helped counteract the lingering odor of Mildred-Jean's perfume.

The one good thing about the roping dream, Duane considered, was that it would give him a good place to start if he did get an appointment with Honor Carmichael. He could tell her how he felt after waking from the dream and she could tell him what she thought about it.

His main worry, when he thought of going to a psychiatrist, was that he'd just sit there and not be able to think of anything to say. After all, he had been brought up *not* to talk about his troubles, which were nobody's business but his. And he never *had* talked about them much. He might get in the doctor's office and find that he was unable to shrug off a lifetime of reticence.

But there were other problems that had to be surmounted before he could even get to that one – how to get to Wichita Falls being the first one. From where he sat in his cabin, it was probably seventeen or eighteen miles to Wichita Falls. He felt sure he could walk it comfortably enough, one way, but what about getting back? Even though he was in good walking trim, thirty-six miles or so was probably too far to walk in one day. If his appointment was in the afternoon it would take him most of the night to get home.

Another problem was Shorty, who would be certain to follow him unless he were restrained in some fashion. No matter how loud Duane yelled at him or how firmly he told him to go home, Shorty would still slink along behind him. Then, once they got to Wichita, he would either get run over or get in all kinds of fights with the local dogs.

'Shorty, you're an impediment to long distance travel,' Duane told him. The dog, feeling vaguely guilty, laid back his ears.

Apart from the problem of Shorty, there was the question of hitchhiking itself. Was it against his rules, or wasn't it? Of course, the rules themselves were not written in granite anywhere. One of the main points about his new life was that he got to make up his own rules as he went along. If he decided that hitchhiking was an acceptable form of travel, then he was free to hitchhike.

Duane was still weighing his options when it occurred to him that he didn't have to make the whole thirty-six-mile round trip in one day. There were motels in Wichita Falls. He could walk in one day, spend the night, and walk back the next day. If he chose a low-end motel, which was his inclination anyway, they probably wouldn't object if he had a pet.

He decided to walk, let Shorty accompany him, stay overnight, and not hitchhike. He would then walk both ways – it would be a way to test his seriousness about the whole business of walking everywhere. Thirty-six miles was a substantial walk. If he did it and liked it, it would sort of confirm his instinct that walking was how he wanted to travel from then on. He couldn't walk to Egypt, of course, but he *could* walk to the airport in Wichita Falls and fly the rest of the way. No automobiles need be involved.

By the time Duane had worked through the options in his mind and made his decision, it was already too late in the day to set out for Wichita Falls. For such a long walk he would need to get an early start; otherwise the doctor's office would be closed before he got there.

Duane felt restless, though. He was primed to walk somewhere, didn't want it to be Thalia, and considered just walking the perimeter of his property, something he had never actually done. He could just follow his own fence, which would mean walking eight miles. Three different creeks crossed the land at various points. If he were lucky he might stumble upon a bee tree; having a source of wild honey would be a welcome thing. One of the few memories he had of his father, who had been killed in a rig explosion when he was five, was of watching his father cut into a bee tree on a property his grandparents had owned. Duane remembered how calm his father had been, as the bees swarmed around him, and how strong the wild honey tasted, so strong that when his father gave him a taste it burned his tongue and he tried to spit it out.

He stepped out to walk his property line, noticed that it was drizzling slightly, and went back in to get his waterproof jacket. Instead of walking his fence he headed for the Corners. He thought he might enjoy a half hour's conversation with Jody Carmichael – he thought he might even tell Jody that he was considering making an appointment with his daughter.

The eight-mile walk seemed to take no time. Except for startling the same two herons out of the same bog, the walk just passed. Before he was really ready to be there he saw the Corners ahead. Three pickups were parked in front of it, which was a little discouraging. Duane had hoped to find Jody alone but seemed to have arrived simultaneously with a large hungry crew, all of whom were inside fueling up on cheap junk foods. He jumped the fence and sat on a big stump for a few minutes – before long, as he had hoped, the crew began to file out. The pickups filled up with dirty, shaggy men and drove away. As they passed, Duane realized that it was one of his own crews – or, rather, one of Dickie's crews. He was glad they didn't notice him, sitting on the stump in the drizzle, which had gotten heavier.

'Why, you just missed your own help,' Jody said, when Duane walked in. 'Just as well you missed them, they'd have probably beaten you up. They weren't in much of a mood.'

'They're never in a good mood,' Duane said. 'Roughnecking's not a good mood kind of job. But I don't know why they would want to beat me up.'

'Oh, for turning them over to your son,' Jody said. 'I guess young Dickie caught a couple of them smoking dope when he got to work this morning. He fired the pot smokers and gave everyone else on the crew a good cussing out.'

'Good for him,' Duane said. 'That's how I was hoping he'd behave.'

'I guess if you made Dickie boss that means it's all off between you and the oil business,' Jody said.

'Right, all off,' Duane said. 'I've got places to walk to now. I've been trying to find that Thoreau book you mentioned, but Karla lost ours. I guess I'll have to walk to Wichita and buy it, unless you've got one you could lend me.'

'Me, read a book?' Jody said – his TV was tuned, as usual, to a soccer match somewhere in the world, and his computer screen had a line of figures on it. 'Nope, I don't have time to read books. The racing form's on-line now, so I can read that right off my computer, and when I ain't reading the form I've got these Portuguese soccer magazines to study. I hear they're publishing a good soccer magazine in Prague now, too – learned about it from my E-mail. I've sent off for it but it ain't shown up yet.'

'Who do you E-mail about stuff like that?' Duane asked. E-mail was a complete puzzle to him.

'Oh, this fellow who told me about the Czech magazine lives up in Siskatoon, B.C.,' Jody said. 'He's a worse soccer nut than me – he even tries to keep up with Communist soccer, or what used to be

Communist soccer. I like South American soccer better myself, but then, to each his own. The point is that between soccer and horse racing I don't have time to sit around reading Yankee assholes like Thoreau.'

'I didn't know he was an asshole,' Duane said. 'Maybe I won't walk all that way to buy it, after all.'

'Being an asshole don't mean he wasn't smart, though,' Jody pointed out. He was eating Fritos at the time, keeping one eye on the soccer match. 'You ought to walk on into town and get his book. He did the same thing you're doing, and he did it over a hundred years ago. He might have figured out a few things you need to know.'

'I was thinking of making an appointment with your daughter while I'm in town,' Duane said. He had not really meant to tell Jody that, or anyone that, but then he did. Jody would undoubtedly mention it to some roughneck, who would mention it to Bobby Lee, who would mention it to Karla. Before he could even reach Wichita and make an appointment everyone in the county would know he was seeing a psychiatrist.

'Want me to call her for you?' Jody asked. 'If you call her you'll be lucky to get an appointment before April or May or sometime – that's how busy she is,' Jody said. 'She might not even take you, if you just call in cold.'

'If she's a psychiatrist, why wouldn't she?' Duane asked.

'Because she's full up with crazies and nuts as it is,' Jody said. 'There ain't many shrinks in Wichita Falls and all the nuts know that my girl's the best.'

'I haven't noticed that many crazies and nuts in this part of the world,' Duane said. 'There's not really that much population.'

'No, but about ninety percent of what population there is is crazy to some degree,' Jody said. 'Of course, most of them are *poor* and crazy. They can't afford one hundred and ninety dollars an hour to let Honor help them with their problems.'

Duane knew psychiatrists were expensive, but he had no idea they were *that* expensive. The news took him aback.

'If that's what she costs I don't know that I can afford it, either,' Duane said. 'It'd be cheaper just to shoot myself.'

'No, you're not the suicide type, Duane,' Jody informed him. 'Besides, you got all those kids and grandkids. You'd be leaving too much grief behind. Better let me call Honor and see if she can slip you into the rotation sometime soon.'

'Well, if it's no bother,' Duane said. 'I'd prefer the afternoon. I'd like to walk over to town.'

Jody chuckled. 'That'll interest Honor,' he said. 'I'll tell her she's got a bad case of pedestrianism to deal with. Honor walks herself – that'll be one thing you two have in common.'

'Mind if I go look at the hardware while you make the call?' Duane asked. 'I need a good wire cutter.'

Jody handed him the padlock key and picked up the telephone.

Duane lingered for nearly an hour in the small shed where the hardware was. He had always appreciated hardware, but now he liked it more than ever. Jody – or his daughter, Honor – had managed to cram an amazing array of tools into a small space. Duane knew what most of the tools were used for, but there were a few that puzzled him until he examined them closely. One of the nice things about being allowed to brood amid the hardware was that he could look at the tools and reason from them to a future. He had always admired fine woodwork, but had never himself done any woodworking. He considered himself handy with tools, and had always made simple repairs, both at home and in the oil fields. But he had never sat down with a few good tools and made something fine, like a cabinet, or a wood carving of an animal or something. He considered that he had a good many years of his life left, during which he would need to occupy himself. It occurred to him that woodworking might be something he could learn.

Poking around in Jody's hardware room, Duane indulged in a pleasant daydream. If he wanted to attempt to master woodworking he would need a workroom in which to do it. The cabin itself wasn't large enough. He would need to build a good strong table to work on; building a little workroom would be his first task and constructing a solid table his second. The thought of having such a room and such a table was very comforting to him. Of course he would have to have the lumber trucked in. He couldn't carry it home. He would need to buy a fair number of tools as well; he would need some sawhorses and a variety of saws and drills. For a moment he considered avoiding power tools, but rejected that notion as silly. He didn't need to reinvent the wheel. Power tools had been available most of his life; if he rejected them he might as well reject electricity and live by candlelight.

Thinking of his room and his table and his woodwork was such a satisfying reverie that it was with reluctance that Duane finally emerged from Jody's hardware room and put the padlock back on the door. Good tools offered one a great deal to look forward to, after all. The prospect of making something appealing was very comforting – it made the whole enterprise that he had embarked on seem less negative. It wasn't merely a walking away that he was involved in. He might also be walking toward a new life – or, at least, acquiring a new attitude. The only sad element in the picture was that he hadn't done it years sooner.

When he walked back into the store Jody was typing on his computer at great speed.

'Hold on, got to get a few bets in, the horses are at the gate,' Jody said. Duane bought a package of peanut butter crackers while Jody clicked away at the computer. As soon as he finished he stood up.

'I like to make about fifty bets a day – it's my organizing principle,' Jody said. 'I guess walking all over the county is *your* organizing principle.'

'For now it is,' Duane said. 'I might develop another one if you give me a while.'

He did not want to reveal his desire to do some woodwork – that was a thing to keep private, a prospect to nurse and enjoy. He was curious as to whether Jody had reached his daughter and secured him an appointment but he felt shy about asking. Jody was absently staring at the TV screen, where, as usual, several soccer players were in hot pursuit of a soccer ball.

Duane paid for the wire cutters. He meant to take them with him to check the fences around his property – and when he handed over the cash Jody handed him another of his daughter's business cards, with a date and a time written on the back. The time was three in the afternoon, this coming Friday.

'That's quick. Thanks, Jody,' Duane said, tucking the card in his shirt pocket.

'Yep – took my daughter by surprise,' Jody said. 'I've never asked her to take anybody on before. I told her you enjoyed walking, like she does.'

'What'd she say to that?' Duane asked.

'Nothing. Honor's closemouthed,' Jody said. 'She just looked at her schedule and gave me the appointment.'

'I didn't expect it to be this quick, busy as she is,' Duane said.

'I know – that surprised me too,' Jody said. 'I guess the person she usually has in this slot was killed in a car wreck yesterday, up by Nocona. Lost control of his vehicle and smashed up against a bridge.'

'Oh my,' Duane said. 'That's one good thing about walking. You don't smash into the bridges.'

'No, but you still have to watch out for the country drivers,' Jody said. 'While you're not smashing into the bridges one of them could always smash into you, if you're not watchful.'

Duane left and walked slowly home with his dog. He felt a little strange. Not only had he decided on a new skill he wanted to master – woodworking – but he also had an appointment with a psychiatrist – the first such appointment of his life.

'There's one good thing about it, Shorty,' he said to the dog. 'It's four days off. I guess I could still cancel it if I change my mind.'

# BOOK TWO

# The Walker and His Doctor

# 28

Karla learned about Duane's appointment the next day, when Duane came home to look for his passport. While he was rummaging in desks and bureaus he casually informed his wife that he had made an appointment with a psychiatrist, namely Honor Carmichael.

'Duane, you don't need a passport to go to a shrink,' Karla informed him. As usual her husband had shown up at an early hour, before anyone else was awake. The sight of him rooting around in drawers at that hour – which meant that he had walked into town while it was still pitch-dark – made her so nervous that she went in the kitchen and poured herself a stiff shot of tequila. Then she poured herself another and went back to the bedroom to help him look.

'I know that, but I might want to go somewhere else besides the doctor,' Duane said. 'I just want to make sure my passport hasn't expired. I haven't used it since those fishing trips I took to South America – that was years ago.'

'It's not my fault; I wanted to go to Norway and see a glacier and sail on up a fjord,' Karla reminded him.

It was true that Karla had once wanted to take a cruise to Scandinavia, a desire inspired by some particularly alluring pictures in a travel magazine, but the family was in a state of crisis at the time and they had had to keep changing the dates until they finally just gave up and canceled the trip entirely, a fact that gave Karla one more thing to resent – or so it seemed to Duane.

'I'm sorry that trip never came off,' Duane said. 'But you can still go, you know? You're not crippled.'

He was a little annoyed – it had been ten years since the trip to Norway had been canceled, but Karla still seized any opportunity to bring it up.

'Take a girlfriend – go to Norway. I'm sure the glaciers are still there,' he said.

His passport was not turning up, which made him feel a little frantic. He had no firm plans for going to Egypt, but, should the mood strike him, he wanted to be able to leave immediately, and he couldn't leave immediately unless he had a valid passport.

'It's strange to me that you'd walk half the night to hunt a passport and not stay to have breakfast with your family.'

'I didn't walk half the night, I only walked two hours,' Duane pointed out. 'Besides, I haven't left yet and all my family's asleep except you.'

'Whatever,' Karla said, before bursting into tears. Everything seemed wrong to her, insupportably wrong. It was an insult to suggest that she go to Norway with a girlfriend when initially the whole trip had been planned as a way of getting some romance back in their marriage. It seemed to her it would be impossible to be sailing on a luxurious boat up a beautiful fjord in Norway without some romance coming about. But the opportunity had been missed; now her husband had gone crazy, and now there was no likelihood that any romantic feelings would ever be aroused again – not between the two of them, at least.

It took Duane another twenty minutes to find his passport, which was in the inside pocket of an old sports coat he hadn't worn for several years. The passport had been expired for the past three years. Karla lay on the bed sobbing the whole time he was looking for the passport, but he hardened his heart, which wasn't difficult to do – maybe she had just ragged him about the lost trip to Norway once too often.

'My passport's expired,' he informed her, sitting for a moment on the bed, where Karla lay amid a pile of Kleenex. 'Put on your tennis shoes and take a walk with me – it's a pretty day.'

Karla was so startled by the invitation that she stopped crying.

'Take a walk how far?' she asked. 'I'm not walking out in the country with you – you're too crazy.'

'Just to the Dairy Queen,' he said. 'I'll buy you breakfast.'

It was a better offer than she had been expecting – not that breakfast at the Dairy Queen, under the watchful eye of the local gossips, was any substitute for a romantic trip to Norway. There had even been a three-day trip to Lapland to ride reindeer included in the tour. Though the suggestion that she make the trip with a girlfriend, rather than him, was a deadly insult, Karla decided to try and make the best of things. She got up, repaired herself as best she could, and went out on the back steps to slip on her tennis shoes – it was only just light.

'I can't get over it that you walk around in the dark,' she said, as they set out. 'It upsets me no end. If all you wanted was your passport why couldn't you have waited till daylight to walk in?'

'Because I can't stand to be around people, and people are milling around when it's daylight,' he said. 'It's nothing personal. The earlier I get in and out and the fewer people I have to deal with, the better.

'It may just be a phase,' he added, by way of comfort.

'Well, if it's forever I'm moving to Santa Fe or somewhere,' Karla informed him. 'Only psychos walk around in the dark – if you're going to be a psycho for the rest of your life I'd just as soon not be nowhere around.'

Duane didn't answer – Karla's position was too absurd. J.T., Dan Connor, and a few other oilmen were already at the Dairy Queen when they walked in. The oilmen were smoking and drinking coffee at their usual table, way in the back.

'Watch them be nice as pie now that you're here,' Karla said bitterly. 'If Dan Connor says anything about my hair not being combed I hope you'll punch him out.'

'Why would he? Your hair *is* combed,' Duane said. He waved at the men, but Karla only gave them a stony stare. She had just remembered a salient fact, which was that the psychiatrist her husband had made an appointment with was a woman. Though she had advised him to seek counseling, it had never occurred to her that he might seek it from a woman.

Now that the fact was staring her in the face, she wasn't sure she liked it.

They got coffee and sat down in a corner booth, as far from the oilmen as possible.

Duane was wishing he had been more efficient about keeping his passport up to date. He knew he could get it renewed through the mail, but that meant having his picture made and getting a certified copy of his birth certificate and perhaps other documents which it would be tedious to have to locate. He thought there might be a copy of his birth certificate in his office, but the thought of having to go there to look for it was a downer.

Karla, blowing on her coffee, was feeling a good deal better. Having breakfast with her husband at the Dairy Queen was pretty much a normal thing – it would shore up her reputation in local eyes.

'I might have known you'd do it with a beautiful woman,' she said – then, from the shocked look on Duane's face, she realized she had been a little sloppy in her choice of words.

'Going to the shrink, that is,' she clarified. 'I might have known you'd choose a beautiful woman to be your shrink.'

'How do you know she's beautiful? We haven't seen her since she was a girl,' Duane said, not completely surprised by the accusation. The minute Karla began to feel better, after a cry, she resumed the line of attack she had been pursuing, or else developed a new one.

'Well, her mother was beautiful,' Karla reminded him. 'Besides, it wouldn't be like you to choose an ugly old boy doctor if there was a pretty woman you could get an appointment with.'

'I just chose her because Jody gave me her card,' Duane said. 'I don't know anything about her at all. But she's a psychiatrist and Jody said he could get me in quick, so I let him try.'

'How quick? Are you feeling more psycho all of a sudden?' she asked.

'I'm not feeling psycho at all,' Duane said. 'I thought you wanted me to get counseling.'

'I did, but not from a beautiful woman who might be smarter than me,' Karla said.

'It's *counseling*,' Duane reminded her. 'It's important that the doctor be smart – otherwise the patient is just wasting time.'

He felt a little dejected. Though he had known that the fact that he was seeing a woman psychiatrist would be a wrinkle Karla wouldn't welcome, he had hoped that the fact that he had agreed to counseling would override that aspect of the matter.

'Your gynecologist is a man,' he pointed out.

'That's because the woman gynecologist I was going to died,' Karla said. 'What's that got to do with the price of peas?'

'Woman, man, it shouldn't matter – the point is she's a doctor,' Duane said. He felt a tightening in his chest. Karla seemed to be in a go-for-the-jugular mood and already he was feeling that it would be nice to be walking down a lonely country road.

'The appointment's not until Friday,' he said. 'This is Tuesday. If you don't want me to go then I guess I could still cancel it and not have to pay.'

Karla shook her head.

'I can't win,' she said. 'If I tell you not to go you'll just get more and more psycho, and if I let you go on and see her you'll be sitting there telling some smart-ass woman doctor that we haven't had sex since my last birthday.'

'Oh, go to hell,' Duane said. 'Why would I be wanting to tell her something like that? That's nobody's business but ours.'

'If she's your shrink it *is* her business,' Karla said. 'Your sex life is the first thing a shrink will want to know about.

'From what I hear it's the *only* thing most of them want to know about,' she added.

Duane stood up and put a ten-dollar bill on the table.

'Be sure and leave a tip,' he said. 'I always leave a tip.'

'Duane, you haven't eaten a bite and you walked all that way – sit down,' Karla said. 'You can go to a woman doctor if you want to – it just took me by surprise at first.'

Duane sat back down but he felt tense and was determined to leave if Karla continued in her go-for-the-jugular mode. Just then their food came and Dan Connor got up from the oilmen's table and walked over. He was chewing two toothpicks simultaneously, one in each corner of his mouth – a small peculiarity of his.

'If you was to swallow one of those toothpicks it would pierce the lining of your stomach and you'd die,' Karla informed him, when it looked as if he meant to join them.

'And no one would care,' she added, to make sure he got the point.

'Oops, I guess Karla ain't feeling sociable this morning,' Dan said, stopping in his tracks.

'Hi, Dan,' Duane said. He didn't particularly like Dan Connor – Karla was correct to suggest that few would lament his passing – but he wanted to preserve at least a semblance of civility for the brief time he had to be in town.

'Howdy,' Dan said. 'Has Bobby Lee still got that one testicle?'

'Why yes, so far as I know,' Duane said.

'Of course he's still got it,' Karla said. 'Why don't you shut up about Bobby Lee's balls? He won't even come in here and have coffee with us because he's so afraid someone will ask him about it.'

It was true that Bobby Lee often went all the way into Wichita Falls to sit in a Dairy Queen and drink coffee, so embarrassed was he by the intense scrutiny his fellow townspeople brought to bear on his condition.

'He needs to get over that; any one of us would be glad to drink coffee with the man,' Dan Connor said. Then he wandered off, looking slightly crestfallen.

'Now you see why I get tense when I'm in town,' Duane said. 'You don't really give people a chance to be friendly.'

'I do unless they're fat ugly slobs like Dan,' Karla said.

'He's not that fat,' Duane said. He had begun to regret his decision to sit back down.

'Will you tell me what you talk to your shrink about?' Karla asked.

'I don't know if I'm allowed to,' Duane said. 'I've never been to a psychiatrist before. I never expected to go to one and I don't really know why I'm going now – it's mainly curiosity, I guess. I don't feel disturbed – at least I don't if I'm left alone.'

Karla thought that over for a while. She looked out the window. A small convoy of cattle trucks was just going by. That was one thing you could count on in Thalia. Cattle trucks would always be going by.

'It's times like this when I wish I hadn't quit smoking,' she said. 'At least I can still drink. This Dairy Queen would be a lot livelier place if they could serve tequila.'

'Honey, if they served tequila half the people who come here would be killed in car wrecks before they could get back to the courthouse,' he said. 'If you could buy drinks at the Dairy Queen it would soon depopulate the town.'

'I feel like crying,' Karla said. 'It's because I don't understand why you're doing what you're doing. You're usually normal, and you're usually more decisive than this. Right now I can't even tell if you want to stay married or would rather get divorced.'

'I want to live in my own little house – that's the main change I feel,' Duane told her. 'But people can live in different houses and still be married. I have no interest in getting divorced.'

'Well, *I* might want to,' Karla said. 'If you want to be a bachelor and live by yourself, then you don't really want to be married much. That fact is plain as mud.'

'It's not plain as mud,' Duane said. 'Will you just keep calm until I've tried this for a while? We've been married forty years. Why is it such a big deal if I want to try something different for a few months?'

'A few *months*?' Karla said. 'You want to live out there in that ratty little cabin for a few *months*?'

Duane edged the ten-dollar bill under his coffee cup, where the waitress could find it.

'I'll see you later,' he said. 'Please don't forget to leave a tip.'

'I'm still gonna want to know what your new shrink thinks of all this,' Karla said, as he was leaving.

# 29

On the way out of town Duane met Bobby Lee, who didn't see the two of them until the last minute and almost ran over Shorty before he could get his pickup stopped. He had been at the rig all night and looked stubbly and depressed.

'I guess that little blue son-of-a-bitch follows you everywhere, don't he?' he said, looking down at the dog.

'Well yes – he has no other occupation,' Duane said.

'What did you say to Dickie? He come out there yesterday and practically drilled us all new assholes, the asshole,' Bobby Lee said.

'I told him he was the boss now – that's all,' Duane said.

'He believed you, too,' Bobby Lee said. 'He ran me ragged yesterday. What's going on in town?'

Duane shrugged.

'I take back the question,' Bobby Lee said. 'What's going on in town is that everybody's sitting around the Dairy Queen talking about what a little freak I am for having only one ball.'

Duane neither confirmed nor denied this analysis. He leaned on the window of the pickup for a minute. The floorboard on the passenger's side was filled with empty beer cans almost to the level of the seat.

'I'm saving those cans for old man Billinger,' Bobby Lee said. 'Scavenging cans is his only means of livelihood, poor old soul.'

'It's good of you to drink beer constantly so old man Billinger will have a way to make a living,' Duane said.

'Well, you know me – I've always gone out of my way to help my fellowman,' Bobby Lee said. 'If there was any justice I'd have the Nobel Peace Prize by now, but I don't have the motherfucker. If you don't have any words of wisdom for me I'm going home and shave.'

He revved his motor a little, but he didn't drive off.

'So, what's new in your life?' he asked.

'Oh, not much,' Duane said. 'I'm thinking of building another room on the cabin, but it's just in the planning stage so far.'

'That place *is* a little confining,' Bobby Lee said. 'If you're interested in taking in a boarder I'd like to apply for the position.'

'Why?' Duane asked. 'You don't seem like the rural type, to me.'

'I wasn't, till I lost my testicle,' Bobby Lee said. 'But I lost that sucker and I'm tired of being the subject of ridicule. I'd rather sit out on a hill and just be weird, like you.'

'Then we'd both be the subject of ridicule,' Duane pointed out. 'Me for being weird and you for having one ball.'

'You didn't say whether I could be a boarder or not,' Bobby Lee said.

'I wasn't planning to build on a bedroom,' Duane said. 'What I had in mind was more a workroom. I'm thinking of doing a little woodwork.'

'Woodwork?' Bobby Lee asked. 'You mean carpentry?'

'No, I mean woodwork,' Duane said. 'You know, building cabinets, or maybe carving animals.'

'Shit, you are weird,' Bobby Lee said, and drove off.

# 30

That night Duane dreamed the calf-roping dream for the fourth time – each time he dreamed it, it seemed to get sharper, more intense, more vivid; and each time he dreamed it, the ache inside him when the dream was over seemed to get worse. This time he saw the calf so clearly that he could almost have counted its hairs. He felt the dash of the well-trained roping horse and saw the loop he threw with perfect clarity. The horse was correctly positioned, the throw was perfect, the rope settled loosely over the calf's head – but instead of the calf hitting the end of the rope and flipping over backward so that it could be quickly tied with the piggin string Duane held between his teeth, something odd happened. The calf's head became Jacy Farrow's head – and then the rope dissolved, Jacy faded, and the calf trotted on across the arena, unroped. Shortly afterward, even as the trotting calf was still visible in his mind, Duane began to wake up, with a deep ache inside him. He felt he had rather not go to sleep again if it meant that he might dream the calf-roping dream another time. The fact that Jacy's face had come into it right at the end of the dream was a new element that he could not account for. He would not even have tried to account for it had it not occurred to him in conjunction with the calf-roping dream, which he had now dreamed four times. He and Jacy had been high school sweethearts, then friends again in their middle age. Though very beautiful, Jacy had not had a very happy life, and now she was dead and frozen, somewhere in the ice of the Arctic. Of course, it was normal enough for dead people to appear in dreams – it was just the fact that Jacy's head had taken the place of the calf's head that had seemed odd.

Beyond that, the thing that was even more odd was that he had kept appearing in his dream as a roper, when he had never roped in his life. So why the dreams, and the ache after the dreams? And why, when he was in excellent position to catch the calf, did he always miss?

Duane didn't know much about psychiatry, but he did know, or had heard, that dream interpretation was one of the things psychiatrists did. Probably the woman he was going to see on Friday could come up with a reasonable explanation for his dream, if there was one. Dreams didn't have to be reasonable – he understood that.

Even so, throughout the day that ensued after his painful dream, Duane wavered about keeping his appointment with Honor Carmichael. Four or five times in the course of the day he decided he would walk over to Jody's and ask him to cancel the appointment. The only thing that stopped him was the fear that such a cancellation would embarrass Jody with his daughter. If he canceled now it was undoubtedly going to seem lame to both Carmichaels. They would probably consider it hick behavior – and it probably would be hick behavior. He had no reason to be the least bit nervous about going in and talking to Jody Carmichael's daughter for an hour. She was a trained doctor – highly trained, evidently. Also, he did not consider himself to be in dire straits. He was not going to be examined for cancer, or some life-threatening illness. He just sometimes felt a little gloomy and, sometimes, grew more angry than the occasion warranted. It might be that all he really needed was a change of scene.

Nonetheless, as Friday approached, Duane grew more and more nervous. He put off walking to Jody's until it was too late to call. On Wednesday night he went to bed early thinking that if he woke up early he could hoof it over to the Corners and cancel the appointment in time for Honor Carmichael to slip someone else into his slot. Some suffering soul could then benefit from his dereliction.

Thursday morning, though still strongly in the mood to cancel the appointment, he didn't spring up and start walking to Jody's, or to Thalia either. There was a pay phone outside the Kwik-Sack he could have used.

But he didn't go anywhere. He spent almost the whole day sitting in his lawn chair, covered by his poncho. Though he could move his arms and legs he felt in some sense paralyzed. All action seemed equally difficult to him. Though he didn't know what was wrong, he did know that he had been lying to himself to think that all he needed was a change of scene. The fact was, he felt awful. The day was neither really sunny nor fully overcast; it was neither really cold nor comfortably warm. Duane felt just as mixed as the weather, just as ambivalent. He was neither desperate nor comfortable, neither at war nor at peace. All appetites seemed to have left him. Lunchtime came and went – it was not until the sun finally dipped down in orange brilliance out of the gray skies to the west that he got up and went in to heat up a bowl of soup – and then he only ate half of it. He felt so listless that he doubted he could walk seventeen or eighteen miles to his appointment.

At three in the morning, though, Duane came wide awake, with no anxiety or dream ache to slow him down. He shaved and put on his last clean change of clothes – the matter of how laundry was to get done was one he had not really addressed since starting his new life. By three-thirty he was out the door, though not out of it as fast as Shorty, who shot out into the darkness barking fiercely. Probably a coon or a skunk was wandering somewhere nearby.

Duane felt that a day had come that he had long been waiting for, without quite knowing that he was waiting. He felt purposeful again and walked at a good clip, so good that he had gone over three miles before Shorty caught up with him, and ten miles before he stopped to take a leak. It was a sunny day, just chill enough that he didn't overheat. As he approached the city he began to pass defunct oil business establishments, old pipe yards, old machine shops, disused oil pumps, old trucks, abandoned storage tanks, all rusting away in weedy ugliness.

By midmorning he was walking east along the Seymour highway, with the few squatty buildings of downtown Wichita Falls dead ahead. A steady stream of traffic flowed by them but nobody stopped to ask him if he needed a ride. Evidently the fact that he had a dog with him convinced them he was on a social amble of some kind.

By 10:30 A.M. he was already so close to his destination that he sat down on a bus bench to contemplate his next move. He was so early that he felt at loose ends, with four and a half hours to kill before his appointment. He was still more or less in the country, but not by much. Another half mile and he would be in the suburbs proper. Two miles more and he would be at Dr Carmichael's door.

Just down the road from where he sat he noticed a dilapidated motel called the Stingaree Courts. He had passed the place many times in his pickup without really giving it a glance. The neon Vacancy sign, which was not lit, had come loose from its wiring and was dangling straight down – a passerby would have to tilt his head to read it. Shorty had his tongue hanging out. He looked bedraggled and thirsty.

'That motel looks like it's about our speed,' he said to the dog. 'Let's proceed over there and see if they'll rent us a room.'

When he entered the motel office he left Shorty nosing around in the parking lot. Duane was hoping the people in the motel wouldn't associate him with the dog, but that hope was soon dashed. The skinny, sharp-eyed old woman behind the counter had no trouble making the connection.

'Is that your dog out there eating gravel?' she asked.

'Yes,' Duane admitted. He couldn't come up with a ready lie.

'Does it bite niggers?' the woman asked.

'No, it just bites babies,' Duane assured her.

'The reason I ask, our maid's a nigger,' the old woman said. 'Did you want a room?'

'I sure do,' he said. 'I'll be staying in town overnight.'

She shoved a registration card toward him, which he promptly filled out. There was a space on the card which read, *Auto: Make, License Plate, State.* Duane left that part blank.

The old woman took the card and frowned.

'You didn't put down your car information,' she said. 'We have to have it so the police can identify you quick if they have to come and grab you.'

'I didn't come in a car, I came on foot,' Duane said.

'Well, I'm Marcie Meeks and I never heard of such,' the old woman said. She came out from behind the counter and scanned the parking lot carefully.

'On foot from where?' she asked.

'On foot from my home,' Duane told her. 'It's a few miles away. I'm supposed to walk for my health, when the distance isn't too great. Doctor's orders.'

Marcie Meeks looked him up and down.

'No luggage, I see,' she said, suspicion in her eyes.

'Well, I brought a toothbrush,' Duane said. 'I'm here for a doctor's appointment. I intend to walk back home tomorrow.

'There's no law against walking,' he added, seeing that the woman was still suspicious.

'No, but there's a law against not putting in no car information when you check into a motel,' she said. 'I'll have to ask Daddy if it's okay to let you have a room. We're not looking for no trouble with the law.'

'Why would there be?' Duane asked. 'I told you, I'm just walking for my health.'

'I better ask Daddy anyway,' the woman said. 'I'm not too sure about that dog, either. He looks like the kind of dog who would bite a nigger.'

Duane waited patiently, and the wait was not brief. He was about to give up and look for another motel when Marcie Meeks came back, trailed by a large old man in a dirty bathrobe and ancient house slippers. His hair wasn't combed and he had the stub of a cigar stuck in his mouth.

'What's this about walking?' he asked.

Duane took the patient approach, though he considered that he had already expended about enough patience on a place as run down as the Stingaree Courts.

'I live a few miles away,' he said. 'I've been advised by my doctor to exercise regularly and walking was the exercise he recommended. I'm here for a doctor's appointment. I thought I'd stay overnight and walk home tomorrow.'

The old man did not have a friendly expression. But the motel was on the wild side of town – the two Meekses, if indeed they were husband and wife, had no doubt seen some things that might induce an attitude of suspicion.

'You could be an illegal alien or from some place like Byeloruss, for all we know,' the old man said. 'A lot of the criminal element has been sneaking in lately from Byeloruss.'

'No, I'm from Thalia, Texas, I'm not an illegal alien,' Duane said. 'I own five or six cars and several trucks. If you don't want to give me a room that's fine, but I don't intend to put up with an interrogation just because I'm out walking for my health.'

'It's not that we're suspicious of you personally, Mr Moore,' the old woman said. 'But a man walking along a public highway with a dog is not a common sight. This is pickup country, mostly.'

'You're right, but I'm a free citizen, and I have a right to walk if I want to – am I correct?' he said.

'It's mainly bums and hippies that walk, or else old folks that have had their licenses taken away because of the Alzheimer's,' the man said. 'You don't fit that description, so you can have a room.'

'I'm not from Byeloruss, either,' Duane added. 'I'm an American citizen, exercising my right to travel in whatever manner I please.'

Though it had not been much of a confrontation, he found that he was shaking.

'The rooms are thirty-two dollars,' the old woman said.

Duane laid the money on the counter.

'That's in case I leave before you're up,' he said.

The old man looked surprised.

'I'd like to see somebody leave before Marcie's up,' he said. 'We've been out here on this godforsaken highway for thirty-eight years and nobody's ever left before Marcie was up.'

'There's always a first time,' Duane said, taking his key. The Meekses watched him without hostility, but without friendliness, either.

'The ice machine's broken, you'll have to do without ice,' Marcie Meeks told him, as he left.

'I won't need ice,' Duane said, a statement that turned out not to be true. His room was even more squalid than he had expected, and he hadn't been expecting much. The mattress was so sunken in that it seemed more like a hammock, and there was no handle on the cold water faucet in the small cramped shower. He turned on the TV, which seemed to be stuck on the porno channel. Two not very attractive people were having sex in vivid color. Duane, embarrassed, tried to change channels but the channel changer didn't work and neither did the volume control. The only way to avoid the sight of loud and vivid sex was to turn off the TV, which he did. He had left the door open, to air out the hot little room – immediately, as if summoned by the sounds of sex, a young whore appeared in the doorway, a girl with a stringy, East Texas look about her.

'Hi, honey, I'm your neighbor,' she informed him. 'You don't have to just watch sex on TV, you could be doing it for real.'

'Oh, no thanks,' Duane said. 'I'm just in town to see my doctor.'

'Shoot, for forty dollars I bet I could make you feel so good you wouldn't need to see a doctor – you could start cutting down on those doctor bills,' the girl said.

'It's just a checkup,' Duane said, feeling awkward.

'Well, I'm Gay-lee, three doors down,' she said. 'Just remember me if you get an urge or an itch. Oh hi, puppy, I didn't see you.'

Shorty, who had been nosing around in the parking lot, slunk in while the young whore was standing in the doorway.

When she left, Duane decided he not only needed ice, he needed whiskey. There was a liquor store a hundred yards or so down the highway; he shut Shorty in the room and started for it. A few doors north of his room a rough-looking young man sat in a battered Buick with the doors open. He had lots of hair, some of which was stuffed under a dirty dozer cap.

'Howdy, cowboy,' he said. 'Want to take a ride over the moon?'

'What?' Duane asked.

'Got meth, got coke, got speedballs,' the young man said. 'Man, I got a drugstore – you name it.'

'Good-bye is what I'll name it,' Duane said.

When he was coming back Duane saw Marcie Meeks, out on the far edge of the parking lot with a lawn edger, clipping a weed here and there. The west side of the parking lot was a wild tangle of tall weeds, short brush, sunflower stalks, and the like – not the sort of foliage you could eliminate with a lawn edger. Duane was still annoyed by his interrogation. He thought about going over to the old woman and pointing out that she had a drug dealer and a prostitute in her motel – and he had only met two guests. But he didn't do it. The old woman looked too forlorn, wandering through the weeds with her inadequate tool.

Duane took a shower – fortunately the hot water was only tepid, because he had no cold water to cut it with. Then he lay on the sagging bed and sipped bourbon out of a little plastic cup. He made another unsuccessful effort to tune the TV to any channel but the sex channel; when that didn't work he merely lay on the bed.

Finally the hour of his appointment drew near. Duane wanted to give himself at least an hour to walk to the doctor's office – he didn't want to be late. He was a little fuzzy from the whiskey but expected to walk off the fuzziness on the way to town. He tried to imagine what he might say to the psychiatrist, and also tried to imagine what sort of questions she might ask him, but both efforts were futile. He had no idea what he was going to say, or what Jody's daughter, Honor Carmichael, might ask. He felt as if he were setting off on a big adventure – an adventure of a sort he had not planned, and didn't know if he was really ready for.

'I'm leaving you here for your own protection,' he said to Shorty. 'I doubt they allow dogs in psychiatrists' offices.'

When he left the motel the whore and the drug dealer were

lounging around the latter's old Buick. Business, for both of them, was slow. Gay-lee waved at Duane, but he didn't wave back.

# 31

Honor Carmichael's offices were in a large, nicely kept white stucco house, on a pleasant street with lots of trees in the yards. There were flower beds all round the white stucco house. It had only taken Duane thirty minutes to walk there from the Stingaree Courts – he felt that he had walked from one world to another. The contrast was so sharp as to be confusing. Which world did he belong in? Or did he belong in either?

He went on into the white stucco house and announced himself twenty minutes early. Usually doctors had you fill out forms, when you saw them for the first time. Duane expected to have to put down his whole medical history, but in this case a nice young woman merely got his address and phone numbers, plus his insurance information, and asked him what medications he was on; then she told him to have a seat. There were heaps of magazines on the tables. Duane picked up an issue of the *Smithsonian* and was reading an article on bats when the receptionist called his name.

At first he thought the receptionist just wanted more information – it couldn't be time for his appointment, already. It seemed to him he had scarcely sat down. Anxiety rose in him like liquid in a straw, but the smiling young woman didn't notice or care. She led him down a short hall to a room where a tall, grave woman waited. The room had lots of plants in it. There was no desk – just several comfortable chairs and a long couch. The woman, Honor Carmichael, was older than he had expected. Her hair was graying at the temples.

'Hello, Mr Moore,' she said, offering her hand. 'I'm Dr Carmichael.'

'Hello. I know your father,' Duane said. He felt absolutely tongue-tied. Honor Carmichael had a nice tan. Either she had just been someplace where it was sunny, or she worked in her yard a lot.

She didn't respond to his mention of her father. Duane didn't know what to do next. Was he supposed to lie on the couch, or just sit in one of the chairs? Where was she going to sit? It was all different from how he had thought it would be – he could not even remember what he *had* thought it would be. Honor Carmichael was comfortably but simply dressed. She didn't have on a white coat or seem like any of the doctors he had ever met before – still, he felt completely intimidated by her. She had a long face, like her father's, only hers was more attractive.

'As you can see there's a couch and there's some chairs,' she said.

Duane had a vague memory of having been told that people were expected to lie on couches when they saw psychiatrists – the couch in the room was clearly meant for stretching out, not sitting. He felt completely awkward, out of his depth.

'Well, where would you like me?' he managed to ask.

'Where you think you'd be most comfortable – most relaxed,' she said.

Duane took a chair, a reclining chair with a comfortable leather seat. He had once owned a Cadillac with a seat as comfortable as the chair, and had always regretted trading the car off, mainly because he liked the seat.

When he sat, Honor Carmichael sat too – or Dr Carmichael, rather. He had to remind himself that he had come to see her because she was a doctor – not because she was Jody Carmichael's daughter.

There was a long silence. Dr Carmichael seemed perfectly relaxed, perfectly content to wait until he began to talk about what was on his mind; but, at the moment, his mind was blank. He had no idea where to start.

'I guess I don't really know how this is supposed to work,' he said finally. 'I've never been to a psychiatrist before.'

'Why do you think you need to see one now?' she said. 'Let's start with that.'

'Well, people think I'm depressed,' Duane said. 'My wife thinks it, and other people too.'

'Do *you* think you're depressed, Mr Moore?' she asked. He noticed she had very large eyes, and long fingers as well as a long face. She wore a ring with a green stone in it.

'I guess everybody's depressed, sometime,' Duane said. 'I doubt I'm that much more depressed than the next man. But people keep mentioning it so I thought I better ask an expert.'

'What have you done to convince all these people that you're depressed?' she asked.

'It's mainly the walking and the fact that I'm living by myself now, in a little cabin,' he said.

'What do you mean, the walking?'

'I parked my pickup nearly three weeks ago,' he said. 'Since then I've walked everywhere I go. I moved to a little cabin on some property I own – and since then I've done a lot of sitting and a lot of walking.

'I walked here today,' he added, after a pause.

'Walked here from how far?' she asked.

'I judge it to be about eighteen miles,' Duane said. 'I started early – about three-thirty.'

The doctor looked him over – if she was surprised by what she had been told she didn't show it.

'You don't look winded,' she said. 'That's a fair distance to walk – you must be in pretty good physical health.'

'I think I'm in good health,' Duane said. 'Some things make me madder than they used to – that's the main difference I notice.'

'What sort of things make you madder?'

'People littering the landscape,' he said. 'They just throw their junk off bridges, into the creek beds. Most of these little creeks don't have much water in them. The stuff don't float away. It just sits there. Sights like junk in the creeks upset me.'

'What do you do about it?' she asked. 'How do you manifest your anger?'

'I mainly just clean it up, if I can,' he said. 'But it makes me angry, and it didn't used to.'

Dr Carmichael didn't change expression.

'What about your parents? Either of them alive?'

'No, both dead,' Duane said.

He went on to explain that his father had been killed in a rig explosion when he was five. His mother had taken in laundry for a living; his grandmother on his mother's side had lived with them until she died – their house was so small and cramped that, as soon as he was able to work and support himself, he had moved out and taken a room in a boardinghouse. His mother, never happy, broken by his father's death, had faded out when she was only fifty-seven. Duane was in the process of explaining that his father had been good to him – he could still remember the smell of his father's work shirts when he would come and sit by him after work; they smelled of starch and cigarettes and sweat – when the doctor stood up and smiled at him.

'I'm sorry, the hour's up,' she said.

Duane was shocked. For a moment he couldn't believe it. It seemed to him that he had only just begun to talk a few minutes before. But when he looked at his watch he saw, to his amazement, that the doctor was right. Somehow, before he had given more than the briefest account of his life, the hour had passed.

It disturbed him – he felt it was wrong to have to cut himself off so abruptly. He liked the doctor and would have preferred to stay in the nice chair whose seat reminded him of his old Cadillac, talking for a long, long time.

'See Natalie ... we'll fit you in on Monday, if that's convenient,' Dr Carmichael said.

Duane stood up – he suddenly felt desperate for information, for some word of counsel or analysis from the doctor.

'That time really passed quick,' he said, feeling very awkward. 'Do you think I'm depressed?'

Dr Carmichael made no attempt to answer the question.

'Natalie will schedule you for Monday,' she said. 'I'll see you next week, Mr Moore.'

# 32

When Duane stepped out of Honor Carmichael's office he still had a sharp sense of having been interrupted. He had just begun to talk about his life to his doctor – it was confusing to have to break off the story so soon; confusing and disturbing. Though he couldn't remember much of what he said to the doctor, the fact that he was finally saying it – indeed, gushing it out – was such a powerful relief that the interruption, for the first few minutes, was nearly intolerable. He couldn't remember the doctor asking more than one or two questions. He had mainly just sat and talked about his parents. It seemed to him he had told the doctor more about his parents in a few minutes than he had told Karla in the forty years of their marriage.

In the anteroom he felt confused. The doctor had told him to see the receptionist, but the receptionist wasn't there. No one was there. He didn't know whether to leave or to wait. Before he could decide the young woman – Natalie – popped back in.

'Sorry, I was just checking the doctor's schedule,' she said. 'We can see you again at three on Monday, if that's convenient.'

'That's fine,' he said.

'How would you like to pay?' she asked. 'It's one hundred and ninety dollars.'

The office seemed so much like a home that Duane had forgotten that it was a kind of hospital – he was a patient, not a guest. He still had the cash from his poker winnings, so he counted out the money, took the little card with his appointment noted on it, and went out into the March sunlight. In his head he was still talking to Dr Carmichael, and he continued to talk to her until he had walked a couple of miles.

Then the one-way interior conversation stopped and a feeling of bleakness and loneliness took its place. He was no longer on Dr Carmichael's pleasant street, either in his head or otherwise. The borders of the road were weedy and strewn with trash, and a constant stream of pickups and oil trucks passed him as he trudged back out the Seymour highway, toward the Stingaree Courts.

About a mile from the Courts he passed a tavern called the Silver Slipper, an establishment every bit as run down as the motel. The sign that spelled out the name had several bulbs burned out. Two or three pickups and a familiar-looking Buick were parked in front of the tavern.

Duane felt shaky, and his legs were leaden. Walking all the way back to the cabin was out of the question – even making it back to the motel was going to be a struggle. It was a weekend – he had meant to go home and look off his hill for two days – but somehow his short conversation with Dr Carmichael had sapped his strength. He decided to go in the tavern, have a drink, and give his legs a rest.

Sure enough, when he went into the Silver Slipper he spotted the young drug dealer with the long hair, sitting with Gay-lee at a booth near the back of the bar. A couple of roughnecks were slamming a tiny puck around on the miniature hockey game.

The bartender, a large, fleshy man, had a white dishcloth draped over one shoulder. Duane sat on a bar stool. It had rarely felt so good just to sit and take a weight off his legs. The bartender, a man about his age, looked vaguely familiar.

'You don't look very peppy, hoss,' the bartender said. 'Is it allergies, or did you just lose someone near and dear?'

Duane didn't know what the man was talking about, but when he put a hand to his face he discovered that his cheeks were wet. Either he had been crying or his eyes were watering from some irritant he hadn't noticed.

'I guess it's the damn ragweed,' he said. 'Could I have a bourbon on the rocks?'

The bartender squirted a jigger into a shot glass and poured the whiskey over ice.

'You're Duane Moore,' the man said. 'You don't remember me, but I remember you.'

Duane looked closely, but still couldn't place the man.

'I played right guard for Iowa Park once upon a time,' the bartender said. 'You were in the backfield for Thalia. We collided on the line in nineteen fifty-four. I stopped you from scoring a touchdown but broke my collarbone in the process. I'm Bub Tucker.'

He held out his hand and Duane shook it.

'Well, you did look familiar, but the damn ragweed's screwed up my vision, I guess,' he said.

Though the man was friendly, Duane wished he had picked a different bar to drink in, just any bar where not a soul knew him. The only person in the world he wanted to talk to was Dr Carmichael, and he especially didn't want to have to relive a high school football game with a man whose collarbone he had broken long ago.

'That collarbone never healed right,' Bub Tucker revealed. 'Lucky thing.'

'Why lucky?' Duane asked.

'Kept me out of the service,' Bub said. 'Accident prone as I am generally, I'd have got killed in Korea or somewhere if they'd let me in the service.'

'That's one way to look at it,' Duane said.

Bub Tucker, once he had reminded Duane of their one moment of contact, seemed no more inclined to reminisce than Duane was. He drifted off to polish glasses, chewing on a toothpick, only drifting back, silently, to refill Duane's glass when Duane nodded at him and held it up.

Duane drank four whiskeys, spreading them over an hour and a half. There was a basketball game on the TV above the bar, but Duane only rarely looked up at it. He sipped his bourbon and crunched the ice in his glass, gradually growing calmer and less shaky as the whiskey took effect. The last time he could remember feeling so shaky was when Karla almost bled to death from an undiagnosed ectopic pregnancy.

That had been a truly scary thing. His wife had been within an hour of death. And yet, walking along the Seymour highway, he had felt just as shaky, though all he had done in this case was talk to a nice doctor for an hour.

'Good to see you, Duane – you ought to get some allergy pills for the ragweed,' Bub Tucker said, when Duane put a bill on the bar and got up to leave. 'Come back to see us sometime.'

'I expect I will – sorry about that collarbone,' Duane said.

Bub Tucker smiled and polished another glass.

'Hey, that's just football,' he said.

# 33

Back at the Stingaree Courts, Duane stayed awake only long enough to drink one more whiskey and to allow Shorty to run around the parking lot for twenty minutes, lifting his leg against fence posts and dead weeds.

Then he took his shirt off, fell back on the sagging mattress, and didn't wake again until the middle of the next morning, when the dog began to whine to go out.

Duane, who rarely slept more than five hours a night, saw that he had just slept nearly fifteen hours – and he still felt that he could sleep some more. He had intended to go to the cabin for the weekend, but quickly abandoned that plan. The eighteen-mile walk that had seemed easy only the day before now became as hard to imagine as climbing Mount Everest. He didn't understand what had happened to him. Somehow a brief talk with a nice doctor had weakened him to the point where he couldn't walk home – or, really, walk anywhere. Normally he would have hated the thought of spending the whole weekend at the Stingaree Courts, with no cold water and a TV that showed only sex, but his lethargy was so profound that he didn't care. Perhaps it meant that he *was* depressed, though he could not remember that Dr Carmichael had used that word at all. At the moment he felt weak, tired, and utterly without appetite or ambition. He didn't want to do anything – the one prospect that meant something was the prospect of seeing the doctor again at three on Monday.

During the long afternoon the thoughts that flickered through Duane's mind as he lay in the hammocklike bed and dozed were inconsistent and disconnected. Several times it occurred to him that he could probably find the Thoreau book at the local bookstore, which was probably about two miles away, but he made no move to walk to the bookstore or even to call and ask if they had the book and would hold it for him. He made no move to do anything until late afternoon, when he began to feel unshaven and dirty. He needed a razor and various toiletries and had begun to feel guilty about Shorty, who had had no food since they had arrived in town.

Finally, as the afternoon was waning, Duane got up. He had decided to ask Marcie Meeks if there might be a better room he could rent – one, at least, where cold water came out of the shower.

When he opened the door to go out he almost walked right into the substantial bosom of a large black woman, who had been about to knock on his door. She had a thin towel and an even thinner wash rag in her hand, plus a tiny bar of soap.

'You all need fresh towels?' she asked, as Shorty sprinted out of the room and went running out into the weed patch.

'I'm Sis,' she added. 'I'd change your sheets but we're low on sheets this weekend.'

'That's okay, I haven't dirtied my sheets much,' Duane said.

'That little dog don't bite black people, do he?' Sis asked, eyeing Shorty with some suspicion.

'No, he doesn't bite grown-ups at all, he just likes to bite babies,' Duane assured her. 'If you're the maid could you tell me if there's a better room to be had in this motel?'

At that the large woman looked wary.

'Better how?' she asked.

'There's no cold water and the TV in this room won't get but one channel,' he said. 'I'm Duane, by the way. I guess I might be living here for a while.'

'You ain't the police, is you?' Sis asked, still more wary.

'No, I'm in the oil business,' Duane said.

He knew there were motels in Wichita Falls that offered a great deal more in the way of creature comforts than the Stingaree Courts, but he was at the Stingaree Courts and didn't feel like moving.

'Well, there's the honeymoon suite,' Sis said. 'Got a water bed. It's high money, though. You talking about luxury when you talking about water beds.'

'I think I'll check it out, even though I'm not on my honeymoon,' Duane said.

Marcie Meeks was behind the registration desk, watching an old Tab Hunter movie on a little TV when Duane walked in. Natalie Wood was in the movie too.

'It looks like I might be staying several days,' Duane said. 'I wonder if I could move to a better room. The cold water in my shower won't turn on, and the TV won't get but one channel.'

'You can't have everything for thirty-two dollars a night,' Marcie said – but she said it sadly rather than angrily. No doubt the state of things at the Stingaree Courts depressed her too.

'The maid said there was a honeymoon suite,' Duane said. 'I think I might like to switch to that one if it's unoccupied.'

Marcie Meeks emitted a dry sound that might have been a laugh.

'The last time we had honeymooners here was the night Cassius Clay knocked out Sonny Liston,' she said. 'Are you old enough to remember that?'

'Just barely,' Duane said. 'But I'll take the suite anyway, if that's agreeable.'

'I doubt Daddy would object,' she said. 'It's forty-eight dollars a night. We're still paying off that water bed.'

Duane paid for two nights.

'I'll just ask you to sign another card, since you're moving,' Marcie said. 'We need to keep close track of you in case the police come looking.'

'Get many visits from the police?' he asked.

'Too many,' Marcie said. 'I despise police. I was in jail once myself, for a crime I never committed.'

Duane waited, expecting Marcie Meeks to describe the crime she hadn't committed, but she said no more about it.

'You look like a married man,' she said, looking him over. 'What do I tell your wife when she shows up?'

'I doubt she'll show up, but if she does she can probably find me by smell,' Duane said. 'You don't have to get involved.'

'She'll show up, I expect,' Marcie said. 'Wives usually show up.'

Sis, the large maid, was just coming out of his old room when he walked by.

'It's the honeymoon suite for me,' he said. 'I hope the shower works.'

'Oh, it'll work,' Sis said. 'Maybe that water bed bring you luck. Maybe you'll find a bride.'

# 34

The room with the water bed was larger, the shower worked, and the TV got several channels. The water bed was comfortable, though it did emit a faint, unpleasant smell that Duane could not at first identify. He thought it smelled a little bit like fish, but how could there be fish in a water bed?

The overall improvement in his living quarters energized him enough that he could walk to the nearest convenience store and buy some toiletries and a large sack of dog food. He used his plastic ice bucket as a dog dish, and Shorty was soon wolfing down the dog food.

Duane lay on the water bed for the rest of the afternoon and all through the night, watching basketball in a hazy, not very involved way. There was no traffic in the parking lot at all – out his window he could see a long stretch of West Texas prairie. He could see almost back to where his cabin was – the contemplation of such a distance made him tired.

Duane lay on the water bed, drowsing and waking, then drowsing some more, for another fifteen hours. Now and then he sipped a little whiskey. There was a telephone by his bed but he didn't touch it. He thought of the Thoreau book, but didn't pick up the phone to call the bookshop.

Several times it occurred to him that he ought to call his family. Dickie or Nellie or even Karla might have gone to the cabin to check on him, found him missing, and drawn dark conclusions. They might conclude that he had left the country, or been the victim of foul play. If Karla knew he was missing she might conclude that he was living elsewhere, with a mystery woman her spies had failed to detect.

Though he had no desire to cause his family distress, Duane did not pick up the phone to inform them of his whereabouts. For reasons he couldn't fathom, he felt completely motiveless. He had no desire to do anything. He didn't want to eat, didn't want to gamble, didn't want to read, didn't want to talk. He seemed to have lost the ability to follow through on even the simplest plan. It wouldn't take twenty seconds to call home and let his family know that he was okay, but even twenty seconds of direct effort seemed more than he was capable of. Calling his family would be a normal thing to do, and it shouldn't be hard – but for some reason it had come to seem irrelevant.

The only thing that *was* relevant, really, was his appointment on Monday afternoon with Dr Carmichael. He could go back to the pleasant office and continue talking to the doctor. An undertaking that he had once been extremely dubious of – psychiatry – had somehow become the only thing he had to live for.

On Monday morning he woke up worrying that the hour would again be too brief – that he would scarcely start talking before he would have to leave. He tried to order his thoughts in such a way that he could ask about or speak about things he really needed to discuss with the doctor, but his attempt to form a mental list of priorities was a total failure. He didn't really know what he needed to talk about most: in a way he needed to talk about *everything*, but how could you squeeze everything into an hour's conversation?

He had scarcely moved all weekend – he didn't even know whether he could walk to the doctor's office. Fortunately there was a phone book in his room – he took down the number of a local taxi, in case he became so weak he had to call for assistance.

Around noon he showered and cleaned up as best he could, but the fact was he had been wearing the same clothes since early Friday morning; the laundry problem, which had seemed minor enough when he was living in the cabin, had begun to seem major now that he had taken up residence at the Stingaree Courts. Somehow or other he was soon going to have to provide himself with some clean clothes. There was a twenty-four-hour Wal-Mart not far from the motel. He could have walked there anytime during the weekend and bought clean clothes, but he had failed to do so, and now it was Monday noon and too late. His shirt was not exactly filthy, but neither was it exactly clean.

Duane was halfway to town before he concluded that one reason he felt so weak and tired was because he hadn't eaten anything since Friday. He had remembered to feed the dog, but had forgotten to feed himself. Fortunately there was a pancake house only a few blocks from the doctor's office. As he was walking to it Duane remembered that he had a small packet of peanuts in his shirt pocket – he had purchased them at the liquor store when he went to get whiskey and ice, but had forgotten about them during his weekend of fasting.

He munched the peanuts as he made for the pancake house. He took a booth and ordered a big breakfast; it was two in the afternoon but any time was breakfast time at the pancake house. Once the food came he found that he wasn't particularly hungry – the idea of food appealed to him more than the reality. His farm fresh eggs and crisp bacon went mostly untouched, though he did eat a few slices of toast as he drank his coffee. The desire for food had left him, along with the desire for almost everything else. Guilty about not cleaning his plate, he left a big tip for the waitress and then went out and walked around and around the block until it became time to present himself at Dr Carmichael's door.

# 35

The minute Duane turned into Dr Carmichael's street he began to feel better. Just the sight of her simple, well-designed house, with its nicely kept lawn and orderly flower beds, made him feel more at rest inside. The house and the yard suggested order and peace of a sort that could be achieved if one paid close attention to the harmonies of life.

There was no one in the waiting room when he arrived – he had come twenty minutes early, hoping he could finish the article about bats. He had almost finished it when the young receptionist, Natalie, appeared, smiled, and ushered him into Dr Carmichael's office.

This time the doctor didn't shake hands when he came in, though she did smile.

'Hello,' she said, indicating that he was to take a seat in the same comfortable chair.

Duane was determined to make a quick start this time, and to keep in mind the fact that the clock was ticking.

'I guess I've been needing this more than I realized,' he said. 'I spent the whole weekend doing nothing – just waiting for it to be time to come for my appointment.'

He stopped and looked at the doctor.

'Do you think that means I'm real depressed?' he asked.

Dr Carmichael regarded him solemnly, with her quiet, grave expression, before she answered.

'It's often a relief to have someone who really listens to what you have to say,' she said finally. 'That's one reason why there are psychiatrists. I don't know yet how depressed you are, or whether you're depressed at all, but if you feel the need to see me strongly enough to put your life on hold, then I imagine we need to meet more than once a week, if you can manage it.'

'Oh, I can manage it,' Duane said. 'Right now I don't have anything else *to* manage.'

'Then probably we should try four times a week, until we learn a little bit more about how you're feeling,' the doctor said.

'Fine with me – or five times a week, if that's not too many,' Duane said, immediately.

'It *is* too many,' the doctor said firmly. 'This process can be tiring at first. Let's stick to four.'

Duane nodded. He felt acutely conscious that his shirt wasn't really clean – he wondered if the doctor noticed that he was wearing the same clothes he had worn on the first visit.

'I take it you didn't walk in the eighteen miles this morning?' Dr Carmichael said.

'Nope, I stayed in a motel,' Duane said.

'Round trip to my office four times a week is about one hundred and forty-four miles, if I'm figuring right,' the doctor said. 'I like to walk myself but I doubt I could manage that.'

'I don't need to go home much,' Duane said.

Dr Carmichael looked at him silently for what seemed a long time. She wasn't tense or threatening – in fact seemed quite relaxed. She kept a notepad in her lap but so far he had not seen her write on it.

'Tell me about the walking,' she said. 'I'd like to know how it started and any thoughts you might have about it.'

Duane told her everything he could remember about the day he had started walking. He had had coffee at a café in Wichita Falls, driven up into southern Oklahoma to talk to one of his crews, driven back home, parked the pickup in the carport, went in his house, hid the keys in the old cracked cup, and walked away. There was nothing very unusual about any of it. His own narration seemed boring to him.

'There was no big reason for me to walk off like that,' he said. 'I don't blame my wife for being upset. I've never done anything like that, and we've been married forty years.

'There was no big reason,' he repeated. 'I just decided to do it, and when I did it, it felt right.'

'That may mean that there *was* a big reason for you to start walking,' the doctor said. 'It just may be that the reason didn't involve your wife. Marital conflict isn't the only reason why people take sudden turns in their lives.'

Duane had not thought of that – at least hadn't thought of it in such simple terms.

'It doesn't seem to have presented any big practical problems, at least not until you started having to keep these appointments,' the doctor said.

'Well, laundry,' he said. 'I need to arrange to get some clean clothes, and I have to be sure to keep food for my dog.'

The doctor looked at him with interest when he mentioned the dog.

'You have a dog with you, at your motel?' she asked.

'Yes, Shorty,' he said. 'He's a blue heeler.'

'Bring him tomorrow, would you?' she said. 'We have nothing against dogs here. You can bring him right into the session.'

Her statement took Duane by surprise. Why would he want to bring Shorty with him to the psychiatrist? The thought of having Shorty there while he tried to talk to the doctor was disquieting, somehow. One thing he liked about the sessions so far was a sense of the privacy of the occasion. With Shorty there it wouldn't be quite as private, although Shorty, of course, would not understand what was being said. It wouldn't be like bringing another person into the session, but it wouldn't be as private, either.

'He's not a good inside dog,' he said. 'He might get nervous and pee on something.'

'I expect we could survive that, if it happened,' the doctor said. 'But if you feel awkward about bringing him, then we won't keep him inside. We'll put him in the back yard. He can bark at my ducks.'

'You have ducks?' he asked.

'Yep, I have a nice little duck pond and four ducks,' she said.

Duane said no more, but he had decided already just to forget Shorty when it came time for his next appointment. Ducks or no ducks, he didn't want to have to worry about any potential misbehavior.

'You were talking to me about your father and mother the other day,' the doctor said. 'I had to cut you off because the hour was up. I have a feeling you might have more to say about your parents.'

'No, not really,' Duane said – but then he slid right back into an account of the last fishing trip he had taken with his father just before the fatal accident. He described how patient his father had been, in instructing him how to remove a fishhook from a fish, or even from a turtle, if they happened to hook a turtle by accident.

Again, it seemed that he had barely begun before the doctor stood up and indicated to him that the hour was over.

'Don't forget to bring Shorty, when you come tomorrow,' the doctor said, as she was showing him out. 'I very much want to meet your dog.'

# 36

Once again Duane found himself outside the doctor's pleasant house, on the rock path that led through her flower beds to the street. Once again, he was dazed, confused by the fact that time seemed to pass so much more quickly when he was talking to the doctor than it did when he wasn't. Not only did he not remember much that he had said, he remembered almost nothing of what the doctor said, because she had said almost nothing. She asked about his parents and suggested that he bring his dog to the next meeting. Otherwise she had been silent.

What he mainly took away from his two hours with Dr Carmichael was how comforting her presence was. If she had formed any opinions about his condition or the turn his life had taken she hadn't revealed them to him. Probably he was foolish to hope that she *would* reveal them so soon but he still wished for at least a comment or two – something that would help him understand whether he was crazy or not. The only indication he had that she thought he needed help was that she wanted to see him four times a week. Surely she didn't see all her patients four times a week. She had been silent while he babbled, and yet all he had talked about was his father, long dead, and what he remembered of his mother's sadness – both things he assumed he had made his peace with years before.

Duane wandered back in the direction of the Stingaree Courts, but slowly. He didn't cover the miles at a steady clip, as he had become used to doing. When he began to feel tired he sat down on a curb and rested. He would never have supposed that chatting for an hour with his doctor would have such an immediate effect on his energies. The effect was so tiring that he began to wonder if he was going to be able to keep to his policy of walking everywhere. There was very little that he needed to do, yet that little – clean clothes, for example – were chores that seemed to take more energy than he had. He had either to buy new clothes or to go to Thalia and get some, and there was no way he could make it to Thalia and back on foot, as shaky as he was. Even diverting himself over to the Wal-Mart, a diversion that would only have taken an hour when he was feeling fit, seemed suddenly to be beyond his powers. He didn't know how to account for such a large, sudden change. On Friday he had easily walked eighteen miles; this was Monday and he was having trouble making it the two miles back to the Stingaree Courts.

There was a Burger King just ahead, right on his route. Remembering that·he had had almost nothing to eat for three days, he went in and ordered a milk shake and some fries. The milk shake, when it came, tasted amazingly good, and so did the fries. Before he left the Burger King he consumed two more milk shakes and another order of fries.

While he was eating it occurred to him that he must be experiencing what had once been called a nervous breakdown. That was what they had called it some years back when Sonny Crawford began to go crazy.

So far Dr Carmichael had not mentioned a nervous breakdown – she had not even confirmed that she considered him to be depressed. Duane had no idea what she thought about his mental state, but he did know that he had ceased to be able to imagine a life that didn't involve regular appointments with Dr Carmichael. The visits were holding him together – at least that was how he felt. They had replaced walking, which had been what was holding him together for the last few weeks.

When Duane finished his meal he headed on back to the motel, walking along briskly for almost a mile. Then, between one block and the next, he ran out of steam, began to feel wobbly, and experienced such overpowering fatigue that he thought he was going to have to give up and call a taxi, even though the motel was now actually in sight, not more than half a mile to the west.

He sat for a time on a large concrete block that had apparently fallen off a truck and been left by the side of the road. There was a pay phone at the liquor store where he had bought the whiskey and ice, and the liquor store was only one hundred yards away, but Duane continued to sit. He told himself it was ridiculous to call a taxi to take him half a mile – besides, for reasons he didn't understand, the principle of walking everywhere was still important to him. Something in him didn't want to give up on the principle of walking – a principle he had evolved suddenly, for no clear reason.

Finally, after spending more than half an hour sitting on the concrete block, Duane got up and walked on to the Stingaree Courts. When he opened the door Shorty immediately went out to race around the parking lot. Duane fell on the bed. He had no memory of letting Shorty back in, but someone must have, because he was there in the early morning when Duane awoke. What brought him awake was the sound of sleet peppering the window of his room. He had slept too heavily to notice that the room had grown chill during the night. The sound of the sleet brought him wide awake – he felt fresh and energetic for the first time since his initial session with Dr Carmichael. He went out into the cold dawn wind, letting the sleet pepper him for a few minutes. Maybe a cold snap was what he needed to put some spring back in his step.

While Shorty was indulging in another run around the parking lot Duane went back in and showered – only to realize, when he finished, that he had no clean clothes to put on. In his fresh, invigorated mood the lack of clean clothes was intolerable. He could put on his dirty clothes and walk through the sleety norther to the Wal-Mart but the thought irritated him, mainly because he hated going in large stores. His wardrobe was simple – for years, when his shirts or jeans began to fray, Karla simply bought him a dozen more of the same size and same brand. When, now and then, she attempted to spiff him up by buying something different, something she and the children considered fashionable, Duane simply ignored the purchases and let them hang in the closet until they found their way into one of the ambitious garage sales Karla staged every few years.

What especially irritated him at the moment was the knowledge that he had a closet full of warm, freshly ironed, neatly folded clothes in his home in Thalia, a mere twenty miles away. What he needed was for someone to bring him some of those clothes. He also had a houseful of children, each of whom made at least one trip to Wichita Falls a day, not to mention plenty of ex-employees who might be willing to bring him clothes.

Duane, unwilling to touch his dirty clothes, wrapped himself in a bedsheet and weighed his options. There were several people who could be persuaded to bring him clothes, but the one person he *didn't* want to make the delivery was Karla. If Karla were ever to glimpse the Stingaree Courts she would have no doubt that he had flipped his wig. The smell of the water bed alone would provoke wild anxiety. Karla could not stand even the slightest bad smell. If a skunk wandered within one hundred yards of their house she smelled it and retreated into her sauna, where the smell couldn't penetrate.

The one thing he didn't want to do was call his house and risk getting Karla – calling the office seemed a far better idea. With any luck Bobby Lee might be there, and Bobby Lee enjoyed espionagelike activities. Sneaking into the house and making off with a few armfuls of Duane's clothes might appeal to the criminal in him.

The sleet finally played out, but the day remained lowering and chill. Duane decided that his principal aim should be to get some clean clothes without risking Karla's appearance at the Courts. The dead-fish smell of the water bed would alone be enough to put her over the edge.

Finally, when 9 A.M. rolled around, Duane picked up the phone and called the office, hoping to catch Bobby Lee while he was still there, drinking coffee. The voice that answered when he dialed was none of the ones he had been expecting to hear – it took him a moment to realize that he had his daughter-in-law, Annette, on the line.

'Hello,' she said three times, before Duane responded.

'Well, hi,' he said. 'You startled me. What are you doing in the office this time of day?'

'Working,' Annette said. 'I run the office now, I guess you could say.'

'Gosh, that's new,' he said. 'What happened to Earlene and Ruth?'

'Dickie fired them last week and just sort of popped me into the job,' Annette said.

Duane was astonished. He had been so focused on his own problems that he had forgotten that he had put his son in charge of the oil company, a move that had already resulted in a complete turnover in office personnel.

'Fired them both?' he said, bemused.

'Yep,' Annette said. 'Earlene had the files so screwed up it's taken me four days to get them like they ought to be.'

'Filing was never Earlene's long suit,' Duane admitted.

'Earlene didn't have a long suit,' Annette said. 'Now she's thinking of suing Bobby Lee.'

'Suing him why?' he asked.

190

'Because he shot off his toe and it caused her to fall into the watercooler and get a scar,' Annette said.

What surprised him was how unsurprised Annette sounded. He had had it in his head that his whole family would have missed him by then and been frantic with worry, but evidently that wasn't the case.

'How is everybody?' he asked. 'I've been out of touch.'

'I know – we all thought you went on off to Egypt to see the pyramids,' Annette said. 'The kids all expect you to bring them back mongo souvenirs.'

'I can't go to Egypt yet, my passport's expired,' Duane said. 'I thought Karla knew that.'

'She may have just forgot – she's in Santa Fe with Babe,' Annette said. 'They got bored and awarded themselves a big shopping trip.'

Duane felt a little let down. He had been assuming that everyone missed him and was anxious about his whereabouts, when in fact nobody missed him, no one was worried; his family had just gone on with their normal lives, unconcerned that he had disappeared.

Annette even seemed a little impatient for him to get to the point of his call, which he did.

'I need to talk to Bobby Lee right away,' he said.

'He's not here but he's got his mobile,' Annette said. 'Dickie got us all cell phones – you want Bobby's number?'

'Hold on a minute until I can find a pen,' Duane said. 'Dickie sounds like he's jumped right into being a boss. First he fires the office staff and then he gets the roving staff cell phones.'

'Yes, and the best part is he's sober as a judge,' Annette confided. 'I can't even get him to have one beer with me at night.'

'That's fine news,' he said.

'Where are you, anyway?' Annette inquired.

'Oh, I'm in Wichita Falls doing some chores,' he said. 'I just need to ask Bobby Lee to do me a small favor.'

'Just call him – he's out at rig two,' Annette said. 'Or you can leave a number and I'll have him call you.'

'No, that's okay, I'll catch up with him,' Duane said. 'I think Dickie made a good choice when he picked you to run the office.'

'Well, thanks,' Annette said.

Then she hung up.

# 37

Bobby Lee answered his mobile phone on the first ring, in his hungover voice. It was a voice Duane had heard hundreds of times, over the years. Usually he could even tell whether he was dealing with a whiskey hangover or a beer hangover – or maybe a woman hangover – just by Bobby Lee's tone. Of course there had been no woman hangovers since the testicle operation, which narrowed the scope of inquiry just to whiskey and beer.

'You had a sound like you had a Jack Daniel's evening,' Duane said, taking a wild guess.

'Fuck you – where are you anyway?' Bobby Lee asked.

'I'm not far away – why do you sound so unhappy?'

'I sound unhappy because I *am* unhappy and that's because you abdicated your solemn responsibilities and now your son's working us all to death,' Bobby Lee said.

'Where did you learn a big word like 'abdicate'?' Duane asked.

'I learned it from a TV show about the King of England, that one that gave it all up for love,' Bobby said. 'Just because I work in the oil fields is no reason for you to criticize my vocabulary. I know plenty of other big words that I don't never use, because there's no one in my life smart enough to use 'em to.'

'Could you do me a favor this morning?' Duane asked. 'I need you to run into Thalia and bring me some clean clothes.'

There was dead silence on the line. The silence continued for some time.

'Are you still there?' Duane asked, finally.

'I'm here – why would I care if your clothes are dirty?' Bobby Lee asked. 'When have you ever brought me any clean clothes?'

'It's not much of a favor,' Duane said, ignoring the question. 'Karla's in Santa Fe, she'll never know.'

'No, but Dickie will know – he might fire me for leaving my post,' Bobby Lee said.

'He won't fire you – I'll speak to him,' Duane said.

'Where is it I'm supposed to deliver your damn laundry?' Bobby Lee asked.

'The Stingaree Courts, on the Seymour highway, room one forty-one,' Duane said. 'I need the clothes within the hour, if you don't mind hurrying a little.'

There was another silence.

'What in hell are the Stingaree Courts?' Bobby Lee asked.

'Just a motel,' Duane said. 'I'd just like some shirts and Levi's and socks and underwear.'

'I was born a slave and I guess I'll die a slave,' Bobby Lee said.

Two hours later, just as Duane was about to get irritated enough to call again, Bobby Lee knocked on the door. He wore his wraparound sunglasses, and, underneath them, a disgusted look.

'There's a filthy little drug dealer in this motel,' he said. 'The asshole tried to sell me speed.'

Duane, still wrapped in his bedsheet, went outside and got his clothes out of Bobby Lee's pickup. When he came back in Bobby Lee was stretched out on the water bed.

'This water bed smells like catfish,' he said. 'Why would you want to stay in a place like this?'

'I'm just staying here because it's convenient to my doctor's,' Duane said. 'I can't walk it from the cabin and back every day. That's thirty-six miles.'

'Good point,' Bobby Lee said. 'I doubt I'll even walk thirty-six miles between now and the millennium.'

He got off the bed, got down on his knees, and sniffed the water bed.

'Catfish,' he said. 'Wonder how it got in there.'

'Thanks for bringing my clothes,' Duane said. 'I was bordering on filthy myself. Did anybody notice you taking the clothes?'

'Just Rag,' Bobby said. 'Julie went to work in the bank and Nellie's down in Arlington interviewing for a job on the Weather Channel. Here you are getting crazier by the day just as your kids are finally shaping up. I guess you must have been inhibiting them with your good behavior or something.'

The remark irritated Duane. He was paying a trained psychiatrist one hundred and ninety dollars an hour to figure him out and now

Bobby Lee, who had never set foot in a college classroom, felt free to pop off about what had been the matter with his children all these years. What was even more irritating was that the comment might be more or less true.

'Seen Karla lately?' he asked.

'I seen her. She wanted me to be a snitch and snoop out your whereabouts but she didn't want to pay me extra so I declined,' Bobby Lee said. 'She said she was going to Santa Fe and look for a rich boyfriend.'

'That might have been bluff,' Duane said. 'I have one more errand I wish you'd run for me while I'm getting dressed. I've been wanting to read this book by Thoreau but the bookstore's kinda out of my way. If you'd run over and buy it for me I'd be much obliged.'

'Who's it by?'

'Thoreau,' Duane said.

'Is that his whole name?' Bobby Lee asked. 'I never heard of the man – or is he even a man?'

'Just ask the clerk for Thoreau,' Duane said. 'They'll know who you're talking about.'

'They don't if you're asking about car books,' Bobby said. 'I went in once to buy a book about a Porsche and none of the dumb fucks even knew what a Porsche was.'

'Why did you want a book about a Porsche?' Duane asked.

Bobby Lee shrugged. 'Why do you want a book by some old dude named Thoreau? Did he write a lot of books, or just one? I don't want to drive all that way and come back with the wrong book.'

'Just ask them for the one about Walden Pond,' Duane said. 'Try to get one that will fit in my hip pocket, in case I want to stop and read a few pages to break up my trek.'

'You sure have got picky,' Bobby Lee said.

Nonetheless, he did as requested – fifteen minutes later he was back with a paperback copy of Walden. It fit perfectly in Duane's hip pocket.

'That drug dealer's still there,' Bobby Lee said. 'Now he's offering crystal meth.'

'Leave it alone,' Duane said. 'That stuff will burn out your sockets in about three days.'

'Yeah, but it might take my mind off my loss.' Duane sighed.

'I'll tell you what,' he said. 'Since you've been so helpful I'll treat you to a free appointment with my psychiatrist. She might have something helpful to say about your loss.'

'How much is she an hour?'

'One ninety,' Duane said.

'You mean one hundred and ninety dollars *an hour*?' Bobby Lee asked.

Duane nodded.

'No thanks,' Bobby Lee said. 'If I start in with her I might like it and then not be able to afford it.'

'Everybody loses something as they go along in life,' Duane said.

'Easy for you to say,' Bobby Lee said. 'All you've lost is your mind.'

'Well, the offer's open,' Duane said.

'You're as bad as a Baptist,' Bobby Lee said. 'You ain't even been seeing that shrink but a week and you're already trying to make converts. Bye.'

'Thanks for helping me out,' Duane said.

He stood in the doorway as Bobby Lee drove off. It wasn't sleeting anymore, but the clouds still looked like snow.

# 38

Having the clean clothes made Duane feel a lot better. After Bobby Lee left he took another shower, got dressed, and headed into town, the Thoreau book in his hip pocket. Just being neatly dressed seemed to renew his energies. He walked as easily and briskly as he had in his first days as a walker.

He also felt hungry. When he got to the pancake house he didn't just toy with his food this time. He ate, nursed his coffee, and began to read. Mr Thoreau announced immediately that he had lived alone in his cabin and earned his living by the labor of his hands for two years and two months, which convinced Duane immediately that he had the right book. He liked the part about people whose misfortune it was to inherit farms and cattle and houses and the like, responsibilities they didn't seek and didn't want. Though he hadn't inherited anything, he knew exactly how it felt to be oppressed by possessions he didn't want or need – the mere sight of the pile of junk in his own carport had played a part in his decision to park the pickup and start walking. When he came to the part about the mass of men leading lives of quiet desperation he closed the book and left the pancake house – the few pages that he had read expressed exactly what he had been feeling or suspecting about his own life: that most of his work had been meaningless, much of his labor pointless, and the majority of his possessions unnecessary. He felt like the very man Thoreau described, the man who went through life pushing a barn ahead of him, and all that went with the ownership of a barn as well. His own three oil rigs and all that went with them took just as much pushing as a New England barn. What did he have to show for it? He wasn't educated, he hadn't traveled. He was in his sixties, and what had it all amounted to?

He had the book with him when he was ushered into the doctor's office – in order to sit comfortably he had to remove it from his pocket, and when he did Dr Carmichael spotted it.

'Well now,' she said. 'Reading that gloomy man's not likely to cheer you up.'

'I just started it,' Duane said, a little nervous. What would he say if she asked him a question about the book?

'I see you've got some clean clothes,' she said. 'You didn't walk all the way home to get them, did you?'

'Had them delivered,' Duane said. 'I leave here tired – real tired. I can barely pick up my feet.'

'That's common for people who have just gone into therapy,' she said. 'They suddenly feel the weight of their history in a different way. I don't doubt that you're tired. I imagine you're expecting too much, too soon. You need to understand that this process we've embarked on is a slow thing. It'll take years, and there's no guarantee it will leave you all that much happier at the end of the road. It might, or it might not.'

'I'm already happier, just from having someone smart to listen to me,' Duane said.

'That's a relief – at least you've found a doctor,' she told him. 'It may take three or four years for you to fully understand what brought you to me in the first place.'

Duane was shocked by the projection.

'I must be awfully sick if it's going to take three or four years to get me cured,' he said.

Dr Carmichael looked at him sternly.

'Mr Moore, you don't have a disease,' she said. 'I think I can bring you to a better understanding of your life and your feelings about it, but I won't let you pay me thousands of dollars in the expectation that I'm going to cure you of anything.

'All there would be to cure you of is life,' she added. 'Which is not to say you don't have things to learn.'

Duane didn't know what to say, or how to take the doctor's remarks. He was silent and so was she – silence stretched out for almost a minute.

'Well, do you want me to keep coming, or am I a waste of your time?' he asked.

'You're not a waste of my time,' she said. 'Therapy's not a miracle cure, but it's not a waste of time, either – not if you believe that

197

understanding has some value. It's an exploration, of a sort. And what we're exploring is you.'

'Okay,' Duane said. He felt relieved – for a few minutes he had begun to fear that the doctor was just going to throw him out.

'Tomorrow's the day we skip,' she said. 'When you come in on Thursday I'd like you to try lying on the couch. I want to try that, for a few sessions. You're a little too braced, at the moment.'

'Okay,' Duane said, though he wasn't sure what she meant.

'I'd also like to prescribe you an antidepressant,' she said.

Duane bristled a little.

'But I thought you said I wasn't sick,' he said.

'I didn't say you weren't gloomy, though,' she said. 'The point of the antidepressant is to keep you from sinking any deeper into the gloom.'

Duane was silent. He didn't want an antidepressant, but he didn't want to flatly refuse, either.

'Let's table that one until Thursday,' Dr Carmichael said. 'I have a final suggestion that is simply practical.'

'What's that?'

'A bicycle,' she said. 'You seem to be philosophically opposed to motor locomotion – I'm not sure why. Maybe we'll uncover the reason in a year or two, or maybe we won't. But a bicycle would give you a lot more mobility. Eighteen miles is nothing to a cyclist. It would give you a good deal more control over your schedule.'

'It sure would,' Duane said. He liked the idea immediately – he couldn't imagine why he hadn't thought of it for himself. On a bike he could probably whistle along at ten or fifteen miles an hour. But he would still be moving at his own pace, and he wouldn't be in a pickup. If he wanted to stop and clean the trash out of a creek bed, he could.

Then he remembered Shorty, whom he had been supposed to bring to the session, but hadn't. Shorty wasn't called Shorty for nothing. He couldn't travel any ten miles an hour on his short little legs.

'You could probably even get a dog seat for that pooch you don't want me to meet,' the doctor said, with a smile. 'Lots of bikes have baby seats, and I guess he's kind of your baby.'

'No, he's kind of my albatross,' Duane said. 'But I think I will get a bike. If Shorty don't want to ride on it he can stay home and guard the property.'

'You mentioned the other day that you were allergic to ragweed,' the doctor said. 'What do you do when this allergy flares up?'

'I've got a pill that works pretty well,' he said.

'You might think of your depression as something rather like an allergy,' she said. 'An antidepressant might work pretty well too.'

Duane didn't answer. He didn't want to appear to be stubborn, yet stubborn was how he felt. The doctor had said she didn't think he was sick, exactly; she had said he couldn't really expect a cure. And yet now she was proposing to give him a prescription, like any other doctor would. It didn't mesh well, in his mind. The whole session was confusing to him. If he wasn't really sick why would it take three or four years to understand his problems? It all left him feeling very off balance.

Besides, he couldn't help associating antidepressants with Lester Marlow and Sonny Crawford, both of whom had taken every mind drug on the market without becoming any less crazy or any less depressed.

'People who have never been happy in their lives sometimes feel happy once they get on the right antidepressant,' the doctor said. 'I want you to think about it until Thursday, okay?'

'Okay,' Duane said.

They chatted for a few more minutes, but did not get into the matter of his parents, or the distant past at all. The doctor asked him about his children and he described them briefly. When he left the office this time he felt energetic, rather than lethargic. He walked straight over to Tenth Street, where he knew there was a good bike shop; within an hour he had spent five thousand dollars on a top-of-the-line bicycle, complete with helmet, biking shoes, goggles, night lights, water bottles, side packs, and a dog seat. He bought shorts, gloves, a windbreaker, and various little trail packs of high-energy foods. He bought a tool kit to repair his bike, and an excellent pump for the tires. He bought an odometer and even a little device that would measure his pulse and his heartbeat as he rode. The young couple who ran the store had been looking lonely when Duane came in, but were looking extremely happy as they totaled up his purchases.

'Is there anything I've forgotten?' Duane asked, as he was getting ready to leave. He had changed into biking garb and was stuffing his street clothes into one of the handy side packs.

'I don't think so,' the young wife said, as he handed her the check. 'But if you think of something, come on back. We're always here.'

.

# 39

Duane had never had a bicycle as a child. He had been too young for one when his father was alive, and his mother was too poor to afford one after that. At one point he had had an intense yearning for a bike, but, before he could satisfy it, he was already supporting himself and instead of buying a bike he bought a run-down pickup. Even though there was a big bike race in Wichita Falls every August – the Hotter-Than-Hell One Hundred – the extent to which the region was a pickup culture, not a biking culture, was brought home to him not three blocks from the bike shop, when a pickup pulling a long horse trailer came within an inch of sideswiping him. The cowboy driving the pickup didn't notice that his trailer had forced Duane up on the curb.

Though the bike was street ready, Duane wasn't. He almost fell over at the first stoplight, unable to get his feet out of the clips easily. Feeling inept, he wheeled into the parking lot of a high school and practiced stops and starts until he felt he understood the gears and the brakes.

When he felt a little more confident he went back to the highway and in only a few minutes was at his door.

Tommy, the young drug dealer, and Gay-lee, the young whore, were chatting when Duane wheeled in. They were so surprised to see him on a bike that they almost took flight.

'Oh my God, you made my heart race,' Gay-lee said, when Duane took his helmet off and she saw that it was only him. 'We thought the cops had decided to hit us on bicycles.'

Without her makeup Gay-lee looked about the age of his daughter Julie, if considerably more weathered.

'I got tired of slow traveling,' Duane said.

'You'll think slow if one of these trucks hits you,' she said. 'People on bikes don't get much respect out here on the Seymour highway.

'That ain't no cheap bike,' she added, looking closely at his new equipment. 'If you can afford a bike like that, why are you staying in a dump like the Courts?'

'Because it's handy to where I need to be,' he said. 'What about you? Why are you staying here?'

Gay-lee smiled, a little tiredly. 'Because it's the first motel you come to if you're driving in from the west,' she said. 'Some of these roughnecks don't have all that much time. If they're after pussy they're gonna stop at the first place they can get some. See what I mean?'

Gay-lee drifted back over to continue her conversation with Tommy, and Duane went into his room. Having such a spiffy new bike put the general shabbiness of the Stingaree Courts in a new light. The look of the place suddenly depressed him. He wanted to leave immediately for the cabin but thought he probably ought to keep the room until the weekend, in case another wave of the immobilizing fatigue hit him when he saw the doctor on Thursday.

When Duane got ready to leave for the cabin he was faced with the problem of Shorty, who absolutely refused to ride in the dog seat. Time and again he wiggled out and jumped off. Gay-lee and Sis, watching from the parking lot, began to laugh as Duane struggled to keep the dog on the bike.

'Your puppy don't want to go,' Sis observed.

'No, but he needs to get used to this dog seat,' Duane said. 'It's eighteen miles to where we live. Short as his legs are, I doubt he can keep up.'

'Shoot, leave him with us,' Gay-lee offered. 'My little girls are coming this afternoon. They'd like a puppy to play with.'

'I won't be back till Thursday,' Duane said. 'I wouldn't want him to be a burden.'

'That puppy won't be no burden,' Sis said. 'I just stick him in your room when nighttime comes.'

Duane wavered. He still felt energetic, and wanted to be off to the cabin – still, there was the fact of Shorty.

'Put him in the room until I'm out of sight,' he said. 'Otherwise he'll follow me and get lost.'

'Or stolen,' Gay-lee said. She looked around at the weedy parking lot. 'People will steal about anything that's loose, out here on the Seymour highway.'

'We'll look after him,' Sis said, again.

'All right, then, you got yourself a dog for a day or two,' Duane said. 'Watch him with your girls. He sometimes nips kids. Thinks he's supposed to herd them.'

Gay-lee smiled. 'My girls are tough,' she said. 'If he's not careful they'll nip him.'

Sis lured the dog into the honeymoon suite, and Duane pedaled away.

# 40

When Duane arrived at his cabin, after a trip of only an hour and a half, he found a brief note from Karla pinned to his door:

Dear Duane:
Back from Santa Fe. No rich boyfriend. Came to check on you. Bobby Lee says you're living in a real scuzzy place. Why hasn't your shrink done something about it?

Karla

Duane went inside and read the note again. The cabin, which had once seemed so peaceful and reassuring, now seemed bleak and empty. Being there brought him no sense of peace. Perhaps if he needed to chop wood he could have worked out of his low feeling, but he already had enough wood chopped to last through the winter. If he had woodworking tools, and some wood to work, he might have soothed himself that way, but he had no wood. It had been fun to sail along the country roads on his new bicycle, traveling thirty times as fast as he could travel on foot. But now he was home, and he felt lonely. The cabin no longer even felt like home – the Stingaree Courts, for all its squalor, felt more like home. There was no sign of life anywhere on the hill – not even a hawk flying by.

Suddenly, as he stood on the old hill in his new biking clothes, Duane began to feel himself leaving. The sensation was so sudden and sharp that at first he thought he might be having a heart attack, or a stroke, so quickly did his spirits sink and his anxiety rise. He felt as if what was left of his real self had just decided to leave: where it was going he didn't know. He felt himself becoming only a faint outline of his old self – then it seemed that even that outline was disappearing, being rubbed out by the passing wind. He felt that somehow he had lived on past his own death, just a consciousness that was now inhabiting his own ghost. Instinctively, he shut the cabin door. He sat on the bed and held tight to a chair. For a moment he had been afraid that he might just be sucked out the door, like a vapor or a smell, to blow away and be dispersed in the wintry air.

Duane clung to the chair, uncertain as to whether he was dying or merely losing his mind. The exhilaration he had felt riding on his new bike had turned to fear. He had no phone, he couldn't call, he was afraid to go out of the house or even to turn loose of the chair. Somehow a dreadful crisis had arrived – a crisis inside him. He felt a huge emptiness, a huge sadness; he felt desperate, and yet he was in his own cabin, with his family just a few miles away.

He wasn't sure what to do to save himself, but then felt a desire to be in water. He stripped off, ran a tubful of hot water, and lay in it. He cupped his hands and sluiced the hot water over his face again and again. The tub was too short – he had to pull his knees up to get the water to cover him. He didn't want to drown himself; he just wanted to be as deep in the warm water as he could get. He kept splashing it over his face. When the water began to cool he ran in more hot water. The heat was as important as the wetness. He stayed in the tub, keeping the water as warm as possible, until only cold water ran out of the tap. The little hot water heater was empty. Duane jumped out, wrapped himself in towels, and got in bed. He stayed there while the heater reheated the water, then got back in the tub and repeated the whole process. He continued that way, waiting for the water to reheat, until he had taken five baths. He felt that somehow the baths were keeping his blood flowing – keeping him alive.

Sometime long after dark, while Duane waited, wrapped in towels and bedclothes, as the water heater slowly warmed another tubful of water, Duane saw a flash of light across his window. There was a car coming along his road. In a moment he was out of bed, convinced that the light he saw was from Karla's BMW. She was coming to check on him. He began to pull on his clothes, anxious to leave before Karla caught him. The biking clothes were unfamiliar to him – he couldn't get into them as quickly as he could into his normal clothes, which were in one of the side packs on his bicycle. He felt a terrible need for haste. He mustn't let Karla catch him – if she saw him in such disarray she would know he was crazy. She would want to take him to a hospital at once. If he meant to escape he had to hurry. The car was approaching from the north – Karla had probably gone to the Stingaree Courts and been told he had left for the day. The car was only about a quarter mile from the turn-in to his cabin. He had to get himself and his bike out of there quick – he didn't wait to tie his biking shoes. He ran out the door and grabbed his bike, then ran back in to switch off the light in the cabin. Maybe if Karla saw the light go out she would conclude that he had just gone to sleep, and leave him alone for the night. He was about to run south into the brush, where it would be easy to hide, when the car lights went right on past the turn-in and continued along the road to the south. Duane felt an immense relief, and also a sense of the absurdity of his behavior. What was he doing, running into the brush at night carrying a bicycle, just to avoid his wife? He felt abashed. What had come over him, that he would spend half a day taking baths and then flee into the darkness because he was afraid his wife might come to see him?

He had run a fair distance south before he realized the car wasn't Karla, and was trudging back, carrying the bicycle – he was afraid to roll it for fear of puncturing a tire on some small cactus – when he saw another flash of light cross the hill. He looked and saw that another car was approaching, this one from the south.

'That'll be Karla,' he said, out loud, but he didn't turn back and he didn't hurry. If it was Karla, let her come, and come she did. She had beat him to the cabin and gone inside and switched on the light before Duane arrived.

In the course of his bathing he had used up every towel in the cabin. When he propped his bike against the wall of the cabin and went inside, Karla was standing by the table, looking at the pile of damp towels.

'Hi,' he said. 'I've been trying out my new bike.'

If the fact that he was in biking garb surprised Karla, she didn't show it, though her glance did take him in from head to foot.

'I don't get it about the towels,' she said. 'Did you just get real dirty, or what?'

'Not real dirty – real crazy,' Duane said.

# 41

'I'm going to make coffee,' Duane said. 'Would you like some?'

Karla shrugged and sat down at the table.

'What I'd like to know is, what the hell is going on with you?' she said. 'I went to that scumbag motel where you're staying. I know there's no Four Seasons in Wichita Falls, but you could do a lot better than that motel. I saw a hooker and a drug dealer before I'd been there five minutes.'

'I know,' Duane said. 'I think there's a fish in my water bed, too.'

'Then why are you there?' Karla asked.

'When I walked in to my appointment it was the first motel I came to,' he explained. 'Then once I started therapy I was too tired to move.'

Karla stepped out the door and looked around. He thought she might be admiring his new bicycle – she had had a bicycle phase herself – but in a moment she came back in and didn't comment on the bike.

'I'm getting convinced there's a girlfriend,' she said. 'This room looks like a room looks when you fuck all day.'

'I didn't fuck all day,' Duane said. 'I felt like I was vanishing – the only thing that helped was to take a lot of baths.'

Karla shook her head.

'I never would have thought that my own husband would lose his marbles to this extent,' she said. 'Is the doctor pretty?'

'She's pleasant looking,' Duane said. 'What's that got to do with anything?'

'It's just a thing I wanted to know,' Karla said. 'Why'd you buy the bike?'

'The therapy makes me real, real tired,' Duane said. 'I could barely even walk back to that crappy motel. I was too tired even to buy new clothes. I finally had to call Bobby and ask him to bring me some.'

'I know,' Karla said. 'Then the little prick didn't want to tell me where you were staying. I practically had to beat it out of him.'

'He never should have told you,' Duane said. 'I've kept plenty of his secrets, over the years.'

'Why does therapy make you tired?' Karla asked. 'If it'll put you to sleep I better try some. I haven't slept through the night since you left home.'

'I don't understand it,' Duane said. 'Dr Carmichael says it makes the past kind of fall in on you. I guess I must have had a pretty heavy past. When I come out of that office I can barely pick up my feet.'

Karla suddenly began to cry. Duane patted her on the shoulder a few times, awkwardly, and then sat across from her and drank his coffee while she had her cry, one of hundreds he had witnessed during the years of their marriage.

'I'm sorry I upset you,' he said, when she had finished and was drying her eyes on a napkin. 'I wish I understood why I feel this way, but I don't. That's why I'm going to the doctor.'

'The school board was real upset that you resigned,' Karla said. 'So was the Chamber of Commerce. You've got the whole damn town feeling guilty. They all think it must be their fault. Elmer Kunkel had the worst idea yet.'

Elmer Kunkel was president of the Chamber of Commerce.

'Uh-oh,' Duane said.

'Elmer thinks the reason you're walking around like a crazy man is because you hate your pickup but can't afford to trade it in for a new one.'

'There's some truth in that but it's not Elmer's problem,' Duane said.

'He thinks it is,' Karla said. 'He don't think a leading citizen ought to be walking around on foot, so he wants to take up a collection from all over the county and buy you a new pickup and then have a big ceremony and give it to you.'

'Oh my lord, that's terrible,' Duane said. 'I've got to stop him. I don't want a new pickup – he's got to return the money, if he's collected any.'

'He's collected a bunch,' Karla said. 'Couldn't you just take the new pickup and let Dickie use it? He needs a new pickup.'

'No, he doesn't, let him use mine,' Duane said. 'I left the keys in that old cracked cup in the cabinet.'

'Oh, I found the keys and let him use your pickup, but he's already broke an axle,' Karla said. 'See how out of touch you get when you don't come home for a week?'

'He broke an axle?' Duane said. 'I know he's always been hard on cars, but that pickup was nearly brand new. How could he break an axle?'

'By being in too big a hurry,' Karla said. 'He tried to drive off the hill over by that west lease.'

'*That* hill?' Duane said. 'But that's insane!'

'No, staying in a motel where there's a fish in the water bed is insane,' Karla said. 'What Dickie done was just stupid.'

'I guess being a boss hasn't made him less reckless,' Duane said. The hill in question was strewn with boulders. He couldn't imagine why his son would have tried to drive down it.

'No, but he's not on drugs,' Karla said. 'Let's count our blessings.'

'I don't have a session tomorrow,' Duane said. 'I might pedal home and see the grandkids – see if they remember me.'

'Don't do us any favors,' Karla said.

Then she went to the door.

'I know you're out there, you little whore!' she screamed into the darkness.

'Karla, there's no one out there,' Duane said, as she was getting into her car.

'Bye, Duane,' Karla said.

# 42

That night Duane couldn't sleep. He knew Karla was shifting from concern to anger. Rather than believe that he was in a shaky mental state she had chosen to believe that he was up to something with a woman – possibly his psychiatrist. For some time she had been complaining that they never talked, husband-to-wife, anymore. But now he was talking regularly to another woman – his doctor. He knew Karla well enough to know that the fact that Honor was a woman would soon come to outweigh the fact that she was a doctor. In Karla's mind he was already giving another woman something he was increasingly reluctant to give her: his attention. That was bound to rankle. He didn't know exactly what Karla might do – but she would do something. Karla wasn't passive. Sooner or later she would come out fighting. It worried him. After tossing and turning for a while, unable to sleep, he decided to phone her at home – but then remembered that he was in his cabin, and had no phone.

Toward morning he did sleep for an hour or two, long enough to have his old calf-roping dream, or at least a snatch of it. The calf was only briefly in the dream. It left the chute and vanished. Duane raced up the length of the arena, swinging his rope. But he never threw it, he just swung it. Then he dismounted and kept swinging his rope. Suddenly there were calves all over the arena, scores of calves. Then the calves turned into jackrabbits and hundreds of children poured out of the stands, to chase the rabbits. Some of the children had tiny ropes. Then the jackrabbits changed into grasshoppers, and the grasshoppers into a flock of egrets, which rose over the bleachers in a white cloud and flew away.

This time when Duane awoke he didn't feel sad. It was a beautiful, crisp day – sunlight beamed into the cabin from every window. He went outside into the sunlight – there was no trace of the vanishing feeling left, but he *was* hungry and Rag and her gourmet cooking was only six miles away. He got into his biking clothes and sped down the road, stopping only at the bridge where the battery and the car seat had been dumped. The river flowed cleanly this time; the litter consisted only of two beer bottles. He didn't want to get his biking shoes muddy, so he decided to leave the beer bottles until he was crossing the bridge in his walking shoes.

'Oh lord, it's Jean-Claude Van Damme, winner of the Tour de France,' Rag said, when Duane came in wearing his biking clothes.

'Jean-Claude Van Damme is an actor,' Duane pointed out. 'What makes you think he won the Tour de France?'

'Because he's got those nice strong thighs, like winners have,' Rag said.

Baby Paul, who was teething and fretful, immediately stopped fretting when Duane lifted him out of his high chair. He began to burble, spewing out carroty baby food.

Little Bascom, wildly excited, started climbing up Duane's leg.

There was a rapid spillage of grandchildren into the room. Loni, Barbi, and Sami came running in from the yard, all of them yelling 'Pa-Pa,' arousing Willy and Bubbles, who stumbled in rubbing sleep out of their eyes. Soon they all clustered around their grandfather, ignoring their breakfast. Several had points they wanted to make, and make immediately.

'I put a spell on Willy and Bubbles and Loni and Sami, so they'll all get Fs in school, because I want them to flunk out,' Barbi said.

'You shut up, you ugly witch,' Bubbles said.

'Shut up, or we'll beat you to a pulp,' Willy added. He had in fact got an F in his math class but had successfully concealed his report card so the news hadn't spread. Now his cousin was spreading it, and to his grandfather at that. His grandfather was the family member who took the most interest in report cards.

'Now, now, let's not beat anybody to a pulp,' Duane said. 'I was hoping we could enjoy a peaceful breakfast.'

Rag went around the table, ladling a thick glutinous gray mass into the children's bowls.

'What's that – it looks like you could pave a road with it,' Duane said.

All of the children burst into fits of giggling, including Baby Paul and Little Bascom, neither of whom knew why they were laughing. The oldest children loved it when their grandfather stood up to Rag, a petty tyrant who caused them much aggravation.

'It's Scottish porridge, which is a roughage, which is what causes people to have good, regular bowel movements,' Rag said. 'Pour some of this maple syrup on it and it will taste just like ambrosia.'

'I never ate ambrosia so I wouldn't know about that,' Duane said. 'If it don't taste good I guess we can pave the driveway with it.'

'Is this *real* maple syrup?' Barbi asked. She had developed an acute product pickiness.

'Sure it's real maple syrup,' Rag said. 'It says so right on the bottle. It came right out of a maple tree.'

'Show me the bottle,' Barbi requested. 'I want to read about it.'

'Shut up, you talk too much, Barbi – I'm getting a headache,' Willy said. He wanted to sit by his grandfather and enjoy the good feeling he got when his grandfather was around, but he couldn't concentrate on the good feeling with Barbi chattering away.

Julie drifted in and gave her father a big hug. She had just washed her face and hair, which made her look about fifteen, too young to be the mother of Willy and Bubbles, though she was. Julie still smelled like a teenager, to Duane. Her smell brought a moment of nostalgia.

'I hear you're working hard at the bank,' Duane said. 'I'm proud of you.'

Julie beamed. 'Leon says I can be an officer at the bank if I go on and finish up my degree,' she said.

'Then do it,' Duane said. 'Who's Leon?'

'Her regional supervisor,' Karla said, entering from the yard. 'He's the latest nerd to get a crush on Julie, which is why he's so anxious to promote her. I wonder, if I left home for a few weeks and ignored all my responsibilities, if everyone would adore me when I showed up again.'

'No, Granny, we wouldn't, because you're too cranky,' Sami said. The comment floored everybody; Sami rarely spoke.

Karla took the comment gracefully. 'Sami's had it in for me ever since I spanked his little butt for trying to run over the cat with his tricycle,' she said. 'Anyway I know I could never be as popular as Grandpa Duane.'

'This oatmeal sucks,' Willy said. 'It makes my teeth stick together.'

'What if it made pavement in your mouth?' Bubbles said, giggling.

'What if it plugged you up so you could never do number two again?' Barbi said. 'Then you'd swell up and burst.'

'Everybody better shut up about my Scottish porridge,' Rag said.

'It's one of the healthiest foods in the world. The whole Scottish nation has lived off it for centuries.'

All the children ignored the comment, and the Scottish porridge too.

'Tardy bell, tardy bell!' Rag warned. 'We need to beat that tardy bell.'

There was the usual mad scramble as the children tried to find book bags, homework, Crayolas, and lunch pails. Bubbles insisted that her mother pin up her hair, although the tardy bell was imminent and all the other children already in the car. Baby Paul began to fret again, biting the tray of his high chair to ease the pain of his emerging teeth.

Duane scraped most of the porridge into the disposal before frying himself three eggs and some bacon.

'If you're going to eat that many eggs you should eat the whites and leave the yolks,' Karla suggested.

'But the yolks are the good part,' he reminded her. 'Besides, didn't you know there's a theory that eating egg whites makes you go blind?'

Rag came back in good spirits.

'Just beat the tardy bell,' she said.

'If you're mad at me why bother warning me about egg yolks?' Duane asked.

Karla lit a cigarette.

'I had quit smoking for almost a month before you pulled this stunt,' she reminded him.

'It's not a stunt, it's a new way of life,' Duane said. 'I think Rag understands that, don't you, Rag?'

Both of them looked at Rag. It was never easy to predict which side she'd come down on in a family dispute.

'I don't officiate, I'm not an umpire, I'm not a referee,' Rag said. 'Even if you pay me ten million dollars I don't officiate.'

'I don't think either one of us was thinking about paying you ten million dollars to decide if Karla's mad,' Duane said. 'She's been mad at me before, once or twice.'

'I looked your doctor up in the yearbook, to see if she was pretty,' Karla informed him. 'You can tell a lot from looking at pictures in a yearbook.'

'What yearbook?' Duane asked. 'She didn't go to high school here.'

'No, but she went here until she was in the sixth grade,' Karla said.

'So she's in the yearbooks, too. She was real cute when she was in the sixth grade.'

'So were you and a lot of other girls,' Duane said. 'I doubt you can really tell much about her from how she looked when she was in the sixth grade.'

'Maybe not, but it's better than nothing,' Karla said. 'All this has stressed me so that I need to be in therapy myself.'

'Then go – it wouldn't be a bad idea,' Duane said.

'Why go? You've already got the best therapist in town. I'd just be spilling out my guts to some dopey man.'

While he was in the den getting a fresh checkbook out of a drawer he noticed a pile of *Monty Python* videos on the floor. *Monty Python* had been one of the first shows he and Karla had watched, when they first got cable, years ago. There was quite a stack of videos on the floor – so many that Duane stopped and counted them. There were twenty-three in all.

'What's with all the *Monty Python?*' he asked, when he went back to the kitchen.

'What do you mean, what's with them?' Karla asked. 'I watch them, that's what's with them.'

'There's twenty-three videos there. That's a lot of videos.'

'Yep, and I have a lot of lonely nights to get through, now that my husband's left me,' Karla said. 'When nighttime comes it's either laugh or cry, and I'd rather laugh.'

'I tried to watch one but it didn't make a word of sense,' Rag said. 'But then, to each his own, I guess.'

'It's comedy, it's not supposed to make sense; it's supposed to make you laugh when otherwise you'd be crying your eyes out,' Karla told her.

'I think you're overreacting, frankly,' Duane said. 'I haven't done anything except take some walks, sleep in my cabin, and go see my doctor. That's nothing to make anyone cry their eyes out. You used to vanish for a week at a time, when you were young and wild.'

'I wasn't vanished, I was just over in a honky-tonk dancing up a storm,' Karla said. 'You took it way too personally.'

'Okay, so why are you taking this personally now?' he asked.

'I'd go into therapy if I could find a Chinese doctor,' Rag said. 'I guess no one liked my gourmet Scottish porridge.'

'Why would you need a Chinese doctor?' Duane asked.

'Because I believe in yoga and meditation,' Rag said. 'The cure for everything is right there in your mind – you just need to know how to get to it.'

'Why can't I be in therapy with you?' Karla asked. 'Lots of marriage counselors see the husband and wife together.'

'But what I'm doing isn't marriage counseling,' Duane said. 'I didn't start all this because I was unhappy in my marriage – I wish you could believe that.'

'You can say that till you're blue in the face and I won't believe it,' Karla said. 'When a woman's husband leaves her to live in a cabin, it's going to cause her to think there's something wrong with her marriage.'

'What if I told you that our marriage is the best part of my life and it's all the other parts that I'm upset about?' Duane asked.

Karla shrugged.

'It's nice to hear but when nighttime comes I still don't have nothing to fall back on but *Monty Python*,' she informed him.

'At least the kids seem to be doing better,' he said, trying another tack. 'Dickie's put the fear of God in all the crews, and Julie's working. I don't know about Nellie and Jack.'

'Nellie's getting a tryout on the Weather Channel and nobody's heard from Jack,' Karla said. 'He leads his own life, like his father.

'I just wish I understood,' she added, sadly. 'I just wish I understood.'

When she began to cry again Rag vanished into the laundry room. Duane went over and hugged his wife until she stopped crying and blew her nose.

'If *I* understood it well enough to explain it I wouldn't need to go to a doctor,' Duane said.

Unable to think of anything more consoling to say, he went outside and checked on the greenhouse – at once he saw that it was in a neglected state. Usually when Karla was depressed she gardened until she felt better, but now the greenhouse was bleak, untended. It was March, time to get the big garden they always planted started too. Normally they grew a great variety of vegetables in the outside garden: corn and peas, green beans, turnips, okra, cabbage, kale, onions, and a fair variety of herbs. They also made sure of an abundance of tomatoes, which they both particularly liked. Sometimes they tried strawberries, and, always, cantaloupe and watermelon.

It looked, though, that if somebody didn't get busy and prepare the ground they would miss their chance to grow much of anything. The thought troubled him sufficiently that he went back in the house. Karla was still where he had left her, smoking and flipping through the morning paper.

'Dickie or Jack or somebody needs to get busy and plow that garden plot,' he said. 'It's planting time, you know.'

Karla seemed cheered by the fact that he had noticed that they were behind on the garden.

'I know it, but the tractor's got a flat,' she said. 'Dickie's so busy now that you've made him the big boss that he doesn't have time to tend to things like gardens.'

'If I take the tire off and carry it to the filling station will you see that somebody picks it up and puts it back on?' he asked. 'I hate to see you lose any more time on that garden.'

'We didn't raise very helpful boys,' Karla pointed out. 'They've both got better things to do than fix the tractor when it breaks.'

'It doesn't take ten minutes to put a tire back on a tractor,' Duane said. 'If the filling station can get the flat fixed in the next hour or so I'll put it back on myself.'

'Why thanks, Duane – that'd be nice,' Karla said.

# 43

Almost immediately, Duane regretted his offer to tend to the flat tractor tire. Gardening was something that *must* be done in a timely fashion, if it was to be done successfully. Once he got the tractor tire off it proved too heavy to be carried on the bicycle. He had to roll it to the handiest of the filling stations, a distance of twelve blocks. While he was rolling the tire along the street, aware that every motorist who passed was gawking at him because he was in his brand-new biking clothes, he began to feel discontent with himself. The kind of chore he was in the process of doing was just the kind of chore he had meant to walk away from when he left home to live in his cabin. The oil company employed twenty-three men, any one of whom could have quickly taken care of the flat tire on the garden tractor. Why employ twenty-three men plus a cook and an office staff if you still had to be the one to roll the tractor tire to the filling station, so that the family garden plot could be plowed on time? It was the long accumulation of such irritating chores that had caused him to park his pickup in the first place – and yet he was doing exactly the kind of thing he had gone away to avoid. The very thing Mr Thoreau warned about had happened: he had become a slave to his machine.

The Fina station where he took the tire was no particular favorite of his – it just happened to be the closest station. It was owned by three brothers: Joe Bond, Bill Bond, and Roy Bond, none of them quick workers. Though they had owned the station for more than forty years they had never arrived at a clear division of labor. The fact that there were three of them meant that the simplest tasks, such as putting gas in a car, or checking someone's oil, became a matter for negotiation. The older brothers, Joe and Bill, thought that Roy ought to do most of the work, since he was the youngest, but Roy often refused to do any work at all. Roy owned a cheap calculator and liked to calculate with it. If left to himself he would sit in the sun on a pile of old tires for hours at a stretch, putting his calculator through its paces. Sometimes he made it add, sometimes he made it subtract; occasionally he even made it multiply and divide. While Roy calculated, Joe and Bill would sometimes take as much as fifteen minutes to service one car. Very often they would be unable to locate the gauge needed to check the air pressure in a customer's tires. They had only one gauge and would pass it from hand to hand until someone mislaid it.

Duane felt himself beginning to tense up, even before he reached the Fina station, just from the thought of having to interact with the Bond brothers. But the other stations were farther away and he was finding it awkward to roll the tire with one hand and his bike with the other. He knew already, from long experience, that none of the three brothers was going to want to snap to and fix the tire. To them their filling station was simply a convenient spot from which to view the world, or contemplate human folly, or something. They were quick to flare into argument, both with one another and with anyone who happened to stop at their station, hoping for services that they might well not be in the mood to render.

Still, the tire needed to be fixed.

Roy Bond, as usual, sat on the pile of tires with his calculator in his hand, involved in an act of pure calculation – that is, one that had no meaning to anyone but himself.

'Why have you got on them funny clothes – is it time for the parade?' Roy asked, when he looked up from his calculating and saw Duane in his biking garb.

'Those are biking clothes, you moron,' Joe Bond said. 'There's no parade, it's March. The parade happens in July, when they have the rodeo.'

'Don't be calling Roy a moron,' Bill Bond said. 'If you hurt his feelings this early he won't do a lick of work all day.'

'He won't anyway – he never does,' Joe said. 'I'll hurt his feelings with a tire iron if he don't snap to the next time a customer shows up.'

'One just showed up,' Duane said. 'I need this tractor tire fixed and I need it fixed now.'

None of the Bond brothers said a word. They all stared into space. 'Now' was not a concept they welcomed around their Fina station.

'If you're too busy to fix it I'll do it myself,' Duane said, hoping the

218

brothers would recognize that he spoke with heavy irony. The road was empty in both directions. Besides himself there were no customers in sight.

There was more silence. The Bond brothers were as passive as possums.

'If I can just borrow your tools I'll fix it,' Duane said. His tensing continued. He couldn't remember why he had come to town, or been foolish enough to eat breakfast at home. He felt like heaving the tire through the plate glass window just behind where Bill and Joe Bond were sitting.

Bill Bond shook his head.

'We ain't insured for customers to use our tools,' he said. 'A nut could fly up and hit you in the eye and blind you and then you'd sue the shit out of us.'

'What nut?' Duane asked. 'I'm just trying to fix a flat. The nuts are already off the wheel. They're back at the house.'

Bill Bond was unmoved.

'Well, but there's nuts laying around here that could fly up and blind you,' he said. 'If one did we'd be in a pickle.'

'Okay then, how soon could you fix it for me? I'm in a hurry,' Duane asked. He attempted to stare them down, but it was hard, since their three gazes wandered willy-nilly over the landscape.

'What do you think, Joe? How soon could we get to it?' Bill asked his brother.

'I guess we can get to it after while,' Joe said. 'Of course we're at the beck and call. We might get busy pumping gas. Anyone could drive up needing gas.'

'Yes, but I'm here now and none of you are doing a damn thing except sitting on your asses,' Duane said. 'I'm a cash customer and this is a job you can do in twenty minutes if you hustle. So what's the holdup?'

The Bond brothers looked shocked, perhaps at the thought of hustling. No one alive had ever seen them hustle.

'I don't see what the hurry of it is,' Bill Bond said, finally. 'You ain't a farmer.'

'I didn't come here to debate you, Bill,' Duane said. 'When can you fix this fuckin' tire?'

'Roy, get to it,' Joe Bond said, without much force.

'No, you called me a moron,' Roy said. 'Anyway I'm trying to add up the years since the Big Bang and it's a lot of years.'

'Here's a big bang for you, you lazy farts,' Duane said. Then he did what he had wanted to do earlier. He heaved the tractor tire through the plate glass window just behind Joe and Bill Bond, who, for once, hustled out of the way. The window exploded with a very satisfying sound, and the tire landed on a messy desk, knocking several ashtrays up in the air. A cat that had been dozing dashed out and ran into the weeds. Ash from the ashtrays blew up to the ceiling of the small office and then filtered slowly down through the rays of sunlight.

'Fix this goddamn tire and then take it up to my house and put it on the tractor,' Duane said in a tone meant to be threatening. 'And send the bill to my office.'

The Bond brothers were all staring dully at what had once been a plate glass window when Duane got on his bicycle and pedaled away.

# 44

When, on Thursday afternoon, Duane told Dr Carmichael what he had done she put her long fingers together and tapped them a few times against her lips, looking directly at him as she did it.

'The interesting thing is the garden,' she said. 'You left your family. You've intimated to me that you think it's unlikely you'll ever go back to your wife. You've changed directions – that's all we know right now.'

She paused and looked out the window. Two blue jays were flitting around on her lawn.

'So why is the state of your family's garden that important to you?' she asked. 'So important that you'd throw a tire through a plate glass window?'

Duane was startled. Dr Carmichael had never questioned him so directly.

'Well, I mainly threw the tire because I was aggravated at not getting any service,' he said.

'Yes, and you still sound aggravated,' she said. 'But it was concern for the garden that prompted you to take the tire to the station. You claim to feel no connection with your family, and you have little curiosity about your children. But when you saw that the garden plot hadn't been prepared you were troubled. If you're so through with family life why do you care so much about the garden?'

Dr Carmichael was looking directly at him, in her grave way. Duane began to feel a little tense. The thing that seemed worrisome to him was that he had lost his temper and thrown a tire through a plate glass window, a very unusual thing for him to do. Even in his wild youth he had never done anything destructive of anyone else's property. He would have to go back to the Bond brothers at some point and apologize. What he had done seemed foolish to him. He should just have taken the tire to another station, where someone might have been more energetic about tending to customers' needs.

It puzzled him that the doctor had chosen to focus on the garden aspect of it all, rather than on the tire throwing. Everyone recognized the importance of growing a garden – or at least everyone had recognized it when he was younger. Growing a good garden meant not having to spend all your money at the grocery store, where the produce was not likely to be as good. Of course there had always been people who *didn't* garden, but they were usually people who were either too shiftless or too rich. Taking good care of one's garden was only common sense, especially in a country that was prone to drought.

'It was just my upbringing, I guess,' he told her. 'I was brought up not to neglect the garden. Maybe it was because of the Depression. My mother always gardened, although she was never much good at it. But at least we always had beans and potatoes and corn to fall back on.'

'But the Depression was sixty years back and your family is now rather affluent,' Dr Carmichael said. 'They no longer *need* to grow their food. Most people don't need to grow food these days. They buy food at the supermarket.'

'You can't buy a tomato with any taste to it at a supermarket,' Duane said.

'Oh, granted,' the doctor said. 'But let's consider what happened. You went home and had breakfast with your family. Then you noticed that the garden hadn't been planted, and that upset you.'

'Not only not planted – it hadn't even been plowed, and it's past time,' Duane said. 'It's way past time, in fact.'

'This is something you would have tended to yourself, if you'd been home, correct?' the doctor asked.

'You bet,' Duane said.

'It's a duty, in your mind, then?' she asked.

'Well, yes … it's a duty,' Duane said. 'We have a good garden plot and all the equipment we need to plow it and plant it. It's just laziness to neglect a garden.'

'It seems as if you want your family to assume the same duties you assumed,' the doctor said. 'But they aren't you – and you've left them. What if they want to live in a different way? What if they never plant that garden?'

For a moment Duane regretted ever coming to see Dr Carmichael.

It was all just talk – he couldn't see that it mattered. There had been some relief in talking to her the first few times he had come, but this visit was just making him feel muddled. Here she was, boring in on the question of his unplanted garden. It made him feel tired.

'Do you plan to plant a garden out at your cabin?' she asked.

'I thought I might have a little pea patch, and some tomatoes,' he said. 'Maybe grow some turnips. I like turnip greens.'

'What interests me is that, where your family is concerned, you've taken away your help but you haven't taken away many of your expectations,' the doctor said. 'You want them to be as responsible as you have been.'

She paused.

'You want them to be a credit to their raising, which is a normal thing for a parent to feel,' she added.

Duane looked at the long couch along the west wall of the room. He thought it would be a relief to lie on it for a while: just lie on the couch and not think. But there were only ten minutes left in the visit, and if he were on the couch he feared he would just embarrass himself by going right to sleep. He remembered that the doctor had wanted him on the couch for this visit – probably he had been so agitated about throwing the tire through the window that she had just let him sit in the chair and babble.

Dr Carmichael saw where he was looking.

'That's okay, we'll get you on the couch next time,' she said. 'It's rather a different experience, being on the couch.'

'I guess I'm just tired,' Duane said. 'I biked in.'

'Are you glad you have the bike?' she asked. 'Is it better than walking?'

'Well, I can get to someplace I need to get to on the bike,' Duane said. 'I can come in and out in a day. But it's not better than walking.'

'Why not?'

'It's just not,' he said. 'I like walking.'

'We'll talk about that a little, next time,' the doctor said.

# 45

Duane had meant to bike right on back to his cabin, but there was the vexed question of Shorty, who had been the sole inhabitant of a semiexpensive room at the Stingaree Courts for two days. When he arrived at the motel and opened the door to number 141 Shorty was so glad to see him that he hopped around in a frenzy for a while.

'If anybody knew I was paying forty-eight dollars a day for a dog to stay in a motel they'd really think I was crazy,' Duane said. Shorty dashed off across the parking lot to chase a tomcat that was lurking around, but the tomcat easily faced him down and Shorty soon returned.

Duane had meant to check out and drag Shorty back to the cabin by one means or another, but he made the mistake of lying down on the water bed for a few minutes. The longing he had felt in the doctor's office – a desire just to lie down and doze peacefully – came over him again, and he nodded off. He had not even fully closed the door to his room.

He awoke, deep in the night, to the sound of a loud argument in the parking lot. Sleep dragging at his muscles, he got up and went to the door just in time to see a tall, skinny young man slap Gay-lee twice.

'Ricky, don't – Ricky, don't!' Gay-lee said.

Before Duane could move to intervene, the young man jumped in a pickup and drove off. Gay-lee stood where she was, sobbing. Shorty barked and barked.

Duane walked over to the girl.

'Are you hurt?' he asked.

'In my feelings I am, because Ricky's a two-timing bastard,' she said.

'I thought I saw him hit you,' Duane said.

'Just slaps, he didn't hurt me,' Gay-lee said. 'Ricky don't know what to do with a woman that's fussing at him other than to slap her and drive off.'

'I guess it's none of my business,' Duane said. 'Thanks for looking after my dog.'

Gay-lee was staring down the road, at the taillights of the departing pickup, still visible a long way down the road.

'You're not going to take our puppy away, are you? My girls love him,' Gay-lee asked.

'Well, I was considering it,' Duane admitted.

Gay-lee looked at him with fresh distress, more distress than she had exhibited over the slapping.

'Me and Sis depend on the puppy to keep us happy,' Gay-lee said. 'Sis has got thirteen children and all her boys are in jail.

'Plus I just got out of jail myself,' she added. 'I been writing bad checks. They *will* put you in jail for that sooner or later. But it's the only way I have to get new clothes. If I can't get new clothes once in a while I'd go crazy. I get over there to Dillard's and I pick up some of them Ralph Lauren clothes and it's almost like I get a religious feeling. So I scribble out a bad check. Shoot, I'd rather sit in jail a day or two than never have nothing pretty to wear.'

Duane had an impulse to help the girl – she was about the age of his youngest daughter, who couldn't resist pretty clothes either. Julie wrote bad checks galore but she never had to go to jail because he or Karla always covered them.

'It's while I was sitting in the slammer that Ricky took up with that slut from Iowa Park,' Gay-lee said. 'I was only in jail two days. You'd think it wouldn't kill him to be faithful for just two days, but oh no, Ricky couldn't do it. I get home and there's a slut from Iowa Park sleeping in my own bed. How's that for ugly?'

'Do you have any education?' Duane asked.

'You bet, I'm only like nine hours from having a college degree,' Gay-Lee said.

'I've turned my whole oil business over to my son Dickie,' he said. 'He fired all the office staff – his wife's running the office by herself. He might want to hire you if you can type and file and help keep an office going.'

'Dickie?' the girl asked. 'Dickie who?'

'Dickie Moore,' Duane said.

'Oh man,' she said, and started laughing. 'You want me to work for Dickie Moore?'

She looked at Duane and saw that he was shocked.

'I'm sorry,' she said. 'I know you're trying to help me and all.'

'My mistake,' Duane said. 'I didn't realize you knew Dickie.'

'I knew him,' Gay-lee said simply. 'Me and Dickie used to run around together when we was both wild – I mean, when we was *really* wild.'

She paused, lost for a moment in memory.

'There's not many people out on this stretch of road who *don't* know Dickie, because this is where the stuff is,' she said. 'You're so quiet and nice – I would never have taken you for Dickie's dad.'

Duane was silent. He felt foolish. Who was he to presume that he could do better for Gay-lee than she could do for herself? She seemed like a nice girl. What was she doing, whoring on the Seymour highway? But then, what was *he* doing, sleeping in a room three doors down from hers? Why did he have on biking clothes in the middle of the night?

Gay-lee looked at him nervously – she seemed embarrassed.

'Oh my lord, now I'm ashamed of myself,' she said. 'I would never have offered you no pussy that first day if I had known you were Dickie's dad.'

'That's over and done with – forget it,' he said. 'If you're all right I guess I'll go back to bed.'

'Okay, Mr Moore,' Gay-lee said. 'If I can ever be of assistance please let me know.'

She said it rather formally, as if her whole relationship to him had changed now that she knew he was Dickie's father.

'You can just call me Duane,' he said.

They continued to stand in the dark, empty parking lot, lit only by the early morning moon, as if there were more that needed to be said, although neither of them knew what.

'I don't know about that Ricky,' Duane said finally, to break the silence.

'He's a devil but I love him to pieces,' Gay-lee said. 'He wouldn't have slapped me if I hadn't got in his face so bad about that slut he slept with while I was in jail.'

Then she gave a little laugh.

'You're itching to reform me, ain't you, Mr Moore?' she said. 'You're aching to make me proper, like Dickie's sisters. What's their names?'

'Nellie and Julie.'

'That's right – Nellie and Julie,' she said. 'I met them once or twice when me and Dickie were doing drugs. They were trying to be wild themselves but they ain't never going to be very wild. You don't have to worry about them. Dickie, I don't know. Did he do rehab, or what?'

'Three times,' Duane said.

'It'll take more than rehab to take the wild out of Dickie – if you don't mind my saying so,' Gay-lee said. 'When Dickie's on a tear he makes Ricky seem like a preacher. Where's Jack now? I knew both your boys at one time. Little Jack's got a few wild bones in him too.'

'He's trapping wild pigs for a living,' Duane said. 'We don't see him for weeks at a stretch.'

Gay-lee laughed.

'Jack's worst tendency is to go in bars and pick fights with people he can't whip,' she said. 'Maybe trapping pigs will take some of the steam out of him.'

'I hope so,' Duane said. He turned to go to his room but before he got there Gay-lee called out to him.

'Mr Moore?' she said.

Duane turned back toward her.

'I just want you to know I was proper once,' Gay-lee said. 'I'm a preacher's daughter from Tyler, Texas. I was even a Rangerette for about half a season, till I got on drugs. I shook hands with President Clinton once, when he was in Texarkana giving a talk. I seen a good bit of the proper side of life.'

'Didn't like it?' Duane asked.

'I guess I just had too much to live up to, my dad being a preacher and all,' she said. 'People can only live up to so much – so here I am being a whore on the Seymour highway. But I'm really sorry I asked you what I asked you that first day. I should have known better.'

'Why? I was a total stranger,' he said.

'Because you don't look like a man who would ever need to pay for pussy, that's why,' Gay-lee said. 'You look like the type of guy who can get it free.'

Shorty was dancing around Gay-lee, standing on his hind legs and trying to get her to pet him, which she did.

'How many children did you say Sis has?' he asked.

'Thirteen. She's had a real hard life,' Gay-lee said. 'Fourteen, if you count me. My mom's dead. Sis is about the nearest thing to a mother that I have.'

'Do you really want this dog?' Duane asked. 'I been thinking of going to Egypt and I wouldn't be able to take him if I do.'

'You bet, we'd love to have him, me and Sis.'

'What if you're busy?' Duane asked. 'Wouldn't it be a little awkward to have a dog?'

Gay-lee giggled. 'Oh, if I'm busy I'll just stick the puppy in my car,' she said. 'It's that Toyota sitting over there. It don't run worth a shit but it would make a fine doghouse.'

'Then he's yours,' Duane said. 'You don't even have to take him to a vet. He's had all his shots.'

'Oh, Mr Moore, thanks,' Gay-lee said. 'Me and Sis will take real good care of him. It'll just sort of pick our spirits up, to have a pet of our own. You know what I mean?'

Then she looked at Duane with concern.

'But what about you, Mr Moore?' she asked. 'You're sure about this? You don't think you'll miss him too much?'

'Shorty and I have had a kind of off-again, on-again relationship, most of the time,' Duane said. 'I think we can get by without one another and not suffer too much.'

He looked down at the dog. Shorty, focused on Gay-lee, was not paying him the slightest attention.

'Shorty, have a happy life,' he said.

Shorty, who had parked himself by Gay-lee's side as if he had been her dog forever, didn't respond.

Later, when he was finally in his room again, Duane felt a little strange. There was no Shorty snoring in the corner. He had grown used to sleeping with the snores – now he would have to get used to sleeping without them.

In a way it seemed that he had just cut his very last tie.

# 46

Duane turned the television set to the Weather Channel and stared at it for three hours, until it began to grow light outside. He remembered that his daughter Nellie had been accepted as a Weather Channel trainee and tried to imagine Nellie pointing with a little pointer and talking earnestly and brightly about high pressure systems and the Gulf Stream or the jet stream and such. He knew Nellie was bright enough to comprehend such meteorological details and she was also prettier than any of the weather girls who had appeared while he was watching, but he still had difficulty imagining Nellie doing what the other girls were doing. It just didn't seem Nellie-like.

He had intended to get up at first light and bicycle out to the cabin, have some soup, and stare off the hill, resting in his spirit, until it was time to bicycle back in to his appointment with Dr Carmichael, his last appointment before the yawning chasm of the weekend.

But when he tired of weather and began to surf through the channels he suddenly struck a commercial in which a number of neatly dressed tourists were looking down on the pyramids from a spacious jetliner. There were the pyramids, there was the Sphinx, there was the Nile. He had just mentioned to Gay-lee that he might go there – but before he could he had to get his passport renewed. He immediately took it out and stared at it. He had had longer hair when his last passport picture had been made. He and Karla had been drinking a lot – they had gone to Mexico several times and Canada twice. But they had never seen the pyramids.

Then he remembered Dr Carmichael, with whom he had just begun a course of therapy. If he told her he wanted to go see the pyramids she might not approve. It would be a serious interruption, just as the treatment itself was getting serious.

Nonetheless, as soon as it came time for the post office to be open, he got on his bike and pedaled to the main post office in downtown Wichita Falls. He wanted to fill out the required forms immediately, get his passport renewed as soon as possible. He didn't know that he really wanted to stop therapy and go away, but he wanted the possibility there in his hand, in the form of a valid passport. He wanted to be able to bike to the airport, chain his bike to a tree, put on his normal clothes, and go to the other side of the world, as far as he could get from where he had spent his life.

The big post office had only been open a minute or two when Duane walked in. There were as yet no customers other than himself, and only one clerk at the window where they took mail and sold stamps. The clerk was an elderly man who kept glancing over his shoulder nervously as he got the cash drawer ready for the day's business.

'I need a form,' Duane said. 'My passport's expired.'

'Well, in that case I advise you not to go abroad,' the clerk said. Then he turned around and stared into the still-dark spaces of the cavernous old post office.

Duane was annoyed. He didn't want advice from a postal clerk. He just wanted the form he had to fill out before he could get his passport renewed.

'Could I just have the form, please?' he asked. 'I have to make a trip abroad.'

'What's wrong with America? Love it or leave it,' the man said testily.

Duane was beginning to feel a little testy himself. He had hurried into the post office at the earliest possible hour. He was the first customer of the day; he was also a tax-paying citizen who needed assistance. At home in Thalia the postal workers were courteous and prompt, eager to keep the tax-paying citizenry happy. But a different ethic seemed to prevail in Wichita Falls.

'Sir, there's nothing wrong with America but I still need to go abroad,' Duane said.

'Why, people are the same everywhere,' the clerk said. He turned back to Duane, but kept glancing around. He seemed to be nearly desperate, although Duane could not even guess at the source of desperation.

'Wherever you go you take yourself with you,' the man added. 'You may think things will be different if you could just get over to some foreign country, but believe me, they won't. Even if you went to Egypt you'd still be your same old self.'

Duane was beginning to be angry.

'This is silly,' he said. 'All I asked for was a simple passport form. My reasons for going abroad are none of your business. I just made a simple, legitimate request. Why can't you just give me the goddamn form?'

The elderly clerk turned around again, carefully scrutinizing the space behind him. Then he turned back to Duane.

'It may seem simple to you, oh sure,' he said. 'Just hand over the passport renewal form. But I assure you it's not as easy as you think. I have to be very careful about this. One false move could mean my life.'

'Why would handing me a form cost you your life?' Duane asked. 'Is there a bomb in your drawer?'

The elderly clerk leaned across the counter and whispered.

'That's right,' he said. 'Bombs. Human bombs. Those passport forms are in the supply room, and the man who runs the supply room is about to blow. Post-office-massacre syndrome – you've heard of that, haven't you? It's what happens when someone who works in a post office finally gets enough and comes in with several handguns or an AK-forty-seven and shoots everyone in the building. It happened right up the road in Oklahoma City, and it could happen here. All it takes is some little thing like asking for a passport form. Then out comes the assault rifle and rat-a-tat-tat, ten or twelve people are dead. Happens in post offices all the time.'

Duane decided the man was crazy. *He* would probably be the disgruntled worker that started the massacre, if one occurred in that post office.

'If you're that worried, then I'd say you're in the wrong job,' Duane said. 'I still need the form. If you're scared to go get it could you ask someone else to do it?'

In the distance, behind the clerk, he saw a couple of young women come in. The sight of them gave him hope, although both of them went to computer terminals and began to get their computers revved up.

'Oh well, if you're just going to insist and insist,' the clerk said. 'Mine not to reason why, mine just to do or die.'

He hurried away. In thirty seconds he was back with the passport form.

'Thanks,' Duane said. 'I'm glad it didn't cost you your life. That would have spoiled my trip.'

'You joke, but you don't know,' the man said. 'There are forty-two employees in this post office and forty-one of them are ticking bombs.'

'Who's the sane one?' Duane asked.

'Oh, that's me,' the man said. 'Do you see anyone else who looks sane around here?'

'Those women don't look too crazy,' Duane said. 'You're sure you're not a ticking bomb yourself?'

'Oh no, not me,' the man said. 'I'm the ticking bomb's victim. It's always been that way. Some people are born to be bombs and others are born to be victims. I expect to be splattered all over this post office any day now.'

Duane felt something of the same immobility he had experienced the night before, while talking to Gay-lee in the parking lot. He had his form. It was time to leave, and yet he didn't go. He didn't really like the nervous postal clerk and yet he found it hard to turn and go.

'Ever think of changing jobs?' he asked. 'You could even leave the country, like I'm about to do.'

'I could, but there's the Islamic fundamentalists to consider,' the man said. 'They're everywhere and they're even more dangerous than postal workers. If I have to get splattered all over it might as well be in Wichita Falls and not in Lebanon or Algeria or somewhere.'

'Well, thanks for taking such a big risk for me.'

'You joke, but it *was* a big risk,' the man said. 'If that fellow in the supply room hadn't been on the potty I doubt I would have made it back alive.'

# 47

Duane bicycled to a nearby park to fill out his passport renewal form. Sure enough, he saw that he would have to present a certified copy of his birth certificate, which would probably mean calling his office. He considered just cycling home and getting the form, but that meant cycling forty miles before his doctor's appointment, which was a trip he wasn't sure he wanted to undertake.

While he was pondering his options he heard some loud squealings from the north side of the little park. The park had a little hill in it, so he couldn't see the animals producing the squeals, but they sounded very much like a herd of wild pigs. Though known to be bold in their behavior, it seemed unlikely that a herd of wild pigs would have wandered into downtown Wichita Falls.

Curious as to what was going on, Duane crossed the park and discovered his son Jack, in the process of transferring eight large wild pigs, with snouts like Russian boars, from his horse trailer to a cattle truck. The truck was parked downhill from the trailer, making it simple for the pigs to walk up a loading ramp into the truck; but, simple or not, the pigs weren't loading. They squealed and balked. Jack wore shorts, a Grateful Dead T-shirt, wading boots, and a dozer cap turned backward. Either he was growing a beard or had neglected to shave for at least a week. He was poking at the pigs with a cattle prod, and held a beer in the other hand.

Two silent Mexicans stood by the cattle truck, keeping a close eye on the hogs. They did not seem eager to take possession of such wild beasts, but Jack was clearly eager to be rid of them. When poking at them with the cattle prod failed to do the trick, he set his beer down, climbed into the trailer, yelled 'Sooey!' at the top of his lungs, and dropped right down among the pigs, using his prod to good effect – scrambling and slipping, the pigs raced up the ramp into the truck. The Mexicans quickly slammed the gates on them.

Duane was amused. Karla had tried to push Jack into either law school or medical school, but Jack, looking nothing like a lawyer or a doctor, was clearly in his element as a professional pig trapper.

'You need to be careful about jumping into the pigs like that,' Duane said. 'Any one of those boars could have made mincemeat of you.'

Jack jumped out of the trailer and gave his father a bone-crunching handshake. Jack belonged to almost every health club in the greater Southwest. When he wasn't trapping pigs he was working out with weights. Duane had shaken many strong hands in his time, but none whose grip seemed to weld his fingers together, as Jack's did.

Whenever he ran into Jack after an absence, Duane always experienced a moment of wonder. Could he and Karla have really produced a creature with such absolute confidence? It was a quality Jack had possessed virtually from the time he could walk. Nothing – not drugs, not drink, not financial setbacks, not women – had ever shaken Jack's confidence for long.

'Aw, pigs will never hurt me,' Jack said. 'My karma's stronger than theirs.'

'Yes, but your head isn't as hard and you don't have tusks,' Duane reminded him, feeling silly even as he said it. Jack was probably right. His karma probably *was* stronger.

'Once in a while I just like to jump in and whale the shit out of them,' Jack said. 'It's just to remind them that they're ugly.'

'What's wild pig worth now?' Duane asked. He knew somebody must be willing to pay well for the pigs, else Jack couldn't have afforded to belong to so many health clubs. He even belonged to one in New York City, where he went to party from time to time.

'Five dollars a pound on the hoof,' Jack said. 'That's nearly ten thousand dollars' worth right there and I've got eight more waiting in my pigpen that I need to rush back and get – be close to twenty thousand before I'm through for the day.

'But what about you, Daddy?' Jack asked. 'I hear you're batching.'

'Yep, I stay at the cabin a lot,' Duane said. 'Your mother's upset about it. I was walking everywhere until I bought this bicycle. I like the walking, but a bike sure gets you there faster.'

'Good for you,' Jack said. 'You should have left that rabble long ago. Let them all get off their lazy butts and get a life.'

'I think your mom thought she *had* a life,' Duane said. 'But then I left. You should go see her once in a while. It might cheer her up.'

Jack adored his mother, though they fought fiercely and held opposite views on a wide range of issues.

'I saw her yesterday and she got in my face because I shaved my head,' Jack said. He lifted the dozer cap briefly, revealing, indeed, a shaved pol.

'Mothers pay a lot of attention to hair,' Duane remarked. 'Wives too.'

His own hair had not been cut since he left home and was now definitely longish, by local standards.

'Fuck, if Michael Jordan can do it so can I,' Jack said. 'Good to see you, Dad. I gotta hustle now – I got eight more pigs to deliver and these people that want 'em ain't patient. They're shipping them to Germany. I wonder if eating too much wild pig is what made the Germans become Nazis.'

In a second he was in his pickup and gone, his last question left unanswered. The truckers evidently meant to wait right where they were until Jack returned with the other load of pigs. One of them was snoring loudly in the cab of the truck – the other walked up into the leafy park carrying a boom box and was soon listening to the wail of lost-love Mexican ballads.

Duane got on his bike and rode twice around the park, trying to decide what to do in the interval of time before his appointment with the doctor. His encounter with his younger son had been altogether too brief. It was always good to see Jack – it made him feel good to think he had fathered at least one healthy son – but they never seemed to have time for a real conversation. Though Jack seemed to approve of his new lifestyle, Duane wasn't sure he meant it. Perhaps his habit of taking the opposite position from his mother's had caused him to say what he said. Perhaps deep down – if there was a deep down with Jack – he thought that his father, too, ought to get off his butt and get a life.

# 48

Feeling aimless, Duane rode his bike north, through a part of town he hadn't visited much since his youth. Wichita Falls had once boasted a professional baseball team, the Spudders – whether the Spudders had been Class B, C, or D, he could not remember; but as a boy of ten or so he and Sonny Crawford and a few other boys would catch rides to Spudder Park with Sam the Lion, the old man who had run the pool hall in Thalia and had been a friend to many boys. Sam the Lion had died suddenly, while he and Sonny were gone on a whoring trip to Mexico. Shortly afterward, Duane had been drafted, but the Korean War ended before he could be sent overseas. He spent his two years of service in Fort Hood, Texas.

Sam the Lion, and Spudder Park, and the summer nights of his boyhood, when he and Sonny and a few other boys had chased down home run balls in the dark field behind the ballpark, were things Duane seldom thought about, seldom remembered. He rode slowly past the old ballpark, now abandoned and weedy, and then drifted back over to the frontage road that ran north toward Oklahoma, just across the Red River, ten miles away.

Duane pedaled on to Burkburnett, a small town on the south bank of the river. He had once known an old man who made excellent fishing lures in Burkburnett; in his fishing days he had visited the old man often. He made his lures in an old trailer house, working on them through the day and evidently on through the night. Fishermen knew of him – some came from as far away as Idaho or New England to buy his lures, but the old man, whose name was Leroy Green, had a great fondness for the fishermen of his native state and saved his best lures for locals such as Duane. Then Duane had stopped fishing, and had stopped visiting Mr Green. Curious to know whether the old man was still sitting in his trailer house, meticulously fashioning his wonderful lures, Duane pedaled over to where the trailer house had been.

But nothing of the little tackle shop remained. The house the trailer had been parked behind had been repainted – a child's bike with training wheels attached to it sat on the front porch. Duane tried to think back to his time as a fisherman, but could not really fix the year when he had paid his last visit to Leroy Green, the old man who had made the best lures in North Texas.

Burkburnett, in 1918 the site of one of the wildest oil booms ever to happen in Texas, was now just a sleepy little town, different from Thalia only because it had the Red River as a northern boundary, and the state of Oklahoma only a mile away.

Duane biked on north and pulled off the road at a little green spot near the long bridge that crossed the river, linking Texas and Oklahoma. He felt a little sad – sorry that he had let the old man, Leroy Green, slip out of his life. Except for his service in the two world wars the old man had lived in North Texas all his life and was as valuable for his stories as for his lures. He told wild tales of the first oil booms, and had known the legendary sheriff Jack Abernathy, who had taken Teddy Roosevelt on a wolf hunt, running down the wolves on horseback and catching them with his bare hands.

Now the old man was gone, and his stories too. Duane left his bicycle and walked down to a little bluff where he could watch the river, its thin reddish channel winding through broad banks of flats of pale sand. As he watched the river the sad feeling grew sharper – it produced as sharp a pain as if one of old man Leroy Green's lures had hooked him in his gut. In coming to the edge of the old, famous river – the river the cattlemen dreaded because of its quicksands, the river the Indians fought to keep and failed to keep, the river young Texas couples once crossed in order to get married quickly, before their parents could catch them and stop them – he had come to the edge of his country, and it felt as if he had suddenly come to the edge of his life. He had gone as far as he could go with the work he knew, with the people he knew, with the family he had helped create. In those spheres little more could be expected.

Mixed in the sudden pain was the feeling that he had arrived at the far edge of himself. The list of things he had never done was far longer than the list of things that might be considered accomplishments. All that he had done in the way of building things had merely slipped away, into the great stream of human effort, gone as silently as the sand below him slid into the flowing water. What had happened to his life? Why, in sixty-two years, had he made so little of it? He was not educated, he had not traveled, he knew nothing of the great cities of the world, he could speak no language except a crude English; he had never visited a great museum, or seen a great picture, or heard a great symphony orchestra, or read a great book. He was ignorant, except at the most general level, of the works of great men and women who had made something in their time as living beings. Duane felt both a sudden need to hurry and a sense of the hopelessness of hurry. How could he now, a sixty-two-year-old man with no education, hope to encompass more than a tiny fraction of what he had missed by casual misapplication throughout decades of wasted time?

Standing above the Red River, watching it flow out of the northwest and pour on eastward, Duane sensed his death. It might not be a near thing; he might live another twenty years, or even thirty – but it lay directly ahead, the next big event, the one thing he still had to accomplish. He had seen several men killed in accidents and car wrecks, had known many others who died of old age, but had never connected any of those deaths with the distant fact of his own; but now, for no reason, against the immediate fact of his strength and good health, he felt that dying was really the only thing he had left to do. Watching the river flow on toward the far distant sea, he suddenly felt that he knew what the calf-roping dream meant – this dream he had not yet even told his psychiatrist about.

The running calf was life – he had had a fine throw at it and missed. The calf ran on, as indifferent as the river to his effort. He should have caught the calf – he had had energy, he was not dumb, he was capable of discipline, he had a healthy will – and yet he had missed and missed and missed. There were no excuses – he had not been forced to live as he had – and there could be no remedy. He just had not seen clearly enough into the arena of life, had not fully appreciated the opportunities it offered, had not tried to rise above his limited upbringing in ways that he could have and should have.

Life – that swift calf – had run right in front of him, and he just hadn't known how to catch it.

The ache of regret that Duane felt as he stood on the banks of the river was as deep and as sharp as anything he had felt in his life. He sat by the riverside for two hours, feeling the river throb within him. Then he pedaled slowly, wiping tears from his cheeks, back into

Wichita Falls, eager for it to be three o'clock. He really wanted to tell his doctor about his dream and what he thought it meant.

# 49

'No dog?' Dr Carmichael asked, when Duane stepped into her office.
'No dog,' Duane said.

'Well, it's frustrating,' the doctor said. 'Why can't I meet your dog?'

'He's not mine anymore,' Duane said, a little impatiently. An hour
wasn't much time. He wanted to tell the doctor about his dream, and
about the sad feeling he had had on the banks of the Red River, just
now. He thought he might have a grip on something important, and
he didn't really want to waste time talking about Shorty.

'He won't ride on a bicycle and my life is too spread out now for me
to do all my traveling on foot,' he explained. 'So I gave him to a girl
and a maid at my motel. The maid's had thirteen children. They're
nice people and the dog likes them so I left him with them. He's used
to change. He lived with some wetbacks before he started following
me around.'

'You're cutting all ties, aren't you?' the doctor said. 'I think we
should try the couch today, if that's all right with you.'

Duane liked the couch – he found he could relax on it. Looking Dr
Carmichael in the face minute after minute might have been what
made him so tired, he decided. He liked knowing she was there, but
he also liked just looking at the wall and the plants when he talked.
That way he didn't wonder what the doctor was thinking, from
minute to minute.

'I've been feeling real sad,' he admitted at once. 'Can I tell you
about this dream I've been having?'

Stretched comfortably on the long couch, looking at the wall and
at the nice tall plants in the corner of the room, Duane told the
doctor about his calf-roping dream. He told her about it in some
detail – the more he talked, the more vividly he remembered the
dream. The horse was a black gelding, the image of one Karla had had
in her barrel-racing days, when they had first been courting. He

remembered the feel of the stiff hemp rope, as he made his loop. He remembered watching the calf he had drawn being eased into the chute from which it would be released. He remembered taking the piggin string between his teeth, remembered the calf charging forward when the barrier was dropped. He remembered being so close to the calf for the first few seconds that he could merely have dropped the rope over its head. He remembered how the calf had just run through the loop as if the rope were not a tangible thing. He even remembered the curious variant of the dream in which the calf had become Jacy Farrow.

All this he told the doctor. Then he stopped talking and waited for the doctor to say something, but the doctor was silent. He could sense her behind him, a presence but a silent presence. He looked at his watch and discovered to his horror that he had only two or three minutes left in the hour – and the weekend loomed. He really wanted to tell the doctor about his sadness that morning by the river, and his feelings about dying, and his sense that he had wasted his life. He didn't understand why an hour in the doctor's office went so quickly, while the hours outside the office took so long to pass.

'I need to know what you think,' he said, twisting for a moment so that he could see her. But the doctor was almost behind him. When he twisted all he saw was her knees.

'It's going to be hard going a whole weekend without knowing what you think,' he said, stretching out again.

'Remember what I told you a few sessions ago,' Dr Carmichael said. 'This is going to be a long process. I realize that you feel in a state of crisis right now, but I can't necessarily relieve you by telling you what I think. What I can tell you is that I *am* thinking. We have a lot more to talk about before I'll know what I think.'

She paused – Duane waited. He didn't know exactly what he was hoping for – maybe just some words that would make him feel a little less troubled.

'When I do know what I think it may be nothing more dramatic than that you've suddenly realized you're getting old – and don't like it,' the doctor said. 'You would like to have back all the possibilities you once had – wouldn't you?'

'I sure would,' Duane said. 'I sure would. I'd do a lot of things different if I could have a few of those possibilities back.'

'Surely you know that you've just described a very common problem,' the doctor said. 'Everyone who survives to a certain age wakes up one day to realize that they're old, or about to be. They wonder where the years went, and why they didn't do more with them. They feel regret. They wish they could have one more chance to ring the bell – realize some ambition, achieve something they might have achieved. No one wants to think it's all just been futile striving.'

'But mostly that's what it has been, hasn't it?' Duane asked. 'Futile striving?'

'Yes, unfortunately,' Dr Carmichael said. 'But not just for you, Duane – that's the human condition. It's been that way for most of the people who have ever lived on this earth.

'I know that's no consolation, unless you can be consoled by the knowledge that you're one with mankind,' she said. 'But that's the state you're in, and now your time's up. You'll just have to hang in there until Monday.'

Duane stood up, but he was reluctant to leave.

'Is there a book I could read about this – I mean about time passing and all?' he asked. 'I've been wanting to read more. I've got all this time on my hands now that I'm not working. If you could just recommend a book that might help me understand it a little better I'd be grateful.'

Dr Carmichael was standing up. She looked a little impatient – maybe she needed to make a phone call, or just go to the bathroom. But she went to her desk, wrote a few words on a notepad, tore off the note, and handed it to him.

'Try this,' she said. 'It's not short, but it *is* great and it deals with some of the feelings you're describing. And if you devote yourself to it and actually read it you won't have so much time on your hands.'

'Thanks,' Duane said. He glanced at the note, saw a name he didn't recognize, and stuck the piece of paper in his shirt pocket.

When he walked up to the desk to pay for his session, Natalie, the young receptionist who took his money, seemed confused. She usually had his receipt ready for him. This time she had to make herself write out the receipt, and her hand was shaking. She seemed on the verge of tears.

'Is something wrong?' Duane asked.

'I'm afraid so,' Natalie said, wiping her eyes hastily. 'There's a man to see you. I'm afraid he has bad news.'

Duane looked around, but saw no one in the waiting room.

'He said he preferred to wait for you outside,' the young woman said.

The man waiting outside was Bobby Lee. The moment Duane looked at him he knew there had been a death. Bobby Lee wasn't wearing his sunglasses. He looked stunned and white and blank.

'Who's dead?' Duane asked. 'Is it Dickie?'

Everyone in his family drove much too fast – always had – but for recklessness on the roads none of them had ever been in a class with Dickie. All through Dickie's teenage years he and Karla had been half afraid to answer the phone at night, for fear that there would be a voice on it telling them their oldest child was dead.

'Not Dickie – it's Karla, she was killed instantly,' Bobby Lee said.

'Killed instantly by what?' Duane asked.

'By a head-on with a truck,' Bobby Lee said. 'The truck driver's dead too. The impact threw him out of the cab and he broke his neck when he landed.'

Duane's bicycle was leaning against the wall of the doctor's house. He got it and turned toward the street.

'All right, I'll be right home,' he said. 'I thank you for coming to tell me. I'll see you at home.'

Bobby Lee was stunned anew. His face showed it.

'Your wife's dead,' he said. 'You mean you're going to ride a bike all the way to Thalia?'

'Bobby, it's just twenty miles – that don't take long on a bike,' Duane said.

'But your kids are crying their eyes out,' Bobby Lee said. 'All except Jack – we can't find Jack.'

'Jack's hauling pigs,' Duane said. 'I know where to leave word for him. You go home now and tell the kids I'll be there in two hours.'

'But if you'd just ride in the pickup with me you could be there a lot quicker,' Bobby Lee said. His lip was quivering. He seemed about to sob, and probably had been sobbing.

'Besides, it would be company for me,' he added. 'I don't know what I'm going to do without Karla.'

'None of us know what we're going to do without Karla,' Duane said. 'But you go on back and tell the kids I'm on my way. I'd just like to be by myself for a little while, before I get into it all.'

He put his arm around Bobby Lee's shoulder, and Bobby Lee gulped and a few tears leaked out of his eyes.

'I guess you're right – she's gone, so what's the hurry?' he said.

'Do we know how fast she was going when she hit the truck?' Duane asked.

'No, but it wasn't slow,' Bobby Lee said. 'The BMW's crumpled up like that car Princess Diana died in.'

'I see,' Duane said.

Duane carefully adjusted his helmet before he got on the bicycle and was about to begin the long ride home when Dr Carmichael came out of her front door and called out to him. He was already in the street but he circled back and drifted up the sidewalk to her front steps. She said something, but he couldn't hear it. He had to remove his helmet in order to be able to hear.

'Duane, I'm very sorry to hear about your wife,' she said. 'It's tragic news for you and your family.'

The doctor's large eyes seemed larger as she looked at him. She didn't try to touch him, but she was clearly upset.

'This is all just topsy-turvy,' Duane said. 'She was the one that was full of life, and I'm the one that's running on empty. It should have been me that died.'

'Well, but it wasn't,' the doctor said.

BOOK THREE

*The Walker and Marcel Proust*

# 50

It was three months before Duane found the little piece of note paper that Dr Carmichael had handed him a minute or two before he learned that his wife had been killed. Amid the flurry of funeral preparations, the wailing of his two daughters, the stunned silence of his grandchildren – at least the older ones – he had absently taken the note out of his shirt pocket, along with his checkbook and a few receipts, and tossed it on the desk in his study. It was not until mid-June, when he was finally getting around to grappling with his income tax, that he opened a letter from his accountant and found the note. He had evidently mailed it with some miscellaneous receipts. The accountant, not knowing what it meant or whether it was important, thoughtfully sent it back to him.

When Duane first looked at the note, written in an unfamiliar handwriting, he was puzzled. He assumed the accountant, being overcautious as accountants were likely to be, had sent him the scrap of paper by mistake. The words on the paper meant nothing to him at all. They read: 'Marcel Proust, *Remembrance of Things Past*, Kilmartin trans.'

Duane didn't understand the 'trans.' Since Karla's death he had been confronted with many things, practical and otherwise, which seemed in no way connected to himself or to his life. The puzzling note seemed only to be another such incongruity. He was about to throw it away when the memory came back to him. Dr Carmichael had been impatient to get him out of her office, but when he asked her for a book he might read to help him combat his sense of futility, she had written the note and handed it to him. Then he had stepped outside, seen Bobby Lee bereft on the sidewalk, and learned that he had lost his wife.

Duane carefully tucked the note with the name of the book on it into his billfold. He had not yet been back to see Dr Carmichael.

Karla's funeral was held on the Monday when he would have had his next appointment, so he had been forced to cancel that appointment and so far had not found time to make another. He meant to, eventually, but felt no real urgency about trying to cure himself now, if that was what he had been doing when he was seeing the doctor regularly. The one rule he had clung to from that time was the rule about not riding in cars, pickups, or other motorized vehicles. After Karla's funeral he had walked from the church to the graveyard, a move that scandalized the town to some extent. As he was walking the short half mile between church and graveyard he glanced at his watch and saw that it was exactly three o'clock, the hour at which Dr Carmichael would have been admitting him had Karla not been killed on the highway. He felt a faint regret – he would rather have been in the quiet peace of Dr Carmichael's office than where he was, but that pleasing, sustaining interlude had receded into the realm of the unattainable. Ahead, in the bare, wind-scoured cemetery, the hundred or so people who had come to pay their last respects to Karla Moore were trying to park their pickups or waiting, stiff in their funeral finery, for him to arrive. Barbette and Little Mike had come from Oregon, but they no longer seemed part of the family, a fact that was sadder even than Karla's death.

He arrived, and Karla was buried, while the strong wind tossed the ladies' hair and blew one or two hats off the heads of those who had been incautious enough to wear them. It was a spring day, but the winter had been dry in the main – the grass in the bare cemetery was only just tinged with green.

Once the last prayer was prayed, the last hymn sung, and the coffin lowered, Duane walked home and began to deal with the maelstrom of detail – practical, legal, familial – that follow upon a human death. At first he stayed at home, in the big house, to reassure the girls and the grandkids. He felt Karla would have wanted him to be there to help the children, although the only children who spent much time with him were Willy, Barbi, and Bubbles. Loni and Sami hadn't been as close to their grandmother, and the babies, Little Bascom and Baby Paul, soon forgot Karla and made Rag into a surrogate grandmother, a role Rag accepted with good cheer. With Karla gone she considered herself undisputed mistress of the household, a claim no one raised much of a challenge to. Nellie had been wooed away from the Weather Channel by a country music station in Fort Worth that needed a female DJ with a sexy voice, which Nellie had – she raced up to see her babies on the weekend and then raced back to her turntables and her microphones. Julie, bored with banking, fell in love with a barbecue magnate from Abilene, a man she met at Mayfest, a local frolic held annually on the courthouse lawn. His name was Walt – he was a kind and rather mournful man who aspired to be a chef but found himself stuck in the unwanted but profitable niche of the region's best barbecue caterer, in constant demand during the warm months at rodeos and family reunions. Walt could seldom resist his own barbecue, and had the belly to show it.

Duane stayed at home because he thought he must, but he could not sleep in his old bedroom, where he had spent so many years with Karla. The bedroom seemed like a cavern where even the air was dead. He kept remembering his last night there with Karla, when he had simply got up at 3 A.M. and walked away. After two nights, raked by memories, he gave up on the bedroom and moved himself onto the big couch in the den, where the big television was. Sometimes Barbi would show up in the middle of the night, dragging her quilt; she had virtually stopped eating since Karla's death, a thing worrisome to everyone except Duane, who thought the little girl was just upset and would eat when she got better. Usually, at night, when she showed up with her quilt, he could get her to eat a bowl of cereal or a peanut butter sandwich. Willy and Bubbles and Barbi all talked to him about their grandmother, all trying in their different ways to puzzle out the meaning of death and the possibility of there being some kind of life beyond it. Bubbles, who had been the merriest of the grandchildren, was starkly realistic about her grandmother, who, in her view, was now becoming a skeleton in a hole in the ground. Willy, softer than his sister, didn't quite want to believe that – he thought his grandmother's spirit might exist and be mainly in the greenhouse, because she had liked to garden so much. Barbi had learned, somewhere, the concept of reincarnation and believed firmly that her grandmother was living already in the body of a great bird. Once Karla had taken Barbi to a lake nearby where there was a flock of pelicans – Barbi was now convinced that Grandmother had become a great white pelican who soared and circled over the house at night, keeping watch on everyone, while living at the lake during the day.

'And she eats frogs,' Barbi assured her grandfather. 'Little green slimy frogs. She scoops them in her scooper and gulps them down.'

Duane slept on the couch in the den for three months. Occasionally Willy or Bubbles would come in, crying, wanting to talk about their grandmother. Once in a while Julie, who was working as a booker for Walt's barbecue business, would stay home for a night or two and come and cuddle with him. Nellie would stay home once in a while too, but when she did she drank too much and went, hungover, back to her job.

Duane asked Rag if she would like to move into the house, so she would be handy in case of emergencies, but Rag declined.

'I need my space – I need my *Nick at Nite*,' Rag said. 'They've been rerunning Davy Crockett at one in the morning. Fess Parker, remember him?'

'I remember old Fess,' Duane said.

He got Rag a beeper and carefully instructed all the older children in its correct use. He also cautioned them not to bother Rag unless they really needed her, an injunction that was constantly disobeyed. Bubbles would beep her if she couldn't find a pair of socks that matched.

'I ought to get more money if I'm on twenty-four-hour call,' Rag complained.

'I'll give you more money,' Duane said.

After three months, when the children were sleeping all night again, and Barbi eating normally, Duane would quietly leave the house about midnight and bicycle out to his cabin; sometimes he would wake up in time to cycle in and help Rag get them through breakfast; but in the cabin he slept deeply and dreamlessly – sometimes he didn't awake until the bright sunlight poured through the windows. He had a phone put in the cabin, in case of dire emergencies, but preferred to rely on a state-of-the-art pager, on which Rag would leave voice mail messages, in case something urgent came up. The first message went: 'These kids are fighting like tigers, how can I reach the SWAT team?'

Duane pedaled in, to find that the kids had made up their differences and were playing video games. Dickie reacted to his mother's death by working around the clock and then around the clock again. Duane gave him a beeper too, in case there were major problems at one of the rigs, but Dickie lost the beeper the next day and never paged him a single time. Jack had driven grimly away from his mother's funeral and disappeared. No one had heard from him since that mournful day, but Duane didn't worry about Jack very much. He might be in Mexico or he might be in China, but Jack would survive.

Time began to do its work. The family began to heal. Things became as normal as they could be, without Karla.

Duane, still walking or pedaling, began to spend more time at his cabin. He had done his best to help his family deal with the death of their parent or grandparent. Now a little time needed to be made for the husband's grief – his own.

# 51

A few days after Karla was buried the spring seemed to die with her. It grew hot; it stayed hot. Two months from the date of her death the temperature hit one hundred and nineteen, the highest temperature recorded in Thalia since records had been kept.

The children wanted to erect a little cross at the curve in the road where Karla had died. Duane encouraged them: he wanted them to keep Karla in their minds and hearts. So he got some boards and helped the children build the cross and paint it. Even Little Bascom and Baby Paul got to swipe at the boards a time or two with the paintbrush, though they had little idea why they were doing it.

Duane and Dickie dug the hole where they set up the cross, just off the road at the fatal curve. Nellie was home from Fort Worth, and Julie – Walt at her side – from Abilene. Bobby Lee was there, and Ruth Popper, and Annette, and even Lester and Jenny. The only family member not present was Jack, from whom not one word had been heard.

Once the cross was planted Duane pedaled out in the late afternoon to renew the flowers; and then did the same by the grave marker in the little cemetery. But the elements exhibited no mercy. The heat climbed day by day. Whatever flowers they put out in the afternoon were burned and dead by ten the next morning. The grass in the cemetery was brown and brittle by the first of June – the skies, day after day, were utterly empty of clouds. The road to the cabin was a hot powder – even pedaling along it on his bicycle threw up a high cloud of dust.

'Well, you're missing a great heat wave,' Duane said once or twice, to Karla's ghost. 'It's ruined the wheat farmers already, and it will ruin the cattlemen if it don't rain in July.'

Every day, without fail, Duane walked in the middle of the

afternoon to the cemetery and sat in the narrow shade of a little cedar tree not far from Karla's grave.

Even though he sat in the one spot of shade in the cemetery, the sweat poured from him as the sun slanted downward in the west. At four it was hot – at five it was hotter still. The heat at its zenith was so powerful it wiped out thought. Duane came with two quarts of water each day and drank them both before he left the cemetery.

He came at the hottest hour because Karla loved such heat. No day was too hot for her. She would lie by the pool for hours, shaded only by an umbrella, reading or listening to music. Duane considered it a small tribute to Karla that he came at the hottest hour – an act of remembrance and respect. When they had been young and poor and had made love in such heat in their hot little room the bedclothes would be as wet afterward as if they had been dipped in a river. Those were the heats of youth, long past but not so long past but that Duane remembered them.

Several times, without the children, he had pedaled the fifteen miles to the curve where the accident had occurred and studied the scene of the two deaths. The curve, badly banked on a narrow farm-to-market road, was known to be treacherous. Twenty years before, two teenagers had been killed on it, rolling their car at almost exactly the same spot. Then, a few years later, a cowboy hurrying home from work had turned both a pickup and a horse trailer over on that curve, killing the best cutting horse in that part of the country, and himself to boot. The deceptive thing about the curve was that the long road beyond it was visible from each direction – drivers sped into the curve thinking it was gentle when actually it was sharp. Both he and Karla had driven around it many times, cutting through the farmlands in order to get over to the road that would take them to Dallas, which was where Karla was going when she was killed.

Duane often sat for an hour by the curve, just thinking. Hay trucks and milk trucks and pickups passed him – but no one stopped. The drivers, many of whom knew him, respected his grief and let him alone.

Death on the highway was as much a part of the culture of that country as rodeos or fistfights. When their children were at the reckless age, all parents lived in terror of the death call, and, for too many of them, it came.

What held Duane's attention, as he sat on his bike well off the pavement and watched people pull into the curve and pull out of it, was the precision that went with fatal timing. The milk truck that killed Karla had been traveling west at a high rate of speed, heading for some nearby dairy, and Karla had been traveling east, just as fast, headed for Dallas and a day of shopping with her friend Babe, who was already there. The two vehicles, speeding in opposite directions, arrived at the sharpest angle of the curve at exactly the same moment. If Karla had hit the curve even a second earlier, or the truck even a second later, the badly banked angle would have been passed or not arrived at, and both drivers would still be alive.

But no: they met head-on, each making, simultaneously, a momentary misjudgment about the angle of the curve, and that was all it took. Karla might have been trying to slip a tape into the tape deck; she may have looked down to set her coffee cup in its holder. The trucker, at the same moment, might have looked out the window, sneezed, yawned. The two small errors came at precisely the same moment and in a blink two lives ended. The driver of the truck was thrown through the passenger window and killed; the truck jack-knifed and split open, flushing thousands of gallons of milk into the ditch. Two weeks later the roadside grass was still pale and milky for some fifty yards. The mangled BMW had to be cut away from Karla, although by then she was dead – killed instantly, as Bobby Lee had said.

Duane looked at the wreckage of the milk truck, looked at the smashed, twisted BMW, and knew that death had come so quickly that his wife had not felt anything. He knew it, and yet his mind kept reaching for her last thoughts. In his first hours of guilt at having deserted her in the last weeks of her life he wondered if there could have been a suicidal element in the accident – but then he thought of Karla's attachment to her children and grandchildren and knew that was wrong. Besides, several people had seen Karla on the morning of her death and all had reported her to be in high spirits. She had helped Rag get the kids off to school and then had gone to Mildred-Jean's to get her hair fixed.

'Oh no, we were laughing and cutting up – I mean, why not? She was going off to Neiman's to shop all day,' Mildred-Jean informed him when he asked how his wife had seemed.

'Mom was fine,' Julie said – she had been home that morning and had helped her mother choose the outfit she wore.

'Grandma didn't even spank me,' Sami volunteered, one day when they were putting flowers by her grave.

Then Sami burst into tears. All the children cried a lot when he brought them to their grandmother's grave, or to the cross by the spot where she had been killed. The only one who didn't cry was Barbi, whose response to the tragedy was more considered.

'I'm going to learn ESP so I can talk to her,' Barbi said. 'I know she's living in a bird. When I learn ESP I'll signal to the bird and when it hears me it will come down and peck on my window. And then I'll go outside and talk to Grandma. Could you get me a book on ESP, Pa-Pa? I want to learn it quick.'

Duane pedaled to Wichita Falls, got Barbi the book, and read most of it to her. Very soon afterward Barbi began to talk to birds, and was unshakable in her conviction that she was talking to her grandmother.

'She moves from bird to bird,' she informed the household. 'Right now she's in a roadrunner and she kills bugs and lizards. But sometimes she's in a crow.'

'Bull,' Willy said. He was deeply grieved by the loss of his grandmother – she had often taken him fishing when no one else had time. He wanted Barbi to shut up about her and just let her be dead, because when they talked about her he began to cry and felt like a sissy all day.

Rag and Bubbles shared that view. Bubbles liked the thought that her grandmother might have wings, but she wanted them to be clean, white angel wings, the color of white sheets just after they were washed. She didn't want to think of her grandmother having dirty old bird's wings – bird's wings, as everyone knew, were filled with lice. Twice she and Barbi had wild fights because Barbi insisted that her grandmother was in an ugly old crow.

Rag sided with Bubbles in these disputes. Karla's death upset her so that she developed a kind of talking hysteria. Although she had not been to church, except for funerals, in more than forty years, she began to read the Bible and attempted to reacquaint herself with Christian doctrine, in which she could find no mention of the souls of good women going into birds. At one point in her life her favorite song had been 'The Great Speckle Bird,' but she searched in vain in the Bible itself for any mention of a great speckle bird. When the talking hysteria hit Rag she would just casually mention something she had remembered about Karla and then, unable to dam up her words, would begin to recapitulate events of her own life – her memories would pour out for hours.

When the talking hysteria took hold of Rag everyone except the two babies left the house. The school-age children poured out of the house and ran to school, often beating the tardy bell by several minutes. Rag would talk on and on for hours, often in competition with whatever happened to be on the Cartoon Channel at the time. Little Bascom and Baby Paul watched the Cartoon Channel most of the day. Since they were too young for play school no one could figure what else to do with them. Baby Paul rolled around on the floor for hours at a stretch, gumming rubber toys. Little Bascom's favorite pursuit, other than watching cartoons, was to sneak out into the garage and pull the stuffing out of an old couch that had once been in Dickie's room. The stuffing stuck to his clothes. Sometimes he would come back in the house looking as if he had been dipped in cotton candy.

Though Karla's absence was felt keenly by everyone every day, somehow the household veered just short of collapse. Meals got cooked and eaten, dirty clothes eventually got washed, minor injuries got treated, and small resentments soothed.

'It makes me sad – she died away! Who'll see me get married?' Bubbles said one morning, before bursting into tears.

Duane took the child in his lap and held her until she felt better.

'You're right, honey,' he said. 'Grandma died away too soon.'

'So did Jesus,' Willy pointed out. 'He was only thirty-something.

'Get it? Thirty-something,' he said, and laughed at his own joke.

'Life goes on,' Rag said, as a familiar cloud of despondency descended over the household.

'If you say life goes on one more time I'll strangle you,' Duane told her. 'It does, but who cares?'

All the children were shocked. Their grandfather had sounded like he meant it, when he said he would strangle Rag. What if he did strangle her?

'Would that be murder, or just manslaughter?' Barbi asked. She was always interested in the technicalities.

'That would just be Rag-slaughter,' Duane said. He smiled, to show that he hadn't meant it, though, for a moment, he *had* meant it.

'It was just an old saying,' Rag said, and burst into tears. In a way, Karla had been her best friend; everything was different, now that she was gone. She was just stuck there with the two babies all day. There was no one she could talk to about hairstyles, or the messy lives of movie stars, or the many catastrophes that would befall mankind once the ozone layer was finally destroyed and the rain forests cut down.

'I don't know what will become of me,' Rag sobbed. Duane and all the children had to hug her and give her many pats of reassurance before she quieted down.

# 52

Even though he was staying at home and wishing he could be living in his cabin, Duane continued to rent the honeymoon suite at the Stingaree Courts, on the Seymour highway west of Wichita Falls. Sometimes, even after the heat came, he would bicycle over to the Stingaree Courts, pay his bill in cash, and lay in his room for a few hours, listening to the whirr of the air conditioner while watching a slow baseball game on TV. Shorty would usually be laying just outside Gay-lee's door when Duane arrived. He would hurry over and yip at Duane a few times, to show Duane that he recognized him, but his response was not really passionate – when Duane left, a few hours later, Shorty rarely did more than lift an ear.

Usually Duane would knock on Gay-lee's door, hoping to chat with her a few minutes. If it was late in the day she would usually be blow-drying her hair. Without makeup she looked like a teenager.

Gay-lee always seemed glad to see him, but she was a little formal with him, perhaps unsure whether to address the fact of his grief.

Sis, the maid, was more forthright.

'I done had two husbands killed off – I know how you feel,' Sis said, when Duane told her he had lost his wife. 'Why do you keep coming back here, Duane? Ain't you got no place better than this to live?'

'I guess I just got used to being at this motel,' Duane said.

Marcie Meeks asked him the same question and he gave the same reply.

'You're an odd one,' Marcie Meeks said. 'Got a big house over there in Thalia that you could live in and you're still spending forty-eight dollars a night on our honeymoon suite.'

Marcie Meeks didn't mince words.

'Everything doesn't have to make sense,' Duane told her.

Marcie disagreed with that sentiment too.

'Maybe not if it's happening to you,' she said. 'But if it's happening to me it needs to make more sense than that. Forty-eight dollars a night adds up quick, even if you are a plutocrat.

'A plutocrat. You know, like Daddy Warbucks in *Little Orphan Annie*,' Marcie Meeks said. 'There was a comic strip of it when I was a kid.'

Duane knew that his desire to keep a room at the Stingaree Courts would seem odd to almost everyone, but having that room was part of an effort that was still important to him. Karla was dead and adjustment to that fact would have to be made, but the tragedy had not changed the fact that he wanted a different life. Perhaps he would fail and have to go back to the old life – but he was not going to do that unless he absolutely had to. He still refused to ride in motorized vehicles, he still spent time alone in his cabin, and he still drew reassurance from the knowledge that he had a room all his own at the Stingaree Courts.

Bicycling around the county – or walking, as he sometimes still did – Duane had Karla almost constantly in his mind. It troubled him that the last few months of her life had not been a very happy time for her, but of course there was no changing that now. At first what he felt most acutely was the fact that there could be no more conversation. Often, in the long spaces of their marriage, he and Karla had stopped talking to one another for long periods of time, though there would be no obvious reason for the stoppage. Sometimes they would just find themselves with nothing to say to each other.

But always, sooner or later, they would casually pick up the thread again and resume their conversation – then, for a year or more, they might be in conversation with one another several times a day, before losing interest again. Duane supposed that was just how a long marriage worked. There were lapses and interruptions of various kinds, but sooner or later the engagement kicked in again.

Now it couldn't. Never again would he hear Karla say 'Duane' in a way that meant she had something on her mind. And yet he kept expecting it, and would sometimes dream that he and Karla were talking. Waking from those dreams made him particularly sad.

The person who helped him most, in the first hot months after Karla's death, was Ruth Popper. Ruth was almost completely blind now, but she was so familiar with her small house, from having lived in it most of her long life, that she was still able to get around and do for herself. She subscribed to the large-print editions of *Time* and *Newsweek* and peered at them through her large magnifying glass.

'I'm pissed off that Dickie fired me,' she informed Duane bluntly, a day or two after Karla's funeral. 'You know why?'

'No, why?' Duane asked.

'Because I miss the gossip,' Ruth said.

'I'd think you'd be tired of gossip,' Duane said. 'I know I am.'

'Now you, you're brokenhearted because your wife's dead,' Ruth said. 'But you're just going to have to get over it, Duane. You had a nice marriage, and everything ends.'

No one had ever put it quite that way: that he had had a nice marriage, which was certainly true.

'Now look at me,' Ruth went on. 'I had ten or twelve boyfriends when I was of courting age, and some of them grew up to be nice men. But I married the worst asshole in the lot. I chose badly and I paid for it in spades. I didn't have a nice marriage like you had. So who's the lucky person?

'Most everybody around here gets killed on the roads, sooner or later,' she went on, without giving him time to reply. 'I'm lucky I'm past the driving age. I might live another ten years, if I can just stay off the roads.'

After that conversation Duane fell into the habit of dropping by Ruth's every day or two, to chat a few minutes and fill her in on whatever gossip he might have picked up. She had a fine sycamore tree in her backyard and liked to sit in its shade, fanning herself, on the long hot evenings when afterglow still lit the sky until nine o'clock or later.

'I've been living in this town for nearly ninety years,' she said, one day. 'You wouldn't think a person with brains would get stuck in a hot little hole like this for ninety years, but I did.'

Usually Duane would manage to bring the conversation around to Karla, at some point. He liked to hear other people talk about her – it made him proud, in a way, because neither Ruth nor Mildred-Jean nor Lester nor Bobby Lee had a bad word to say about her now, however much they may have quarreled with her when she was alive.

Also, hearing people talk about Karla meant that she was alive, in a way – alive, at least, in the memory of the town.

'Well, she had that energy,' Ruth said one day. 'Most people get sort of ground down, you know. I was ground down myself for about twenty-five years. I didn't have no zip – I was just going through the motions. Karla never seemed to lose her zip – that's gotta be good genes.'

'I ran out of it,' Duane commented. 'Just getting the kids off to school does me in for most of the day.'

'Yes, and I've been meaning to talk to you about that,' Ruth said.

'About what?' Bullbats were swooping over the pond next door.

'You,' Ruth said. 'Why are you raising your grandkids? It's not your job.'

The comment took him by surprise. Most of his grandkids had lived in or near the big house their whole lives, while their parents got in and out of various kinds of trouble. Karla had just seemed to want it that way; he could not remember that it had ever been discussed. The house was large; there was room for everyone. Having the grandkids there seemed like part of the natural order.

But Ruth was right – it *wasn't* part of the natural order.

'Your kids ain't perfect but they're healthy enough and none of them are morons,' she said. 'They *had* those children. It's their job to raise them, not yours.

'You ain't a baby-sitter service,' she went on. 'You'll be needing to marry again yourself, and I doubt your bride will want all those grandkids underfoot.'

'I agree that the kids should raise the grandkids,' Duane said. 'That *is* their job. But I won't marry again. I can't imagine it. Forty years is long enough to be married.'

'I know, I oughtn't to have said that while you're still in mourning,' Ruth said. 'I ought to have said that next year, or the year after. But I'm an old woman – I may not be around next year or the year after. I have to advise you while I can, even if the advice is a little premature.'

The thought of being married to someone other than Karla was so odd that Duane could scarcely grasp it. The strange thing was that two or three days ago he had overheard Rag say the same thing; she had been talking to Julie. He had just happened to step in the door at the right moment to overhear them. Julie had been insisting that her father would never marry again – even if he wanted to, the kids wouldn't stand for it, Julie told Rag.

'Yes, but honey, a grown man can't live on memories forever,' Rag said. 'Unless your dad's dead as a stump he'll marry again.'

The remark struck him with particular force because he remembered that Karla had said almost the same thing when she was complaining about their lack of a sex life.

'Sweet memories ain't enough,' she had said.

It was odd that Ruth and Rag, who had no use for each other, would have the same thought about him.

'Ruth, why would you think that?' he asked. 'Why would I want to marry again?'

But Ruth, embarrassed, refused to discuss it further.

'You'll know when the time comes,' she said.

# 53

In the next few days Duane learned that Ruth and Rag were not alone in their speculations about his future. Everyone in town seemed to be of the same opinion, which was that in a year or two – if not sooner – he would marry again. Mildred-Jean admitted as much the next day, while she was giving him a haircut.

'Yep, there ain't been no messy divorces lately, so you're the main topic of conversation,' Mildred-Jean said. 'Some people think you've got a girlfriend already.'

'They better not think it out loud in my hearing,' he told her. 'Karla's just been dead three months. What kind of man do they think I am?'

Duane was disgusted by such talk. He had been married forty years, and had loved his wife to the end, even if he had wandered off and pursued a lonely lifestyle at the end. Did they think he held her memory so cheap that he would just turn around and get married? Every day now he felt the urge to talk to Karla. Though she was dead, in some way he felt more married to her than he had when she was alive. The thought of being with another woman didn't appeal to him at all – in fact, it repelled him. Karla was a dead wife, the only one he had ever had, the only one, he felt sure, that he would ever need.

The local speculation troubled him so much that he even managed to convene three out of his four children, in order to reassure them on that score. He didn't want them to listen to the talk and get any silly ideas.

'People are talking about me getting married,' he said, to Dickie, Julie, and Nellie. There had been no solid reports of Jack's whereabouts, but rumor had it that he was in South America, trying to canoe down the Amazon.

'This talk is just silly gossip,' he said. 'I'm not going to get married.'

To his annoyance all his children avoided his eye. He saw that not one of them believed him, which annoyed him even more.

'We just want you to do what's best for you, Daddy,' Nellie said.

'If you find someone you love we don't want to stand in your way,' Julie said.

'Hell, why should you have a lonely old age just because Mom hit the milk truck?'

'What did I just say?' Duane said. 'I said I wasn't getting married. I've got nine grandkids and a few good friends. Why should I be worried about a lonely old age?'

No one spoke, but he saw that his children were as convinced as everyone else that he meant to marry again.

'Okay, think what you want, but from now on I'm going to be staying in the cabin at night,' he said. 'You'll have to figure out a way to raise your own kids.'

With that he left, leaving the children looking stunned. That night he sat late in front of his cabin, feeling the heat rise up from the ground. When he thought about it more calmly he realized that the speculation about his future was probably normal. For most of those doing the speculating, marriage was the norm by which all activity was measured. Just as nature abhorred a vacuum, society – at least as it was constituted in Thalia – abhorred the odd man out. Bad enough that he had given up pickups, but that one eccentricity the people might eventually accept. Giving up pickups while remaining single was more than the home folks were prepared to cope with. They needed to *think* Duane was going to marry again, even if in the end he never did.

The next morning Bobby Lee showed up at the cabin just as Duane was scrambling some eggs – Duane scrambled a couple more and set his visitor a plate.

'I guess you've come to talk to me about my forthcoming marriage,' Duane said.

Bobby Lee looked blank. He proceeded to empty about half the pepper shaker onto his eggs.

'I like visible pepper,' he explained, when Duane raised an eyebrow. 'I like visible salt too, but I've had to go light on the salt since I lost my ball.'

'Yes, they say a low-salt diet is good for people with one ball,' Duane said, nodding gravely.

'What's this about getting married?' Bobby Lee asked.

'It's the talk of the town,' Duane said. 'I don't know who I'm supposed to be marrying. I thought you might know.'

'I close my ears when there's gossip being said,' Bobby Lee said. 'I don't care whether you marry or don't marry – I got my own problems.'

'Good, I'm glad somebody's neutral,' Duane said.

'If there was another room on this cabin I might just move in with you,' Bobby Lee said. 'I'm sick of human society – all it does is make fun of my condition.'

'That's the main reason I don't have but one room – so you can't move in,' Duane said.

'Wait a minute – something ain't right about this situation,' Bobby Lee said. 'Where's Shorty?'

'I gave him away – he couldn't tolerate the travel,' Duane said.

'My God, you are a lost soul,' Bobby Lee said. 'I didn't know you was so far gone that you'd give your only dog away.'

'I gave him to a whore and a black lady,' Duane admitted. 'I saw him yesterday, though – he was in fine spirits.'

'Shorty may be, but Sonny Crawford ain't,' Bobby Lee said. 'They hauled him off to the hospital last night.'

'The crazy hospital, or the regular hospital?' Duane asked.

'The regular hospital,' Bobby Lee said. 'They're thinking of cutting both his feet off.

'They're black as oil,' he added. 'Sonny don't move around much and I guess his circulation just finally gave out.'

'You mean he's got gangrene?' Duane asked.

'Well, his feet are black as oil, they say,' Bobby Lee said. 'It might be gangrene. Whatever it means, his dancing days are over.'

'They were over anyway – I haven't seen Sonny at a dance in twenty years,' Duane said.

The news sobered him – the thought of Sonny sitting there, year after year in his little convenience store, hardly moving, hardly walking, until his feet began to rot, was not a pleasant thing to contemplate.

'You ought to go see him, Duane,' Bobby Lee said. 'You and him was best friends once. If they cut off both his feet he's going to be pretty depressed.'

Bobby Lee left and Duane washed the dishes. He liked everything in the cabin to be clean and in its ordered place. It was so peaceful not being in the big house, with Rag ranting and the children bickering and the TV blaring, that he had looked forward to a day of doing not much other than sitting in his lawn chair and looking off the hill. It was mainly when he was alone that he could think about Karla almost in a tranquil way, letting incidents from their life together sort of rise out of his memory and sink back into it. It was utterly still, not a breath of breeze even on his hilltop; the temperature was rapidly climbing toward one hundred. The distant horizon, which had been clear and sharp at sunrise, was already hazy from heat. He had the Thoreau book with him and looked through it idly now and then, but could not really get up enough momentum to read it straight through. There was one sentence he liked so much that he had underlined it and stuck a little piece of paper in the book to mark the place. 'I went into the woods because I wished to live deliberately, to front only the essential facts of life,' the sentence read, 'and see if I could not learn what it had to teach, and not, when I came to die, discover that I had not lived.'

Duane read that sentence over and over again, forty or fifty times; it was that sentence that explained exactly what he himself was trying to do – explained it so clearly that he didn't really want to read the rest of *Walden*. He had parked his pickup, left his family, and settled in the cabin to attempt to learn about life and not feel that he was just plodding through it. He knew most of his acquaintances would consider such an ambition puzzling and unnecessary. He had had a long marriage, four children, and nine grandchildren. How could he possibly think he hadn't really lived?

It was a question Duane couldn't easily answer himself. All he knew was that in his fifties he had begun to lose his sense of purpose and had merely gone on for several years, going through the motions, until finally he couldn't do that anymore – so he had stopped and was attempting to start a life that – detail by detail – meant something. He wanted to feel that at least some of what he did was worthwhile, in and of itself – even if it was nothing more than cleaning the trash out from under one bridge. Indeed, he felt that the smaller and more local the attempt, the better chance he had of accomplishing an action that had value. He didn't know enough to change anything large. Whatever he worked on had to be small, and within the sphere of his competence.

Already, it seemed to him, he had let his confusion and depression deflect him from even that modest goal. He had begun seeing the doctor, which had turned out to be unexpectedly tiring. Then, just as

266

it promised to become less tiring, Karla smacked into the milk truck and three months had been sucked into the attempt to keep his family's head above water. Ruth Popper had done him a very good turn when she reminded him that his children were grown and should be expected to be the hands-on parents of their own offspring. His wife was dead – giving up his new life, or at least his attempt to make a life that had some purpose, would not bring her back. He was not going to forget Karla, not ever, but being a widower was not a profession. He didn't intend to marry – didn't want to – but, as he thought about it, he became more and more sympathetic to the town's hope that he would marry. In gossiping about his next wife the townspeople were just saying, in effect, what he had threatened to strangle Rag for saying: that life goes on. Though it seemed disloyal to think that his life would eventually go on completely out of relation to Karla, or her memory, the likelihood was that it would. When he had been young his mother had sung him a song, popular in that day, called 'Time Changes Everything.' As he sat in his lawn chair, letting the heat soak into him, he realized as never before what a powerful truth that was.

It might even be that the gossipy townspeople were right. Time, which changed everything, might even change him so much that he *would* want to marry again.

It just wouldn't happen soon – that much he knew.

That evening he didn't go into town. He walked around the hill until the afterglow faded and it was too late to check on the grandkids. Checking on the grandkids every few hours, was, after all, the habit he was trying to break. He ate no supper and didn't miss it. The concept of fasting one day a week had begun to appeal to him. Frequently he ate out of habit, rather than hunger – it seemed to him that it was time to eliminate that habit. The day he had bought Barbi her book on ESP he had also bought himself a small book on woodworking, which he studied for half an hour, just before he turned his light off. He hadn't yet used many of the tools he had bought at Jody Carmichael's, the first time he had gone there. He didn't want to buy a bunch of specialized woodworking tools and then never do anything with them. He meant to buy just three or four tools and actually try to use them to work a piece of wood, shaping it into something of his own devising.

That night, to his extreme surprise, Duane had a wet dream. He was kissing a woman. At first he only felt sensation – he could not identify the woman. But then, very clearly, he saw that the woman he was touching and kissing was Honor Carmichael. He saw her large eyes, and smelt her breath. When he woke his sheets were so sticky with semen that he had to get up, clean himself, and change them. For the rest of the night he was wakeful. It had been many months, perhaps even a year, since he had felt any sexual stirring at all, and yet suddenly, unbidden, a dream came in which he was making love to his doctor.

When he dozed off again, as light was breaking, Karla came into a dream.

'Duane, I told you so,' his dead wife said, before she dissolved into the clear morning light.

# 54

When Duane left his cabin the little thermometer by his window read one hundred and two, and yet it was only eight-fifteen in the morning. He had turned his radio on for a few minutes – speculation from the weathermen was that the temperature might reach one hundred and twenty by the middle of the afternoon. Far away, in Phoenix, the Sky Harbor airport had had to close because the temperature had risen so high that planes could not get enough lift to ascend.

He got on his bicycle and pedaled slowly toward Wichita Falls, intending to visit Sonny Crawford in the hospital. It had been many years since he and Sonny had been able to talk companionably, or really be friends, as they had once been; but he had known Sonny all his life and had shared many early pleasures and early miseries with him. Duane had even been the cause of Sonny losing the sight in his left eye, in a sudden violent fight over the affections, such as they had been, of Jacy Farrow.

Duane felt he ought at least to visit Sonny. There was a time when Sonny had been a kind of honorary uncle to his own children – Julie and Jack in particular had doted on him once, and Sonny had been a good honorary uncle, easing them through many rough spots in their relationships with their parents. The least he could do now was check in on Sonny. The thought of a man so depressed that he couldn't even move around enough to sustain circulation in his feet was a grim thought.

As he rode along the country road, keeping in what shade he could find, moments of his wet dream began to replay themselves in his mind. The images that came to him were momentary, but they all involved Honor Carmichael: her breasts, her mouth, her legs. The images annoyed him. He didn't want to be having sexual thoughts about his doctor. It seemed particularly disloyal, somehow, both to

Dr Carmichael and to Karla. If he had to have sexy dreams, why couldn't they be of Karla, the wife he had just lost? Once or twice, bored, he had even tried to build a fantasy about Karla – but it didn't work. When he thought of Karla she was always fully dressed, ready for shopping, not sex. He was unable to retrieve a sexual image of his wife of forty years, with whom he thought he had had a pretty good sex life, even if it had tailed off quite a bit in the last few years; yet he could produce exciting sexual images of his doctor, whom he scarcely knew and in fact had quit seeing. It was troubling, not because there was anything much wrong about having a sexual fantasy about an attractive woman, but because it made him feel silly. He was on his way to see a very sick old friend. Why wouldn't his mind let the sex alone?

When he passed in sight of the Corners he decided on the spur of the moment to stop in and chat with Jody for a few minutes – he had had no breakfast and felt like a bottle of Gatorade might improve his pace.

Three depressed roughnecks, all from one of his own crews, were sitting on the tailgate of a pickup, eating microwaved burritos when Duane rode up.

'Morning, boys,' he said. 'Enjoying your breakfast?'

All three stopped eating and stared at him. Seeing him in biking garb seemed to render them speechless; or perhaps they were just too tired to talk. One, a boy named Gene, had a big piece of burrito sticking out of his mouth but seemed too weary even to chew it.

'Mr Moore, Dickie's killing us. Make him stop,' one man said. 'Ever since you put him in charge it's just been work, work, work.'

'Shit, I wish he'd just go back to being a dope addict,' Gene said, removing the wad of half-chewed burrito from his mouth in order to say it.

'My girlfriend's about to quit me because I don't never get no time off,' the third man said. 'It's got to be a serious situation.'

'When are you going to take over again?' Gene asked. 'It might save our lives.'

'I'm not going to take over again,' Duane said, and went inside.

Jody Carmichael was in shadow behind his counter, illuminated only by the green light of his computer screen.

'Excuse me just a minute,' he said. 'The horses are at the gate and the Queen's got a filly running.'

'Which queen?' Duane asked.

'Queen Elizabeth, the only queen that's got any horses that are worth a shit,' Jody said. He clicked on his keyboard a few more times and then swiveled around to face Duane.

'That's terrible about your wife,' he said. 'I always liked Karla.'

'Yes, most everybody did,' Duane said.

'The minute you start paving these goddamn little dirt roads that don't need to be paved you start losing valuable members of the population,' Jody said. 'People don't smash into milk trucks on these dirt roads.'

Duane didn't answer. He was momentarily stunned by the spiffed-up condition of Jody's store. Instead of being a dark, untidy mess in which double-A batteries might be shelved behind the Fritos, the store was now brightly lit, clean as a pin, and arranged in such a way that the potato chips, not the double-A batteries, were next to the Fritos. The general store was now as neat and clean as the hardware store had been.

'It looks as if your daughter's been here,' he said.

'Yes, there's been a revolution since you've been here,' Jody said. 'You lost an old wife and my daughter cleaned my store, and neither you nor me expected such a thing to happen.'

'Don't all this orderliness scare people?' Duane asked.

'Scares the roughnecks,' Jody said. 'It even scares me a little. I'm apt to see my own reflection on a can and think an old madman's snuck in on me. When did you adopt the bicycle as your mode of transportation?'

'When I started having appointments with your daughter,' Duane said. 'Eighteen miles is just a little too far to walk.'

'Oh, have you been visiting Honor?' Jody asked. 'That's good. No wonder you look in good health.'

'I saw her for a while,' Duane said. 'Didn't she tell you?'

'Nope, she's a psychiatrist,' Jody said, a little testily. 'She don't go around mentioning who's crazy and who ain't.'

'No, I guess that wouldn't really be the right thing,' Duane said.

Still, he felt a little disappointed. For some reason he had assumed that Dr Carmichael would have at least mentioned to her father that he had become a patient. It struck him that he wanted her to be more interested in him than she actually was. If that weren't true, probably there would have been no wet dream.

Even though he felt vaguely disappointed, Duane could not but be struck by the improvement Honor Carmichael had made in her father's working environment. The Corners had been a dark, dirty hole – now it was bright, clean, cheerful, and well ordered. Honor had obviously given some thought to how things should go, to how the toiletries and snacks and groceries should relate on the shelves to the lightbulbs, fishing lures, and bug spray.

Jody saw Duane admiring the smart arrangement, and smiled.

'Honor's got that organized mind,' he said. 'I guess that's why she's a good psychiatrist. She can figure out what kinds of things ought to sit next to one another on a shelf.'

'She sure can – you're lucky,' Duane said.

'Yes,' Jody said simply. 'I'm lucky. Having a daughter like Honor frees up my mind so I can pay attention to my betting. There's this new Albanian soccer team they're trying to get going. I never thought I'd live to see an Albanian soccer team. Old King Zog must be dancing on his grave.'

'Who's King Zog?' Duane asked.

Jody gave him a startled look.

'He was the King of Albania until the Commies took over,' Jody said.

Jody's response made Duane feel like an uneducated hick. Not only had he never heard of King Zog, he had never really even heard of Albania. All he could remember about Albania was that a bunch of Albanians had tried to escape to Italy somewhere on a boat, and – he thought he remembered – had been turned back. They had been sort of like the Vietnamese boat people, only they weren't Oriental.

'I didn't know you kept up with all the royalty, Jody,' he said.

'Oh, just the Queen, really,' Jody said. 'The Queen's got a couple of nice fillies and some two-year-olds that look like they might be picking up speed.'

Duane bought a bottle of Gatorade and some peanuts to nibble on his way to visit Sonny Crawford.

'Your daughter's really done a good job here,' he said. 'You already had the neatest hardware store in this part of the country, but now you've got the neatest grocery store to go with it.'

'That's not the end of it, either,' Jody said. 'Any day now she claims she's going to paint the outside.'

'If I was her I'd wait till fall to start in on that job,' Duane said. 'This heat will dry her brushes before she could even get the paint on the board.'

'No, it won't, because she'll be out here at first light and paint for an hour and leave,' Jody said. 'Then she'll be out the next morning and paint for an hour and leave. Once she starts a job, Honor don't let up.'

Duane wanted to ask Jody to tell her hello for him, but, at the last minute, he didn't make the request. If Dr Carmichael hadn't even mentioned to her father that he had become her patient, then asking Jody to tell her hello was probably quite inappropriate. He realized, as he pedaled away, that he didn't know much more about the rules of psychiatry than he did about the kings of Albania. Perhaps, in Honor Carmichael's view, he was still her patient, in which case it would probably be much more appropriate for him to make a new appointment and go tell her hello himself.

# 55

'You don't want to look at my feet, or smell them either,' Sonny said, when Duane came into his hospital room. 'Your best bet is to sit right under the air conditioner.'

'That's the best bet in this heat anyway,' Duane told him.

Sonny looked out the window at the baking hospital lawn.

'I guess it is hot, isn't it?' he said. His eyes didn't really fix on Duane – they didn't really fix on anything. They reminded Duane of the eyes of old dogs. Wherever Sonny Crawford was looking was a place no one normal could hope to see.

'It's so hot airplanes can't take off,' Duane said. 'They had to close down Phoenix.'

Sonny smiled his vague, impersonal smile.

'That's okay, I wasn't going to Phoenix anyway,' Sonny said. 'The seasons don't really mean much to me anymore. I don't mind if it's hot and I don't mind if it's cold.'

To Duane's eye, Sonny looked awful. He hadn't shaved for three or four days, and his graying hair was messed. When Duane reached to shake his hand Sonny had no grip at all. Duane might as well have been shaking his elbow, or his knee. He might just as well be shaking the hand of a man who had died. He felt awkward even being in the room with Sonny, and was sorry he had come. All the two of them shared was a town and a past. They had lived their lives in the same place, but any interest they had had in knowing each other had evaporated over time.

'The whole town misses Karla but I guess you probably miss her most,' Sonny said. He had been at the funeral, his necktie poorly knotted. Duane remembered seeing him talking to the girls.

'I do miss her,' Duane said.

'I hadn't really talked to Karla in years,' Sonny admitted, looking out again at the burning lawn. 'It was my fault. Karla was always into self-improvement – she kept trying to get me to jog, or eat right, or look for a girlfriend, but I didn't. I guess she just got pissed off and gave up on me – can't blame her.'

'That was her way,' Duane said.

'How come you started walking everywhere?' Sonny asked.

'I don't know, really. I guess it just came to seem like a better use of my time than riding in pickups. I've ridden millions of miles in pickups and yet I've never really seen the world – I've just seen the pickups.'

There was, after that, a long silence. Duane felt he had done his duty, by coming to see Sonny, but couldn't tell that Sonny much cared.

'It's strange, isn't it?' Sonny said. He had noted Duane's unease.

'What, that your feet have gone bad?' Duane asked.

'No, that's not strange, that's just what happens if you sit on your ass all night and don't exercise. If I'd just listened to your wife my feet would probably be fine. What's strange is us – you and I have known one another all our lives and don't have a thing to say to one another.'

'That may not be so strange,' Duane said. 'There may just not be that much to talk about if two people live their whole lives in Thalia.'

'Well, there's life, and there's high school football, and there's Jacy Farrow,' Sonny said. 'I guess that only takes you so far.'

'I think Ruth means to come and see you, if she can get someone to drive her,' Duane said. 'She asked about you yesterday.'

'Old Ruth,' Sonny said. 'She might come to visit me but she can't come to see me because she can't see. She's another one who tried to get me into self-improvement. Remember when Ruth used to jog?'

'Yep, during the boom,' Duane said. 'That was when everybody was into jogging. Then the bust happened and everybody went back to real life.'

'I had an affair with Ruth, remember?' Sonny said. 'Her husband was that fat-ass coach. He asked me to take Ruth to the doctor one day and we started sleeping together.'

Duane did remember. At the time he had been going with Jacy, the prettiest girl in town, and had thought it rather odd that his friend was shacking up with an old lady – Ruth would have been in her mid-thirties, at the time. Not only that, he thought it was dangerous. Everyone in town knew about the affair – how the coach failed to notice it was a mystery to everyone; but the consensus was that he would catch them in the act someday and kill them both with his deer rifle.

'When you come right down to it, I guess Ruth Popper was my only real girlfriend,' Sonny said. 'I married Jacy but her parents caught us and had the marriage annulled before I even slept with her. I guess Ruth was it for me, so far as romance was concerned.'

'You could have done worse,' Duane said. 'Lots of people have.'

Sonny looked startled. His face was puffy and he seldom changed expression but he did shift his eyes and look at Duane when Duane told him he could have done worse.

'You know, that's true,' Sonny said. 'Ruth is a nice woman. I should have run that fat coach off and married her. I knew Ruth cared about me and I knew Jacy didn't – but Jacy was prettier. I never really got over Jacy. *You* got over her and married Karla and had four kids, but look at me. All I married was a Kwik-Sack.'

Duane was beginning to feel low and sad, which is how he always felt when he was with Sonny Crawford for more than a few minutes – Sonny just had the ability to shift the weight of his lifelong gloom onto whomever he was with. Now it was happening again, and the reason it was happening was because what Sonny was saying was true, and also sad. If Duane considered that he was bad off for having wasted so much time riding in pickups, how much sadder was Sonny's case? The aging man in the bed with the ruined feet had been blocked all his life from mature happiness because he couldn't get over his failure to win one girl, Jacy Farrow, who, in the years when Sonny had such a terrible crush on her, had just been a pretty, selfish, small-town rich girl. Jacy had grown beyond some of those faults, it was true – in her middle years, when she had returned to Thalia after a very modest career in movies, Duane had grown to like her a lot. But the Jacy who had transfixed Sonny and somehow arrested his growth had had nothing to offer but her looks. Of course the pull of beauty in a small town where there was little of it was no slight pull. He himself had been as in love with Jacy as Sonny had been – and more successfully – and had needed three or four years to get over her himself, after she was sent away to school and went on to have her small success in Hollywood and Europe.

Then Karla showed up and he moved on – only, for Sonny, there was no Karla. Dickie or one of the kids told him that Sonny was still cutting pictures of Jacy out of magazines when *Dickie* was in high school, twenty years or more after Jacy had left Thalia.

Yet Sonny was not dumb. Even now, despite his puffy face and his black feet, he gave the impression of being an intelligent man, intelligent enough to notice that Duane's spirits were sinking.

'Sometimes I think it's Jacy's fault that my feet are rotting,' Sonny said, with a little smile. 'She bewitched me and I stayed bewitched.'

'It don't do to dwell in the past,' Duane said.

The remark sounded stupid, but he had to say something and could come up with nothing better. All he wanted was to be out of the building, on his bike, off in the country feeling the comforting heat. Sonny's room was chill, so chill that Duane had goose bumps on his arms. He wondered if they kept the room so cold in order to drive visitors out sooner, or because most of the building was filled with people who were dying. Keeping them chilled down probably made the undertaker's job easier.

'I guess that's been my problem,' Sonny said. 'I've always dwelled in the past. I'm just one of those country boys who never got out of high school – not really. My happiest times were when you and me and Jacy ran around together. You know, when Sam the Lion was alive. That was back before the picture show closed, remember?'

'Oh, I remember,' Duane said. 'I had to work my ass off, in those days. Sometimes I would have to roughneck forty-eight hours, straight through. I worked for Jacy's daddy, mostly. That's why they never wanted me going with her. I was just oil field trash, to them.'

As he was leaving, Sonny stuck one of his black feet out from under the sheets and looked at it.

'So long, toes,' Sonny said. 'I'll be rid of you tomorrow.'

Duane was so glad to be out of the hospital that all he did, for a time, was stand and soak up the heat. Being with Sonny made him feel suffocated, smothered by the past that meant so much to Sonny and so little to himself.

Later, buying a milk shake at the Burger King, Duane took a dollar bill out of his pocket and happened to notice the little slip of paper with the name of the book on it – the note Honor Carmichael had made for him the last time he had seen her. He wished he had thought to make an appointment with her, but he hadn't. In view of the dream he had had about her, he didn't even know if he should make an appointment. Falling in love with his doctor, if that was what he was doing, didn't make any sense. For all he knew she was married, or had a boyfriend. The last thing he needed was to get hung up on a woman he couldn't have.

On his way out of town he pedaled over to a bookstore in one of the larger malls and handed the slip of paper to a clerk, a skinny young woman in a green blouse.

'Oh, Proust,' she said, as if it were an everyday name. 'We don't get many calls for Proust. I don't think we have this in stock but we could order it for you, if you like.'

'Why don't you do that?' Duane said, writing down his name and address.

'Wow, Proust,' the girl said. 'I've been meaning to read him myself, but it just looks so long.'

'Do you know what it's about?' Duane asked.

'Wow, France, I think – or Paris or something,' the girl said. 'We'll call you when it comes in.'

'Thanks,' Duane said. He wondered, as he pedaled home, why his doctor thought he ought to read about France.

# 56

For the next year and a half Duane devoted himself to the task he had chosen to undertake, which was to pare his life down to essentials. He bicycled less, walked more. Much of his time he spent alone, in or near his cabin. He bought a few simple woodworking tools and built a shed onto the east side of his cabin, in which to do his woodworking. He had a small assortment of woods and lumber delivered to him, which he kept covered with a tarp. With some difficulty – involving many failed efforts – he learned to make boxes. He made a box for each of his children, and then one for each of his grandchildren.

He did not enclose his shed, but worked in the heat and the cold, desisting only when winter rain slanted in and wet his workbench. He tried carving animals out of knotty mesquite, but found that he could not get the proportions of the animals right – his best creations were boxes. He gave a box to Rag, one to Ruth Popper, one to Bobby Lee, and one to Lester and Jenny Marlow. Even so his stock of boxes increased faster than he could give them away.

The books that he had ordered – the ones the salesclerk thought were about France – came in less than a week: three fat silver-and-black paperbacks. Duane took them home and put them on a shelf next to the coffee can, but he didn't try to read them. Twice he pedaled over to the Corners in the predawn hours because Jody Carmichael had said his daughter intended to paint the store. Jody had been right. Honor Carmichael was there, in shorts, with her long hair tied up in a bun; but she was not there alone. A short, dumpy woman was helping her. Duane pulled his bicycle into the ditch and watched the two women through a screen of brush. He didn't want to be seen. Though he knew it was weird that he was peeping at his doctor, he couldn't resist. When he came back a second morning he saw the same scene: Honor Carmichael was painting, with the help of a short woman who wore a kind of pushed-down hat.

On a third morning he rode halfway to the Corners and then turned and went back home. Spying on his doctor as she tried to make her father's store presentable just seemed too weird – if Dr Carmichael should happen to catch sight of him he knew he would feel dreadfully embarrassed.

What he ought to do was simply call the doctor and start a new sequence of appointments. The doctor had said his therapy might take years – that meant that, for a price, he could have her company four times a week indefinitely. But he didn't call to make an appointment and he didn't ride back to the Corners, either.

When he did go back, months later, he marveled at the transformation. Both the store and the hardware shed had been painted white, with green trim. The debris had been cleaned up and a low fence built around the yard. Flowers had been planted all around the house, and the mud hole where customers had once parked was blacktopped. The store that had for so long been a mess and an eyesore was now one of the more attractive places of business in the whole county.

Meanwhile, in Thalia, the big house where Duane and Karla had lived much of their lives slowly emptied of children and grandchildren. Dickie decided he could run the oil company more efficiently if he lived in Wichita Falls, so he and Annette and Loni and Barbi and Sami moved into a house in the western suburbs. There was increased oil and gas activity in southern Oklahoma and Dickie wanted to be closer to the action.

In the fall after his mother's death Jack returned from wherever he had been, only to leave again immediately. Duane came home to the cabin one day to find a note on the table which read:

Hi, Dad.
Sorry I missed you, I'm moving to Montana.

Jack

After that the family heard of him mainly through Rag. Sometimes Jack would call her in the middle of the night – the two of them would talk for hours about the state of the world. In January Duane got a postcard informing him that Jack was going to college in Bozeman. By the next summer he had a job as a sheep detective, catching sheep rustlers up on the Wyoming-Montana border, employed, so Rag claimed, by a rich woman who owned half a million acres in that part of the world.

'Why would a rich woman hire Jack?' Duane asked Rag one day. 'Why would a rich woman bother with sheep? It sounds fishy to me.'

'Okay, doubt my word,' Rag said. 'If you don't believe me I guess you could hike up there in a year or two and check it out. Of course, by the time you get there Jack may be back in the Amazon. People who travel at a snail's pace can't expect to know everything.'

Nellie, the most popular country DJ in the whole of the Dallas-Fort Worth metroplex, fell in love with the rich man who owned the station she worked at, plus eighty-two others and various cable enterprises. His name was Zenas Church; he was a widower with five children and a Learjet which he piloted himself, whizzing around to his eighty-three radio stations. Nellie was soon spending weekends in Nashville and New York, where she attended lavish parties. She had a nanny whose exclusive responsibility was Little Bascom and Baby Paul; the nanny's main job was keeping the little tykes from being trampled underfoot by Zenas Church's five boys, all of whom were large and clumsy.

Julie moved into north Dallas, or south Plano, where Jeanette, her best girlfriend, lived. The two of them ranged as far north as Tulsa and as far south as Padre Island in pursuit of parties, at one of which Julie met Goober Flynn, a flamboyant native of Texarkana who liked to wear Western shirts with pearl buttons and two-thousand-dollar cowboy boots but in fact had graduated from the Wharton School of Business and had been one of the first Texans to buy stock in Microsoft. Goober Flynn and Zenas Church were soon in competition to see who could get richer. Goober put Julie to work in one of his several craft malls, where the years she had spent with her mother, shopping wildly and at random, stood her in good stead. Soon she was traveling to New England, Kentucky, the Pacific Northwest, and even as far afield as Afghanistan, seeking out native craftsmen. Goober insisted that she finish her education, which she did at a junior college in Garland. Duane rode down on his bike to see her graduate; the trip took him two days each way. Goober Flynn, a man of some polish, did not seem to regard Duane's determination to avoid motorized transport as being in any way unusual. He thought it might be a good way for stressed-out executives to unwind, and even suggested that Duane go up to the Wharton School of Business and give a seminar in how to get around without motor transportation.

Willy and Bubbles were soon enrolled in a private school in Highland Park, where they were required to wear uniforms – even, in Willy's case, a tie.

Back home in Thalia, Rag ruled forlornly over a big empty house. The only sign that a large family had once lived there was the pile of junk that still filled much of the carport.

'Couldn't you just have a garage sale and get rid of it?' Duane asked. 'It's been there for years. There could be snakes living in it.'

Rag received the suggestion with indifference.

'Better yet, you ought to sell this whole place, Duane,' she said. 'Nobody wants to live here anymore. I'm getting to be a drunkard just from sitting here by myself.'

'You could get a pet,' Duane suggested.

'A pet ain't as good as human company,' Rag insisted. It was true that she was drinking a lot. She and Bobby Lee had formed the habit of playing video games with each other – sometimes their games raged deep into the night. Though Bobby Lee had eventually broken down and acquired a prosthetic testicle, it hadn't made him any less shy with women.

'I think I *could* have sex,' Bobby Lee said often. 'But the thing is, I can't get up my nerve to try.'

Then he joined a health club and became an exercise addict, lifting weights, climbing StairMasters, rowing on rowing machines, playing racquetball with all comers.

'I can't figure out why you exercise so much,' Duane said one day. Bobby Lee came to the cabin to visit with him at least twice a week.

'You work hard all day,' he added. 'Then you go to a damn health club and work harder. What's the point?'

Bobby Lee pondered the question for a long time, before answering. The hair at his temples had turned white; otherwise he was almost bald.

'I guess it's because all those machines are so clean,' he said, finally. 'We've got machines at the rig but they're oily and greasy or muddy and yucky. But those machines at the health club are spotless. I mean, spotless. They clean those suckers every day.'

'I don't care how clean they are, they're still just machines,' Duane said. 'Dickie pays you to work with the dirty machines and then you turn around and give your hard-earned money to a damn health club just so you can get all sweaty and smelly working with a clean machine. I don't guess I get it.'

'There's not much to get,' Bobby Lee said, a little sadly. He was prone to low spells, during which, without warning, his spirits would plummet to serious depths.

'I guess I go to health clubs for the same reason people go to art museums,' he added.

'Art museums?' Duane asked.

'Sure,' Bobby said. 'People go to art museums to see pretty pictures and I go to health clubs to see those pretty machines. You know, they're even so clean they gleam.'

'Now I've heard everything,' Duane said.

# 57

In the spring after Karla's death Duane raised a splendid garden behind the big house. Discouraged by the tragedy and the overpowering heat wave that followed it, he let the previous year's hasty garden burn up. Blister bugs got into the greenhouse and ruined the tomatoes; the drought and the heat took care of everything that had been planted outside. Even the peaches on their four nice peach trees shriveled up before they ripened – the birds got most of them. Duane, trying to hold the family together, discovered that he lacked the energy to hold the family together and garden too. Now and then in the late afternoon he would go out and make a stab at weeding the garden, but about the only things he took from it that summer were a few good onions and a bucket or two of unblemished peaches.

The problem of the garden nagged at his conscience all summer. He remembered that Dr Carmichael had been particularly interested in his attitudes toward the garden – they had been probing those very attitudes not long before Karla got killed and he left therapy. With Karla alive he hadn't fretted about the garden too much, because it was her responsibility as much as his; and Karla was, if anything, the better gardener. Once she was killed the whole responsibility became his, and the fact that he immediately failed at it and let the garden burn up was one of the things that troubled him most from day to day. The children had no interest in helping him, and somehow it didn't feel right just to hire a gardener. It was his garden, and Karla's. Hiring a gardener would have destroyed the whole point; though, when he thought about it, he couldn't easily say why. If hiring a gardener for a few weeks would save the garden, why not do it?

Duane could formulate no clear answer to that question – perhaps he hesitated out of nostalgia. He and Karla had always gardened together – they both took great satisfaction not only from doing the work but from discussing the success or failure of this crop or that with each other. Karla was always eager to test the latest horticultural products or techniques – she and Duane spent many pleasant hours drinking margaritas on their patio and discussing their eggplants or their rutabagas. One reason they both looked forward to the summer months was because the gardening absorbed them and brought them together. In a way it was to their late middle age what sex had been to their youth: something they never got tired of; something, even, that kept them feeling like a couple.

So, after the accident, one of the most difficult adjustments Duane had to make was to accept the fact that he would never have Karla to garden with again. He would have to go it alone or not go it at all. If he had been blessed with a wetter spring or a cooler summer he might have adjusted in time to at least make a respectable job of it, but the elements were unforgiving and his energies drained by the effort to comfort his family and deal with the daily crises that Karla had once dealt with as competently as she had once dealt with the blister bugs and the tomato plants. He gave up, and the garden burned.

When spring came again – the spring after Karla's death – Duane determined to do better. He didn't hire a gardener, but he did pay a competent young farmer to plow the garden plot. As soon as the weather was warm enough for planting, Duane began. In the greenhouse they kept a huge pile of seed catalogues, more of which arrived every week. Duane took a sheaf of seed catalogues back to his cabin and pored over them at night, looking for new varieties of vegetables to plant. He sent off his orders and seeds began to arrive. When the time came to plant he was ready, and from then on, every day until full summer, he worked in the garden, carefully keeping watch over every plant. In the last few years he and Karla had become more interested in organic gardening – after some thought Duane decided to keep this year's garden fully organic. He planted three varieties of corn, he planted kale, he planted leeks, he planted three kinds of tomatoes and eight kinds of onions. One corner of the garden was reserved for herbs.

This year, as if repentant, the spring provided him with an ideal combination of warm days and slow rains. The garden flourished, and so did the weeds, although no weed was long safe from Duane's hoe. There were a number of gardening buffs in Thalia, people he and Karla had compared notes with over the years. Though busy with their own gardens, some of these neighbors would drop by in the late afternoon to admire Duane's vegetables, by far the greatest variety to be found within the city limits of Thalia. The one who came by most often was Jenny Marlow, Lester's wife. Jenny loved to garden, but had had a hard time satisfying herself in the last few years because of Lester's many legal problems.

'Every time I think I've finally got a good garden going, we have to move to a smaller house,' Jenny told Duane. 'We're just living in four rooms now. I don't know how much smaller these houses can get.'

Duane admired Jenny. She had carried on gallantly although her husband was a nearly insane person who had been jailed twice and might yet be jailed again. It could not have been easy to be the wife of a man who was constantly the butt of local jokes, but Jenny held her head up, did her job, and stood by Lester unwaveringly. Despite her troubles she preserved a serene demeanor.

One day in June with a nice little drizzle falling, Duane and Jenny walked up and down the long rows of his garden, admiring this vegetable and that. Standing amid the green abundance Jenny looked at Duane sadly for a moment. Though they had never discussed it Jenny seemed to understand that he had made a special effort with this year's garden as a way of showing his devotion to Karla's memory. The wonderful garden was Duane's way of paying tribute to his late wife.

'I guess you miss her like I'd miss Lester, if he died,' Jenny said, putting her hand on his arm for a moment.

'Yes, I do,' Duane said, though he was guiltily aware that he was not telling the whole truth. He *did* miss Karla, sometimes acutely; but the fact was that it was easier to miss her than it had been – at times – to live with her. Alive, her energy, her questing was so unceasing that it was impossible to ignore it – for long stretches Karla went through life as charged as a naked wire. It was easy to love her but hard to find quietness with her. Often he had not had the energy for the level of engagement Karla wanted; often he just reached a point where he had nothing to say. Being a widower was not a better state, but it did take less energy. He could think of himself a little while working in Karla's garden.

But he didn't want to talk about complications of that nature with Jenny – perhaps she sensed them anyway, guessed that there were times when he *didn't* miss Karla, when he was happy just to be working alone in the garden, or walking at his own pace along the country roads.

There were aspects of widowerhood Duane just did not want to get into, particularly not with someone as smart as Jenny Marlow. He was grieved, but he wasn't devastated, and he liked to think that Karla would have understood that and considered it a healthy attitude – the attitude he liked to think *she* would have had if he had been the one to smack into the milk truck. Karla too would have been grieved, perhaps devastated for a time; but she wouldn't have been stopped. 'Shoot, we're all just passing through,' she liked to say – it was one of her favorite expressions. If he had been the one to pass on through, Karla, in time, would have coped.

'This is the biggest garden I've ever seen, Duane,' Jenny said. 'Who are you going to feed all this stuff to? You've got more food here than five families could eat, and there's not a single one of your children at home. There's just you.'

The question Jenny asked was one that had begun to nag Duane himself. Who was he going to feed all these healthy vegetables to? He might occasionally drop off a few vegetables with Dickie and Annette, in Wichita Falls, and of course any of the children were welcome to drop by and pick what they wanted, but the fact was they never did. Both Julie and Nellie had rich boyfriends who fed them in the best restaurants in Dallas or Nashville or Los Angeles or New York or wherever their airplanes took them. Jack was in Montana and Rag had died in the winter, a victim – in only six weeks – of cancer in both lungs. The last time Duane visited her in the hospital she expressed amazement at the swiftness of her own demise. 'This stuff's got me nearly killed off before I even knew I had it,' Rag said. 'Reckon it was the smoking?'

'I have no idea what it was,' Duane said.

'If there's shopping malls up in heaven maybe I'll meet Karla and we'll go on a spree,' Rag said. 'Sonny Crawford lost both feet and he's still stumpin' around. I guess you can spare both feet but you can't spare both lungs.'

Once Rag was buried Duane closed and locked the big house and sold all the unwanted cars his children had left in the driveway or the carport. The big house, filled with life for some thirty years, was now only filled with shadows.

The fact that he had a huge garden, but no one to feed the

vegetables to, was an irony he had been thinking about even before Jenny Marlow mentioned it to him.

'I think I may just open it to the public,' he told Jenny. 'There's poor people in this town who would be glad to get these vegetables.'

'I think that's a fine idea,' Jenny said. 'And you know what, I may be one of them. Can you spare a little kale?'

'You can have a little of anything,' Duane assured her. 'Or a lot of anything, for that matter.'

'I don't need a lot of anything,' Jenny said. 'Lester hates veggies. He's managing to stay alive on Fudgsicles and barbecue potato chips.'

The next day Duane bought some plywood, and painted it white. Then he rummaged in the trailer house until he found an old set of child's paints that had once belonged to Barbi. With the paints he wrote several signs and stuck one by each of the four roads into Thalia. The last one he put up right by the garden itself. The sign read:

KARLA LAVERNE MOORE MEMORIAL GARDEN
*Organic Vegetables Free to the Public*
*Please Be Neat with Your Picking*
*Duane C. Moore*

He ran a similar notice in the local paper for three weeks. The response was immediate and gratifying. Since the garden needed all but full-time attention Duane had taken to working in it early and late and spending the hot hours in Dickie and Annette's old trailer house, which was still parked at the back of the property. He had tried resting in the big house at first but found he could not be at ease there. Dickie and Annette had taken everything but one old couch, an air conditioner, and a few glasses out of the trailer – what they abandoned was exactly what he needed. But the best thing about the trailer house was that its rear window allowed him to keep an eye on the garden and observe the people that came to it. The trailer was a perfect observation post – no one need suspect that they were being watched.

The first people who visited the garden were not poor – most of them were neighbors he had known for years – but these first visitors either took nothing at all or limited themselves to a few tomatoes and an ear or two of corn. They paid close attention to the garden, though – it was clear that they regarded it with wonderment, almost with awe. Nine people came the first morning, all but two of them elderly neighbors.

Then, late that afternoon, a black family came – the only black family in Thalia.

'My lord,' the mother of the family said – she was a woman in late middle age. 'Been a long time since I seen a garden like this, Mr Moore.'

'Thanks, Gladys – I'm proud of it,' Duane admitted.

Gladys and her husband and grandchildren took mostly green beans and a variety of greens. The next day they came back and got more. They looked nervous when they saw Duane working, perhaps nervous that he might chide them for reappearing so soon. But he just joked with them a little and let them know they were welcome to take what they needed.

There were a few Hispanics in town, most of whom worked in the farming country to the east – it was not long before they began to arrive to check out the garden. They paid Duane many compliments and rewarded his generosity with modest smiles. They took corn, peppers, radishes, a few spring onions, and an eggplant or two.

Often old couples would pull off the highway and check out the garden – strangers, travelers, people on their way from someplace south to someplace north, or vice versa. These passers-through rarely took anything from the garden, but they didn't treat it cursorily, either. Many of them walked slowly up every row, stooping now and then to inspect the quality of the vegetables.

'A garden this big is a passel of work,' one large-handed old man said. 'Momma and me put up a garden nearly this size when we was younger, but hell, I wouldn't be up to it today.'

'There's things growing here that I don't even know the name of, and I know the names of plenty of vegetables,' his wife said.

Though most any kind of person was apt to stop by and admire the garden and pick themselves a mess of this or that, by far the most regular users were the disadvantaged young white families of the town – roughnecks or pipeliners who had been laid off, food stamp mothers with two or three unkempt children with bewildered eyes. They all came to the garden tentatively, on the first visit, not investing much hope, as they might stop by a garage sale hoping to pick up a usable hot plate for fifty cents. Often they would mope around the garden for an hour or so, confused by the abundance, not knowing quite what to choose, perhaps not yet convinced that they *could* choose. Some Duane had to encourage by offering gatherings of whatever had just come ripe. He had overplanted tomatoes – he had enough, he felt, to feed the whole town, so he urged a pound or two of homegrown tomatoes on everyone who stopped by. The young mothers quickly became convinced that Duane meant what he said: that the food was free. They perked up a little, and made sure their children said thank you, when they got back into their cheap cars, laden with peaches and corn and snap peas, and drove off.

Soon young farmwives from the circle of farm communities just to the east began to visit the garden. These women were not so much poor as curious, eager to find out about vegetables they could try in their own gardens, when it came time to plant again.

Word soon spread to the nearby communities – Duane was even pestered by reporters and TV crews, but he refused all requests for interviews and hid out in the trailer house when the reporters became too persistent. He had a big garden, but it wasn't big enough to feed the whole area. He wanted it to be a resource mainly for the local poor, who needed it most.

One day, to his surprise, Gay-lee and Sis drove up, with Shorty in the car. He had finally given up his room at the Stingaree Courts. Once he started his garden he went to the Courts less and less, until he finally came round to Marcie Meeks's view, which was that it was absurd to pay forty-eight dollars a night for a room he never used.

He felt a little sad when he turned in his room key, even so.

When the women drove up Shorty hopped out of the car and ran around the outside of the house, lifting his leg on every second bush. When Duane walked over to Sis and Gay-lee and gave them each a big hug they both looked shy and a little scared. Neither seemed comfortable to be standing in the middle of nowhere, on the outskirts of a small town.

'Duane, you sure got a big garden,' Sis said. 'My grandma, she used to garden like this – she grew every kind of thing that grows. But after she passed ain't nobody had time to put in this much garden.'

'If I was a vegetarian this would be heaven, I guess,' Gay-lee said.

'Well, but you don't have to be a vegetarian to enjoy a good garden,' Duane said. 'I'm real glad to see you two. What's been happening over at the Courts?'

Both of the women hesitated. They seemed tongue-tied.

'This my day off,' Sis said. 'Gay and me just decided to get out into the country and take a little drive.'

290

'Is that where you live?' Gay-lee asked, pointing at the big house.

'No, I live in a little cabin about six miles out,' Duane said. 'This house is where I used to live when my wife was alive and all my kids were living at home.'

Duane walked them through the garden, showed them what was good, and piled their car with his choicest produce before he let them leave. He knew Sis had many children – she could use all the vegetables she could carry. Though Gay-lee didn't cook he insisted that she take some fresh peaches and a box of dewberries for her girls.

The gift made Gay-lee choke up.

'We miss you,' she said, wiping a tear.

'Sure do,' Sis said. 'We don't get too many gentlemen out at the Stingaree.'

'We don't get *any* gentlemen, now that you're gone,' Gay-lee said.

'You two are the first people ever to refer to me as a gentleman,' Duane told them, as he was putting a final sack of roasting ears into their car.

In response Sis came over and gave him a big tight hug.

'Well, you is one,' she said. 'You is one even if you didn't know it.'

'You may miss me but my dog don't,' he said.

Shorty hopped in the front seat of Gay-lee's car as if he had been riding in it all his life. He was riding in the middle, between Sis and Gay-lee, his paws on the dashboard, when the three of them drove away.

# 58

Duane was deeply gratified by the way the big garden was received. Particularly, he was pleased by the fact that everyone who took vegetables from it – young, old, and middle aged – took care to obey the sign and do their picking neatly. There was no wastage. Young mothers kept tight control of their little ones, so that few plants were trampled. Only once or twice had he even found a cigarette butt in the garden rows.

Karla, he felt sure, would have been very pleased by the offering he had made in her name. He liked to think she might have planted a public garden in *his* name, if he had been the one to die.

In July the good slow rains ended and the temperatures began to climb. Despite constant picking the garden still flourished, but it began to need regular watering. Duane spent the early mornings and the late afternoons here and there in the garden with his hose or his watering can.

Near midday one Wednesday, when he was resting under the whirr of the air conditioner in the trailer house, he heard a car drive up. It parked, and two doors slammed, but Duane was in a half doze and did not immediately get up from the couch to see who was in the garden. But in a few minutes curiosity got the better of him – he was always interested in what kind of people came to see the garden. He got off the couch, splashed water in his face, and peered out his back window at the two visitors. Two women in khakis and shorts were on the far side of the garden plot. One wore a floppy hat with a large brim and the other a little mashed-down green cap of a kind he had seen only once before: the morning when he had spied on Honor Carmichael and her friend as they painted Jody Carmichael's store.

The visitors were, in fact, Honor Carmichael and the same friend. Honor carried a large straw basket and would occasionally stoop down to inspect a vegetable – sometimes she would kneel down and sniff it. Her friend had a slight limp – she steadied herself with a cane. Duane could not remember that she had used a cane when the two were painting the store, but perhaps he had missed it in the early dimness.

The sight of Honor Carmichael took Duane aback. He was accustomed to having pretty much anybody show up at his garden – a couple from Auckland, New Zealand, had stopped and picked a few vegetables one day – but the one person he had not expected to see there was his psychiatrist, the woman he had wanted in his dream. The two women seemed to be having an animated conversation as they inspected the garden. The little short woman seemed to be agitated – perhaps even annoyed. She kept gesturing with her cane, and raising her hands as if in despair.

After watching the two for a few minutes Duane began to feel like a Peeping Tom. He washed his face again and hastily ran a comb through his hair before stepping out to greet them. Though Honor Carmichael saw him at once and walked over to greet him, the little short woman, who was boldly lipsticked, took not the slightest notice of him.

'I don't believe you grew up here – it's a lie you told me to make me believe you're some kind of hick,' the small stout woman said. 'This is the end of the earth. I don't believe you grew up here, and if you did I have no idea why I'm living with you. No wonder we don't get along.'

Honor came over and shook hands with Duane, evidently quite unperturbed by her friend's protest, which was delivered in a strange, gravelly-voice accent that Duane couldn't place – all he knew was that it was not a Texas accent.

'Hi,' Honor said. 'We've come to raid your garden. It's really wonderful.'

'But have you got any squash? I'm not finding any squash and I live for squash,' the stocky woman said, looking at Duane suspiciously. Evidently her appetite for squash took precedence over her views about whether Honor had grown up in Thalia because she dropped that subject and never mentioned it again.

'Duane, this is my friend Angie Cohen,' Honor said. 'Angie Cohen from Baltimore, the squash lover.'

'Well, if she's a squash lover she's landed in the right garden,'

Duane said. 'We've got eight or nine kinds of squash and they're ready to go.'

He had shaken hands with Honor and now reached out to shake hands with her friend. Angie Cohen extended her hand for a moment but turned away before he really had time to shake it.

Honor looked lovely under her wide-brimmed hat. Her arms and legs were tanned, though Angie Cohen's were a fish-belly white.

Duane was glad the little woman with the cane had asked for squash, because he had planted several varieties that could not be found in the local supermarkets. Karla had always loved squash, both to eat and to look at. Throughout the summer she always kept a big tray of squashes on the kitchen counter, and a bucket or two of them on the small porch inside the back door, to distribute to guests.

Though it was Angie Cohen who had asked about the squash, it was Honor who actually squatted down and selected a dozen or more, putting them in her large straw bag.

'Leave that one, it looks mealy,' Angie said – otherwise she made no comment.

'I'm afraid you've missed the peaches,' Duane said. 'Everybody who showed up last week took peaches.'

'What about cucumbers?' Angie asked, when she considered that they had enough squash. 'I haven't had a decent cucumber since we left Maryland.'

Honor looked at her friend and wrinkled her nose.

'Angie, we left Maryland fifteen years ago,' she said. 'I've had plenty of decent cucumbers since then.'

'Oh, you – you've got no sensitivity,' Angie Cohen said. 'You could eat wallpaper and like it. The best cucumbers grow on the eastern shore of Maryland and you won't find anyone who knows cucumbers who disagrees with me.'

Honor ignored that remark, but she followed Duane to the cucumber row and picked several. Angie Cohen did not join them – she seemed convinced that no Texas cucumber could be worth the walk.

'This garden is wonderful,' Honor told him. 'What a very generous way to honor your wife.'

'Well, she always liked gardens,' Duane said. 'We gardened together for quite a few years. When the kids were home we ate most of what we grew, but now our kids have moved away. I can grow a lot more than I can eat. Giving it away seemed like the best plan. How'd you hear about it?'

'Oh, from a patient,' Honor said.

Angie Cohen was limping along impatiently, several rows away. Every time Duane glanced at her she glared back at him, balefully – she seemed to be in a very quarrelsome mood. The fact that he and Honor were chatting for a moment clearly didn't please her.

'Honor, get over here and pick some of these beets,' she said – it came out almost like a growl.

'It's inhumanly hot,' she added, pulling a handkerchief out of her pocket and mopping her face.·

'We'll go in a minute, Angie,' Honor said.

'Beets!' Angie said, pointing at the plants. 'Beets, beets, beets!'

'I heard you the first time, Angie,' Honor said.

She didn't hurry to obey her friend. Instead she stood looking at Duane.

'It seems to me you found the right cure for yourself,' she said. 'You planted a garden, and it solved some of your problems. So I suppose you won't be needing a psychiatrist again.'

'Oh, I will, though,' Duane said. 'I've just kind of been trying to get adjusted to not having my wife.'

Honor Carmichael gave her friend a casual wave, as if to say hold your horses, and then looked straight at Duane.

'You were looking for something that felt essential, as I remember,' she said. 'Something whose value was undeniable. Well, you found it. A garden is essential. It's simple and it's good, and you're feeding the poor, which is also good.'

'Honor, goddamit, what about these beets?' Angie Cohen growled.

Honor was now the one to look impatient.

'She won't let me alone,' she said to Duane. Then she went over, knelt down, and picked a dozen beets.

'Well, beets have iron and I really need the iron,' Angie said, as if someone had questioned her right to iron.

By the time the two women finished going through the garden the straw basket was bulging – Duane persuaded Honor to let him carry it to their car.

'I sure hope you ladies will come back sometime,' he said. 'This garden is a long way from played out.'

'We missed the asparagus, though,' Angie said glumly, as she limped around to the passenger's side of the vehicle – it was an old green Volvo, its backseat littered with books and papers.

'Well, you did,' Duane said. 'I had some fine white asparagus back in June.'

'Too late – every goddamn thing we do is too late,' Angie said, as she got in the car. She didn't thank him for the vegetables, and she slammed the car door hard.

'Don't mind her, she lives for complaint,' Honor said. 'Thank you very much for the wonderful vegetables. We're going to have fine eats for the next few days, thanks to you.'

She stood by the open trunk, looking at Duane with her head tilted slightly back. She took off the floppy hat and let her long hair spill over her shoulders.

'Did you read that book I recommended to you, the last time I saw you?' she asked. For a moment, because the trunk lid was up, they were concealed from her companion.

'Well, I bought it,' Duane said. 'But that's as far as it's gone. It looks way over my head.'

Honor shook her head, frowning a little.

'It's a very long book, but it's not over your head,' she told him. 'You just need to take it slow.'

'Slow is the only way I could take it,' Duane said.

Angie Cohen honked loudly, but Honor ignored her.

Duane began to wish he could spend more time with Honor – a lot more time. He felt confused but was glad, at least, that she was allowing him a moment.

'Honor, let's go!' Angie Cohen said loudly. 'I'm melting in this goddamn car.'

Honor walked around the car and looked in at her friend.

'Then melt,' she said. 'I'm having a word with my patient. Do you mind?'

'Well, can't he make an appointment?' Angie said. 'Why should I have to sit in this end-of-the-earth town all day?'

But her complaint had lost much of its force.

Honor came back to Duane and closed the trunk.

'You still consider yourself my patient, do you not?' she asked.
He nodded.

'We've lapsed, that's all,' Honor said. 'You've planted your garden – you're okay for now. But someday you may want to go on with your therapy.'

296

'I'm sure I will,' Duane told her.

'Good, because we've only just got started,' Honor said. 'If I'm still your doctor then I have the right to write you prescriptions, correct?'

Duane thought she might be talking about antidepressants and started to protest, but Honor stopped him with a look.

'Nope, I'm not prescribing Prozac,' she said. 'I'm prescribing Proust. I want you to sit down and read this great book. Read just ten pages a day – no more. It'll take you an hour.'

Duane had looked into the three fat volumes a few times. They looked completely tedious, to him.

'I'm kind of a slow reader,' he said.

Honor fanned herself with her big hat.

'An hour and a half, then,' she said. 'You can spare an hour and a half a day, I hope. The whole thing is about thirty-five hundred pages. If you read ten pages a day you'll be through in a year. Then call and make an appointment with me and we'll resume our talks.'

'But what if I need to call you before then?' Duane asked.

Honor didn't answer. Instead she turned and looked at his garden again.

'Do you intend to do this next year?' she asked. 'Next year and all the years thereafter?'

Angie Cohen, unable to tolerate the delay, honked again but Honor stood as she was, looking directly at Duane, waiting for him to answer her question – it was a question he had already begun to ask himself as well. Such a garden was a big responsibility – he knew that already.

'I don't know,' he said. 'I was lucky with the rains this spring. I doubt I'll be that lucky two years in a row.'

'Not the point,' Honor said. 'People who receive great blessings expect the blessings to continue. And a garden such as this, where poor people are allowed to take what they want, is a great blessing indeed.'

'I guess it is,' Duane said. 'I've thought about that too. But I don't know about next year. I was hoping to travel some.'

'You should,' Honor said. 'But good deeds are tricky – once you start being saintly it's not too easy to stop.'

'Oh, I'm not saintly,' Duane said. 'I just started my garden at the right time and then got lucky with the rains.'

Honor laughed at the remark – she had a pleasing, throaty laugh.

'Now you're trying to shift the burden of your good deeds onto

God, or nature, or something – that's smart, actually,' she said. 'I haven't done many good deeds, but the few I have done have got me in more trouble than my bad deeds.'

Angie Cohen honked a third time – long and loud.

'Honor, get in this car!' she yelled.

Through the window they could see Angie, twisted around to look at them as she mopped her sweaty face.

'Can you believe her?' Honor said. 'She's honked three times now. Only someone from Baltimore or points north and east would be that rude.'

'I guess she's hot,' Duane said.

'Yes, and if she was cold she'd do the same thing,' Honor said. 'She just won't let me alone.'

She reached out her hand and he shook it.

'Take your prescription now – ten pages of Proust a day,' she said. 'And thanks again for the vegetables.'

'You're welcome,' Duane said.

Honor got in the Volvo and turned it around. He could hear Angie Cohen, complaining volubly, as they drove away.

# 59

When Honor Carmichael and her friend Angie drove off, Duane felt so unsettled that he could neither work nor rest. The unexpected visit had been deeply disquieting. He had never expected to encounter Honor outside her psychiatric offices, had never expected to converse with her except as a patient converses with a doctor. Now that she was gone, having given him a strange assignment which she expected him to take a year to complete, he felt both pleased and frustrated. He felt that the woman liked him – that at least she seemed to want him to continue as her patient. And yet she had told him he should call her in a year, or whenever he finished reading the fat, three-volume French book. That Honor could casually posit a gap of that sort in their acquaintance disturbed him. It meant that she didn't feel the need to establish a relationship with him immediately – not even a professional relationship.

His own response to Honor Carmichael, on the other hand, was so strong that he couldn't imagine going a year without seeing her. He knew that he was attracted to her as a woman – more strongly attracted than he had been to any woman for a long time. Yet he felt doubly blocked: first by the fact that she was his doctor, meaning that a professional relationship was the only kind he was supposed to expect, and secondly by her imposition of the year-long wait.

Also, he was puzzled by Angie Cohen's role in Honor Carmichael's life. The remark Honor made when Angie was bragging on Maryland cucumbers indicated that they had been together a long time. He wondered if Angie Cohen might be a psychiatrist too – the two women might be partners.

What Duane really wanted to do was call Honor up and ask her if she would go out with him. He was ready to forget the doctor-patient relationship. Honor had looked at him acutely several times –

perhaps she harbored some feelings for him that were not so different from those he felt for her.

But he didn't call her. The fact that she still considered him her patient inhibited him. He had the sense that, at this stage of things at least, Honor Carmichael would be severely displeased if he suddenly called her up and asked her for a date.

He went into the trailer house and fidgeted for a while, unable to get Honor Carmichael off his mind. The thoughts he had about her were not professional thoughts, either. They were sexual thoughts.

Then it occurred to him that perhaps the solution to his powerful need to see Honor again, and quickly, was just to get the three fat French books and read them straight through – it couldn't be that hard.

Once, twenty years ago, when speed-reading was in vogue, he had let Karla drag him to a course in it. Her enthusiasms in the way of self-improvement varied – she might want yoga one day and speed-reading the next. She scanned the papers and signed them up for whatever was available. In most cases Duane would go to a few meetings and then quietly drop out, using the pressures of the oil business as an excuse. But he had not dropped out of the speed-reading course. At one point he got so good at it that he could read a whole issue of the newspaper, or even a copy of *Time*, in about forty-five seconds. He had been much better at speed-reading than Karla, a fact that pissed her off.

'Duane, you're just supposed to go to the classes to keep me from getting raped in the parking lot,' she explained. 'You're not supposed to get better grades than I do.'

The memory of his skill as a speed-reader gave Duane a surge of hope. If he could remember how to speed-read he might be able to rip through the French books in a week or two. His spirits high, he immediately bicycled out to the cabin, where he kept the books. But his half hour of optimism proved to have been foolish. The key-word technique that had been so helpful when reading *Time* was completely useless when applied to the book he had in his hand. The sentences seemed to run on for pages – often he could not even find the verbs. Within half an hour he gave up – he had been unable even to discover the name of the character who was telling the story, and nothing about the story, if there was a story, interested him in the least. He was convinced that what Honor Carmichael wanted of him was simply beyond his powers. It was hopeless. If he was required to read the books by Proust all the way through before he could see Honor again, then he would never see her again.

In frustration he closed the book and then threw it at the wall. What kind of doctor would do such a thing to a patient? Though working in the garden had relieved him of much of his depression, the summer would soon end and his depression might return. It seemed deeply irresponsible on her part. What if he fell into real despair? Was he supposed to despair for a year just because he couldn't read a huge book that held no interest for him?

Though finally Duane calmed down enough to pick the book up and put it back on the shelf with the other two, he could not stop thinking about Honor Carmichael. That night he stayed in the cabin, thinking about her. He slept little and woke up with an erection – his first morning erection in years. It made him feel a little silly. Here he was, a sixty-three-year-old man who had the hots for his doctor. Probably it wasn't even legal for a patient to sleep with his psychiatrist. And the psychiatrist, in any case, seemed to be living with an unpleasant little woman with a growly voice. What was that about?

Duane felt much too restless just to sit around the cabin, so he jumped on his bicycle and pedaled over to the Corners, to have a chat with Jody Carmichael. It was early – he thought he might catch Jody alone. But as he was nearing the intersection where the store stood he heard the sound of a lawn tractor – far ahead he saw the stumpy figure of Angie Cohen, riding the lawn tractor in her mashed-down hat. She was cutting the weeds in the ditches around the store. If Angie was there, Honor must be somewhere around, but he didn't see her. He turned around and pedaled all the way back to his cabin and had some coffee. Angie Cohen was the last person he wanted to see.

While he was having coffee he flipped through the French book again, hoping to find some dialogue or something that he could be interested in, but, as he feared, it was hopeless. The book was an impenetrable mass of words.

Two hours later, when the sun was well up and the day too hot for anyone sane to be riding a lawn tractor, Duane rode back to the Corners again. This time there was no Angie, no Volvo, no lawn tractor.

The first thing he saw when he entered the store was a tray of the vegetables that Honor had taken from his garden the day before – cucumbers, squash, radishes, carrots, and even a few beets.

'I think I've seen those vegetables before,' he told Jody, who was peering intently at his computer screen.

'Yep, the girls just brought me all that rabbit food,' Jody said. 'They say you've replanted the Garden of Eden, over here in Thalia.'

'It's not the Garden of Eden but it's a pretty good garden,' Duane said. 'I hope they'll feel free to come back.'

'They might, but it won't be anytime soon,' Jody informed him. 'They're leaving for China next week on a big vacation.'

Duane got a sinking feeling. Honor Carmichael was going away, leaving him with nothing but an unreadable book and the vague promise of seeing him in a year. His impulse was to call and try to get an appointment with her before she left. He didn't think he would be able to stand the wait.

'They wanted to take me with 'em but I can't stay away from my betting that long,' Jody said. 'This computer betting gets in your blood. They were just lecturing me about it this morning. Angie thinks I ought to get out more.'

'What's the story on Angie?' Duane asked. He felt that Jody's comment had given him an opening to ask.

'Angie Cohen is richer than God,' Jody said. 'She's a princess of the city. Her grandpa worked with old man Rockefeller. Her family owns most of Maryland and a lot of Pennsylvania. I think her grandpa helped invent the drilling bit. If it hadn't been for Angie's grandpa there wouldn't be much of an oil business and this part of the country would still be all just cowboys.'

'I don't think she likes Texas much,' Duane said. 'She wasn't too happy when they were over in Thalia, but she did brag on Maryland cucumbers.'

He paused – Jody had turned back to his computer screen.

'I guess your daughter's been friends with her a long time,' Duane said.

Jody immediately gave Duane a funny look. Duane had supposed he was being subtle when he asked the question, but he had not been subtle enough to fool the old gambling man.

'Oh, they're not friends – it's more than that,' Jody said. 'Angie is Honor's husband – if you know what I mean.'

# 60

Later, Duane had a hard time remembering the rest of that day. He could not recall exactly what he had said to Jody Carmichael when Jody told him that Angie Cohen was Honor's husband. To cover his shock he had got himself a bean burrito and put it in the microwave. Jody now stocked a whole line of vegetarian burritos that Duane could not remember seeing in the store before. Perhaps they too were the work of 'the girls,' as Jody called them.

Mainly, when that bombshell burst, Duane just wanted to get out of the store as quickly as possible. He needed to be away, to be alone. Whether Jody realized he had exploded a bomb in Duane's consciousness was not clear.

'Honor's mother left me for a woman,' Jody informed him, as he was paying for the burrito. 'Honor's mother wasn't as rich as Angie – I doubt the Hunts or the Basses are as rich as Angie. But Grace was rich and so was the woman she left me for.'

'Are they still together?'

'No, the woman Grace took up with died,' Jody said. 'They lived in Upperville, Virginia. She was a Mellon.'

'I see,' Duane said, although he had only vaguely heard the name.

'Rich women don't have to put up with us old hairy men and all our spitting and farting,' Jody said. 'They can do without us and plenty of them *do* do without us. It's hard on the ego, though, to be left for a woman. I'd probably still be fretting about Grace if I didn't have this computer betting to occupy my mind.'

I'm a big boy, I oughtn't to be shocked, Duane told himself, as he pedaled home. He kept telling himself that all day, and for most of the next day. He was a big boy; he knew that some men and women were homosexual in orientation, by inclination or whatever. At some point he and Karla had wondered if Jack might be gay; the notion

303

crossed their minds because Jack seemed so much more interested in trapping pigs than he did in women.

Besides that, there had been times, twenty or thirty years back in their marriage, when Karla had formed such intense friendships with women that Duane, on a few occasions, wondered exactly what went on between Karla and her girlfriends. It had crossed his mind once or twice that Karla might even leave him for a woman.

But those episodes were far in the past, and the anxieties they bred had subsided decades ago. Neither he nor Karla had had much in the way of outside interests for the last fifteen years – he had all but forgotten that sometimes girls preferred girls.

If, in those past years, he *had* discovered that Karla was having a love affair with a woman, he didn't believe it would have shocked him half as much as the discovery that Honor Carmichael and Angie Cohen were lovers. Jody had come right out and said that Angie was Honor's husband. Honor was tall and graceful and lovely, Angie short, bossy, and rude: if Honor did prefer women, why would she choose a disagreeable little person such as Angie for a mate?

Of course, he did not have to think long to realize that plenty of attractive and appealing women married males who were every bit as ill featured as Angie. Beautiful women often took up with ugly men; he didn't know why it should seem peculiar that a beautiful woman would take up with an ugly woman, but it did.

For the next day and a half Duane went around in a daze, so distracted that he did a poor job of watering his garden. He almost drowned some plants, while leaving others to burn up. He tried to tell himself it was probably for the best – what business did he have, getting the hots for his doctor, anyway? But the fact was he still had the hots. He wanted Honor Carmichael more than ever.

Although he told himself he should do exactly what she had asked him to do – read the French book, wait a year, then call for an appointment – in the end he couldn't check his impulse to try and see Honor before she left for China. To the astonishment of everyone he suddenly appeared in the offices of his oil company and sent a fax to Dr Carmichael:

Dear Dr Carmichael:
I saw your father and he said you were going to China. I don't think I
can read those books you wanted me to read. I'm not educated enough.
Would it be possible for me to have an appointment with you before you
leave on the trip? I believe I need it.

Duane Moore

He scribbled the office fax number on the note and went outside to
await a reply. One came within twenty minutes.

Dear Duane:
I'm sorry but I'm completely booked until I leave for the Orient.
    In any case I think it's best that we leave it where we left it. I'll see you
when you've taken your prescription: that is, when you've read Proust.
    It's nonsense that you're not educated enough to read it. I'm only
asking for ten pages a day. Pretend it's exercise, which it is, in a way. Give
it an hour or so a day and call me when you're through.
    Thanks again for the vegetables. I'm afraid we've gorged ourselves.

Honor Carmichael

Duane folded the fax and pedaled over to Ruth Popper's. He
stopped by his garden on the way and picked her a little sack of
okra and a few radishes. Ruth loved okra. When he came in
she was watching a baseball game on her ancient black-and-white
television. The television set produced only a faint picture, the
players moving like ghosts across the surface of the screen. Duane
had to look closely even to discern that a ball game was in progress. The picture being projected was as faint as Ruth's vision.
Yet Ruth sat placidly on the couch, watching something she
couldn't see.
    'I brought you some okra,' Duane said. 'Okra and some radishes.'
    'Radishes make me belch but thanks for the okra,' Ruth said.
'When I was growing up they thought okra kept you from having
rickets. I guess it does, because I've never had rickets.'
    Duane put the vegetables in her kitchen and came back and sat in
the rocking chair.
    'Why are you discouraged?' Ruth asked.
    'Who said I was?'
    'Nobody, but I can tell by your demeanor,' she said.

'I'm discouraged because I've done something stupid,' he admitted.

'Well, we all knew it was just a matter of time before you fell in love,' Ruth said. 'I hope it's not some little slut who just wants your money.'

'Nope, it's my doctor,' he said.

'That's nice,' Ruth said. 'If she's a doctor she's probably got plenty of her own money. I would hate to see you get taken for a cleaning this late in life. You don't have much judgment when it comes to women.'

'I won't get taken for a cleaning,' Duane said. 'As a matter of fact I don't think I'm likely to get anything at all.'

'Well, if there's not going to be any sex, what's the point?'

'There doesn't have to be a point,' Duane said. 'The point is I'm in love with my doctor and she's gay.'

Ruth absorbed that information in silence for a few minutes.

'Good lord,' she said finally. 'The things we get ourselves into. How's your prostate?'

'My prostate's fine – what's that got to do with anything?' he asked.

'All men get prostate cancer sooner or later,' Ruth told him. 'You just need to have regular checkups. What kind of doctor is your doctor?'

'A psychiatrist,' Duane said. 'She's Jody Carmichael's daughter. She lives with a woman who's richer than the Hunts and the Basses.'

'Well, then there's that much less likelihood she'll skin you out of your money,' Ruth said.

'Ruth, you're missing the point,' Duane said. 'She's gay and I'm in love with her – and she's my doctor besides. What am I going to do?'

'Suffer, I guess. Love's mostly suffering anyway,' Ruth replied.

'You're no help,' he said.

Ruth shrugged. 'If you do something stupid, like falling in love with your gay doctor, what am I supposed to do about it?

'Does she know you're in love with her?' she asked, after peering at the ghostly baseball game for a moment.

'She's a psychiatrist, she might have figured it out,' he said. 'I'm not sure. Anyway she's going to China next week and doesn't want to give me another appointment for a long time. I'm supposed to read this long French book before I see her again.'

'That's interesting,' Ruth said. 'We all ought to read more.'

'Ruth, I can't read that book – it's thirty-five hundred pages long.'

'Oh, sure you can,' Ruth said. 'I zoomed right through *Gone with the Wind* and it was pretty long.'

'It's all about France,' Duane said. 'I've never even been to France.'

'So what? I've never been to Atlanta but I read *Gone with the Wind*,' Ruth said. 'Maybe you could hire a tutor to help you get started.'

'I'm sixty-three,' he reminded her. 'I'd feel silly hiring a tutor.'

'Karla would have hired one in a minute, if she was in love with her doctor and he told her to read some old book before he'd sleep with her,' Ruth pointed out.

'But my doctor won't sleep with me anyway – she's gay, I told you that,' he said.

'I know, but sometimes people slip,' Ruth said.

'Did you ever slip?' he asked.

'Almost,' Ruth said. 'I had my best friend, Naomi. It was the Depression. We had no money and we were both married to jerks. We used to go to movies together.'

'That's all – just movies?' Duane asked.

Ruth hesitated a moment, staring out the window across the plains of the past.

'There was more,' she said, finally. 'I'm not telling you how much more.'

Then she sighed.

'I don't think I would have made it without my friend Naomi,' she said.

'What happened to her?' Duane asked.

'Oh, nothing,' Ruth said. 'She moved to Odessa. Her husband got killed. She married again and that one got killed too. After that we lost touch.'

'I guess life's always more complicated than people think it's going to be,' Duane said.

'Just while you're young and still after sex,' Ruth said. 'Now that I'm not after sex my life is perfectly simple – you bring me little sacks of okra and I sit here watching ball games. But that's no consolation to you, because you're not at that stage yet.'

'I wish it hadn't happened,' Duane said. 'I wish it had just stayed simple.'

'Shut up; that's foolish,' Ruth said. 'It's always foolish to wish for less. Even if you don't get to sleep with her the two of you might touch one another in some way. It might be good, even if it isn't everything you want it to be right now.'

Later, sitting in his lawn chair under the white moonlight, Duane decided Ruth might be right. He didn't want to totally lose Honor Carmichael. Something good might happen, even if it wasn't what he was hoping for, exactly. He knew he did need to slow down his wanting, not an easy thing to do.

The next morning he pedaled in before dawn and watered his garden. An old couple from a neighboring town, early risers who had been there several times before, were making a modest selection: green beans, some squash, an eggplant.

'Is that all you can find in this whole garden?' Duane asked. He liked the old couple and persuaded them to take a little fresh spinach before they left.

'We don't really eat much,' the old lady said. 'It's just a pleasure to be in a fine garden early in the morning. We're retired. Coming here gives us something to get up for.'

Duane had left the first volume of the French book in the trailer house. He found the keys to the big house, went in, turned on a few lights, and after a good deal of searching, found the dictionary the kids had used when they were in high school and had themes to write. The cover was almost torn off, from rough use, but the dictionary seemed to be all there.

He decided he ought to make a new start with the Proust books and thought the dictionary might help him with many words he did not understand. He had reconsidered the whole matter during the night and decided he ought to at least try to do what Honor Carmichael wanted him to do. Honor was probably the best-educated person he had ever had to deal with. If she thought the three books could help him understand why he felt that his life's effort had been futile, then, if he could just read them, perhaps they would. After all, he *could* read pretty well, and the books were made of words. He had read and reread the doctor's fax several times. She wanted an hour a day of his attention and wanted it to be applied to the three Proust books. There was no real cause for panic, on his part. Even if he didn't enjoy a single page of what he read – and he didn't expect to – still, now that he had his dictionary he ought to be able to read them through. Also, by doing what Honor asked – or at least trying to do it – he could still feel a little bit connected with his doctor.

Perhaps he overestimated the difficulty when he first looked into the books. Perhaps it wouldn't take a year, quite. Anyway, he couldn't work in his garden all day long – the reading could be a kind of break in his routine. It might be that after he had read a few hundred pages he would begin to enjoy the book, or at least to understand why Honor wanted him to read it. Besides, she was right that it wouldn't hurt him to exercise his brain. If he came to enjoy the books he might even want to stop in France, on his way back from Egypt, though Egypt was still where he wanted to go first, when he finally did go away – far away, to where the pyramids were.

# 61

Though Duane was determined to try to read the book by the man named Marcel Proust, he had a very hard time actually sitting down and addressing himself to the task. He had rigged up a little irrigation system for part of the garden, and now some of the nozzles were plugged up. Replacing them took two hours. By then it was close to lunchtime – he decided he might as well go eat. Usually at lunchtime he just had a fresh tomato, with an onion or two and perhaps a radish, but this time he rode to the Dairy Queen and ate a chicken-fried steak and some mashed potatoes.

'Duane, you're feeding yourself up like you're going to do some heavy work,' Billie, the waitress, said. 'I thought you had about given up on the heavy work.'

'Nope, I'm just about to start some real heavy work,' he said, but he didn't enlighten Billie as to what the heavy work was.

By midafternoon he had finally run out of chores to distract himself with, so he was forced to sit down with the book, and also with his dictionary and a pad and pencil. He had decided to keep a list of all the words he had to look up – once he learned what they meant he thought he might try to dazzle Ruth and Bobby Lee by dropping them casually into some conversation.

At least it was something to make the proceedings a little more interesting.

The first ten pages took him almost two hours. The first word he had to look up was 'vetiver' – he looked it up and discovered that it was the fragrant root of a grass he had never heard of. That seemed like a word that might dumbfound Bobby Lee – he could ask him if he'd sniffed any vetiver lately. Duane thought that if he kept his cool he might succeed in starting the rumor that a new strain of marijuana had just arrived in the county.

Despite that fantasy, the two hours were hard going. Some of the sentences were so long that even after reading them five or six times he still could not retain the sense of them. Also, he found that reading even the comparatively simple passages required extreme concentration. If a fly buzzed in the kitchen window, or a horn honked somewhere down the street, these slight sounds threw him off entirely. The only way he could regain his focus was to go back to the top of the page and start over. Sometimes he would get nearly to the end of a page only to have his mind drift off into a daydream having nothing to do with the task at hand. But, for the time, at least, he was determined not to cheat. When he lost his grip on the narrative he went back to the top of the page and started over.

Several of his daydreams that afternoon involved Karla, and they were not helpful daydreams. He felt absurd for even attempting to do what he was doing, and no one had ever been better at calling attention to the absurdity of what he was doing than Karla.

'Duane, I can't believe you're doing this,' she would have been sure to say. 'You can't read a book that long. The only long book you ever read was *Lonesome Dove*, and if the mini-series had been on first you wouldn't have read that one, either.

'Just because some gay doctor wants you to, you're going to waste a whole year reading a book that don't interest you,' she would tell him. 'You always just let women push you around any old way, Duane.'

Still, even though he felt silly, Duane pressed on and finally came to the end of the tenth page. Relieved, he immediately went out into his garden and thought no more of Proust that day.

On the second day he had every bit as much trouble getting himself to sit down with the book as he had had the day before. Again, he felt silly, and when he went to his cabin and got the two other volumes of the book he felt even sillier.

But then, halfway through the second day's reading, after he had looked up 'Merovingian,' 'transvertebration,' and a few other words that would not fit easily into a conversation with Bobby Lee, while reading a page that he had had to start on for the third or fourth time – at one point a tractor stalled in the alley right behind the trailer house; he had to let the driver into the big house so he could call for help – Duane was rereading a passage about an old man whose wife had died: '*It's a funny thing, now; I often think of my poor wife, but I cannot think of her for very long at a time.*'

Duane, who had read the passage at least twice without attending to anything that was going on – he had not, so far, been able to keep any of the characters except the maid straight in his mind – stopped at that passage and reread it with a different attention. What the old man said was a precise description of how his own memory worked when he thought of Karla. He might remember Karla a dozen times a day, but he remembered her briefly, in flashes, for a second or two, or half a minute at most. His reveries about Karla were frequent, but they were also brief.

The family in the book made a little joke of what the old man said about remembering his dead wife – 'often, but for only a little' became a kind of catchphrase, a joke but an affectionate one.

That evening – his reading done, his garden watered – Duane decided to walk to the cabin, rather than bicycling. It had rained a little in the midafternoon and the country still smelled of rain. While he walked he thought again about the passage about the old man, his dead wife, and the little joke the family had made about him. It reminded him of the way people in Thalia – people who had known him all their lives, people who cared about him – had begun to joke about his marrying again. Those jokes too, he realized, were kindly meant. Probably it was also healthy – after all, death hung over his neighbors too. Joking about an old widower who was looking for a young woman who would give him a lot of sex probably protected them somewhat from the thought that they too might be widowed and alone. What would these neighbors who wished him well think if they knew he had been foolish enough to fall in love with a woman who would never be likely to give him any sex – perhaps would never even know that he wanted her? Falling in love with a gay psychiatrist was not the future any of the jokers were predicting for him.

The old man who thought of his wife often but only for a little while had unwittingly stated a truth that Duane had arrived at but had not articulated, which was that grief was intermittent, momentary, and private. Once he had had an intense memory of Karla while he was standing in the street gossiping with an old man about the greedy Arabs and the low price of oil. The conversation went on predictably, the oilman never suspecting that Duane had just been riven by a vision of his wife as he had seen her once years before, getting out of the shower, one leg cocked up because she had a sticker in her heel. It was just a moment on the street, and it soon passed, but it was also the most intense spasm of regret and longing that he

312

had felt since Karla's death – and yet it didn't even derail a conversation on that most familiar of topics, the price of oil.

Reading that little passage that connected so precisely with something he himself had felt made Duane feel a little hopeful about reading Proust. Perhaps the long effort ahead would not be completely barren. Even so, he was glad to be walking through the rain-freshened country, and not reading. He was happy just to be out in the air, smelling the country, hearing the birds, inspecting the creek beds. To the west huge thunderheads were still rolling in off the Staked Plains, with now and again snake tongues of prairie lightning shooting out beneath them. No smell was quite as pleasing to him as the smell of the grassy prairies after a summer rain.

That night he sat late in front of his cabin, watching the immense white clouds move in slow battalions across the sky. Thunder rumbled in the far distance, and lightning continued to flicker. Now and then there would be a few splattering drops of rain, but the rain was not continuous enough to drive him inside. To the north, beneath the clouds, he could see the glow of lights from Wichita Falls. Honor was still there, perhaps packing for her coming trip to China. Duane wondered whether Honor thought of him at all, or realized that he was interested in her as a woman. The clouds passed and the night became clear. Duane dozed a little in his chair, but he did not go to bed. At 4 A.M., with the sky still dark, he walked back to town and began to water his garden.

# 62

At the beginning of October Duane picked the last of his tomatoes – the summer of the great garden was over. He rolled up the little irrigation system that he had installed himself and stored it in the garage. He did some raking and tidying up and then had the same young farmer come back and turn the land over with his plow. Next summer he meant to preserve what vegetables the people didn't take. Whatever he preserved he meant to sell for modest prices. He had picked up a book about bee culture and was considering getting some bees. Though the Karla Laverne Moore Memorial Garden had been a wild success, Duane didn't intend to rest on his laurels. He had been blessed with ideal weather, a thing not likely to happen two years in a row. He knew he needed to think about a better irrigation system, and to keep studying his seed catalogues assiduously, for new varieties of vegetables he might grow. A young man from Wichita Falls showed up, wanting Duane to invest in a vegetarian restaurant, just on the basis of what he had heard about the garden – Duane wished the young man well, but declined to invest. During the fall he got letters from a number of environmentalist groups, wanting him to give them money, or come to their meetings, or – in one or two cases – accept awards. Duane ignored the letters, declined the awards. A man from as far away as Mississippi called and tried to convince him that bullfrog farming was the coming thing, but this proposition also failed to interest him. He was becoming adept at the graceful refusal.

From time to time he saw this child or that. Julie came home one day because she only trusted her old family dentist to pull her wisdom teeth. Then Nellie showed up to attend a bridal shower for an old friend. 'How's Zenas?' Duane asked. 'How's Goober?'

'Still competing,' Nellie said. 'Goober's opening a new restaurant in Dallas and he's bringing a chef over from France.'

'How does Zenas plan to compete with that?' he asked.

'Investing in a Broadway show,' Nellie informed him.

Dickie he saw on the road now and then. Usually Dickie would be traveling at top speed and, once he noticed his father, would brake so hard that Duane would be engulfed in a cloud of dust. After gossiping amiably for a few minutes Dickie would speed off, engulfing Duane in another cloud of dust.

Jack, still in Montana, had not been heard from, which was nothing new.

Every time Duane stopped in to visit with Ruth Popper she quizzed him about the book his psychiatrist had wanted him to read – she was invariably dissatisfied with the brevity of his answers.

'All I know so far is that it's about some people in France,' he told her.

'Be more specific,' she demanded. 'I can't read. It's spiteful of you to tease me this way.'

'Ruth, I'm not teasing you,' Duane said. 'It's a long book and so far I'm not understanding much of it. Some of the sentences are as long as old Preacher Jenson's sermons. Remember old Preacher Jenson? One of his sermons lasted nearly two hours.'

'Who cares? I didn't go to his church,' Ruth said. 'Besides, no sentence is that long.'

'If you could see, I'd show you,' he told her.

'Bring the book and read one of the sentences to me,' she said. 'If it takes you two hours to read it I'll apologize.'

This Duane resolutely refused to do. He felt silly enough just reading some of the sentences to himself.

In November he turned sixty-four. The girls came home and conspired with Dickie and Annette to give him a big surprise party, catered by Goober's new French chef. Bubbles and Willy showed him their school pictures: there they stood in their smart uniforms. The chef babbled in French to the two French girls who were helping him serve. The chef refused to make spaghetti, which prompted Barbi to give him the finger. Duane had a sense of unreality. The older kids now seemed like children from a family other than his own. A steady stream of French poured out of the kitchen – it was as if Proust had tried to come to Thalia in order that Duane would have a better chance to understand his book.

Then the next morning they were all gone again. Though Duane had been happy to see them, he was also deeply relieved that they were gone. A strong norther was blowing; he put on a coat and walked to the cabin. He loved his family, but even the brief time he had spent with them made him long for the simplicity of his solitude.

That winter Duane stayed mostly in his cabin, going into Thalia rarely and Wichita Falls not at all. From one of the gardening-equipment catalogues he ordered a small wagon and used it to haul supplies out to his cabin. He had saved a certain amount of produce from his garden – onions, carrots, potatoes, turnips – and kept it stored in the little shed, where he occasionally still did a little woodworking.

But woodworking didn't engage him, that winter. He wanted more vigorous exercise and so began to cut wood. He worked his way through a sizable mesquite thicket, cutting the wood into burnable chunks and hauling them to the road in his wagon. He stacked the wood in neat piles along his fence line and put up a sign that said: *Firewood, Help Yourself!* He worked at his woodcutting even on the coldest days. The woodpile, though, attracted few takers. Traffic along the little country road consisted mostly of roughnecks or hunters, few of whom had fireplaces.

In the winter, at his daughters' insistence, he had a complete physical, which revealed him to be a sixty-four-year-old man in perfect health. His blood pressure was normal, his cholesterol low, his PSA scarcely registered.

On his way home from the physical he stopped by Jody Carmichael's to buy some twenty-two shells. Now and then he bagged a squirrel or a rabbit and made himself a good stew, using the vegetables in his storeroom. He told himself he was not going to inquire about Honor Carmichael, but he didn't have to. While he was paying for the twenty-two shells Jody handed him several photographs.

'The girls made it to the Great Wall,' Jody said. 'I tried to talk them into going to Macao – that's the gambling island – but they didn't want to go to Macao.'

It was clear from the pictures that the girls had made it to the Great Wall and a good many other places too. There was a picture of them on a tour boat in Hong Kong harbor, a picture of Honor on a camel, a picture of them in a huge square of some sort, a picture of Honor on a bicycle. In all the pictures Honor looked lovely and happy – Angie looked sour and bored. Duane politely worked his way through the photographs and then handed them back to Jody. Even seeing a

316

picture of Honor Carmichael was disquieting – but he couldn't tell her father that.

That afternoon, restless, he walked the creeks for several hours, carrying his twenty-two. It was cold – he was in the mood for squirrel stew and was keeping his eye out for squirrels, but ended up shooting a wild turkey instead, making a lucky shot on a big hen turkey. Duane dressed the turkey – it was a lot more meat than he needed. But it was only a week until Christmas. The children were all going to Vail – Jack had even consented to come down and ski with his siblings. They all urged Duane to go but he declined. He had planned a Christmas dinner with Ruth and Bobby Lee – now he wouldn't even have to buy a turkey.

Two days before Christmas he got a Christmas card from Honor Carmichael. It was merely a standard Christmas card, of the sort doctors sent to their patients, but Honor had signed it and added a little note that said, 'I hope your reading's going well.'

Duane had supposed that his crush on Honor Carmichael was finally wearing off, but the sight of her handwriting on the card told him otherwise. He was as smitten as ever. He thought of sending her a Christmas card in return, but it was too late, the mails were clogged, and he didn't think that he had the nerve to hand-deliver it.

On Christmas Eve Bobby Lee got the news that his PSA had soared. The news – understandably – plunged him into a deep depression. He arrived for the Christmas dinner so drunk he could barely stand up.

'I'll soon be dead and up in heaven, where my other ball is,' he said, several times. Duane had bought him a deer rifle for Christmas, but began to regret the gift. In his present mood Bobby Lee might just shoot himself with it.

For the past several Christmases Ruth had spent the whole day telling everyone good-bye. She was fond of insisting that the present Christmas would undoubtedly be her last. She meant to do it this time too, but Bobby Lee's bad news upstaged her.

The two of them bickered rancorously while Duane cooked the turkey.

'Why would you think your testicle would be in heaven?' Ruth inquired. 'The Lord – if there is a Lord – is not going to waste his time storing people's body parts – particularly not body parts from down there.'

'Down where?' Bobby Lee asked, very drunk.

'You know where I mean,' Ruth said. 'I doubt you'll get to heaven anyway, but if you do you can forget that other testicle being there.'

'Can't we talk about something besides dying?' Duane asked. 'It's Christmas.'

'It's hard being without a sex life when everybody else is celebrating,' Bobby Lee said.

'*I'm* without a sex life,' Duane pointed out. 'Ruth's without a sex life. You ain't the only one.'

Ruth took offense at the remark.

'Speak for yourself, Duane,' she said. 'You aren't privy to my intimate secrets.'

Her rejoinder took both of them aback.

'Excuse me,' Duane said. 'I didn't know you had a boyfriend.'

'If an old crone like you can have a sex life when I don't get one, then I'm moving away,' Bobby Lee said. 'I don't want to live in a town where such things can happen.'

'Duane's the one who really needs a sex life,' Ruth said. 'He's in perfect health. What's the point of perfect health if there's no sex? It just means it ain't perfect health – it's wasted health.'

'I'd prefer it if we dropped the whole subject,' Duane said.

In fact, though, he had begun to ask himself the same question. An appealing Mexican woman, who worked in a small café where he sometimes ate on his rare trips to Wichita Falls, had been flirting with him lately. Occasionally, if the café wasn't too busy, she'd sit and chat with him for a minute. The woman's name was Maria – she was in her late forties, unpretentious, frank, cheerful. Lately her image had begun to come into Duane's mind at night, competing in his fantasies with Honor Carmichael's. The flirtation, so far, had been light. Duane knew very little about Maria – didn't know whether she was married, a widow, or what. He just knew that she liked him. She was there, a possibility – indeed, the only possibility.

Toward the end of dinner Ruth grew lachrymose, saddened by the thought that her last Christmas dinner was nearly over. She insisted they all drink brandy. She and Bobby Lee got drunker, tried to dance, cried, forgave each other for a lifetime of mutually insulting behavior. Duane sat on the couch and watched a football game he had no interest in. He began to miss Karla. Whatever her faults, Karla always managed to pull off splendid Christmases. At her Christmas dinners everybody ate so much that they lacked the energy to be hostile. Duane didn't have the skill, or even the interest.

While Ruth and Bobby Lee indulged in an orgy of forgiveness he washed the dishes.

When he left, Bobby Lee had passed out on the couch and Ruth was asleep in her rocking chair, snoring loudly.

Before he pedaled away Duane took the precaution of hiding Bobby Lee's pickup keys. Bobby Lee was not popular with the local constabulary – if he woke up and drove off in his drunken state they would be sure to pounce on him.

Duane rarely drank brandy – he was drunker than he realized, so drunk that he pedaled right off one of the low wooden bridges, smashing his bike and gashing his forehead. He had to walk the rest of the way to the cabin, bleeding freely. He thought of Karla. She always liked it when he did something foolish. She would laugh her head off if she saw him as he was then.

What Honor Carmichael would think of such behavior he didn't know.

# 63

Throughout the winter, usually in the afternoon, when he was done with woodchopping and errands, Duane, each day, read his ten pages of Proust. Reading the ten pages became his balance to woodchopping. It was mental woodchopping, though he did not always feel that he was getting the wood cut, where the Proust books were concerned. Even after three and a half months, when he finished volume one, he still could not rid himself of the feeling that he was doing something inappropriate. He knew that if Bobby Lee, or one of his own children, discovered him reading such a book they would have been completely bewildered. People would think he was trying to pretend to be smarter than he was.

Duane, though, knew that he wasn't pretending to be smarter than he was, because often he would sit with the book for two hours and come away with almost no sense of having understood what he read. Sometimes he would sit down with the best of intentions – even with a little pleasurable anticipation; he liked the sense that he was being faithful to his chore – and yet be almost totally unable to concentrate on the page in front of him. He would start one of Mr Proust's long, looping sentences only to have his mind simply drift off before he had read even halfway down a page. Sometimes he would have to start a given page over six or seven times; his concentration just kept slipping, and he grew lazy about looking up words that he didn't really understand. Sometimes he would spend most of his hour and a half on the first three or four pages and then hastily scan the last several pages, eager to be free of the book for the day. The minute he finished, if he happened to be at the cabin, he would take a long walk, meandering along one of the creek beds with his twenty-two.

At first he was consciously resentful of the book he was reading, and consciously resentful of Honor Carmichael for forcing it on him.

He wanted *her* – perhaps she realized that, perhaps she didn't – and she had given him Proust as a substitute.

Of course, she couldn't really force him to read the book. He had had no appointments with her since the death of his wife – though she seemed to consider that he was still her patient, he himself wasn't too sure about it. But if he wasn't her patient, then he wasn't in her life at all – which was not what he wanted. Her insistence that he read the three books was not unlike Karla's insistence that he take the speed-reading course, or yoga lessons, or a course in Latin dancing. Both women seemed determined to improve him in ways of their own choosing, a similarity that annoyed him when he thought about it, and he did think about it from time to time.

Still, in a way that he could not have described, he eventually developed a more welcoming attitude toward the reading. Having to sit down and concentrate his mind for an hour or two every day came to seem like a positive thing. His resentment toward the task wore off sooner than his resentment toward the book itself. Very gradually, his reading improved. There were still many days when he took nothing from what he read – those days were, in fact, still the majority – but on the whole his mind wandered less and, now and then, he would have a moment of recognition, of the sort he had had when the old man mentioned that he thought of his dead wife, but not for long. Often his recognition would involve no more than a description of weather, or of some natural or social condition that he had observed himself, though without grasping what he had seen as intelligently as Proust grasped it. The reading was not wholly barren, though the people that Proust described were mostly as foreign to his own experience as people could be.

Sometimes it seemed to him that the very foreignness of the material was what had prompted Honor Carmichael to prescribe it to him. He had told her he wanted to travel to foreign places and she had supplied him with a book that was definitely about a foreign place. Practically the only things he could relate to in the whole first volume were the plants and foodstuffs; he thought that might be because he was paying such close attention to his own garden when he began to read. He was surprised by the care Proust took in the description of asparagus; Duane happened to be particularly fond of asparagus himself. He had grown some asparagus as fine as any described in the book, and yet he had had to urge them on the local people, many of whom had never eaten asparagus and didn't know how to cook them. Some of his own asparagus went to waste, which clearly would not have been the case if he had been growing it in France.

Still, most of what he read as he did his daily ten pages was tedious stuff. Few of the people interested him and most of the conversation seemed pointless. The maid and the old aunt interested him a bit, the latter because her pickiness reminded him of Ruth Popper; but then the old woman died and the family went back to Paris. It was soon obvious that social life in Paris was a thousand times more complicated than social life in Thalia, but Duane didn't care. Once in a while he felt amazement that people would go on so about such trifles; but then he would remember that Karla had been almost as bad, when it came to obsessing about trifles. Some days he wished she were still alive so he could tell her that she really ought to move to France.

In the winter, when he finished the first volume, he immediately developed a resistance to opening the second. The book he had just finished was by far the longest he had ever read in his life. He had made his way through more than a thousand pages, only twenty or thirty of which had anything in them that really interested him. Though he liked devoting an hour and a half a day to reading, he resented having to read that particular book. His work in the garden had given him a renewed interest in botany, something about which he had a great deal more to learn. He owned a plant dictionary and several books on shrubs, weeds, and grasses; an hour and a half with any of those books would have taught him more that he could use than anything he was getting out of the French books.

Also, he knew that he was being foolish to base so much of his life on Honor Carmichael. Even thinking about Honor had become painful to him. Once, cycling home from a trip to the dentist, he glanced over and happened to notice her in a parking lot. It was a windy day. Honor's long hair was loose; bending to get in the Volvo she had trouble controlling her skirt – Duane caught a quick glimpse of her legs. Then she was in the car and gone – yet the little that he had seen haunted him for two weeks. It produced the kind of excitement that stray glimpses of women had produced when he was a teenager.

But he wasn't a teenager. He was a sixty-four-year-old man. What was he doing obsessing about the fact that he had seen a little ways up a woman's skirt as she was getting into a car? It was absurd, and he knew it. He knew that his momentary glimpse of Honor Carmichael's legs was the kind of thing that Mr Proust could have written two hundred pages about. But he wasn't Mr Proust. He was a retired oilman who happened to still be horny. Why didn't he just go and seduce Maria, a nice woman who liked him and would readily have taken him into her bed? Why was he hung up on a woman he couldn't have when there was a nice woman right there in the same town who was hoping he would make a move? Why had he bound himself into such a circle of frustration? In earlier life he had not been one to frustrate himself in that way.

The second volume of Proust lay unopened for ten days. Though it was winter, Duane set out on his bicycle to visit Julie and Nellie and his grandkids. Willy and Bubbles entertained him with their few words of French, and the chef at Goober's new restaurant cooked some of the food Mr Proust had been writing about. Duane bought bicycles for Willy and Bubbles, and then rode to Arlington and bought bicycles with training wheels for Little Bascom and Baby Paul. Zenas had decided to invest in health clubs. Nellie, the laziest of his children, had become an exercise professional, whose job it was to train exercise personnel in Zenas's health clubs in Tulsa, Midland, Hot Springs, Tyler, and other cities.

Duane contemplated bicycling north to see Jack, who was living in a small trailer with three dogs and two horses, somewhere near the Wyoming-Montana line, still pursuing sheep rustlers when he wasn't going to college. According to his sisters, who had flown up with their boyfriends to visit him, Jack was heavily armed at all times, even taking a saddle gun with him when he took them all horseback riding. The news didn't surprise Duane, or bother him. Jack had always been happiest when heavily armed – if there was a part of the Wild West that was still wild, Jack would find it and live in it.

On the way back to Thalia from Fort Worth Duane ran into a February ice storm. A warm rain fell most of one night and then a freezing wind sliced down from the plains, dropping temperatures almost to zero. The roads acquired a glaze of ice. Duane, who had spent the night at a small motel in Jacksboro, took one look at the highway and concluded that it was not a good day for bicycling. A few vehicles crawled along the road, but not many. A few hundred yards to the south an eighteen-wheeler had skidded into a ditch and turned over. He had difficulty even walking to the motel office to request his room for another day. The wires of the barbed-wire fences along the roads were sheathed in ice.

Duane spent the day reading fishing magazines. The Weather Channel informed him that certain parts of Wyoming had received more than thirty inches of snow – more than enough snow to bury his bicycle but nothing his son Jack couldn't handle. Jack had once gone to a survivalist camp above the Arctic Circle and learned to build an igloo. If he happened to be abroad in the thirty-inch snow, no doubt he had a snug igloo to camp in.

In view of the weather Duane decided that his visit to Jack could wait until summer. The winds were still gusting. That night he heard sleet peppering the window; the icy roads received a nice dusting of sleet. But the wind blew itself out and the sun came out warm the next day. The trees and the fence wires soon began to drip. Riding home, Duane tried to imagine how cold it must be in Wyoming.

When he got back to his cabin he built a good fire in the fireplace and spent some time studying a map of the western United States.

Then, reluctantly and resentfully, he opened the second volume of Proust.

# 64

In March of that year Sonny Crawford died. A roughneck coming into the Kwik-Sack to buy a six-pack found him slumped against the cash register, dead. He had not adjusted well to his prosthetic feet, or become adept at getting around on crutches. Often the shelves of the Kwik-Sack would be almost bare of foodstuffs, because Sonny simply neglected to restock them. He had been eating a bag of Fritos when he died. Cause of death was thought to be a heart attack.

'No, it wasn't a heart attack; he died of discouragement,' Ruth said, when Duane walked over to chat with her, after the funeral.

Behind the big house the young farmer was once more plowing the big garden plot. It was time to think of gardening. Duane had ordered a great many seeds, some of them for vegetables that, so far as he knew, had never been planted in the county before. He was in a mood to experiment, and did not stint on seeds.

'I guess you're right – but what was he so discouraged about?' Duane asked.

Ruth glared at him for a moment.

'You wouldn't understand,' she said. 'You've never been discouraged.'

'The hell I haven't,' Duane said. 'Why do you think I stopped riding in pickups and started walking everywhere?'

'Just to show off,' Ruth said. 'You've always been a vain person. You want everybody to know how different you are from them.'

'I don't think I'm very different from "them," depending on who you mean by "them," ' Duane said.

'You should have kept going to that psychiatrist,' Ruth said. 'I thought she was helping you a little, but then you stopped going.'

'I mean to start seeing her again this summer,' Duane said.

'Just because you're in love with her and she's gay is no reason to give up on your therapy,' Ruth said. 'She's your doctor, remember – just get all that other stuff out of your mind.'

'I'm trying to,' Duane said. 'It's not that easy to do.'

'It wasn't easy for Sonny, either,' Ruth said. 'He never got over Jacy – isn't that sad?'

Duane didn't answer. In his view it was not so much sad as self-indulgent, an excuse to give up young.

While they were chatting Bobby Lee came roaring up. He had been having bad back spasms lately and had been coming to Ruth for massages. She had once studied massage therapy and was good at unknotting muscles.

'Here comes a customer,' Duane said. 'Bobby's spasming again.'

Bobby Lee had his pager in his hand, the expensive pager Dickie had given him. It not only made him reachable, it gave him instant access to the latest news developments, not to mention sports scores and other odd tidbits of information.

'Did you hear?' he asked, when he came in the door.

'Hear what?'

'They found Jacy – at least they think so,' Bobby Lee said. 'They're checking dental records now. She was in a snowbank. An ice fisherman found her.'

'The old gang is dying off,' he added, looking as if he might cry. Although the over-the-top PSA reading had turned out to be a mistake – a lab assistant had forgotten to insert a critical decimal point – Bobby Lee was still prone to ferocious outbreaks of self-pity. The slightest mention of sex, or groins, or anything below the waist would usually cause him to burst into tears.

'It's typical that she was found on the day Sonny was buried,' Ruth said. 'Even dead he can't escape her, the hussy. He and I might have gone on longer if it hadn't been for her.'

She looked coldly at Bobby Lee, who was experiencing a fierce back spasm. He was tilted so far to the left that it seemed he might topple over.

'If that pager of yours is so wonderful, why can't it tell you what's wrong with your back?' she asked.

'My pager don't diagnose illnesses,' Bobby Lee said. 'It just keeps up with things like dead movie stars.'

He sat down in front of Ruth and she began to knead his back in a professional fashion.

'I think I'll go,' Duane said.

'You must feel odd, Duane,' Ruth said. 'Sonny was your first friend and Jacy was your first girlfriend. Bobby's right. The old gang is dying off.'

'Yes, but it hasn't been a gang in a long time, if it was ever a gang,' he said.

'Don't you be cynical – of course it was a gang,' Ruth said.

'It might have been a gang when I was about fourteen,' Duane said.

'I had my first car wreck when I was nine,' Bobby Lee said. He hated to be left out of any conversation, even momentarily.

'It's about time for me to go,' Ruth said. 'When you've lived as long as I have you don't have much of anybody left. Just ghosts.'

Duane stood up to leave but didn't leave. He had not read his Proust that day and also needed to go check on the plowing, but he felt reluctant to leave Ruth and Bobby Lee.

'If there was more of us left we could have a wake,' Bobby Lee said. 'I might be able to scare up a few drinkers if I cruised by the Dairy Queen.'

'You need to practice meditation,' Ruth told him, kneading his shoulder muscles. 'Your back wouldn't knot up like this if you took time to do a little meditation.'

'All I've got to meditate about is the fact that I've only got one ball and it's hanging by a thread,' Bobby Lee said.

Duane left them to their quiet bickering, checked briefly on the plowing, bought a bottle of whiskey, and walked out toward his cabin.

The cemetery was not much out of his way, so he veered by it, though to visit Karla, not Sonny – his grave was a raw scar near the west end of the cemetery. The twilight was lengthening; it would not be dark for a while yet. The air was unusually soft for March, though there was still plenty of opportunity for chilly weather.

He sat by his wife's grave for an hour, getting quietly drunk, wondering what it might be that Karla would be happiest about if she were still alive. The fact that both her daughters had rich boyfriends would probably be one thing, presenting her, as it would, with fine trips in private jets as well as shopping opportunities on a world scale. The fact that Bubbles and Willy were taking French and wearing uniforms was more dicey – Karla had thought they were uppity even before they left Thalia.

'We'll never be sophisticated, will we, Duane?' she asked him once, while she was leafing through an issue of *W*, a publication that fascinated her. 'Just look at all these people having a party in Paris. Nearly every single one of them looks sophisticated.'

'It doesn't mean they're happy,' he said.

'It might not be total happiness but I'd be happier if I had a few of those clothes,' Karla said.

That conversation had occurred during the boom, when Karla had subscribed to many fashion magazines. She had even flown off to fashionable spas occasionally, once or twice with Jacy Farrow as her traveling companion.

'Planes fly from Dallas to Paris every day,' he pointed out. 'I guess we could afford a few French clothes. Go, if you want to see Paris that much.'

'Duane, I can't go, I don't even speak the language,' Karla said. 'Besides, Jacy says French people are snippy.'

'You're snippy yourself, and so is Jacy,' he had pointed out.

'Just with you,' she said. 'I'm nice as pie to the general public,' Karla said.

Karla had never gone to Paris. What French clothes she owned had been bought at Neiman Marcus, in Dallas. She had gone to New York several times, but mainly, when she left home, she went to Los Angeles or Santa Fe.

But she had kept up her subscription to *W* long after the boom ended, by which time French clothes were well out of their reach. To the end, though, Karla had loved to look at pictures of elegant people at fancy parties in the expensive cities of the world: beautiful people, rich people, titled people, famous people – they all fascinated her.

In the cemetery where she lay there were no such people – there were just the humble people who had lived their lives in a small country town.

Duane felt a sadness settle over him, as he walked home. He felt that he ought to have done more for Karla, ought to have seen that she got to Paris, even if the French *were* snippy. He had got as far as investigating it once. They could have flown from Dallas straight to Paris. But one of the kids got sick and the Paris trip fell by the wayside; it became just one of those things that they never quite got around to.

Of course, they hadn't foreseen the milk truck hurtling around the curve.

When he got to the cabin he tried to get back to his Proust, but he was too drunk to make sense of the long sentences. Instead he sat in his lawn chair most of the night, watching the clouds.

# 65

The second and much of the third volume of Proust Duane took in gulps, between long and often tiring sessions in his garden. The spring and summer were both as harsh as he had expected them to be. No rain fell in April; only a little fell in May. Duane was forced to lay a more extensive irrigation system and be vigilant with his hose and his watering can. Thanks to his attention, many of the new vegetables he planted flourished. He had become interested in the Native Seeds movement – some of the varieties of corn he planted, as well as a few root vegetables, probably hadn't been grown in that part of the country since the time of the Kickapoos. The fact that he had brought back crops that hadn't been grown in or around Thalia in more than one hundred years was something he felt very good about.

By now his garden had become almost too famous. Many more people stopped than had stopped the year before, some of them knowledgeable gardeners who had come specifically in hopes of talking to him. Scarcely a day passed without his having to spend an hour or more in conversation with some passerby. People from ag schools began to show up, intense young agronomists from Texas A&M, Texas Tech, and the University of Oklahoma. Often their questions were so technical that Duane couldn't answer them. At times his own ignorance left him abashed – he even toyed with the idea of enrolling in school, in order to take a few courses in botany. He didn't, probably because it was just the day-to-day gardening that he liked most.

With the garden occupying most of the daylight hours he had less and less time for the long book about spoiled and finicky people in Paris. He imagined them to be much like the people whose photographs Karla had studied so closely in the pages of W. He found little to interest him in their quarrels and their peculiarities. Only now and then a description of a garden or a park would catch his attention.

He considered simply abandoning the book and also the notion of going back to see Honor Carmichael. When he did leave his garden it was mainly to pedal to Wichita Falls and flirt with Maria. Their flirtation was pleasant, but it was also slowly growing more intense. Duane asked her once about her husband – he wanted to know if there was a rival he should be aware of.

'Husband? Which one?' Maria asked. 'I've had three and you know how I feel now? *No mas,* that's how I feel now. *No mas.*

'Doesn't mean I don't like fun,' she added, leaning closer to him. 'Husbands, no – fun, that's always good if you can get it.'

Duane knew that he and Maria were moving steadily closer to the moment when all that would be left to do would be to take each other to bed. He had begun to think about it a lot – so, clearly, had Maria.

And yet he kept on, irregularly, with Proust, gulping down thirty or even forty pages in the hot afternoons when to be in the garden was to risk sunstroke. He had read more than two-thirds of the books by then – he didn't want to give up. Nor had he stopped thinking about Honor. His consciousness seemed to be saturated with plants and with women. When he wasn't thinking about one, he was thinking about the other. In fantasy he switched restlessly back and forth, between Honor and Maria.

'Come by, you know,' Maria said, one day. She had a small house near the café. 'My kids are grown. Come by – we could watch TV, you know.'

Duane was ready to take her up on it, but before they fixed a date Maria's mother died and she had to rush back to Sonora, to look after her old father and an equally aged aunt. A month passed, and she had not returned. When Duane asked about her the people she worked with were vague.

'Oh yeah, she's coming back,' they said, but one month stretched into two.

Meanwhile his garden, in only its second year as a public garden, had changed into something Duane didn't really like. It became too famous. Poor people still came and took food, but the easy attitude they had about it the first year changed. Some came and picked their vegetables defiantly, as if they were robbing the rich. Only rarely could he persuade them to try any of the new vegetables – they rejected anything that smacked of the exotic. They just grabbed a few beans, a few tomatoes, a little corn. The more unusual vegetables went to travelers or to the more knowledgeable gardeners who stopped by. Duane began to be troubled by the local people's attitude toward the garden. Why did the poor people slink away so meekly if he happened to be there when they came to do their picking?

'Because you're the squire,' Ruth said. 'Nobody wants to risk upsetting the squire.'

'But I'm not a squire,' Duane protested. 'Those people know better than that. They know me. I've lived here with them my whole life.'

'Don't care, you're still the squire,' Ruth insisted.

'If it's going to be this way, then I won't plant a garden next year,' Duane said. 'I didn't set out to be a famous gardener. Maybe I'll go see the pyramids next summer. Let somebody else plant a damn garden.'

'Go ahead,' Ruth told him. 'Maybe you'll find a girlfriend over there in Egypt.'

'Ruth, I'm going because I want to see the pyramids,' he reminded her. 'I'm not going halfway around the world just to look for a girlfriend.'

'I don't know that you need an Egyptian but you do need to get married,' she told him. 'You weren't meant for solitude.'

'I think I've been doing pretty well with it,' he said.

'No you haven't, you're still in love with that gay shrink,' she said. 'That's never going to come to anything.'

Duane dropped the subject – in fact, he didn't disagree.

As the summer waned, so did the number of pages he had left of Proust. When he dropped below two hundred he began to feel a little sad and also a little anxious – the anxiety arose from the knowledge that it would soon be time for him to call Honor Carmichael and request an appointment. Much of Proust he didn't remember at all, but he did remember how anxious the young boy telling the story had become at the thought that his mother would soon come up and kiss him good night – kiss him good night and then be gone. Duane felt some of the same mixture of anticipation and apprehension when he thought of visiting Honor Carmichael again. He remembered how swiftly his hour with her passed, so swiftly that, like the boy in Proust, he would begin to miss her before she even arrived. Just a few words, a few moments, and he would be out on her front steps again, faced with a long gap of time before his next appointment.

Also, even though he only enjoyed about one page out of one hundred of the many pages he had read, he did not really want the reading to end. Reading Proust had become a habit – he didn't want to lose it from his life. The feelings he had about the books were so complicated, so mixed up with feelings he had about Karla or Honor, that he could not understand them. He would sit in his lawn chair at night, watching the distant lightning flicker, unhappy, but not for any clear reason. Something was lost – he had not the skills to say what was lost, or how the loss had occurred, or whether he could expect to save or capture anything.

It struck him that perhaps Honor had wanted him to read that particular novel because it was so long and complicated that – if he stayed faithful to his task and finished it – it would arouse feelings in him so complicated that he would have to come to her if he sought explanations of those feelings.

Perhaps Honor Carmichael hoped to help him understand the kinds of things that Mr Proust understood about the losses that come to one in life. Perhaps she thought he, particularly, needed to understand the nature of such losses – surely she didn't ask all her patients to read such a long book about a foreign place. She had picked the book particularly for him and he hoped, when he saw her again, to ask her why.

Thinking about the matter in those terms made him feel a little more hopeful, although, within the hopefulness, his sadness still hung, like an old coat in a closet.

The evening when he finally read the last few pages of Proust was very hot. Thunder had rumbled all afternoon. He closed the book and took it with him outside. He wanted to sit a minute in his lawn chair. When the shower broke, the raindrops at first were hot too, but they soon cooled. As the rain began to fall harder he rose and took the Proust book back inside. It had taken him more than a year to read the whole of the three books – he did not want the last volume to get wet.

Then he took his clothes off and went back to the lawn chair for a few minutes, letting the cool rain pelt him. It had been a sweaty day – it was nice to be showered by the fresh-smelling rain before he went to bed.

# 66

The next morning, his assigned task done at last, Duane rode into Thalia, meaning to water his garden and then call Honor Carmichael and make an appointment. He felt it was time to start again where he had stopped the day Karla was killed.

But he dawdled over his watering, did a little weeding, pulled up a few onions, chopped them with some tomatoes and a good cucumber, and had an excellent salad for breakfast. Several travelers stopped at the garden during the morning. Three frizzy-haired old ladies showed up from Anadarko, Oklahoma, chattery as birds. Duane indulged them, showing them this and that – something he rarely did, anymore. In only a year's time the general public had come to irritate him. Mainly he hid in his trailer if a car showed up with an out-of-state license plate.

Though he had waited a long time for his chance to see Honor Carmichael again, he found himself unable to simply pick up the phone and make the call. He had been depressed when he had seen her before, but he didn't consider that he was particularly depressed anymore. In fact, all that was depressing him that morning was the thought of seeing Honor in such a limited way. A patient-to-doctor relationship wasn't what he wanted.

Around noon, the call still not made, he cycled over to Wichita Falls and ate at the diner where Maria had worked. Maybe, by a miracle, she had come back; maybe he could initiate a normal relationship with an appealing woman, rather than pursuing an expensive and ultimately futile relationship with a woman who didn't want him and never would.

But Maria was not back. When he asked about her the young man behind the counter just looked vague. The cook, a wiry little woman, came out of the kitchen and gave him a shrewd look. She knew what he wanted, knew why he was always making inquiries about Maria.

'We don't know,' she said. 'She had to go home. She'll be back, but we don't know when. She can't get no papers on her father.'

Thwarted at the diner, Duane pedaled out the Seymour highway to the Stingaree Courts. He thought he might rent the honeymoon suite again, just for one night. He could visit with Gay-lee and Sis and Shorty. Maybe being back at the Stingaree Courts would help him to decide whether to resume the life of a psychiatric patient again.

To his shock, the Stingaree Courts was closed. There was a For Sale sign in the window of the office – the gravel parking lot was empty of cars, except for an ancient Mercury with all four wheels missing, rotting in the weeds by the outer fence. There was no Sis, no Gay-lee, no Shorty. The line of low cabins seemed to be sagging already, sinking back into the earth.

Duane peered in the window of the office, but the windowpanes were so heavy with dust that he could see little. The office was completely empty – even the counter where guests had once registered had been removed.

He cycled back down the road to the bar where the man who had once played football for Iowa Park tended bar. But his former opponent was not there, or at least not there yet. Instead an old man with a cigarette dangling from his mouth was wearily pushing a mop across the floor.

'Do you know anything about the Stingaree Courts?' Duane asked. 'I used to stay there sometimes but it looks like they're closed for good.'

'Yep, closed for good,' the old man echoed. 'The Meekses are gone. It's the same old story. The old man died and the old lady left. That business about the fish got in the papers, though – it even made the television.'

'What business? What fish?'

The old man chuckled – when he did his cigarette fell out of his mouth. He bent slowly down, picked it up, looked at it, and flipped it in the general direction of a big trash can.

'There was a catfish in one of the water beds,' he said. 'How it got in there, don't ask me. What it lived on, don't ask me. When the old boy who bought the water bed drained it, the next thing you know a catfish was flopping around on the ground.'

'That's amazing,' Duane said. 'Was it a big one?'

'No, it wasn't what you'd call big,' the old man said. 'How big could a catfish get, living in a damn water bed? But, like I said, it made the TV.'

# 67

The next morning, disgusted with his own wavery behavior, Duane picked up the phone and made an appointment with Dr Carmichael for the next afternoon at three. Even if he only ended up seeing Honor once, at least he wanted to tell her he had done what she ordered him to do: he had read the Proust books.

That afternoon, after his work in the garden was done, looking at the three fat silver-and-black paperbacks piled up on his table, he began to grow nervous. He *had* read the three books – at least he had turned every page – but he had no confidence that he understood even a tenth of what he had read. What did Honor mean to do? If she started asking him questions about Proust he felt sure he would embarrass himself immediately. If she quizzed him about the characters he wouldn't even be able to say the names correctly. It all seemed like folly. He had finished the book only two days ago, but already it was just a jumble of names, places, and descriptions in his mind.

That night he rode out to the cabin and sat in his lawn chair, wavering between excitement and despair. One moment he would decide he ought to just give up.

'There *is* a time to just plain give up, Duane,' Karla had said to him, many times. It was one of her maxims. 'There's times when you can't move the world just by being bullheaded.'

Then he would remember his glimpse of Honor the day the wind blew her skirt and, despite himself, would grow excited. He told himself he ought to calm down. He was just making a visit to a doctor. But he couldn't calm down and was relieved when he saw the headlights of a pickup coming across his hill. It was Bobby Lee, stopping for his bi-nightly chat.

A few weeks before, Bobby Lee had impulsively proposed marriage to a young woman he had just met. The woman had been putting gas in her car at one of the local Kwik-Sacks, when Bobby Lee drove up to the pump just behind her. The young woman, whose name was Jennifer, had been humming 'The Yellow Rose of Texas' while pumping gas. She had blonde hair and two babies in her car.

'The minute she set that nozzle back in the pump it was like I knew, Duane – it was like I knew!' Bobby Lee said. 'It was sort of the way she was humming that got me.'

'Just because she can hum pretty tunes don't mean she would make a good wife for a man your age,' Duane said, but his words of caution came too late – much too late. Bobby Lee had walked right up to Jennifer; there was no hesitation at all. He gave her a shy kiss and told her he wanted to marry her for life – all this before he even met her kids. What's more, he got away with it – somehow the impulse worked. The girl had just been passing through on her way to Abilene, where she hoped to get a job working in an old folks' home. She was twenty-six and had never been married – the two kids, as she put it, had just kind of arrived. Nobody in Thalia could call to mind a more striking example of love at first sight.

'He probably just liked her butt,' Lester Marlow speculated. 'She probably had her cute little butt turned to him while she was pumping gas.'

So far, two weeks into the relationship, love had not dimmed – Jennifer seemed not to have experienced the slightest problem with the fact that one of Bobby Lee's balls was a fake.

'As long as one of them's yours, that's fine with me,' Jennifer said – it was a statement that seemed likely to bind him to her forever.

Or, perhaps, *not* forever. The nuptials had yet to be celebrated and Bobby Lee had begun to exhibit traces of nervousness, which is one reason he had taken to showing up at Duane's for bi-nightly chats.

'What's new?' Duane asked, when Bobby parked and got out.

'I've been thinking of driving off a cliff – what do you think of that option?' Bobby Lee asked.

'It would depend on the cliff,' Duane said. 'If it was a low cliff you might just get crippled up for a while. That might be your best out.'

'Out from what?' Bobby Lee asked.

'Out from marrying a girl you just met at a gas station and don't know from Adam,' Duane said. 'Haven't you ever heard about courtship?'

'I know, but I'm too old to date,' Bobby Lee said. 'The minute I saw Jennifer I knew that was it, the whole question was settled.'

'If it's so settled why are you running out here to bother me every other night?' Duane asked. 'Why aren't you home changing diapers?'

'Fuck, that's the whole problem, I hate to change diapers,' Bobby Lee said. 'I got two grown children. What am I doing starting over with two little pissers whose daddies have been lost track of?'

Duane said nothing.

'Do you think it's a sign of loose morals that she didn't bother to keep up with the daddies?' Bobby Lee asked.

'It could be,' Duane said.

'Her mother's a Seventh-Day Adventist – that's another bad sign,' Bobby Lee said.

'I'm not a marriage counselor,' Duane reminded him, in case he had forgotten that fact.

'I know, but I ain't married yet either,' Bobby said. 'I'm using you as a prenuptial counselor. Another thing that gets me is the thought of having to buy those kids braces. Then right after that they start getting girls pregnant.'

'Right, girls like Jennifer,' Duane said.

'You think I'm doing it because she don't mind that I've only got one ball, don't you?' Bobby said. 'That's what everybody thinks. I can feel it in the air.'

After that Duane refused all comment.

'If only Karla hadn't smacked into that milk truck,' Bobby Lee said. 'It's times like this when I need a shoulder to cry on.'

'I doubt she'd lend you a shoulder to cry on if she knew you'd started proposing to girls you meet in filling stations,' Duane said. 'She might take the view that you've always ignored her advice anyway.'

'Ruth's right,' Bobby said.

'Right about what?' Duane asked.

'About you getting cynical,' Bobby said. 'Ruth thinks it's all because of that psychiatrist you want to sleep with, only she's gay.'

'That first plan of yours sounds better to me all the time,' Duane said.

'Which plan?'

'The one where you drive off a cliff,' Duane said.

# 68

On the way to his appointment with Honor Carmichael, Duane got butterflies in his stomach. He felt the same almost sick anticipation he had begun to feel after his first session or two. He knew that his time with the doctor would be too brief – it would be like the mother's kiss, in the first volume of Proust, a pleasure so brief that one would begin to dread its absence even before it happened. But the sight of her house, once he turned into the street, with its nice lawn and nice flowers, soothed him a little. It was a house that bespoke peace of mind. He tried to get a little better control of his feelings. He needed to calm down and let the doctor do her work.

Honor was wearing a dark blue blouse and a necklace of rough amber. She had cut her hair – her new hairdo was sporty, made her seem younger.

She smiled at him and shook his hand when he came in, hesitating a moment as she considered the couch versus the chair.

'Hmm,' she said. 'As I remember you had just graduated to the couch when your wife had the accident. Do you want to go right back on the couch, or would you prefer to sit in the chair and sort of ease back into this?'

'Let's ease back into it, if you don't mind,' Duane said.

In fact he just wanted to look at her, which he would not get to do if he lay on the couch.

'How's the garden?' she asked.

'Well, it's been drier this year,' he said. 'It's done okay.'

'You don't sound convinced.'

'I guess I'm getting a little tired of that garden,' he admitted. 'People have made it into something it wasn't intended to be.

'Seems like I spend half my time growing it and the rest of the time explaining it,' he added. 'I never meant it to be such a big deal. It was just a garden for the neighbors – particularly the ones who are needy.'

Honor Carmichael folded her long fingers, put her chin on them, and looked at him.

'Noble efforts always produce complications,' she said. 'I guess it's more or less true that no good deeds go unpunished. Humans are just so pesky. They don't want to let a good thing alone, to be what it is. I'm not surprised that you find that annoying.'

'I may not do it next year,' he said. 'The people I did it for are scared to come there, because of all the publicity.'

Duane shrugged.

'I felt good about it last year,' he said. 'I don't feel so good about it this year.'

'I meant to come back, but my friend's a pill,' she said. 'You'd think we crossed the Sahara, to hear her describe that trip.'

Duane didn't say anything. The doctor unfolded her fingers and put her hands in her lap.

'I was a little surprised that you made this appointment,' she said, looking up suddenly and meeting his eye. 'I didn't expect to see you here again.'

She paused, considering her words.

'I thought you'd back off,' she said.

Duane was startled. Back off from what? His therapy?

'No, I always meant to come back,' he said. 'I thought you were helping me. But then Karla got killed. You told me to read that book. You said it would take a year, and it did.'

'I'm glad you kept on with it,' Honor said. 'It's a great book but I know it's not everybody's cup of tea. When did you finish it?'

'A few days ago,' he said. 'I don't think I got much out of it.'

'You need to let it soak in,' she said. 'You may find that it's left something with you, even if you can't quite put your finger on what it is.'

She looked directly at him, frowning a little, as if in perplexity. Duane had no idea what to do or say, but he was glad he had come.

'I've had a thought that's rather unprofessional,' she said. 'You're my patient and I should leave it at that. But you're not the average patient, so I'm tempted.'

Though she had just said what he had hoped to hear, Duane was a little shocked. Tempted to what?

'I belong to a little reading group,' the doctor said. 'There are six or seven of us. Proust is who we've been reading. We've been working through him for the past six months. I'm tempted to ask you to join the group – it's informal. We're meeting here tomorrow night. I'll make a salad or something. It might help the soaking-in process if you came to a meeting or two.'

'Will your friend Angie be here?' he asked.

The doctor looked startled, as if the thought were too odd to contemplate. Then she laughed.

'Oh lord no, Angie's in Oyster Bay,' she said. 'Angie can't tolerate literature. Having to listen to people talk about Proust would infuriate her – it would be worse than a trip to Thalia.'

She giggled.

'We only meet at my house when she's safely out of the way,' she said.

Then she seemed to become slightly apprehensive.

'Of course, that's just an invitation – it's not a command,' she said. 'You may not want to come, or you may feel it's not wise. After all, you're the patient. It's only because you've just finished your reading that I thought you might want to come.'

There was a pause.

'If you prefer you can remain a pure patient,' she said. 'Proust *will* soak in, if you give him time. You might want to read it again, after a while. The second time around you notice a lot of things you miss the first time.'

Duane could not imagine reading the book again, but he didn't say so.

'Do I have to talk, if I come to the meeting?' he asked. 'I've never studied French. I wouldn't even know how to pronounce the names.'

'No, you don't have to talk, you can be a silent observer,' the doctor said. 'I suspect that's what you are in real life anyway – a silent observer.'

'I was until I grew this public garden,' Duane said. 'Now I have to talk all the time, explaining it to anyone who stops by.'

Dr Carmichael pushed back her chair and stood up. Duane was startled – surely the hour wasn't up. He had only been there thirty minutes.

'I know – I'm rushing you off,' she said. 'I'm not going to charge you for this session, because it really wasn't a session. We've just been catching up. If you do decide that you want to go on with your therapy, then from now on I want you on the couch. Do you understand why?'

'No,' Duane said. 'I don't mind, though, if that's what you prefer.'

'It is,' she said crisply. 'I want you to talk to me, not look at me. And I want to listen to you, not look at you.'

There was a moment of silence. Dr Carmichael was gazing out the window.

'I'm going to put in a greenhouse,' she said. 'I want to grow orchids. Do you know anything about orchids?'

He remembered that he had bought Jacy an orchid corsage when he had taken her to the senior prom. It had been the flower all the girls wanted. Though he had gulped at the expense, he had bought her the orchid.

'I don't know a thing about them,' he said.

'They're beautiful but rather sinister, like some of the people in Proust – or like Angie, for that matter,' she said.

Then she sighed and rubbed a pencil against her upper lip.

'The reading group meets at seven,' she said. 'Do you think you might like to come, at least this once?'

'I would like to,' Duane said. 'Do I have to dress up?'

Honor shook her head, as if the very notion of people dressing up irritated her.

'Any peppers in your garden?' she asked. 'I don't mean bell peppers. I mean the hot kind.'

'Oh sure – I have plenty of peppers,' Duane said.

'Bring me a few,' she said. 'I've changed my mind about the salad. I think I'll just make salsa. Come about ten till seven. I'll start the salsa and then just chop in the peppers.'

'I'll be here,' Duane said.

# 69

The next evening Duane showed up right on time at Honor Carmichael's door. It was ten minutes until seven. He carried a small bag of peppers, and felt extremely silly. Though he had biked over, he wore no biking clothes, except his helmet. He felt like a fool for agreeing to come to the reading group anyway. He knew he was going to look out of place, feel out of place – indeed, be out of place – and he didn't want to add to his embarrassment by showing up in biking garb.

When he knocked a skinny girl in shorts with very short hair and a wide mouth let him in.

'Hi, I'm Nina, I guess you're Duane,' she said. 'I'm glad you're prompt – Honor needs those peppers.'

He followed the girl down the hall to a pleasant kitchen. The kitchen opened onto a tiled patio. Honor was chopping scallions. She too was in shorts, and wore a sleeveless blouse that left her shoulders bare.

'Good man, you're on time,' she said, taking the sack from him.

She shook the peppers into her hand, sniffed them, and immediately sneezed. A moment later her eyes watered.

'Wow!' she said. 'I wanted them hot but I didn't know they'd be *that* hot.'

'It's just that one – that little *habermo*,' Duane said. 'You have to watch that one. It'll scorch you.'

Before he had time to say more the rest of the reading group poured in. There was a prominent doctor named Jake Lawton, whom Duane had bumped into quite a few times over the years, at one civic event or another. His wife, Jacqueline, was a tiny woman wearing lots of makeup and an expensive-looking silk dress. Though Duane had met Jacqueline Lawton many times over the years he had never exchanged two words with her. Perhaps she was French. At least her name sounded French.

The only other guests were a young couple named the Orensteins – they looked more like siblings than husband and wife. Reuben Orenstein wore a bow tie with dots on it, set off by seersucker pants. His wife, Joanie, wore seersucker shorts and a T-shirt that said *Brandeis* on it.

'Hi, I'm Joanie Orenstein, I went to Brandeis, as I guess you can tell,' she said, shaking Duane's hand.

Her husband shook hands too.

'I *didn't* go to Brandeis but I might as well have because I have to hear about it every day,' he said.

'Hello – are you doctors too?' Duane asked.

'Reuben is,' Joanie said. 'He's a neuro-ophthalmologist. We live in Oklahoma City.'

'Yep, they're young and eager,' Honor said. 'They drive four hours a month just to hear a little talk about Proust.'

'No, just to hear a little talk about *books!*' Reuben insisted. 'It isn't always going to be Proust – in fact the sooner we get through with the long-winded little fag, the happier I'll be. I'm waiting for Canetti. Now, there's a writer worth driving from Oklahoma City to talk about.'

'Who's that, Reuben?' Dr Lawton said. He winked at Duane and gave him a firm handshake. When Jake Lawton had been younger he had done a little team roping at local rodeos. He owned a small ranch and let it be used frequently for charity barbecues. He was a surgeon – the surgeon, in fact, who had relieved Bobby Lee of his cancerous ball.

'I think he won a Nobel Prize, that's about all I know about Mr Canetti,' Honor said. 'I don't think I ought to put this little scorcher in my salsa, Duane. My nose is still stinging and all I did was sniff it.'

'How'd you rope Duane into coming to this soiree?' Jake Lawton asked. 'I'm used to seeing Duane at rodeos and auctions, not Proustathons.'

'Nonetheless, he's read the book,' Honor said, 'and he also furnished the peppers for the salsa.'

'It's good he came, we need new blood,' Nina said. 'Did you read it in French, or English?'

'English,' Duane said.

Honor still had to fling tears out of her eyes, from her incautious sniffing of the peppers, but the salsa she made was excellent. Duane noticed that Jacqueline Lawton had put away three gin and tonics before they even sat down on the patio.

'Elias Canetti is a Bulgarian who wrote in German,' Reuben Orenstein informed the company. 'His masterpieces are *Crowds and Power* and *Auto-da-Fé*, which is a novel. I move we read it next.'

'Oh shut up, Reuben, you can't move anything,' Nina said sharply. 'Tell him to shut up, Joanie. This is not a business meeting, he's not a director of anything.'

'Shut up, Rube,' Joanie said dutifully. There was no heat in her voice, but there had been some heat in Nina's.

'Okay, but I'm not driving a four-hour round trip to talk about another faggy Frog,' Reuben said.

Duane had not brought his book, but he noticed both the Lawtons and the Orensteins had the same silver-and-black paperbacks as he had. Honor and Nina, though, had skinny little paperbacks with tattered covers. Their paperbacks were in French.

Honor caught him looking at her book. She smiled.

'Nina and I are still trying to keep up our miserable French,' she said.

'Speak for yourself, Honor,' Nina said immediately, with a touch of annoyance. 'My French isn't miserable. My French is excellent.'

Honor ignored the annoyance. She was drinking gin and tonic, though more slowly than Jacqueline Lawton.

'Anyway, those fat little English books are too heavy,' she said. 'My hand gets tired.'

'Jake tears his in two,' Jacqueline revealed. It was the only time she spoke, during the entire evening.

Everyone looked at Jake Lawton's paperback, which was not torn in two. He looked mildly annoyed, at having been exposed as a book tearer.

'Well, they *are* heavy,' he said. 'I keep a half of one in the pickup, in case I want to dip in when I'm out at the ranch, relaxing.'

'We've been looking at a ranchette,' Joanie Orenstein said. 'Rube works so hard. I think it would be good for him to get out in the country once in a while.

'Maybe we could fish,' she added, without much conviction.

'Let's get started,' Reuben said. 'This is excellent salsa, Honor. You can't get salsa this good in Oklahoma City and Joanie can't make salsa this good.'

346

'Rube, I'm just learning,' Joanie said. 'Give me a break.'

'I hate the Guermantes,' Reuben said. 'If the man was going to be obsessed with aristocrats all his life you'd think he'd have found some better ones – or made up some better ones, or something.

'They're coarse,' he added. 'They're just like the oil millionaires, and yet they're from families that have been around for thousands of years.'

'Hundreds,' Nina corrected. 'Even France isn't that old. Nobody's been there for thousands of years.'

'Oh shut up, Nina – you know what I mean,' Reuben said.

Nina whirled on the little man with the dots on his bow tie.

'Don't tell me to shut up, you pipsqueak!' she said. 'Is it wrong to ask for a little precision? Isn't that what Proust is all about, precision? Nobody's been there for thousands of years.'

'Calm down,' Honor said. 'Reuben's got a point, even if he exaggerated. The Guermantes are pretty awful.'

'Oh, they weren't that bad,' Jake Lawton said. 'At least they know what they want, which is more than you can say for a lot of these characters. Swann's the one that bored me. He could barely figure out if he wanted to kiss a girl.'

'So? Maybe he's gender challenged,' Nina said. 'He doesn't just run off and fuck every woman in sight.'

'Well, the prostitutes … ,' Joanie said vaguely. She didn't finish the sentence.

'Can't you even finish a sentence?' her husband said at once. He looked around the company in mock despair.

'She *never* finishes her sentences,' he said. 'She talks in phrases. Sometimes clauses. But never sentences. You'd think Brandeis would have at least taught her to finish her sentences.'

'I do finish them, if you don't make me defensive,' Joanie said, flushing. 'That was a complete sentence, wasn't it, Rube? Wasn't it?'

'If nobody's going to say a kind word for the Guermantes, I will,' Honor said. 'They're blunt, which is more than you can say for anybody else in Proust. They're not as hypocritical as the rest.'

'No, but that's the point,' Reuben said. 'They're aristocrats – they're secure. They don't have to *bother* to be hypocritical.'

'Swann is the modern man,' Nina said, ignoring the fact that everybody else was talking about the Guermantes. 'Swann is ambivalence, doubt, paranoia. He's the reason the book seems so modern. He embodies the dilemma of the sensitive man in a crass age.'

'Still bores me shitless,' Jake Lawton said, getting up to refresh his wife's drink. Jacqueline Lawton sat on the edge of a footstool, swaying slightly. The late sunlight shone on her silk dress, creating an effect of iridescence. She was too drunk to speak, or even to sit up straight, but her husband kept refilling her drink. Jake Lawton had once taken Duane into his house, during a lawn party for some charity. He was a hunter – he had killed everything from Kodiak bears to lions. The house was like a natural history museum, filled with mounted heads and whole stuffed animals. A stuffed wolverine glared down at you when you entered the main trophy room.

'I think the fact that the Guermantes didn't quite exhibit the graces we like to think of aristocrats as having was an interesting element in the book,' Honor said. 'You rather feel that Proust was disappointed in them too. I think he *had* expected them to have these graces but when he looked closely at them he had to admit they didn't. He didn't want to admit that great aristocrats were as selfish as anybody else, but then he did admit it.'

'Charlus is my man,' Jake Lawton said. 'He'd have done fine in the oil business, don't you think, Duane?'

'Or he would have until he made a pass at some roughneck and got his head bashed in,' the doctor said.

Duane didn't answer – he saw that Jake Lawton didn't really care whether he answered or not.

'I thought you could read French, Dr Lawton,' Nina said. 'I thought you had a house in France.'

'Yes, in the Dordogne, but we sold it,' Jake Lawton said. 'Once we bought the ranch here we got too busy to be running off to France.'

'But you *do* read French, don't you?' Nina asked. The point seemed to trouble her.

'Honey, I read it fine when I was in Princeton,' Jake Lawton said. 'But that was a long time ago. Jacqueline and I have been trying to learn Japanese – we both love Japan – but I guess we're too old. We don't have the head for it now.'

'I thought we were supposed to talk about Proust,' Reuben Orenstein complained. 'My point is it's all hypochondria – it's the epic of hypochondria. It's about people who constantly think there's something wrong with them when in fact they're healthy as horses.

'Who needs it?' he added. 'I don't.'

'If you don't need it, then why did we drive all this way down here?' Joanie asked. 'If you don't like the stupid book, then why do you bug me every night if I haven't read as many pages as you've read?'

She had spoken with real anger – her husband seemed taken aback.

'It's just that if you say you're going to read it you should *read* it,' he said mildly.

'Oh yeah, you always say you're going to do things you don't do,' Joanie said, growing more angry as she spoke. 'You say you're going to have sex with me but then you never do.'

To her husband's horror Joanie burst into tears and ran off the patio into the house. They heard the front door slam. Reuben sighed, picked up their Proust books, and got ready to leave.

'I guess that's Joanie's way of letting me know it's time to go back to Oklahoma City,' he said.

'No it isn't, you fucking idiot!' Nina said, her face red with anger. 'It's her way of letting you know she'd like you to have sex with her.'

Reuben ignored Nina completely – he acted as if she didn't exist.

'Thanks for having us, Honor,' he said. 'That's great salsa. I can't remember when I had salsa this good.'

Then he left.

'I've never been fond of neuro-ophthalmologists,' Jake Lawton said. 'I guess we need a few, but I'll tell you one thing: I wouldn't marry one.'

'I wonder what would happen if Proust should come to Oklahoma?' Honor mused.

'Honor, Proust is never going to come to Oklahoma,' Nina said.

'It was a rhetorical question,' Honor said. 'Can't I even ask a rhetorical question?' She had poured herself another gin and tonic.

'Yeah, well, Reuben Orenstein is a little jerk,' Nina said hotly. 'Everything he said about Proust was idiotic. Now he's going to try to get us to read some Bulgarian? Oh please!'

She got up and flounced into the house, highly indignant.

Darkness fell, and Proust was forgotten. The Lawtons were planning a trip to Tibet – Jake Lawton got very excited, talking about it.

'We did Nepal long ago,' he said. 'But you couldn't get into Tibet, in those days. Now you can. Jac and I are heading out as soon as we hold our longhorn auction.'

'Tibet's too high for me,' Honor said. 'I get dizzy if I even go to Wyoming.'

'What about Angie?' the doctor asked. 'I heard she was a traveler.'

Honor made a face.

'Only to countries with three-star restaurants and four-star hotels,' Honor said. 'The Michelin is Angie's holy book. The only way she'll ever see Tibet is if she sails over it on her way to heaven.'

She chuckled and sipped her drink.

'Which is a slim likelihood,' she added, and chuckled again.

'You think Nina's gone for the night – should we go and say good night to her?' Jake Lawton asked, when he stood up to leave.

'Let her be,' Honor said. 'Tolerance is not Nina's long suit.'

'I suppose that's youth,' the doctor said.

Honor glanced at the house. A light had come on in an upstairs bedroom. They saw Nina pacing back and forth, a cell phone pressed to her ear.

'She's calling Angie, to tell her what a jerk Reuben is,' Honor said.

The four of them walked out to the street. Jacqueline was so drunk her husband had to keep a firm grip on her arm to keep her from wobbling off the sidewalk.

'Jac, you're in your cups,' he said. 'Way down deep in your cups.'

Honor carried the Lawtons' books, while the doctor practically carried his wife. Honor walked beside Duane. Now and then her arm brushed his.

'In case you're wondering, Nina is Angie's niece,' she said, as they eased down the sidewalk.

Just as they got to the curb Jacqueline Lawton's knees buckled, but Jake Lawton, in one smooth motion, opened the car door and rolled his drunken wife gently into the backseat.

'She's out,' he said. 'Jac can't really drink, anymore. I think it's those hormones she's on.'

'It was nice of you to come,' Honor said. 'We'll see you before you leave for Tibet.'

'Oh, that's not until after the longhorn auction,' Jake said. 'Why don't you come this year, Duane? Bring Karla. Buy your wife a longhorn for a pet.'

'Karla's dead, Jake – car wreck,' Duane said. 'About two years ago.'

'Oh dear, I'm sorry,' the doctor said. 'Jac and I must have been traveling and I missed it. I guess that explains why I haven't seen her around.

'My God,' he added. 'I had no idea Karla had been killed. I liked Karla.'

Then he shook Duane's hand, kissed Honor, got in his car, and drove off. The car was almost out of sight before Honor remembered that she was still holding the Lawtons' books in her hand.

'Shit,' she said. 'Now I've given Jake Lawton an excuse to come back. It was the fact that he mentioned your wife that threw me off.'

The mention of Karla had thrown Duane off too. He assumed that everyone local who had known Karla even slightly knew by then that she was dead. But the Lawtons *did* travel a lot and he and Karla had only seen them once or twice a year, at public events. No one had happened to mention it to the Lawtons – the doctor's surprise had been genuine.

But the fact that Karla had been dropped into the evening jangled Duane a little. He had been standing near Honor – he wanted to kiss her as soon as the Lawtons left. He had persuaded himself that Honor might want him – why else would she invite him? But then Jake Lawton mentioned Karla – it spoiled the moment, in a way.

Honor still stood there, the heavy paperbacks in her hands. She looked down the street, perhaps hoping Jake Lawton would realize his mistake and come back for the books. But the car didn't reappear – the two of them were alone. Duane stepped closer – he was afraid there might not be another such moment. When he leaned nearer to kiss her, Honor didn't move away, but she inclined her head slightly, so that the kiss missed. He just brushed her cheek – he could smell the gin on her breath.

'Nope – you mustn't,' Honor said, in a pleasant voice.

'Honor, I'm in love with you,' Duane said. 'I can't lie about it. I'm in love with you.'

Again he leaned forward to kiss her and again Honor Carmichael deftly inclined her head. She did not seem agitated. She was not even looking at him. She still gazed down the street.

'I'm in love with you,' he said, a third time.

'I heard you,' Honor said. 'It's mainly my fault. I'm afraid I crossed the line.'

'But it isn't a fault,' Duane said. 'It's just a fact.'

'Duane, there are two of us here,' Honor said, in the same pleasant voice. 'What's a fact from your point of view might be a fault from mine.'

She looked at him in silence. She did not seem to be upset – indeed, she seemed as calm and friendly as she had been when he arrived that evening. But she was not going to kiss him, and he didn't know what that left them, exactly. It was too bad Jake Lawton had mentioned

Karla – it seemed to him the kiss might have worked if he hadn't become slightly jangled.

'Your helmet's in the house,' Honor reminded him. 'I don't want you getting brained on your ride home. I'm afraid it wasn't such a high-minded evening, either. This reading group has seen better days.'

When he retrieved his helmet and got ready to pedal off to his cabin, Honor once more accompanied him back down the sidewalk. She seemed serene, and perfectly at ease with him, which annoyed him slightly.

'Thanks for coming,' Honor said. 'Your appointment is tomorrow at the customary time. Perhaps we'll talk a bit about this thing called love.'

'I hope so,' Duane said.

Honor did not appear to be offended, or anxious, or even nervous.

'Going to your cabin?' she asked.

'Going to my cabin,' Duane said.

She was still standing in her yard when he pedaled away. She watched him but she didn't wave.

# 70

Duane grew more and more agitated, as he pedaled home through the dark pastures. It was a still night – he could smell the dust his wheels threw up. At first he merely felt a little embarrassed. He had gone to the gathering afraid of saying something foolish in front of a bunch of people who were better educated than himself, which hadn't happened. Even though the guests were supposed to talk about Proust they barely got around to it and the kind of things happened that could happen at any party. An old woman got drunk, a young couple quarreled, the salsa was good. Jake Lawton showed off a little but did nothing outrageous. It was, in the main, a normal party and he had fit in well enough.

He hadn't embarrassed himself intellectually, but then, as the evening was ending, he had embarrassed himself emotionally by trying to kiss a woman who didn't want to kiss him – a woman he should have known wouldn't want to kiss him.

Although he kept telling himself that it was silly to think that way, he still felt that Karla's sudden appearance in the conversation had doomed his attempt to kiss Honor. At the mention of Karla his own confidence evaporated, his effort carried no conviction. It was as if Karla had inserted herself just in time to prevent him from having any real contact with the one woman he really wanted. She had done it often enough while she was alive, and now she was doing it from the grave.

By the time he reached his cabin he was far too agitated to sleep. A chance to touch a woman had seemed to glimmer there, in the warm summer night – and then had flickered and flown away, like a firefly. It seemed to him that he had bumbled terribly – a teenager could have done better.

A little later, though, his mood shifted and he just felt a fool. Why had he ever supposed there was a chance, where Honor was concerned? Her own father had made it plain that she was gay. What had he been thinking, to stand there and tell her three times that he was in love with her?

That night, when he finally dozed, Honor and Karla mixed erratically in his dreams. He seemed not only to smell the gin on Honor's breath; he smelled her sweat. He heard Karla say his name: 'Duane, Duane.' She said it as only she said it, changing the intonation to match her mood. She might say 'Duane' in such a way as to make it an invitation, or a threat, or a tease, or a condemnation. Sometimes she said it just to let him know she had her suspicions.

Duane awoke unrested. So much emotion had coursed through him during the night that he felt a little shaky. He didn't know what he ought to do. He had an appointment with Honor, in only a few hours. She had even said, pleasantly, that they might talk about this thing called love.

He rode into Thalia to get clean clothes and stopped to chat with Ruth for a moment, but he did not mention his evening. His attempted kiss wouldn't disturb her but if he told her he had sat around with a bunch of people attempting to talk about Proust she would have considered the whole thing absurd.

Nor did he mention it to Bobby Lee, who was so deep in the doldrums that he would have been unlikely to be moved by any troubles other than his own. Jennifer and her mother, in what Bobby regarded as a conspiracy of silence, had secretly drawn up a list and sent out wedding invitations.

'The trap's closing – the trap's closing,' Bobby Lee muttered, to anyone who would listen.

'You don't have to get married if you don't want to. I don't care how many invitations they've sent out,' Duane said.

'I don't know – some of the people they've invited live as far away as Missouri,' Bobby Lee said, as if that fact alone sealed his doom.

'You better stand up for yourself now,' Duane warned. 'If you don't you'll be changing diapers when you're ninety.'

'I won't make no ninety,' Bobby Lee said. 'If I even make eighty-six I'll be lucky.'

'Okay, but you still may not feel like changing diapers,' Duane said.

He poked around in his garden for most of the morning, doing a little watering and hoeing, pulling up a dead plant here and there, picking a few tomatoes. He had begun to leave a bushel basket of tomatoes out by the road every day – always, the basket was empty by nightfall.

Where Honor Carmichael was concerned, he told himself, he should just give up. He could not have what he wanted, which was Honor as a lover. She had a companion and seemed to be living happily with her. The fact that her companion seemed to him a spiteful little person didn't mean anything. In houses all over Thalia men and women were living more or less happily with spiteful and quarrelsome mates. Karla had exhibited no shortage of spite, and yet he had lived happily with her for four decades. The ways in which people got along, or didn't, were unfathomable, at least to him.

All morning he wavered about whether to keep his appointment. On impulse he went to the bank and drew out ten thousand dollars in cash. He made sure he had his passport and his reading glasses. Then he pedaled to Wichita Falls and stopped at a travel agency. He thought he might just leave – he might do what he had been telling himself he would do for two years: go to Egypt, see the pyramids. The summer was almost over, his garden almost gone. In two weeks it would be time to plow it up.

The travel agent, a skinny woman in her seventies with a lot of blue hair, quickly sketched out his options. He could go Wichita Falls–Dallas–New York–Cairo, or Wichita Falls–Dallas–London–Cairo, or Wichita Falls–Dallas–Paris–Cairo, or Wichita Falls–Dallas–Frankfurt–Cairo. Which would it be?

Duane didn't know, couldn't choose. The important thing was that he knew he could get to Cairo quickly, once he decided to go. The planes, as the travel agent assured him, flew every day. He wavered until the lady grew impatient.

'Duane, do you want to travel, or do you just want to sit there and daydream about the land of the pharaohs?' she asked.

'Oh, I want to travel – I just have to talk it over with my wife first,' he said.

'Oh goodness, I'm sorry,' the agent said. 'I didn't know you'd married again.'

'I didn't – I meant my old wife,' he said.

He left the lady looking puzzled, a mass of travel folders spread out on her desk. He had mentioned his wife mainly to back the lady off, but in fact he still had occasional little dialogues with Karla – it was just that when he had the dialogues he spoke both parts. Where Karla was concerned, he felt sure she would approve of his trip. Anything to break his ridiculous fixation with Honor Carmichael would be fine with Karla.

He arrived a few minutes early for his appointment, very nervous. Nina was the receptionist.

'Oh hi,' she said. 'I'm sorry I ran off last night without saying good-bye. Reuben Orenstein really pisses me off. You sat through the whole evening without saying a word.'

Duane didn't tell her that that was how he wanted it. He poked through the magazines, trying to find the one with the article about the pyramids – it didn't seem to be there.

Honor smiled at him when he came in. To his surprise she was wearing a white doctor's smock over a blue Western shirt and Levi's. She had on boots.

'I know – mixed messages today,' she said. 'Am I a doctor, or am I a cowgirl? Jake Lawton talked me into letting him show me his precious longhorns, but then there was an emergency at the state hospital and I had to rush back.'

'I almost didn't come,' he admitted – he felt a need to say it.

'Then I guess that's what we'll talk about – why you almost didn't come,' she said, motioning toward the couch.

Duane lay down. He felt nervous and began to hyperventilate. Honor started to sit down and then went to the door.

'Excuse me,' she said. 'I'll only cheat you of a minute or two. I can't think in these clothes. I keep thinking of the Lone Ranger, for some reason. Whatever your problems, I don't think you're the Lone Ranger.'

In less than five minutes she was back, wearing a green blouse and white skirt.

'That's something I guess I ought to talk to my shrink about,' she said. 'I can't function as a psychiatrist unless I'm dressed like a psychiatrist. What does that say?'

Duane didn't answer – though seeing her in cowboy clothes *had* jangled him a bit. Seeing her in normal clothes relaxed him; more than that, life seemed to swing back into perspective. He stopped feeling quite so weird.

'Tell me why you almost didn't come,' she asked.

'I feel embarrassed about last night,' he said. 'Real embarrassed.'

'You mean you were thinking of abandoning your therapy altogether because you tried to kiss me and I didn't let you? Is that right?' she asked.

'I guess,' he said.

'Now do you see why I said I had crossed the line?' she asked. 'You hadn't been a patient in such a long time that I wavered and asked you to join the reading group for one evening. But I was wrong. You still *were* a patient, and I should have left it at that.'

'I think it would have come to the same thing, sooner or later,' Duane said.

'No, I disagree,' Honor said. 'Context very often determines not only how things happen but what happens. In this office I'm your doctor. That may not be what you want, but I think you respect it. What you did last night, in a different context, was normal. We were sharing a friendly moment, you were attracted, you tried to kiss me. It's not unheard of. Jake Lawton tried to kiss me in the barn this morning, for that matter.'

Duane wasn't surprised. He had seen the doctor eyeing Honor, the night before.

'What'd you do?' he asked.

'I socked the old fart in the kisser – cut my knuckle on his tooth,' Honor said. She held her hand in front of his face – there was a small cut on the knuckle of her middle finger.

'It wasn't the first time Jake's misbehaved,' she added. 'That's why I felt I had to be emphatic – not to mention that I was mad. But you were very nice. I don't expect to have to slug you and I would be sorry to see you abandon your therapy just because you've run into a little rejection. That would be smallminded, and I don't think you are small-minded, Duane.'

Duane didn't immediately answer. He lay on the couch, looking at the tall green plant in the corner of the room. He wished Honor would talk some more. He liked the sound of her voice, and the reasonableness and courtesy of what she said. He felt she liked him and believed she could help him. Now she was asking to be allowed that opportunity. Everything she said was reasonable. He was sixty-four. He had had a sex life, he thought a fairly good one. Was he really ready to put Honor out of his life because he couldn't sleep with her?

Still, there were his feelings, and they were strong enough to have kept him awake most of the night.

'I think I can do this but it's tricky,' he said. 'Maybe too tricky.'

'And it's because you're in love with me that you think it might be too tricky?' she asked.

'I am in love with you and that's going to make it tricky,' he said.

'All right, so it's tricky,' Honor said. 'Had you rather deal with something that's legitimately tricky, or would you rather just ride your bicycle, sit in your cabin, walk your roads, and be bored for the rest of your life?'

Duane didn't answer. He felt tired and confused.

'I don't think this feeling arose just because I invited you to a garden party,' Honor said. 'I hadn't seen you for over a year. If you're in love with me, when did it start?'

'Way back,' Duane said.

But when he tried to think exactly when he had begun to suspect he might be in love with Honor Carmichael he could not really fix a date. He remembered that he had had a sexual dream, and that Honor was the woman in it. But he didn't want to talk about that with the doctor. In his mind he grew more and more confused about how to think about the woman sitting behind him. In his mind he thought of her as Honor, but she was also Dr Carmichael. He didn't know whether it was proper to be on a first-name basis with your psychiatrist. She had not invited him to call her Honor. But Honor was how he thought of her – he thought it was a lovely name, and one that fit her well.

'Would you try to back up just a bit?' she asked. 'Let's wind the reel backwards until we reach a time when you *weren't* in love with me. Will you try to do that?'

'All right,' he said.

'You were married – would you say happily?' she asked.

'Happily,' he said.

'Well, but even so you were sufficiently depressed that you walked off and began to live in your cabin,' Honor said. 'Yet as I recall you didn't seem to regard this as a criticism of your marriage. It reflected a more general dissatisfaction, right?'

Duane began to feel very tired. The lassitude that had hit him the first few times he had a therapy session with Honor suddenly came over him. Why was the doctor talking about the past, talking about his marriage, trying to pinpoint the time when he had fallen in love with her? Probably she didn't take the fact that he was in love with her seriously at all. Many of her male patients probably fell in love with her, or thought they did.

From overwhelming lassitude Duane sank into hopelessness. He regretted ever coming to Wichita Falls to keep the appointment. Why hadn't he just got on an airplane and flown away? Why did he have to think about his marriage? He wanted to forget Karla, so he wouldn't miss her. Now he would have to learn to forget Honor as well. If he could forget her, then he wouldn't yearn for her and be unhappy all day.

'I shouldn't have come here,' he said. 'I can't do this. I should have gone right on to Egypt. I started … to leave …'

Then his lungs seemed to swell, his eyes to tear up. A storm rose in him – it arrived before he could move. He made a motion to get up from the couch but he was too tired, and then he was crying – crying, crying, crying. He was silent about it, but his chest heaved and tears poured out of his eyes, ran down his cheeks and down his neck, wet his collar. He cried so hard that it seemed as if his whole body was crying, that tears were coming out of his pores. It was as if all the sadnesses he had ever felt, and those he had not known he was feeling, had suddenly turned to water, had become tears, a bath of tears, a waterfall of tears, pouring out of him and, it seemed to him, pouring on him.

In the midst of his crying he tried to get up and leave but Honor Carmichael calmly put a hand on his shoulder and pressed him back down.

'No … no … don't fight it,' she said. 'You've probably been fighting this since your father died, and that's a long time. Now you need to let it come. Just lay there and cry.'

Duane obeyed – he had no control over the flood of tears. The whole front of his shirt was wet. When he put his hands to his face it was like putting them in a stream.

'It's all right, Duane,' Honor said. 'Just let it come.'

He cried, he sighed. Once he stopped and felt the tear storm was over, but then started crying again. He had no idea how long he had been crying. Surely he should try and stop – Honor had other patients. His hour must be up.

When he tried to say that, Honor just said, 'Shush. You don't have to leave. Nobody's coming. Just cry until you stop.'

At first she offered him Kleenex, but when she saw that tissues were going to be inadequate she stepped into the bathroom and got him a small hand towel.

'You look like you've been in a washing machine,' she said. 'I think I better loan you a T-shirt.'

'I'll dry when I go outside,' Duane said. 'It's hot.'

'I had a feeling this storm might break,' Honor said. 'That's why I gave you the last appointment of the day.'

Duane sat up and looked at her gratefully.

'How could you know it was coming?' he asked. 'I've never done nothing like this. Not when my wife died. Not when my mother died.'

'Psychiatrists don't know everything, but we do know some things,' Honor said. She wasn't bragging. She just stated it as she would state a plain fact.

'I better go home,' Duane said. 'I'm weak as a kitten.'

'If that's true, how do you expect to get home?' Honor asked. 'I'm not sure it's safe for you to be cycling around right now.'

Duane didn't answer. He wasn't sure, himself, that he could ride home.

'Here,' Honor said, handing him his passport.

'But how'd you get it?' he asked.

'Duane, your whole shirt is soaked,' she said. 'I slipped it out of your pocket to keep it from getting wet.'

Rather somberly she walked him to the door of her house. When Nina started to say something Honor stopped her with a look.

'You're a tricky one,' she said, when they were outside, standing on the sidewalk, not far from the spot where, just last evening, he had tried to kiss her.

'What do you mean?'

'You had your passport with you,' she said. 'You meant to slip away to Egypt and give me no chance. That possibility occurred to me last night. I was actually a little surprised when you showed up today.'

'Give you no chance to what?' he asked.

'No chance to help you understand why you're sad,' Honor said. 'Please don't do that. Don't slip away just yet. Those pyramids have been there a long time. They can wait, but this can't. Please come back tomorrow. It would be good if you could at least give me a few more days.'

Duane didn't say anything. He didn't want to lie to her, and yet, at that moment, he didn't know if he would ever come back to her house.

'I'll come tomorrow if I can,' he said, finally.

'Okay, I'll take that,' Honor said. 'Be careful now. Don't get run over. Watch out for trucks.'

# 71

Duane had not been exaggerating much when he said he was weak as a kitten. He had hardly any strength in his legs and had barely ridden out of sight before he came within an inch or two of doing what Honor had warned him not to do. He drifted into a turn and was almost hit by a teenager barreling up the street in a black pickup. The teenager honked, swerved, and yelled 'Motherfucker!' at him. When the pickup passed, Duane pulled up on the sidewalk and got off the bike. If he couldn't tune in enough to at least see pickups on the street, then he had better not ride at all.

Besides, he had a sharp pain in his side, in a place where he had never had a pain before. He wondered if, in his violent crying jag, he could have broken a rib. He had heard of people coughing so hard they broke ribs, but he had never heard of anyone breaking a rib crying.

But the pain was sharp, he felt very weak, and, though it seemed impossible that he could have any more tears in him, he felt like crying again. There was no question of riding eighteen miles to his cabin – fortunately there was a strip of motels only a few hundred yards up the way. Afraid to get back on his bike, he pushed it to the nearest motel, got a room, and fell on the bed, feeling as tired as he had ever been in his life.

Sometime in the night he woke from a dream in which he and Karla were drifting in a canoe, watching a small plane fly over the river they were on. The plane sounded like a lawn mower. He went back to sleep only to have the screech of air brakes wake him. The motel was on a crosstown throughway, near the northernmost traffic light in Wichita Falls. Once through that light the big trucks could pour on up the highway, unchecked, to Oklahoma City or St. Louis. Some trucker had considered running the last light, but then had thought better of it and hit his brakes.

Duane opened the curtain a little and sat at the foot of the bed, watching the big trucks pass. In young manhood, right after he got out of the army, Duane had considered being a long-haul trucker. It seemed a romantic life, and the pay was good – at least it was if you put the pedal to the metal and kept rolling. Once or twice he had gone on cattle truck runs to South Dakota, running night and day from Thalia to Sioux Falls.

But then Karla came along and he gave no more thought to the trucking life.

He watched the big trucks pour through Wichita Falls for an hour, as the traffic light blinked red and green and yellow. There was never an end to trucks. They rolled north from the Gulf Coast, from Houston and Dallas, from Mexico. To amuse himself he counted trucks for a while – one hundred passed his motel in less than fifteen minutes, huge trucks, rimmed with lights, their cabs vast as castles. There were hundreds of thousands of trucks, rambling over the prairies where the buffalo had once been.

Duane had an impulse just to step out of his room, stick out his thumb, and get in with the first trucker who offered him a ride. Egypt seemed like a fantasy, but the trucks passing through Wichita Falls were real, and the truckers mostly country boys, men not unlike himself. He had always felt at home with truckers. Even the fact that he had only biking clothes presented no huge problem. Truckers were tolerant of eccentrics, up to a point, and he was country born, whatever clothes he wore. Besides, he had ten thousand dollars in his pocket – he could buy some Western duds at some Wal-Mart or Kmart up the road.

What kept him in the room was the fact that he felt too drained to move, and wasn't even sure that he was done with the draining. He still felt tearful. Long ago, if one of the children burst into tears for no apparent reason, Karla would look at them and say, 'Who pushed your cry button?'

Something had pushed his cry button, and was still pushing it. What had occurred in the doctor's office had been a flash flood, sweeping all his defenses before it; now he felt empty and helpless. If Honor Carmichael thought she understood what had made him so sad, that was fine – he himself didn't understand it or even have the energy to worry about understanding it. A flood had come and swept him away, and he – insofar as he was a personality – was still away. He didn't reject hitchhiking because of his decision not to ride in motorized vehicles any more – he rejected it because he was too weak to walk to the bathroom and pee.

When the sky reddened and he saw the new sun bracketed by the buildings of downtown Wichita Falls, he walked two blocks to a convenience store and bought a toothbrush, toothpaste, a razor, and shaving cream. He was back at the motel before he realized he didn't have a comb. When he showered he just patted his wet hair down as best he could.

Then he lay on the bed in his room, the television off, lulled by the whirr of the air conditioner. It occurred to him that he hadn't gone home to water his garden, a thought that produced only a slight stirring of guilt: it was the first day he had missed, in all the time he had been attending to the garden.

When he got ready to pedal over to Honor's office for his appointment he had a nagging sense that something was missing – some component that he usually took to their meetings was not there. He had just turned onto the street where Honor lived and worked when he realized what the missing component was: it was that thing called love. He wasn't in love with Honor Carmichael anymore. The flash flood of tears that had swept his personality away had taken all romantic feeling with it.

If Duane had had more energy he would have been astonished by such a realization. A sense of being in love with Honor had been the one feeling that had been constant for the last year. Only the day before, on his way to see her, he had been so agitated by love that he could hardly steer his bicycle. So it had been almost from the first time he had gone to see her. Her image, her way of being, her womanliness had distracted him for more than a year. Honor Carmichael had been his focus almost from the first time he had met her – because of her, he had had foolish thoughts, nursed foolish hopes; and yet now, headed for her house, he felt perfectly calm. He had even recovered his physical stability – he didn't steer his bicycle in the direction of any pickups. His heart wasn't pounding; he didn't hyperventilate as he walked up to her door. He was purged of sentiment, free from the distracting rhythm of anticipation and anxiety that he had usually felt at the prospect of seeing her.

When he stepped into her office he thought he saw some anxiety in *her* face; no doubt he had worried her with his violent tear storm. But then, as soon as he lay on the couch his hands began to tremble – in a minute or two, with nothing being said, he began to cry again.

He did not pour tears, as he had the first day: that had been a cloudburst, this was only a shower. Honor didn't have to get a towel this time – a few Kleenex sufficed. He would think he was all right and start to talk, only to immediately choke up again. At first he could hardly finish a sentence without crying, but finally the tears lessened and Honor led him back to the subject of his father. He mentioned again, as he had once long before, that when he remembered his father he always remembered the smell of his father's plain cotton work shirts, a smell composed of sweat and starch and tobacco. The shirt Duane's father had been wearing the day he died hung in the closet throughout Duane's boyhood – his mother either forgot to launder it or didn't want to.

'Every time I went in the closet and smelled that shirt, he'd come back to me,' Duane said. 'That is, his memory would. If he came off work in the middle of the night he'd always come in and sit on my bed a minute – even if I was too sleepy to really wake up, I'd smell his smell.'

'That smell means love to you,' Honor said gently, handing him another Kleenex. 'Your father's love. You trusted him, didn't you?'

'I trusted him,' Duane said. 'I don't think I've ever trusted anybody that much – unless it's you.'

'I think you also trusted him not to die, but he died,' Honor said. 'The first time you came to me you mentioned your father's shirt.'

'Seems like a lot's happened since then,' Duane said.

'Yes, you grew two gardens,' she said, with a grin. 'You became a philanthropist – you fed the poor for two years. And yesterday, probably for the only time in your life, you cried your heart out.'

Duane was silent – he was crying again, but not violently. Only a little.

'Here's a small observation,' Honor said. 'Trust and love are a smell to you, the smell of those shirts your father wore when he took you fishing or came and sat by your bed at night. You weren't aware of how deeply you held on to that memory. We *don't* know those things until something touches us in a certain way and memory comes flooding back. What happened to you yesterday is not so different from what happened to the young man in Proust who ate the madeleine and was swept back into all the anxieties and insecurities of his childhood.'

'Ate the what?' he asked.

'The cookie,' Honor said. 'The cookie dipped in tea. But never mind. You suddenly connected with something you hadn't allowed yourself to connect with in a very long time. All that pain was lurking there, and suddenly it came out.'

'Was it because I fell in love with you?' he asked.

'Oh, I don't know,' she said. 'Perhaps that played a part. It's generally when people are touched unexpectedly but powerfully that their defenses suddenly crumble completely, as yours did yesterday. Being with someone who doesn't judge you, or at least doesn't judge you conventionally, can sometimes bring that about.'

They were silent. Duane had stopped crying, but his hands still trembled and he knew that if he stood up he wouldn't be very steady on his legs.

'I'm glad you trust me,' Honor said. 'I've tried rather hard not to play you false – I hope you know that. I didn't sock you in the kisser when you tried to kiss me, and I didn't run you off, either.'

'What do you mean?'

'Just that if you really want to be my *patient*, I'm ready to begin,' she said. 'We've only skirmished and feinted a little, so far. This is only the third time you've trusted yourself on my couch. We've a very long way to go together, if you're ready to make the trip.'

'Four times a week, maybe for years?' he asked.

'Four times a week for however long it takes,' she said.

'What do I know, that's worth years of talk?' he asked. 'I don't even have much of a memory.'

'Memory isn't really the measure of what we'll do,' Honor said. 'A good analysis will take you to places you don't know are there. You didn't know your tears were there, but they were.'

Duane didn't respond. The thought of being able to see Honor four times a week for several years was appealing. Even though he no longer felt that he was in love with her there was no other woman whose company pleased him so much. Seeing her regularly in the afternoons, in private, would be, in a way, like having a love affair. It would be a love affair only of the mind, it seemed, but that was not necessarily a reason to cast it away. He smiled to himself, at the thought of a love affair of the mind, and Honor saw the smile.

'What's so amusing?' she asked.

'Just a dumb thought,' he said.

'Tell me,' she said. 'What's dumb to you might seem eloquent to me.'

'Yesterday I was in love with you and today I don't guess I am,' he said, sheepishly. 'I was thinking that coming to see you nearly every afternoon for several years would be kind of like keeping a girlfriend.'

Honor considered the comment. She didn't seem offended.

'It's more like keeping a call girl – isn't that what you were thinking?' she said. 'Because of the money involved?'

Duane saw the point. Men paid Gay-lee for the use of her body – he would be paying Honor for the use of her mind. But he thought it was a dumb point. Laying on a couch in a room with an attractive woman wasn't much like keeping a call girl. It was like seeing a doctor who also, in a way, happened to be a friend.

'Let's work a little, shall we?' Honor said. 'I don't want those tears you shed yesterday to be wasted. If you could choose one word for the feeling you felt when you parked your pickup and started walking, what would it be?'

Duane couldn't come up with a word. He could no longer really remember what he had felt at that time.

'I'm just the patient,' he said. 'You tell me.'

'I think the word would be "disappointment," ' Honor said, without delay. 'The reason I made you read Proust is because it's still the greatest catalogue of the varieties of disappointment human beings feel.'

Duane felt a little irritated by the comment.

'I don't know what I have to be so disappointed about,' he said. 'I had a good marriage. I raised a nice family. I even did well enough in my business.'

'Yes, I know all that,' Honor said, a little angrily. 'But the point you're not considering is that you didn't get to choose your life. You had your father only for five years. Your mother was very poor – you had to work from the time you were old enough to work.'

'Thirteen,' Duane said.

'Thirteen,' she said. 'You made it through high school but college was out of the question, right?'

'Pretty much,' he said. 'My mother was in poor health. I thought I ought to see after her, a little.'

'That's right – you did the decent thing,' Honor said. 'You took care of your parent but you didn't really take care of yourself. You were born with a good brain but you didn't train it. Then one day you noticed that you were sixty-two and you and your good brain had spent a lifetime riding around in pickups, not thinking about much. You haven't been to Egypt. You haven't been anywhere. What you ended up with was hard work and family life. That's enough for some people but I don't think you really feel that it was enough for you, Duane.'

There was a silence.

'People who realize they had the capacity to do more than they've done usually feel cheated,' she said. 'Even if they mainly have only themselves to blame, they still feel cheated when they come around a curve in the road and start thinking about the end of their life.

'I think you feel profoundly cheated, Duane,' she added. Then she stopped.

There was a long silence, but it was a restful silence, as far as Duane was concerned. He was trying to think about what Honor had just said, and it seemed to him she had just said a lot. It was a surprise – in their other sessions she had hardly talked at all.

'You've never talked that much to me,' he said.

'No, and there are people who have been coming to me for five years that I haven't talked that much to,' she said. 'Some of them are fairly disturbed, too, but none of them ever cried as hard as you cried yesterday. I figure if I say something maybe I can keep you coming in.'

Duane didn't know how much of what Honor said was true, but he did know he wanted to keep his mind away from his father. He was afraid to think of his father: the hard crying might start again. His father had not even lived to see him into the first grade.

'It would be a big expense,' he said, thinking out loud about the therapy she was proposing.

'You're right – it would be a big expense,' she said.

'What good would it do to talk about the past that much?' he asked. 'No matter how much you talk, you can't get it back. My life's been what it's been.'

'Yes, but it hasn't been what it might be,' Honor said. 'You still have two decades to live – maybe three.'

Then she fell silent again, pondering the same issues he was pondering.

'I suppose it depends on what value you place on understanding, and its power to heal our wounds,' she said. 'Obviously, I place a lot, or I wouldn't have chosen to do this. But I'm not you. I don't know how interested you are in understanding your own life, or whether you think it would help you do more satisfying things with the time you have left.'

Duane saw that his time was up. He stood up to leave and Honor stood up too.

'Still have your passport with you?' she asked, as he stood at the door.

'Yep, still got it,' he said.

'Then use it,' Honor said. 'Take your trip to Egypt. If you like Egypt, go to Greece. See some old places.'

'I'd like to,' Duane said.

'Yes, and you should,' Honor said. 'This place is all present – it's barely a hundred years old. Go take a look at some of the places where human beings have been living together for three or four thousand years. Or more. I visited a couple of places in China where people have been living for about six thousand years.'

She paused and looked out her window – two grackles were walking around in her yard.

'There's a grace that you find in some of the old places that you won't find here,' she said. 'Even though the people may be very poor, there's still that grace. They've lived together long enough to figure out a thing or two.'

She drew out a couple more Kleenex and handed them to Duane – despite himself he was still dribbling out tears, as if, somewhere inside him, there was a faucet that wouldn't turn off properly.

'When you come back I'd like to see you,' Honor said. 'Maybe by then you'll have figured out whether you want to be my patient.'

She walked him to the door and held out her hand. He shook it.

'Good-bye, Duane,' she said. 'I hope you have a good trip, and I hope you come to see me when you get back.'

Then she closed the door.

# 72

Duane's blue-haired travel agent was just about to close her shop and go home when Duane came pedaling up.

'Why is it that it's always the people who want to go around the world who show up at ten till five?' she asked. 'People like you deserve to end up in Mongolia.'

Nonetheless, in a very short space of time, she issued him a ticket for the next day. The ticket would take him from Wichita Falls to Dallas to London to Cairo.

'That'll get you to the pyramids,' she said. 'How did you want to come back?'

'I hadn't got that far with my planning,' Duane admitted. 'Is it out of the way to come back through India?'

The woman looked at him as if he were a complete dolt.

'Haven't you ever seen a globe?' she asked.

'Not in a while. I think the kids had one when they were in school.'

'If you're that ignorant I don't know what to think of you,' the woman said. 'Of course it's out of the way. Texas is west of the pyramids. India is east.'

'Okay – what's an old place I could stop at on my way home?' he asked.

'How about Rome?' she asked.

'Which is better, Rome or Paris?' he asked.

'I like 'em both, myself,' she said. 'You're taking this trip, not me. I was hoping to go hit a few golf balls before the sun sets but I won't get to if you don't make up your mind.'

Duane decided on Rome and, in a very few minutes, left with his ticket in his pocket.

On impulse he cycled back to the street where Honor lived. He thought he might just stop in for a moment, to tell her he had made up his mind, not just about where to go on his trip but that he had decided to be her patient when he returned. He knew that the opportunity to have that much of her company and counsel was something he didn't want to miss.

Riding back toward Honor's house he felt a sudden surge of optimism. He had his tickets, he was going to see the pyramids, the big step had been taken. Although Honor had already said good-bye to him and told him to have a good trip he had an impulse to let her know he was actually going, leaving the next day, to be gone almost a month.

As he turned into the shady street where Honor lived he saw two women ahead of him, walking along the sidewalk under the great shade trees, their arms companionably linked. Duane immediately braked. He got off his bike and removed his hot helmet. Ahead of him Honor Carmichael and Angie Cohen were taking a stroll in the cool of the evening. Honor had put on tennis shoes, Angie had her cane. He could just hear the low murmur of their conversation, hear Honor's pleasant voice and Angie's growl. Horrified at the thought that Honor might turn and see him, he quickly pulled his bicycle behind a shrub. The sight of the two women walking arm in arm, in harmony, stirred some old memory of a revival meeting he had gone to when just a boy. His grandmother and her only sister had walked arm in arm like that, when they went to church. In the years since he could not remember seeing two women stroll along so happily, arm in arm.

Honor and Angie went on past their house, still talking. Finally they were so far down the sidewalk that Duane could no longer distinguish them, one from the other; they became a moving dot – their voices, too, merged into one sound, soon lost in the general hum of a summer evening, of distant cars, of children yelling from a nearby ball field, of cicadas in the trees. When Duane could no longer see them, as they walked deep into the dusk, he put his helmet back on and pedaled away.

# 73

Duane rode out to his cabin and spent most of the night sitting in his lawn chair, enjoying the starlight. He had read that the early Egyptians were fine astronomers. He wondered if the stars would be different in Egypt, or if they would be the same. One of the big questions he hoped his travels would answer was how much would be different, in the old places of the earth, and how much would be the same.

In the morning he tidied up his woodworking shed a little. His woodworking hadn't really come to much – he hadn't focused on it to the extent that he had planned to. The very best thing he had made was a nice redwood box, whose joints fit perfectly. It was just a plain box, but Duane was pleased with it. After some thought, he took the box inside, sat down with his tablet, and began to write a letter to his wife.

Dear Karla:
Well, honey, I've finally done it. Yesterday I bought my ticket for Cairo, Egypt. In a day or two I'll be at the pyramids.

As you know the pyramids are something I have always hoped to see.

The kids all seem to be fine. Willy and Bubbles go to a private school in Highland Park. They have to wear uniforms – Willy even has to wear a tie, which doesn't please him much. They are taking French, I guess they will grow up a lot different from how their grandparents grew up.

I don't see too much of the girls, they both have busy lives, and Jack has not come back from Wyoming since he went up there to live.

I will try to bicycle up to visit him when I get back from overseas.

I am happy to say that Dickie has been clean this whole time – he goes to his AA meetings religiously and would seem to be in fine health.

Barbi had a poem published in a national magazine for schoolchildren – I guess she is our creative grandchild. It was a poem about cannibals ...

wouldn't you know?

The last two summers I have grown a good garden in your memory and given the produce away to the poor folks, or just whoever happened by. It has been a great success but of course a large garden is a big responsibility. Honey, so many times I have wished you were there to help me with it.

I don't know that I will have a willingness to take it on next year. It will depend somewhat on the rains.

Well, Karla, it was a tragedy for me that you smashed into the milk truck – the BMW was a total loss too.

After that I stopped seeing my doctor – there was just too much to do – but I am thinking of trying the therapy again when I get home from Egypt.

Before I quit therapy Dr Carmichael assigned this big French book for me to read. It was over three thousand pages long – you would laugh your head off if you saw me trying to read a book that long. I have been studying seed catalogues and reading a good deal about botany too.

I have not ridden in a motorized vehicle since the day I parked that pickup that Dickie proceeded to ruin by driving it off the hill.

Honey, I can't explain why – it is one of those mysteries that will never be explained, but if I can't get there walking I ride my bicycle.

My cholesterol is low, probably it is the healthy exercise and diet – I eat whatever vegetables I can't manage to give away.

Honey, I believe this is the longest letter I have ever written, there is no more to say except that I miss you ... I think of all those good years we had. I am going to leave this letter in this little box, it is the best I could do as a woodworker, at least the joints are tight.

Your loving husband,
Duane Moore

P.S. Sonny died last summer, it was blood poisoning, he just wouldn't exercise and his feet went bad. About the same time they found Jacy's bones, an ice fisherman found her. So those two stories are ended.

Duane put the letter in an envelope, put the envelope in the box, and sealed the box with a small nail. Then he rode into Thalia, to his garden shed, and got a trowel. He thought of stopping at Ruth's to say good-bye, but saw that Bobby Lee's pickup was there – no doubt Bobby was getting a back rub. Not wanting to hear the two of them bicker, Duane just decided to go. Ruth had already told him in no uncertain terms that, if he did go, she expected him to hurry back in case she died.

'You're my head pallbearer, all the others are flakes,' she said. 'You need to be there to keep them in line. I don't want to be sliding around in my coffin, and I don't want to be dropped, either.

'Those pyramids are just tombstones, anyway,' she added. 'It shouldn't take you that long to look at a few tombstones.'

Duane pedaled on through town to the cemetery, keeping to the backstreets. He didn't want some garrulous gardener to stop him, in order to chat about Israeli melons or what variety of cabbage made the best sauerkraut. He wanted to deliver his letter, and be alone with his wife for a few minutes before traveling over the ocean.

Nobody was in the cemetery except the elderly caretaker, who was puttering around with a spade at the far end of the burying ground. Only three days earlier an old farmer had been killed when his tractor flipped over on him – the caretaker was leveling the pale clods above the fresh grave.

It was a hot noon, the sky white, the heat waves shimmering across the lands that stretched to the west.

Duane knelt by the gravestone that said, *Karla Laverne Moore*, and, with his pocketknife and the trowel, dug a hole just large enough to contain the redwood box. Then, very carefully, he covered the box with earth and smoothed the earth with his trowel.

'Duane, you be careful; they say there's pickpockets in those airports,' he imagined Karla saying. He had never left, even on the simplest trip, without her warning him about the criminal element, which, in her opinion, was sure to be numerous wherever he went.

'Honey, I'm always careful,' he said aloud, in response to the comment he felt sure his wife would have made, were she not dead.

At the Wichita Falls airport he chained his bicycle to a sapling in the parking lot, and, the very next afternoon, he was able to look down on many, many white boats, all of them floating on the Mediterranean Sea.